THE SECOND OMNI
BOOK OF SCIENCE FICTION

Here are seventeen amazing works of finely crafted
science fiction. For an imaginative grasp of ma
future—and the kinds of men and women who w
live in that future—experience some of the most
highly acclaimed science fiction writers of our time,
including Harlan Ellison, Spider Robinson, Ray
Bradbury, Orson Scott Card, and many others.
They'll take you to new dimensions of time and
space as they describe both the beauty and the terror
of all our tomorrows . . . .

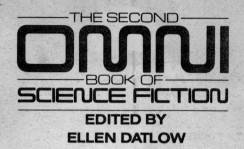

THE SECOND
OMNI
BOOK OF
SCIENCE FICTION

EDITED BY
ELLEN DATLOW

ZEBRA BOOKS
KENSINGTON PUBLISHING CORP.

ZEBRA BOOKS

are published by

KENSINGTON PUBLISHING CORP.

Omni is a registered trademark of Omni Publications International, Ltd.

THE SECOND
OMNI
BOOK OF
SCIENCE FICTION

CONTENTS

FOREWORD

In over five years, OMNI's fiction has achieved a reputation for excellence and has established itself as a leader in the field of science fiction. The magazine's enormous success has encouraged writers like Robert Silverberg to return to short fiction and has provided a select group of talented new writers with the opportunity to publish their best works before a much larger audience than they could have reached with traditional science fiction magazines.

I am particularly pleased to include in this second anthology stories by Harlan Ellison and Ray Bradbury—for personal reasons. As a girl, it was these two writers who turned me on to science fiction and fantasy. And throughout the years, I've continued to read and cherish their work.

The lead story of this anthology is Ellison's "On The Slab." It is an imaginative retelling of the Greek myth of Prometheus and demonstrates Ellison's extraordinary powers as a storyteller as well as his own very personal style. "Colonel Stonesteel's Genuine Home-Made Truly Egyptian Mummy" likewise epitomizes Bradbury's magical renditions of life in smalltown, U.S.A.

Robert Silverberg has dropped in and out of the science fiction field over the years. We'd like to think that OMNI nudged him back this most recent time. His novelette, "Waiting for the Earthquake," first appeared in 1981, and will be included in the book *Medea: Harlan's World.*

The stories "Blind Spot," by Jayge Carr and "Forever," by Damon Knight included in this volume made it into *Best of Year* anthologies in 1981. Two other distinguished OMNI stories published that same year are included here: Barry Malzberg's short, sharp satire "Icons," and Orson Scott Card's "A Sepulcher of Songs," a story tragic on its surface (as is much of Card's fiction), but one that ends in triumph for its young protagonist.

Also presented here is one original story never before published in the United States. Written by Dmitri Bilenkin, a prominent Soviet science fiction writer, it is called "The Genius House," and is a tale of technology gone awry.

To round out this collection, we've chosen stories by several promising writers who are already causing readers to take notice. They are: Michael Bishop, who won the Nebula Award in 1981; Michael Swanwick and William Gibson, both 1981 Nebula finalists; and Dan Simmons, who you're going to hear a lot more about. His first story, "Eyes I Dare Not Meet in Dreams," debuted in OMNI in 1982 and appears here.

Every one of the stories in this anthology reveals why OMNI fiction has already made such an enduring impression on the science fiction community and why it continues to do so.

Ellen Datlow
Fiction Editor

ON THE SLAB

By Harlan Ellison

Lightning was drawn to the spot. Season after season, August to November, but most heavily in September, the jagged killing bolts sought out George Gibree's orchard.

Gibree, a farmer with four acres of scabrous apple trees whose steadily diminishing production of fruit would drive him, one year later, to cut his throat with a rabbit-skinning knife and to bleed to death in the loft of his barn in Chepachet, near Providence, Rhode Island, *that* George Gibree found the dismal creature at the northeast corner of his property late in September. In the season of killing bolts.

The obscenely crippled trees—scarred black as if by fireblight—had withstood one attack after another; splintering a little more each year; withering a little more each year; dying a little more each year. The MacIntoshes they produced, hideous and wrinkled as Thalidomide babies. Night after night

11

the lightning, drawn to the spot, cracked and thrashed until one night, as though weary of the cosmic game, a monstrous forked bolt, sizzling with power, uncovered the creature's graveplace.

When he went out to inspect the orchard the next morning, holding back the tears till he was well out of sight of Emma and the house, George Gibree looked down in the crater and saw it stretched out on its back, its single green eye with the two pupils glowing terribly in the morning sunlight, its left forearm—bent up at the elbow—seeming to clutch with spread fingers at the morning air. It was as if the thing had been struck by the sky's fury as it was trying to dig itself out.

For just a moment as he stared down into the pit, George Gibree felt as if the ganglia mooring his brain were being ripped loose. His head began to tremble on his neck . . . and he wrenched his gaze from the impossible titan, stretched out, filling the thirty-foot-long pit.

In the orchard there could be heard the sounds of insects, a few birds, and the whimpering of George Gibree.

Children, trespassing to play in the orchard, saw it; and the word spread through town, and by stringer to a freelance writer who did occasional human-interest pieces for the Providence *Journal*. She drove out to the Gibree farm and, finding it impossible to speak to George Gibree, who sat in a straight-back chair, staring out the window without speaking or even acknowledging her presence, managed to cajole Emma Gibree into letting her wander out to the orchard alone.

The item was small when published, but it was the beginning of October and the world was quiet. The item received interested attention.

By the time a team of graduate students in anthropology arrived with their professor, pieces of the enormous being had been torn away by beasts of the field and by curious visitors. They sent one of their group back to the University of Rhode Island, in Kingston, advising him to contact the University's legal representatives, readying them for the eventual purchase of this terrifying, miraculous discovery. Clearly, it was not a hoax; this was no P.T. Barnum "Cardiff Giant," but a creature never before seen on the earth.

And when night fell, the professor was forced to badger the most amenable of the students into staying with the thing. Coleman lanterns, down jackets, and a ministove were brought in. But by morning all three of the students had fled.

Three days later, a mere six hours before the attorneys for the University could present their offer to Emma Gibree, a rock concert entrepreneur from Providence contracted for full rights to, and ownership of, the dead giant for three thousand dollars. Emma Gibree had been unable to get her husband to speak since the morning he had stood on the lip of the grave and stared down at the one-eyed being; she was in a panic; there were doctors and hospitals in her future.

Frank Kneller, who had brought every major rock group of the past decade to the city, rented exposition space in the Providence Civic Center at a ridiculously low rate because it was only the second week in October and the world was quiet. Then he assigned his public relations firm the task of making the giant a national curiosity. It was not a difficult task.

It was displayed via minicam footage on the evening news of all three major networks. Frank Kneller's flair for the dramatically staged was not wasted:

The thirty-foot humanoid, pink-skinned and with staring eye malevolently directed at the cameraman's lens, was held in loving close-up on the marble slab Kneller had had hewn by a local monument contractor.

Pilbeam of Yale came, and Johanson of the Cleveland Museum of Natural History, and both the Leakeys, and Taylor of Riverside came with Hans Seuss from the University of California at La Jolla. They all said it was genuine. But they could not say where the thing had come from. It was, however, native to the planet: thirty feet in height. Cyclopean, as hard as rhinoceros horn . . . but human. And they all noticed one more thing:

The chest, just over the place where the heart lay, was hideously scarred. As though centurions had jammed their pikes again and again into the flesh when this abomination had been crucified. Terrible weals, puckered skin still angrily crimson against the gentle pink of the otherwise unmarred body.

Unmarred, that is, but for the places where the curious had used their nail files and penknives to gouge out souvenirs.

And then Frank Kneller made them go away, shaking their heads in wonder, mad to take the creature back to their laboratories for private study, but thwarted by Kneller's clear and unshakable ownership. And when the last of them had departed, and the view of the Cyclops on its slab could be found in magazines and newspapers and even on posters, *then* Frank Kneller set up his exposition at the Civic Center.

There, within sight of the Rhode Island State House, atop whose dome stands the twelve-foot-high, gold-leafed statue of the Independent Man.

The curious came by the thousands to line up and pay their three dollars a head, so they could file past the dead colossus, blazoned on life-sized thirty-foot-high posters festooning the outer walls of the Civic Center as *The 9th Wonder of the World!* (Ninth, reasoned Frank Kneller with a flash of wit and a sense of history uncommon to popularizers and entrepreneurs, because King Kong had been the Eighth.) It was a gracious *hommage* that did not go unnoticed by fans of the cinematically horrific; and the gesture garnered for Kneller an acceptance he might not have otherwise known from the cognoscenti.

And there was an almost symphonic correctness to the titan's having been unearthed in Providence, in Rhode Island in that Yankee state so uncharacteristic of New England; that situs founded by Roger Williams for "those distressed for cause of conscience" and historically identified with independence of thought and freedom of religion; that locale where the odd and the bizarre melded with

15

the mundane: Poe had lived there, and Lovecraft; and they had had strange visions, terrible dreams that had been recorded, that had influenced the course of literature; the moral ownership of the city by the modern coven known as the Mafia; these, and uncountable reports of bizarre happenings, sightings, gatherings, beliefs that made it seem the Providence *Journal* was an appendix to the writings of Charles Fort . . . provided a free-floating ambience of the peculiar.

The lines never seemed to grow shorter. The crowds came by the busloads, renting cassette players with background information spoken by a man who had played the lead in a television series dealing with the occult. Schoolchildren were herded past the staring green eye in gaggles; teenagers whose senses had been dulled by horror movies came in knots of five and ten; young lovers needing to share stopped and wondered; elderly citizens from whose lives had been leached all wonder smiled and pointed and clucked their tongues; skeptics and cynics and professional debunkers stood frozen in disbelief and came away bewildered.

Frank Kneller found himself involved in a way he had never experienced before, not even the most artistically rewarding groups he had booked. He went to bed each night exhausted, but uplifted. And he awoke each day feeling his time was being well-spent. When he spoke of the feeling to his oldest friend, his accountant, with whom he had shared lodgings during college days, he was rewarded with the word *ennobled*. When he dwelled on the word, he came to agree.

Showing the monstrosity was *important*.

He wished with all his heart to know the reason. The single sound that echoed most often through the verdant glade of his thoughts was: *why?*

"I understand you've taken to sleeping in the rotunda where the giant is on display?" The host of the late-night television talk show was leaning forward. The ash on his cigarette was growing to the point where it would drop on his sharply creased slacks. He didn't notice.

Kneller nodded. "Yes, that's true."

"Why?"

"*Why* is a question I've been asking myself ever since I bought the great man and started letting people see him . . ."

"Well, let's be honest about it," the interviewer said. "You don't *let* people see the giant . . . you charge them for the privilege. You're showing an attraction, after all. It's not purely a humanitarian act."

Kneller pursed his lips and acceded. "That's right, that's very true. But I'll tell you, if I had the where-withal, I'd do it free of charge. I don't, of course, so I charge what it costs me to rent space at the Civic Center. That much; no more."

The interviewer gave him a sly smile. "Come *on* . . ."

"No, really, honest to God, I mean it," Frank said quickly. "It's been eleven months, and I can't begin to tell you how many hundreds of thousands of people have come to see the great man; maybe a million or more; I don't know. And everybody who comes, goes away feeling a little bit better, a little more important . . ."

"A religious experience?" The interviewer did not smile.

Frank shrugged. "No, what I'm saying is that people feel *ennobled* in the presence of the great man."

"You keep calling the giant 'the great man.' Strange phrase. Why?"

"Seems right, that's all."

"But you still haven't told me why you sleep there in the place where he's on display every day."

Frank Kneller looked straight into the eyes of the interviewer, who had to live in New York City every day and so might not understand what peace of mind was all about, and he said, "I like the feeling. I feel as if I'm worth the trouble it took to create me. And I don't want to be away from it too long. So I set up a bed in there. It may sound freaky to you, but . . ."

But if he had not been compelled to center his life around the immobile figure on the marble slab, then Frank Kneller would not have been there the night the destroyer came.

Moonlight flooded the rotunda through the enormous skylights of the central display areas.

Kneller lay on his back, hands behind his head, as usual finding sleep a long way off, yet at peace with himself, in the presence of the great man.

The titan lay on his marble slab, tilted against the far wall, thirty feet high, his face now cloaked in shadows. Kneller needed no light. He knew the single great eye was open, the twin pupils staring straight ahead. They had become companions, the man and the giant. And, as usual, Frank saw something that none of the thousands who had passed before the colossus had ever seen. In the darkness up there near the ceiling, the scars covering the chest of the giant glowed faintly, like amber plankton or the minuscule creatures that cling to limestone walls in the deepest caverns of the earth. When night fell, Frank was overcome with an unbearable sadness. Wherever and however this astounding being had lived . . . in whatever way he had passed through the days and nights that had been his life . . . he had suffered something more terrible than anyone merely human could conceive. What had done such awesome damage to his flesh, and how he had regenerated even as imperfectly as this, Kneller could not begin to fathom.

But he knew the pain had been interminable, and terrible.

He lay there on his back, thinking again, as he did every night, of the life the giant had known, and what it must have been for him on this earth.

The questions were too potent, too complex, and beyond Frank Kneller's ability even to pose properly. The titan defied the laws of nature and reason.

And the shadow of the destroyer covered the skylight of the rotunda, and the sound of a great wind rose around the Civic Center, and Frank Kneller felt a terror that was impossible to contain. Something was coming from the sky, and he knew without looking up that it was coming for the great man on the slab.

The hurricane wind shrieked past the point of audibility, vibrating in the roots of his teeth. The darkness outside seemed to fall toward the skylight, and with the final sound of enormous wings beating against the night, the destroyer splintered the shatter-proof glass.

Razor-edged stalactites struck the bed, the floor, the walls; one long spear imbedded itself through the pillow where Frank's head had lain a moment before, penetrating the mattress and missing him by inches where he cowered in the darkness.

Something enormous was moving beyond the foot of the bed.

Glass lay in a scintillant carpet across the rotunda. Moonlight still shone down and illuminated the display area.

Frank Kneller looked up and saw a nightmare.

The force that had collapsed the skylight was a bird. A bird so enormous he could not catalog it in the same genus with the robin he had found outside his bedroom window when he was a child . . . the robin that had flown against the pane when sunlight had turned it to a mirror . . . the robin that had struck and fallen and lain there till he came out of the house and picked it up. Its blood had been watery, and he could feel its heart beating against his palm. It had been defenseless and weak and dying in fear, he could feel that it was dying in fear. And Frank had rushed in to his mother, crying, and had begged her to help restore the creature to the sky. And his mother had gotten the old eyedropper that had been used to put cod-liver oil in Frank's milk when he was younger, and she had tried to get the robin to take some sugar-water.

But it had died.

Tiny, it had died in fear.

The thing in the rotunda was of that genus, but it was neither tiny nor fearful.

Like no other bird he had ever seen, like no other bird that had ever *been* seen, like no other bird that had ever existed. Sinbad had known such a bird, perhaps, but no other human eyes had ever beheld such a destroyer. It was gigantic. Frank Kneller could not estimate its size, because it was almost as tall as the great man, and when it made the hideous watery cawing sound and puffed out its bellows chest and jerked its wings into a billowing canopy, the pin-feathers scraped the walls of the rotunda on either side. The walls were seventy-five feet apart.

The vulture gave a hellish scream and sank its scimitar talons in the petrified flesh of the great man, its vicious beak in the chest, in the puckered area of scars that had glowed softly in the shadows.

It ripped away the flesh as hard as rhinoceros horn.

Its head came away with the beak locked around a chunk of horny flesh. Then, as Kneller watched, the flesh seemed to lose its rigidity, it softened, and blood ran off the carrion crow's killer beak. And the great man groaned.

The eye blinked.

The bird struck again, tossing gobbets of meat across the rotunda.

Frank felt his brain exploding. He could not bear to see this.

But the vulture worked at its task, ripping out the area of chest where the heart of the great man lay under the scar tissue. Frank Kneller crawled out of the shadows and stood helpless. The creature was immense. *He* was the robin: pitiful and tiny.

Then he saw the fire extinguisher in its brackets on the wall, and he grabbed the pillow from the bed and rushed to the compartment holding the extinguisher and he smashed the glass with the pillow protecting his hand. He wrenched the extinguisher off its moorings and rushed the black bird, yanking the handle on the extinguisher so hard the wire broke without effort. He aimed it up at the vulture just as it threw back its head to rid itself of its carrion load, and the virulent Halon 1301 mixture sprayed in a white stream over the bird's head. The mixture of fluorine, bromine, iodine, and chlorine washed the vulture, spurted into his eyes, filled his mouth. The vulture gave one last violent scream, tore its claws loose, and arced up into the darkness with a spastic beating of wings that caught Frank Kneller across the face and threw him thirty feet into a corner. He struck the wall; everything slid toward gray.

When he was able to get to his knees, he felt an excruciating pain in his side and knew at once several ribs had been broken. All he could think of was the great man.

He crawled across the floor of the rotunda to the base of the slab, and looked up. There in the shadows . . .

The great man, in terrible pain, was staring down at him.

A moan escaped the huge lips.

What can I do? Kneller thought, desperately.

And the words were in his head. *Nothing. It will come again.*

Kneller looked up. Where the scar tissue had

22

glowed faintly, the chest was ripped open, and the great man's heart lay there in pulsing blood, part of it torn away.

Now I know who you are, Kneller said. *Now I know your name.*

The great man smiled a strange, shy smile. The one great green eye made the expression somehow winsome. *Yes,* he said, *yes, you know who I am.*

Your tears mingled with the earth to create us.

Yes.

You gave us fire.

Yes; and wisdom.

And you've suffered for it ever since.

Yes.

"I have to know," Frank Kneller said. "I have to know if *you* were what we were before we became what we are now."

The sound of the great wind was rising again. The destroyer was in the night, on its way back. The chemicals of man could not drive it away from the task it had to perform, could not drive it away for long.

It comes again, the great man said in Kneller's mind. *And I will not come again.*

"Tell me! Were you what we were . . .?"

The shadow fell across the rotunda and darkness came down upon them as the great man said, in that final moment, *No, I am what you would have become . . .*

And the carrion crow sent by the gods struck him as he said one more thing . . .

When Frank Kneller regained consciousness, hours

later, there on the floor where the scissoring pain of his broken ribs had dropped him, he heard those last words reverberating in his mind. And heard them endlessly all the days of his life.

No, I am what you would have become . . . *if you had been worthy*.

And the silence was deeper that night across the face of the world, from pole to pole, deeper than it had ever been before in the life of the creatures that called themselves humans.

But not as deep as it would soon become.

LOBOTOMY SHOALS

By Juleen Brantingham

Sharks followed the school of fish, as sharks have been doing for millions of years. The new element was the submarine, an oversized coffin, within the shark pack, following the fish.

From time to time, sharks would dart out of the pack, to the right or the left, driving in stragglers. In the crannies of the rock piles on the bottom, moray eels watched this action as dogs might watch for crumbs to drop from the master's table. But there were no crumbs. These sharks were not feeding.

The morays also watched the submarine as it passed. Its shape was like that of a shark but, from its actions, the morays categorized it as not immediately dangerous. Its smell/taste was thin and bitter, not like that of the soft thing on which the morays fed.

But the eels continued to watch until the school, pack, and intruder faded from sight. An ocean predator seldom knows where its next meal is coming from until the scent of blood spreads in the water.

Tinkertoy was nuzzling my submarine's rear stabilizer. Just before burn-out, old hammerheads get as friendly as puppies. A pony is designed to withstand abuse; that's the word from topside. But that's *topside*. Up there they don't have to worry about getting too close to playmates with lots of teeth.

This promised to be a tough patrol. I'd relieved Tindall, my alternative, off the eastern tip of Cuba.

I was sweeping a school of mackerel up the shelf to Atlantic Fisheries Corporation's Station Number Seven at Grand Abaco. Tindall had reported the school to be losing mass. Down an estimated 700 kilos since the spotters had tagged it out in the Deep. Something was slipping in under the noses of the pack and the scopes of the pony.

Civilians seem to think a pack can protect the school against anything, but that just shows how little they know about conditions out here. Throwing a pack against healthy cetaceans or a good-sized great white would be mass murder. The pack's job is to herd the school into the catch pens before word gets around that a free lunch is in the neighborhood.

Besides losing mass in the school, the pack was down to 37. Tindall had reported four losses. Two, he said, had been rammed by porpoises. But Tindall's been my alternate for three years now and I know him. He likes to play with the pack. So his burn-out rate is way too high and he tries to hide it from the cost accountants. He probably burned all four, plus Tinkertoy. There's no mistake, the way

26

the old boy's acting. He's close. I'll hate to see him go. I was running the pack a year and a half ago when the trainer delivered Tinkertoy and a couple of tigers.

First thing he did was shimmy through the pack, wagging his head like it wasn't enough that he had an eye at each end of that ridiculous deformity and he was afraid of missing out on something.

There was a bump from amidships. Tinkertoy had seen me come out of the lock often enough to make a lie of its name on the parts list—Emergency Escape Chamber.

There's something about a hammerhead. I don't think any herder feels neutral about them. They look like a cross between a nightmare and an abortion, but they have brains that can be conditioned and programmed to herd fish, just like any other shark. Some herders would run all-hammerhead packs if they could. Others have threatened to torp the trainer if he ever delivers one.

I've had some minor troubles with hammerheads. And I've had some good experiences, mostly with Tinkertoy. He's always the first to go into action when I use the Voice. When there's a predator for my command to go at it.

I haven't named any of the others in the pack and Tindall wouldn't. We're warned not to do that, not to get emotionally attached. Sharks may not seem lovable to civilians, but when you work with them day after day, you learn their little quirks. It's hard to see a friend nearing brain death.

There was another nudge from amidships. He was acting like a little boy. I could almost read his mind.

27

"Can Petey come out and play?"

Cancel that. Erase. I could not read Tinkertoy's mind, did not know what he wanted. Could not. Did not. The Voice only works one way.

I steered the pony through the pack. Warned by the pressure wave, sharks scooted right and left, never crossing the invisible barrier that their conditioning set up between them and the school. I'd hoped Tinkertoy would turn his attention to one of the others, but a rasp along the hull testified to his loyalty.

"Please, Petey. Let's play."

Wrong. He wasn't thinking that. He wasn't thinking at all. He was just a big, dumb fish. Maybe he was horny and had mistaken me for a female hammerhead. How would *I* know?

The Voice only works one way.

I reached hesitantly for my mike switch. Tinkertoy was close to burn-out. One more command might trigger it, and the pack was understrength now. But I *did* reach for the switch. I'd been in the pony for over 24 hours, and before that I'd had two weeks of the violence and filth of topside.

I *needed* to go out. I was carefully not thinking about the rumors. *My* brain was all right. I just needed to go out for a swim.

The bars in the ports are full of rumors and stories and things that have to be pure myth. God knows where they all come from. There's no such animal as an *old* fish herder.

Once in a while a wild shark will swim with the

pack. Sharks aren't like dogs or wolves or even lions. They don't hunt cooperatively. But where the food supply is good, they gather in groups, especially hammerheads.

When a wild shark joins a guard pack, it never stays long. Even if the pack doesn't drive it away, the wild one becomes more and more skittish and bad-tempered. The Voice hardware doesn't show on a shark's head, but apparently the wild ones can sense *something*.

It's the same with fish herders and civilians.

In every port city close to a harvesting station, there are one or two special bars. There is no canned music, the voices are hushed, and the light is sort of green and peaceful. The customers move slowly, and there's a blasted look in their eyes. Those are the fish herders' bars.

The owners of those places aren't going to get rich. The stuff they sell doesn't have much of an effect compared to the smoothed-out feeling we carry over from our jobs. The only reason we need the bars at all is as a retreat.

When a civilian wanders in by mistake, we don't chase him away. We'll talk about our jobs if he wants to listen, or about the happenings topside— though that's harder because most of us are deliberately out of touch. But the civilians don't stay long. They become more and more nervous, as if they can sense some kind of hardware in our heads, something that changes us.

There is no hardware. Our heads are as clean as theirs. But we're not sorry to see them go. Civilians are too loud, too tight, too scared.

When fish herders are alone we talk about the most important things in the world; the packs, the predators, the ocean. And sometimes we wonder why there are no old fish herders. Why is it that nearly every week at least one pony fails to meet its okay schedule?

Civilians pity us. They're always talking about the loneliness and the danger. They talk about the sacrifices we have to make to feed the millions topside. They ought to take a good look at *their* world: crowds, noise, shortages, tension, rules, ugliness, hostility, and more rules. They can have it.

Pass through the surface of the ocean and you leave all that behind. Herders are the last of the free people. It's clean down here. It's peaceful. It's beautiful.

Sure, there's danger. Hulls crack, systems fail, and outside there's an ocean full of predators with an appetite for red meat. But that's just the way things even out. Maybe what topside needs is a little more danger, a few more predators.

The packs themselves are right at the top of the list of dangers. Oh, they've been conditioned to avoid a human body in the water, but conditioning works best with an animal that's at least semi-intelligent. You need the Voice of guarantee control and you can't use it from outside. I guess the Atlantic Fisheries Corporation figures they'll lose fewer of us if they keep us in the ponies. Scared like all topsiders.

Herders aren't the first to find the ocean more attractive than topside. Cetaceans used to be land animals, too.

There's no sacrifice involved in being a herder, in spite of the stuff they spout in the training sessions. We're down here because this is where we want to be. But sometimes we wonder why no one has ever beaten the odds. Sometimes, when too many of our friends have missed the okay schedule, we speculate in whispers about the Voice.

We're just herders, not scientists or trainers. We know that even sharks can be conditioned to avoid certain things, like the schools they're supposed to be guarding. We know that hardware can be planted in a shark's brain to stimulate certain areas. It's like pulling a puppet's strings. But they don't tell us too much about how it works. We're just supposed to give the orders and the Voice does the rest.

We do know about burn-out. The Voice is a clumsy tool. Repeated commands damage neural tissue, and sooner or later, usually within a year or two, the animal suffers brain death.

When the ocean ranges began to be managed and harvested intensively, when the big harvesting stations replaced the energy-hungry fishing fleets, herders used porpoises to steer the schools. Cetaceans are intelligent and can be trained. But they're also intelligent enough to resent being turned into slaves. Sometimes the whole pack would take off, leaving the herder with a scattering school and a hole in the harvesting plan.

So the scientists started cutting open the porpoises' heads and implanting their hardware. After all, there were quotas to meet.

Thank God that was stopped. It was like turning our brothers into zombies.

Sharks are just killing machines, ugly, vicious, unpredictable devourers, according to civilians. Yet, there isn't a herder who doesn't wish there was another way.

Burn-out.

I've seen it happen a few times. It's nothing dramatic but I've happened to be looking in the right direction once in a while. Just after a command, one shark gives a little quiver. That's it. Most of a shark's systems are so primitive that it's a while after brain death before the body gives up. But that quiver is the end. Even if the body continues to move, there's nothing there.

I guess every herder has had nightmares of looking down and seeing his own body quiver like that.

There *is* no hardware in a herder's head. The Voice only works one way.

That's what they tell us.

Why are there no *old* herders? Why are bodies almost never recovered, even when the ponies are intact?

I touched the switch on my mike and the box translated my words into a command for Tinkertoy to swim to the east and circle around the school. His appearance would keep it bunched up. And why was I thinking about waste? This school was a big one in spite of the loss of mass, so I should have plenty of time. I really needed a swim to wash off the stink of topside.

He swam away below the eyes of the pony, giving me a good view of sinuous locomotion. He seemed regretful. "Aw, Petey, I wanted to play!"

Cancel that. Erase. I don't know what he was thinking.

When Tinkertoy faded into the distance, I took a last look at the scopes and put the pony on automatic. I was slipping into the escape gear as I stepped down to the lock. The pony is home, but outside is heaven.

The touch of the water made me euphoric. I don't know what it is, but I feel more alive there than anywhere else. In a way it doesn't make sense because I'm completely dependent on the air packs. My senses are limited to vision—dim—and hearing—almost useless. I can't sense a pressure wave until it's too late to be any use. I can't taste/smell the odors in the water, probably the most important sense to fish. I can't swim very fast, and I have to depend on my suit to prevent dangerous loss of body heat. In the world under the surface I'm better prey than predator.

But I can move, glide, fly—effortlessly. I am part of the ocean, as it is a part of me.

I forgot about the air packs and the suit. I was alert and aware of the danger every second but it was unimportant. Every part of my body was functioning, not like being in the pony, or topside, where I am mostly useless meat supporting a brain that in turn functions as a puppet of the Atlantic Fisheries Corporation.

I could fly. I was alive. I was whole.

I swam from the lock directly into the school, counting on the pack's avoidance conditioning to protect me there. It is possible to swim with the pack, even to play with them if they've been fed recently. I've done it often. But around the pack you have to be doubly alert, and on this first swim after my return, I didn't want to be alert. Not that way.

Why do they force us to go topside for R and R every two weeks? I'd stay on the job forever if they'd keep giving me air packs. I'd take my R and R outside if they'd give me air packs. Why won't they turn us loose? Why keep binding us with their own fears?

Maybe they're afraid we won't come back.

Change course. Think of something else. That's the way a shark would think.

Erase.

I soared through the school. It was like swimming through a shower of gigantic confetti that parted to make a path for me. They're even dumber than the sharks. If I'd been hungry I could have reached out and grabbed one.

I flew, trying to breathe shallowly, hoarding every breath in my pack.

Time was running out. I called my usual curse down on the heads of the Atlantic Fisheries Corporation and began my return to the pony. Thirty hours of air in a pack and one pack per pony. For emergency use only. I had to make this one last two weeks. Damn them. With this slender thread they hold me. Topsiders.

At the edge of the school I stopped dead in the water. Something had changed out there. The aura was different.

The pack was making its usual near-aimless sweeps, but they seemed nervous, their movements jerky. The school was calm, but then, the school is always calm until they approach the catch pens. I could see no predators. But something had changed. I could feel it.

Then I saw him. Gliding from the dimness at the edge of my vision. Tinkertoy.

He was returning from the east.

From the *east*. The shock raised my respiration rate but I no longer thought about hoarding the air in my pack. A shark cannot disobey a command. The puppet can't cut its own strings. Either a shark obeys or its brain is dead and it is not capable of initiating an action. But Tinkertoy was returning from the east. If he had finished his sweep, if my time sense could have been that far wrong, he would have returned from the northwest.

A shark could not disobey a command. But if something had changed since I gave Tinkertoy that last order, he would expect a new order. He could not function without the correct order. If predators were attacking the school on the east side, Tinkertoy could not complete his sweep and he could not attack without my command.

There must be predators in the school. It was the only explanation. If I'd been in the pony I would have seen them on the scopes. Alarms must have been flashing all across the board as I indulged in that forbidden pleasure.

Tinkertoy circled the pony, caressed it with his hide, tasting. "Here I am. Petey. What do you want me to do?"

My suit suddenly felt like a quilted overcoat. As long as I stayed where I was, Tinkertoy would not "see" me. His conditioning blinded him to the main body of the school, to prevent him from lunching on the things he was supposed to protect. While I was hidden in the school I was safe, and the way he'd been acting, I needed that protection. Maybe he wouldn't attack me.

Maybe. But a friendly shark is no better than a hungry one. A flick of his tail could break my spine. A caress from that hide would rip away my suit and half my skin. Blood in the water would bring the rest of the pack down on me.

I had to get back to the pony. I had to find out what was hitting the school. If it was a few small sharks I could send the pack to attack. If it was more than the pack could handle, I might be able to save part of the school by turning it with the pony.

Tinkertoy rounded the pony's stern and started up the other side. I swam out of the school, trying to reach the lock before he made a complete circuit. No good. I threw out my arms to stop myself. He was soaring over the top, almost as if he'd planned this maneuver to trick me out of hiding.

"Petey! I've been looking all over for you!"

Erase. He just seemed a little excited, that's all. I didn't know what he was thinking. I swam back into the school and Tinkertoy lost interest again.

I felt dizzy. Hyperventilation. I had to slow down. I had to *think*.

I couldn't get back to the pony but I could swim *through* the school. At least get to the east and check out the situation for myself. I had no weapons, but if it was a small shark or a single porpoise—fat chance—I might be able to chase it away.

That still left the problem of getting back to the pony. But save that for later.

36

If I lost an entire school because I was outside, against regulations, I could get fired. Exiled topside for the rest of my life.

Forget that. Breath slowly.

I couldn't go straight through the school or I'd lose my sense of direction. Fish all look alike and sections of the school are always changing orientation, though the school as a whole was heading north.

If I swam over the school and there were any wild sharks around, they might be drawn to attack. Even a careful diver makes some jerky movements and the closer these are to the surface, the more exciting to sharks.

I went under the school, gliding like a ray, inches from the bottom.

Swimming like that gives a diver a dangerous sense of power. It's not narcosis. Biochemistry has taken care of that. But the movement is almost effortless. You look down and you see the bottom passing so rapidly you feel jet propelled. The light is confusing.

The world was small enough to clasp in my arms.

I hadn't solved my problem; I was running away from it. And not from any sense of duty to the Atlantic Fisheries Corporation. My brain was a prisoner in an organism that had returned to its natural element.

Cancel that. Erase.

It wouldn't erase. I'd been a herder for years, using the Voice almost daily. If there was feedback, if the experts were wrong, my brain must be riddled with holes. Maybe I was as much a puppet as Tinkertoy. Who was pulling my strings? The Atlantic Fisheries Corporation? Or something older, more primitive?

I remember what a sculptor said when asked about a piece of his work. "Why, I just took a block of marble and cut away everything that wasn't lion."

Cancel. Cancel. Cancel.

I was swimming to the east of the school to see if it was being attacked and by what. Cut off from my pony, I still had an obligation to my employer. I was protecting a vital food crop for millions of topsiders.

Oh, hell. That wasn't any better. Cancel.

I was trying to save my job, my life. My only opportunity to live where I belonged.

Why bother? I didn't care about the topsiders, the Atlantic Fisheries Corporation, *or* my job. Why not let it all slip away? I didn't *have* to go back to the pony.

Swimming was no longer effortless. I was moving fast, pushed by adrenalin. Thinking like a shark again. I didn't even bother to cancel that one.

When the school started to thin out, I rose just inside the curve of its flank, hoping it would cover me from whatever it was that had disturbed Tinkertoy. I could see nothing but the bottom, the fish, and the blue-green curtain at the edge of my vision.

Nothing. No sharks. No cetaceans.

I pushed out of the school and let my body drift north. The ocean was calm, as if nothing existed but the fish and me, suspended in the quiet. I decided I was still suffering from the effects of hyperventilation. I was seeing spots.

Or rather, one spot. I shook my head and looked straight at it. It didn't go away. It was a man-shaped thing hanging so deep within the curtain that I could hardly see it. But man-shaped. No air pack.

My breath went in and out; the school drifted away from me. I stared at the dark spot in the curtain while the world turned over and crushed something.

Maybe after years on the job, the Voice riddled a herder's brain with pinholes. Maybe we start to see things, imagine impossibilities.

Humans can't breathe water like fish. We can't survive underwater without complicated support systems, air packs. We have the word of the experts on that. That couldn't be a man out there, waving at me. No air packs. Impossible.

Cetaceans used to be land animals, too. Maybe something has been working on me like that sculptor, cutting away everything that isn't—what? I wanted to find out. I wanted to believe it was possible.

But there was my job. The world I knew, the packs and the pony and a fresh air pack every month.

The man-shaped thing beckoned.

I think I'm going to miss Tinkertoy.

FIVESIGHT

By Spider Robinson

I know what the exact date was, of course, but I can't see that it would matter to you. Say it was just another Saturday night at Callahan's Place.

Which is to say that the joint was merry as hell, as usual. Over in the corner Fast Eddie sat in joyous combat with Eubie Blake's old rag "Tricky Fingers," and a crowd had gathered around the piano to cheer him on. It is a demonically difficult rag, which Eubie wrote for the specific purpose of humiliating his competitors, and Eddie takes a crack at it maybe once or twice a year. He was playing it with his whole body, grinning like a murderer and spraying sweat in all directions. The onlookers fed him energy in the form of whoops and rebel yells, and one of the unlikely miracles about Callahan's Place is that no one claps along with Eddie's music who cannot keep time. All across the rest of the tavern people whirled and danced, laughing because they could not make their feet move one fourth as fast as Eddie's hands. Behind the bar Callahan danced with himself, and bottles danced with each other on the shelves behind him. I sat stock-still in front of the bar, clutched my third drink in fifteen minutes, and concentrated on not bursting into tears.

Doc Webster caught me at it. You would not think that a man navigating that much mass around a crowded room could spare attention for anything else; furthermore, he was dancing with Margie Thomas, who is enough to hold anyone's attention. She is very pretty and limber enough to kick a man standing behind her in the eye. But the Doc has a built-in compass for pain; when his eyes fell on mine, they stayed there.

His *other* professional gift is for tact and delicacy. He did not glance at the calendar, he did not pause in his dance, he did not so much as frown. But I knew that he knew.

Then the dance whirled him away. I spun my chair around to the bar and gulped whiskey. Eddie brought "Tricky Fingers" to a triumphant conclusion, hammering that final chord home with both hands, and his howl of pure glee was audible even over the roar of applause that rose from the whole crew at once. Many glasses hit the fireplace together, and happy conversation began everywhere. I finished my drink. For the hundredth time I was grateful that Callahan keeps no mirror behind his bar: Behind me. I knew, Doc Webster would be whispering in various ears, unobtrusively passing the word, and I didn't want to see it.

"Hit me again, Mike," I called out.

"Half a sec, Jake," Callahan boomed cheerily. He finished drawing a pitcher of beer, stuck a straw into it, and passed it across to Long-Drink McGonnigle, who ferried it to Eddie. The big barkeep ambled my way running damp hands through his thinning red hair. "Beer?"

I produced a very authentic-looking grin. "Irish again."

Callahan looked ever so slightly pained and rubbed his big broken nose. "I'll have to have your keys, Jake."

The expression *one too many* has only a limited meaning at Callahan's Place. Mike operates on the assumption that his customers are grown-ups—he'll keep on serving you for as long as you can stand up and order 'em intelligibly. But no one drunk drives home from Callahan's. When he decides you've reached your limit, you have to surrender your car keys to keep on drinking, then let Pyotr—who drinks only ginger ale—drive you home when you fold.

"British constitution," I tried experimentally. "The lethal policeman dismisseth us. Peter Pepper packed his pipe with paraquat . . ."

Mike kept his big hand out for the keys. "I've heard you sing 'Shiny Stockings' blind drunk without a single syllabobble, Jake."

"Damn it," I began, and stopped. "Make it a beer, Mike."

He nodded and brought me a Löwenbräu dark. "How about a toast?"

I glanced at him sharply. There was a toast that I urgently wanted to make, to have behind me for another year. "Maybe later."

"Sure. Hey, *Drink!* How about a toast around here?"

Long-Drink looked up from across the room. "I'm your man." The conversation began to abate as he threaded his way through the crowd to the chalk line on the floor and stood facing the deep thick fireplace. He is considerably taller than somewhat, and he towered over everyone. He waited until he had our attention.

"Ladies and gentlemen and regular customers," he said then, "you may find this difficult to believe, but in my youth I was known far and wide as a jackass." This brought the spirited response, which he endured stoically. "My only passion in life, back in my college days, was grossing people out. I considered it a holy mission, and I had a whole crew of other jackasses to tell me I was just terrific. I would type long letters onto a roll of toilet paper, smear mustard on the last square, then roll it back up and mail it in a box. I kept a dead mouse in my pocket at all times. I streaked Town Hall in 1952. I loved to see eyes glaze. And I regret to confess that I concentrated mostly on ladies, because they were the easiest to gross out. Foul Phil, they called me in them days. I'll tell you what cured me." He wet his whistle, confident of our attention.

"The only trouble with a reputation for crudeness is that sooner or later you run short of unsuspecting victims. So you look for new faces. One day I'm at a party off campus, and I notice a young lady I've never seen before, a pretty little thing in an off-the-shoulder blouse. *Oboy,* I sez to myself, *fresh blood! What'll I do?* I've got the mouse in one pocket, the rectal-thermometer swizzle stick in the other, but she looks so virginal and innocent I decide the hell with subtlety, I'll try a direct approach. So I walk over to where she's sittin' talkin' to Petey LeFave on a little couch. I come up behind her, like, upzip me trousers, out with me instrument, and lay it across her shoulder.''

There were some howls of outrage, from the men as much as from the women, and some giggles, from the women as much as from the men. "Well, I said I was a jackass,'' the Drink said, and we all applauded.

"No reaction whatsoever do I get from her,'' he went on, dropping into his fake brogue. "People grinnin' or growlin' all round the room just like here, Petey's eyes poppin', but this lady gives no sign that she's aware of me presence atall, atall. I kinda wiggle it a bit, and not a glance does she give me. Fnially I can't stand it. 'Hey,' I sez, tappin' her other shoulder and pointing, 'what do you think *this* is?' And she takes a leisurely look. Then she looks me in the eyes and says, 'It's something like a man's penis, only smaller.' ''

An explosion of laughter and applause filled the room.

". . . wherefore,'' continued Long-Drink, "I propose a toast: to me youth, and may God save me from a relapse.'' And the cheers overcame the laughter as he gulped his drink and flung the glass into the fireplace. I nearly grinned myself.

"My turn,'' Tommy Janssen called out, and the Drink made way for him at the chalk line. Tommy's probably the youngest of the regulars; I'd put him at just about twenty-one. His hair is even longer than

45

mine, but he keeps his face mowed.

"This happened to me just last week. I went into the city for a party, and I left it too late, and it was the *wrong* neighborhood of New York for a civilian to be in at that time of night, right? A dreadful error! Never been so scared in my life. I'm walking on tippy-toe, looking in every doorway I pass and trying to look insolvent, and the burning question in my mind is, 'Are the crosstown buses still running?' Because if they are, I can catch one a block away that'll take me to bright lights and safety—but I've forgotten how late the crosstown bus keeps running in this part of town. It's my only hope. I keep on walking, scared as hell. And when I get to the bus stop, there, leaning up against a mailbox, is the biggest, meanest-looking, ugliest, *blackest* man I have ever seen in my life. Head shaved, three days' worth of beard, big scar on his face, hands in his pockets."

Not a sound in the joint.

"So the essential thing is not to let them know you're scared. I put a big grin on my face, and I walk right up to him, and I stammer, 'Uh . . . crosstown bus run all night long?' And the fella goes . . .'" Tommy mimed a ferocious-looking giant with his hands in his pockets. Then suddenly he yanked them out, clapped them rhythmically, and sang, *"Doo*-dah, *doo*-dah!"

The whole bar dissolved in laughter.

". . . fella whipped out a joint, and we both got high while we waited for the bus," he went on, and the laughter redoubled. Tommy finished his beer and cocked the empty. "So my toast is to prejudice," he finished, and pegged the glass square into the hearth, and the laughter became a standing ovation. Isham Latimer, who is the exact color of recording tape, came over and gave Tommy a beer, a grin, and some skin.

Suddenly I thought I understood something, and it filled me with shame.

Perhaps in my self-involvement I was wrong. I had not seen the Doc communicate in any way with Long-Drink or Tommy, nor had the toasters seemed to notice me at all. But all at once it seemed suspicious that both men, both proud men, had picked tonight to stand up and uncharacteristically tell egg-on-my-face anecdotes. Damn Doc Webster! I had been trying so hard to keep my pain off my face, so determined to get my toast made and get home without bringing my friends down.

Or was I, with the egotism of the wounded, reading too much into a couple of good anecdotes well told? I wanted to hear the next toast. I turned around to set my beer down so I could prop my face up on both fists, and was stunned out of my self-involvement, and was further ashamed.

It was inconceivable that I could have sat next to her for a full fifteen minutes without noticing her—anywhere in the world, let alone at Callahan's Place.

I worked the night shift in a hospital once, pushing a broom. The only new faces you see are the ones they wheel into Emergency. There are two basic ways people react facially to mortal agony. The first kind smiles a lot, slightly apologetically, thanks everyone elaborately for small favors, extravagantly praises the hospital and its every employee. The face is animated, trying to ensure that the last impression it leaves before going under the knife is of a helluva nice person whom it would be a shame to lose. The second kind is absolutely blank-faced, so utterly wrapped up in wondering whether he's dying that he has no attention left for working the switches and levers of the face—or so *certain* of death that the perpetual dialogue people conduct with their faces has ceased to interest him. It's not the *total* deanimation of a corpse's face, but it's not far from it.

Her face was of the second type. I suppose it could have been cancer or some such, but somehow I knew her pain was not physical. I was just as sure that it might be fatal. I was so shocked I violated the prime rule of Callahan's Place without even thinking about it. "Good God, lady," I blurted, "what's the *matter?*"

Her head turned toward me with such elaborate care that I knew her car keys must be in the coffee can behind the bar. Her eyes took awhile focusing on me, but when they did, there was no one looking out of them. She enunciated her words.

"Is it to me to whom you are referring?"

She was not especially pretty, not particularly well dressed, her hair cut wrong for her face and in need of brushing. She was a normal person, in other words, save that her face was uninhabited, and somehow I could not take my eyes off her. It was not the pain—I *wanted* to take my eyes from that—it was something else.

It was necessary to get her attention. "Nothing, nothing, just wanted to tell you your hair's on fire."

She nodded. "Think nothing of it." She turned back to her screwdriver and started to take a sip and sprayed it all over the counter. She shrieked on the inhale, dropped the glass, and flung her hands at her hair.

Conversation stopped all over the house.

She whirled on me, ready to achieve total fury at the slightest sign of a smile, and I debated giving her that release but decided she could not afford the energy it would cost her. "I'm truly, truly sorry," I said at once, "but a minute ago you weren't here and now you are, and that's the way I wanted it."

Callahan was there, his big knuckly hand resting light as lint on my shoulder. His expression was mournful. "Prying, Jake? You?"

"That's up to her, Mike," I said, holding her eyes.

"What you *talkin'* about?" she asked.

"Lady," I said, "there's so much pain on your face I just have to ask you, How come? If you don't want to tell me, then I'm prying."

She blinked. "And if you are?"

"The little guy with a face like a foot who has by now tiptoed up behind me will brush his blackjack across my occiput, and I'll wake up tomorrow with the same kind of head you're gonna have. Right, Eddie?"

"Dat's right, Jake," the piano man's voice came from just behind me.

She shook her head dizzily, then looked around at friendly, attentive faces. "What the *hell* kind of place is this?"

Usually we prefer to let newcomers figure that out for themselves, but I couldn't wait that long. "This is Callahan's. Most joints the barkeep listens to your troubles, but we happen to love this one so much that we all share his load. This is the place you found because you needed to." I gave it everything I had.

She looked around again, searching faces. I saw her look for the prurience of the accident spectator and not find it; then I saw her look again for compassion and find it. She turned back to me and looked me over carefully. I tried to look gentle, trustworthy, understanding, wise, and strong. I wanted to be more than I was for her. "He's not prying, Eddie," she said at last. "Sure, I'll tell you people. You're not going to believe it anyway. Innkeeper, gimme coffee, light and sweet."

She picked somebody's empty from the bar, got down unsteadily from her chair, and walked with great care to the chalk line. "You people like toasts? I'll give you a toast. To fivesight," she said, and whipped her glass so hard she nearly fell. It smashed in the geometrical center of the fireplace, and residual alcohol made the flames ripple through the spectrum.

I made a little gasping sound.

By the time she had regained her balance, young Tommy was straightening up from the chair he had placed behind her, brushing his hair back over his shoulders. She sat gratefully. We formed a ragged half-circle in front of her, and Shorty Steinitz brought her the coffee. I sat at her feet and studied her as she sipped it. Her face was still not pretty, but now that the lights were back on in it, you could see that she was beautiful, and I'll take that any day. Go chase a pretty one and see what it gets you. The coffee seemed to help steady her.

"It starts out prosaic," she began. "Three years ago my first husband, Freddie, took off with a sculptress named, God help us, Kitten, leaving me with empty savings and checking, a mortgage I couldn't cut, and a seven-year-old son. Freddie was the life of the party. Lily of the valley. So I got myself a job on a specialist newspaper. Little business man's daily, average subscriber's median income fifty kay. The front-page story always happened to be about the firm that had bought the most ad space that week. Got the picture? I did a weekly Leisure Supplement, ten pages every Thursday, with a . . . you don't care about this crap. I don't care about this crap.

"So one day I'm sitting at my little steel desk. This place is a reconverted warehouse, one immense office, and the editorial department is six desks pushed together in the back, near the paste-up tables and the library and the wire. Everybody else is gone to lunch, and I'm just gonna leave myself when this guy from accounting comes over. I couldn't remember his name; he was one of those grim, stolid, fatalistic guys that accounting departments run to. He hands me two envelopes. 'This is for you,' he says, 'and this one's for Tom.' Tom was the hippie who put out the weekly Real Estate Supplement. So I start to open mine—it feels like there's candy in it—and he gives me this *look* and says, 'Oh *no,* not *now.*' I look at him like *huh?* and he says, 'Not until it's time. You'll know when,' and he leaves. *Okay,* I say to myself, and I put both envelopes in a drawer, and I go to lunch and forget it.

"About three o'clock I wrap up my work, and I get to thinking about how strange his face looked when he gave me those envelopes. So I take out mine and open it. Inside it are two very big downs—you know, powerful tranquilizers. I sit up straight. I open Tom's envelope, and if I hadn't worked in a drugstore once, I never would have recognized it. Demerol. Synthetic morphine, one of the most addictive drugs in the world.

"Now Tom is a hippie-looking guy, like I say, long hair and mustache, not long like yours, but long for a newspaper. So I figure this accounting guy is maybe his pusher and somehow he's got the idea I'm a potential customer. I was kind of fidgety and tense in those days. So I get mad as hell, and I'm just thinking about taking Tom into the darkroom and chewing him out good, and I look up, and the guy from accounting is staring at me from all the way across the room. No expression at all, he just looks. It gives me the heebie-jeebies.

"Now, overhead is this gigantic air-conditioning unit, from the old warehouse days, that's supposed to cool the whole building and never does. What it does is drip water on editorial and make so much goddamn noise you can't talk on the phone while it's on. And what it does, right at that moment, is rip loose and drop straight down, maybe eight hundred pounds. It crushes all the desks in editorial, and it kills Mabel and Art and Dolores and Phil and takes two toes off of Tom's right foot and misses me completely. A flying piece of wire snips off one of my ponytails.

"So I sit there with my mouth open, and in the silence I hear the publisher say, 'God *damn* it,' from the middle of the room, and I climb over the wreckage and get the Demerol into Tom, and then I make a tourniquet on his arch out of rubber bands and blue pencils, and then everybody's taking me away and saying stupid things. I took those two tranquilizers and went home.''

She took a sip of her coffee and sat up a little straighter. Her eyes were the color of sun-cured Hawaiian buds. ''They shut the paper down for a week. The next day, when I woke up, I got out my employee directory and looked this guy up. While Bobby was in school, I went over to his house. It took me hours to break him down, but I wouldn't take no answer for an answer. Finally he gave up.

'' 'I've got fivesight,' he told me. 'Something just a little bit better than foresight.' It was the only joke I ever heard him make, then or since.''

I made the gasping sound again. ''Precognition,'' Doc Webster breathed. Awkwardly, from my tailor's seat, I worked my keys out of my pocket and tossed them to Callahan. He caught them in the coffee can he had ready and started a shot of Bushmill's on its way to me without a word.

''You know the expression 'Bad news travels fast'?'' she asked. ''For him it travels so fast it gets there before the event. About three hours before, more or less. But only *bad* news. Disasters, accidents, traumas large and small are all he ever sees.''

''That sounds ideal,'' Doc Webster said thoughtfully. ''He doesn't have to lose the fun of *pleasant* surprises, but he doesn't have to worry about unpleasant ones. That sounds like the best way to . . .'' He shifted his immense bulk in his chair. ''Damn it, what *is* the verb for precognition? *Precognite?*''

"Ain't they the guys that sang that 'Jeremiah was a bullfrog' song?" Long-Drink murmured to Tommy, who kicked him hard in the shins.

"That shows how much you know about it," she told the Doc. "He has *three hours* to worry about each unpleasant surprise—and there's a stRickly limited amount he can do about it."

The Doc opened his mouth and then shut it tight and let her tell it. A good doctor hates forming opinions in ignorance.

"The first thing I asked him when he told me was why hadn't he warned Phil and Mabel and the others. And then I caught myself and said, 'What a dumb question! How're you going to keep six people away from their desks *without telling them why?* Forget I asked that.'

" 'It's worse than that,' he told me. 'It's not that I'm trying to preserve some kind of secret identity—it's that it wouldn't do the slightest bit of good anyway. I can ameliorate—to some extent. But I *cannot* prevent. No matter what. I'm not . . . not permitted.'

" 'Permitted by who?' I asked.

" 'By whoever or whatever sends me these damned premonitions in the first place,' he said. 'I haven't the faintest idea who.'

" 'What exactly are the limitations?'

" 'If a pot of water is going to boil over and scald me, I can't just not make tea that night. Sooner or later I *will* make tea and scald myself. The longer I put off the inevitable, the worse I get burned. But if I accept it and let it happen in its natural time, I'm allowed to, say, have a pot of ice water handy to stick my hand in. When I saw that my neighbor's steering

54

box was going to fail, I couldn't keep him from driving that day, but I could remind him to wear his seatbelt, and so his injuries were minimized. But if I'd seen him dying in that wreck, I couldn't have done *anything*—except arrange to be near the wife when she got the news. It's . . . it's especially bad to try to prevent a death. The results are . . .' I saw him start to say 'horrible' and reject it as not strong enough. He couldn't find anything strong enough.

" 'Okay, Cass,' I said real quick. 'So at least you can help some. That's more than some doctors can do. I think that was really terrific of you, to bring me that stuff like that, take a chance that I'd think you were—hey, how did you get hold of narcotics on three hours' notice?'

" 'I had three hours' warning for the last big black-out,' he told me. 'I took two suitcases of stuff out of Smithtown General while they were trying to get their emergency generator going. I . . . have uses for the stuff.' "

She looked down into her empty cup, then handed it to Eddie, who had it refilled. While he was gone, she stared at her lap, breathing with her whole torso, lungs cycling slowly from absolutely full to empty.

"I was grateful to him. I felt sorry for him. I figured he needed somebody to help him. I figured after a manic-oppressive like Freddie, a quiet, phlegmatic kind of guy might suit me better. His favorite expression was, 'What's done is done.' I started dating him. One day Bobby fell . . . fell out of a tree and broke his leg, and Uncle Cass just happened to be walking by with a hypo and splints." She looked up and around at us, and her eyes fastened on me. "Maybe I wanted my kid to be safe.'' She looked away again. ''Make a long story short, I married him.''

I spilled a little Bushmill's down my beard. No one seemed to notice.

''It's . . . funny,'' she said slowly, and getting out that second word cost her a lot. ''It's really damned funny. At first . . . at first, there, he was really good for my nerves. He never got angry. Nothing rattled him. He never got emotional the way men do, never got the blues. It's not that he doesn't *feel* things. I thought so at first, but I was wrong. It's just that . . . living with a thing like that, either he could be irritable enough to bite people's heads off all the time, or he could learn how to hold it all in. That's what he did, probably back when he was a little kid. 'What's done is done,' he'd say, and keep on going. He *does* need to be held and cared for, have his shoulders rubbed out after a bad one, have one person he can tell about it. I *know* I've been good for him, and I guess at first it made me feel kind of special. As if it took some kind of genius person to share pain.'' She closed her eyes and grimaced. ''Oh, and Bobby came to love him so!''

There was a silence.

''Then the weirdness of it started to get to me. He'd put a Band-Aid in his pocket, and a couple of hours later he'd cut his finger chopping lettuce. I'd get diarrhea and run to the john, and there'd be my favorite magazine on the floor. I'd come downstairs at bedtime for vitamins and find every pot in the house full of water, and go back up to bed wondering what the hell, and wake up a little while later to find that a socket short had set the living room on fire before it tripped the breaker and he had it under control. I'd catch him concealing some little preparation from me, and know that it was for me or Bobby, and I'd carry on and beg him to tell me—and the *best* of those times were when all I could make him tell me was, 'What's done is done.'

"I started losing sleep and losing weight.

"And then one day the principal called just before dinner to tell me that a school bus had been hit by a tractor-trailer and fourteen students were critically injured and Bobby and another boy were . . . I threw the telephone across the room at him, I jumped on him like a wild animal and punched him with my fists. I screamed and screamed. 'YOU DIDN'T EVEN TRY!' " she screamed again now, and it rang and rang in the stillness of Callahan's Place. I wanted to leap up and take her in my arms, let her sob it out against my chest, but something held me back.

She pulled herself together and gulped cold coffee. You could hear the air conditioner sigh and the clock whir. You could not hear cloth rustle or a chair creak. When she spoke again, her voice was under rigid control. It made my heart sick to hear it.

"I left him for a week. He must have been hurting more than *I* was. So I left him and stayed in a crummy motel, curled up around my own pain. He made all the arrangements, and made them hold off burying Bobby until I came back, and when I did, all he said was . . . what I expected him to say, and we went on living.

"I started drinking. I mean, I started in that motel and kept it up when I went home. I never had before. I drank alone. I don't know if he ever found out. He must have. He never said anything. I . . . just started growing *away* from him. I knew it wasn't right or fair, but I just turned off to him completely. He never said anything. All this started happening about six months ago. I just got more and more self-destructive, more crazy, more . . . hungry for something.''

She closed her eyes and straightened her shoulders. ''Tonight is Cass's bowling night. This afternoon I . . .'' She opened her eyes. ''. . . I made a date with a stockboy at the Pathmark supermarket. I told him to come by around ten, when my husband was gone. After supper he got his ball and shoes ready, like always, and left. I started to clean up in the kitchen so I'd have time to get juiced before Wally showed up. Out of the corner of my eye I saw Cass tiptoe back into the living room. He was carrying a big manila envelope and something else I couldn't see; the envelope was in the way. I pretended not to see him, and in a few seconds I heard the door close behind him.

''I dried my hands. I went into the living room. On the mantel, by the bedroom door, was the envelope, tucked behind the flowerpot. Tucked behind it was his service revolver. I left it there and walked out the door and came here and started drinking, and now I've had enough of this fucking coffee. I want a screwdriver.''

Fast Eddie deserves his name. He was the first of us to snap out of the trance, and it probably didn't take him more than thirty seconds. He walked over to the bar on his banty little legs and slapped down a dollar and said, ''Screwdriver, Mike.''

Callahan shook his head slightly. He drew on his cigar and frowned at it for having gone out. He flung it into the fireplace and built a screwdriver, and he never said a mumblin' word. Eddie brought her the drink. She drained half at once.

Shorty Steinitz spoke up, and his voice sounded rusty. "I service air-conditioning systems. The big ones. I was over at Century Lanes today. Their unit has an intermittent that I can't seem to trace. It keeps cuttin' in and out."

She shut her eyes and did something similar to smiling and nodded her head. "That's it, all right. He'll be home early."

Then she looked me square in the eye.

"Well, Jake, do you understand now? I'm scared as hell! Because I'm here instead of there, and so he's not going to kill me after all. And he tells me that if you try to prevent a death, something worse happens, and I'm going out of my mind wondering what could be worse than getting killed!"

Total horror flooded through me; I thought my heart would stop.

I *knew* what was worse than getting killed.

Dear Jesus, no, I thought, and I couldn't help it. I wanted very badly to keep my face absolutely straight and my eyes holding hers, and I couldn't help it. There was just that tiny hope, and so I glanced for the merest instant at the Counterclock and then back to her. And in that moment of moments, scared silly and three-quarters bagged, she was seeing me clearly enough to pick up on it and know from my face that something was wrong.

It was 10:15.

My heart was a stone. I knew the answers to the next questions, and again I couldn't help myself: I had to ask them.

"Mrs.—"

"Kathy Anders. What's the *matter?*" Just what I had asked her, a few centuries ago.

"Kathy, you . . . you didn't lock the house behind you when you left?"

Callahan went pale behind the bar, and his new cigar fell out of his mouth.

"No," she said. "What the *hell* has that—"

"And you were too upset to think of—"

"Oh, *Christ,*" she screamed. "Oh, no, I never thought! Oh, Christ, *Wally,* that dumb cocky kid. He'll show up at ten and find the door wide open and figure I went to the corner for beer and decide it's cute to wait for me in bed, and—" She whirled and found the clock, and puzzled out the time somehow, and wailed, *"No!"* And I tore in half right down the middle. She sprang from her chair and lurched toward the bar. I could not get to my feet to follow her. Callahan was already holding out the telephone, and when she couldn't dial it, he got the number out of her and dialed it for her. His face was carven from marble. I was just getting up on my hind legs by then. No one else moved. My feet made no sound at all on the sawdust. I could clearly hear the phone ringing on the other end. Once. Twice. Three times. "Come on, Cass, damn you, answer me!" Four times. *Oh dear God,* I thought, *she still doesn't get it.* Five times. *Maybe she does get it—and won't have it.* Six times.

It was picked up on the seventh ring, and at once she was shrieking, "You *killed* him, you *bastard.* He was just a jerk kid, and you had to—"

She stopped and held the phone at arm's length and stared at it. It chittered at her, an agitated chipmunk. Her eyes went round.

"Wally?" she asked it weakly. Then even more weakly she said to it, "That's his *will* in that manila envelope," and she fainted.

"Mike!" I cried, and leaped forward. The big barkeep understood me somehow and lunged across the bar on his belly and caught the phone in both hands. That left me my whole attention to deal with her, and I needed that and all my strength to get her to the floor gently.

"Wally," Callahan was saying to the chipmunk, "Wally, *listen to me*. This is a friend. I know what happened, and—*listen* to me, Wally, I'm trying to keep your ass out of the slam. Are you listening to me, son? Here's what you've got to do—"

Someone crowded me on my left, and I almost belted him before I realized it was Doc Webster with smelling salts.

"No, *screw* fingerprints, this ain't TV. Just make up the goddamn bed and put yer cigarette butts in yer pocket and *don't touch anything else*—"

She coughed and came around.

"—sure nobody sees you leave, and then you get your ass over to Callahan's bar, off 25A. We got thirty folks here'll swear you been here all night, but it'd be nice if we knew what you looked like."

She stared up at us vacantly, and as I was helping her get up and into a chair, I was talking. I wanted her to be involved in listening to me when full awareness returned. It would be very hard to hold her, and I was absolutely certain I could do it.

"Kathy, you've got to listen carefully to me, because if you don't, in just another minute now you're going to try and swallow one giant egg of guilt,

61

and it will, believe me, stick in your throat and choke you. You're choking on a couple already, and this one might kill you—and it's not fair, it's not right, it's not just. You're gonna award yourself a guilt that you don't deserve, and the moment you accept it and pin it on it'll stay with you for the rest of your life. Believe me, I *know*. Damn it, *it's okay to be glad you're still alive!*"

"What the hell do you know about it?" she cried out.

"I've been there," I said softly. "As recently as an hour ago."

Her eyes widened.

"I came in here tonight so egocentrically wrapped up in my own pain that I sat next to you for fifteen minutes and never noticed you, until some friends woke me up. This is a kind of anniversary for me. Kathy. Five years and one day ago I had a wife and a two-year-old daughter. And I had a *Big Book of Auto Repair*. I decided I could save thirty dollars easy by doing my own brake job. I tested it myself and drove myself a whole block. Five years ago tonight all three of us went to the drive-in movie. I woke up without a scratch on me. Both dead. I smiled at the man who was trying to cut my door open, and I climbed out the window past him and tried to get my wrists on his chainsaw. He coldcocked me, and I woke up under restraint." I locked eyes with her. "I was glad to be alive, too. That's why I wanted to die so bad."

She blinked and spoke very softly. "How . . . how did you keep alive?"

"I got talking with a doctor the size of a hippo

62

named Sam Webster, and he got me turned loose and brought me around here.''

She waited for me to finish. ''You—that's it? What is that?''

''Dis is Callahan's Place,'' Eddie said.

''This place is magic,'' I told her.

''Magic? *Bull*shit, magic, it's a *bar*. People come here to get blind.''

''No. Not this one. People come to this bar to see. That's why I'm ashamed at how long it took me to see you. This is the place where people care. For as long as I sat here in my pain, my friends were in pain with me and did what they could to help. They told stories of past blunders to make it a little easier for me to make my annual toast to my family without embarrassing myself. You know what gives me the courage to keep on living? The courage to love myself a little? It's having a whole bunch of friends who really give a Goddamn. When you share pain, there's less of it, and when you share joy, there's more of it. That's a basic fact of the universe, and I learned it here. I've seen it work honest-to-God miracles.''

''Name me a miracle.''

''Of all the gin joints in all the world, you come into this one. Tonight, of all the nights in the year. And you look like her, and your name is Kathy.''

She gaped. ''I—your wife?—I look—?''

''Oh, not a ringer—that only happens on *The Late Show*. But close enough to scare me silly. Don't you see, Kathy? For five years now I've been using that word, *fivesight,* not in conversation, just in my head, as a private label for precognition. I jumped when you said it. For five years now I've been wishing to

God I'd been born with it. I was wishing it earlier tonight.

"Now I know better."

Her jaw worked, but she made no sound.

"We'll help you, Kathy," Callahan said.

"Damn straight," Eddie croaked.

"We'll help you find your own miracle," Long-Drink assured her. "They come by here regular."

There were murmurs of agreement, encouraging words. She stared around the place as though we had all turned into toads. "And what do you want from me?" she snapped.

"That you hold up your end," I said. "That you not leave us holding the bag. Suicide isn't just a cop-out; it's a rip-off."

She shook her head, as violently as she dared. "People don't *do* that; people don't act this way."

My voice softened, saddened. "Upright apes don't. People do."

She finished her drink. "But—"

"Listen, we just contradicted something you said earlier. It seems like it *does* take some kind of genius person to share pain. And I think you did a better job than I could have done. Two, three *years* you stayed with that poor bastard? Kathy, that strength and compassion you gave to Cass for so long, the imagination and empathy you have so much of, those are things we badly need here. We get a lot of incoming wounded. You could be of use here, while you're waiting for your own miracle."

She looked around at every face, looked long at Callahan and longest at me.

Then she shook her head and said, "Maybe I

already got it,'' and she burst finally and explosively into tears, flinging herself into my arms. They were the right kind of tears. I smiled and smiled for some considerable time, and then I saw the clock and got very businesslike. Wally would be along soon, and there was much to be done. "Okay, Eddie, you get her address from her purse and ankle over there. Make sure that fool kid didn't screw up. Pyotr, you Litvak Samaritan, go on out and wake up your wheels. Here, Drink, you get her out to the parking lot; I can't hold her up much longer. Margie, you're the girl friend she went to spend the weekend with yesterday, okay? You're gonna put her up until she's ready to face the cops. Doc, you figure out what she's contracted that she doesn't want to bother her husband by calling. Shorty, if nobody discovers the body by, say, tomorrow noon, you make a service call to the wrong address and find him. Mike—''

Callahan was already holding out one finger of Irish.

"Say, Jake,'' Callahan said softly, "didn't I hear your wife's name was Diane? Kinda short and red-haired and jolly, gray eyes?''

We smiled at each other. "It was a plausible miracle that didn't take a whole lot of buildup and explanation. What if I'd told her we stopped an alien from blowing up the earth in here once?''

"You talk good on your feet, son.''

I walked up to the chalk line. "Let me make the toast now,'' I said loudly. "The same one I've made annually for five years—with a little addition.''

Folks hushed up and listened.

"To my family,'' I said formally, then drained the

Irish and gently underhanded my glass into the hearth.

And then I turned around and faced them all and added, "Each and every one of you."

ICONS

By Barry N. Malzberg

"My Hemingway keeps mumbling about the ulti mate *nada,*" Smith said, "and the darkness and the light. It keeps trying to go upstairs to lock itself in the bathroom with my carbine. I have to shut off the power, but one of these days I'm not going to be home when it happens."

Jones nodded glumly. *"My* Hemingway wants to go running with the bulls," he said, "calls it the ultimate quest and so on, but what it really wants is to be gored. It keeps on looking out the window, staring at the pavement, and I have to pull it back inside."

I shrugged. There was no point in admitting that *my* Hemingway slipped off while I was at the slaughtering docks yesterday and put a hole in its Plexiglas head. I had the same warnings as Smith and Jones: No one to blame. "Not good," I said.

"It's always the same damned things," Jones said bitterly. "They send these things out glistening with their white beards and fiery eyes, and they're marvelously entertaining for a few weeks, typing and drinking away and speaking of the clean and the just, and next thing you know they're off in corners whispering about telescopic sights. I say it's disgusting."

"Design defect," Smith said knowingly, "built into the machines. Planned obsolescence. Self-destructing. Good turnover. A need for replacements all the time. It's all planned."

"Well, I won't take it anymore," Jones said. "You have to take a position, make a stand."

"That's the ticket," Smith said. "Draw the line. Fight for truth. Stand up to the bastards once and for all."

They looked at me expectantly. I have their trust. In a way I am the ringleader, by unspoken consensus.

"Agreed, gentlemen," I said. "One must take a stand."

We left the Juicer and took the tramway to the central offices of Icons, Inc., located in the packing district. As soon as we arrived, we could see the dimensions of the problem. The offices were ringed by thousands of demonstrators, chanting in an ugly way for justice. Barricades had been established, and the police were restraining the crowd. Many had brought their defective or imploded Hemingways to wave above their heads. The problem, as we had suspected, was quite widespread.

"Who would have known?" Smith said reverently. "There is still some spirit left in us—and outrage."

"There are limits," Jones agreed. "They cannot sell us defective icons indefinitely. We can only take this stuff for so long."

We established positions at the rear and joined in the chant. Smith's face flushed with accomplishment. Jones seemed timorous; he lacks physical courage—a quality that he had hoped his Hemingway might have given him, more's the pity.

"New Hemingways!" we shouted. "Hemingways that live, not Hemingways that die!" Gunshots were heard as, here and there in the crowd, defective Hemingways found their masters' weapons and did away with themselves on the spot.

An employee of Icons, Inc., came out on a balcony. Even from this distance we could see him shaking. They usually assign a minor functionary to address rioters. "Be reasonable," the junior shouted. "Disperse! You are breaking the law."

"Justice!" we shouted. The police, with their weapons holstered, stood looking in the opposite direction. After all, many of them had Hemingways, too. "Go home!" the junior said, but he was pelted by debris. He recoiled under a hail of garbage.

"All right," he bellowed suddenly, "we'll make an adjustment."

"No adjustments!" we shouted, quite caught up in the moment. "Justice!" We knew that we would prevail. We always do in these confrontations. After all, Icons is dependent upon our goodwill. Remember the Monroe riots and their outcome.

"Very well," the junior said, "we accept return of all Hemingways. For full credit."

We cheered.

"And we will apply the full cost of each toward the purchase of a Kennedy. Only taxation differential will be due."

We cheered again. Everyone thinks of the Kennedy with anticipation. Rumors are that models had been in production for years but were being held back purposely to manipulate greater demand.

"A Kennedy for everyone!" the junior screamed. "Everyone, *all* of you will know that they will fight any battle, share any cause in the struggle for freedom. Friend and foe alike will know that a new generation, forged from a hard and bitter peace—"

But he could no longer be heard, so great now were the cheers.

I can't wait for my Kennedy. He will put strength in my spine, sparkle in my eyes, purpose in each dreary day. It will be like the early days with the Hemingway before the terrible design defect manifested itself.

Smith fears, however, that the Kennedy will also prove defective. "You can't trust these corporations," he points out. "They probably have an obsolescence factor in the Kennedy as well. But Icons is clever."

"What do you mean?" I ask.

"I mean, this time, when it breaks down, they'll have it arranged so it looks like *our* fault," Smith says bitterly. "Wait and see."

Jones and I, however, disgusted with Smith's pessimism, have threatened to do him damage if he doesn't shut up. If you can't trust a Kennedy, what then?

THE GENIUS HOUSE

By Dmitri Bilenkin
Translated by Antonina W. Bouis

"After you," Yurkov said with an expansive gesture.

"Here?" Smolin asked again, clumsily getting out of the jetcar.

"If you like it."

Yurkov's speckled eyes were heavy lidded, indifferent, yet a hidden mischief splashed around in them. Smolin cleared his throat and looked around.

The grass on the meadow glistened with such bright patterns of color that he wanted to hug it to his chest. A few birches threw a translucent, shimmering shadow. The forest approached from three sides, the river opened on the fourth, and the distant foothills showed blue. The bright snowcaps of the peaks cast a pure reflection, sky-clear, over everything.

Smolin took a deep breath.

"It's wonderful here . . ."

"Then let's get on with it," Yurkov said, business-like.

His thin body leaned over the side of the jetcar. He pulled a heavy bag out from under the seat, extracted a crystal that gave off a dull glint, and handed it to Smolin. The shape of the semitransparent crystal vaguely reminded Smolin of a crystal egg with facets on the sides that he used to play with as a child.

"Catch!"

The "egg" turned out to be unexpectedly light. Smolin clutched it awkwardly to his chest. It felt warm and, despite its hardness, supple. When he turned the facets vague waves rolled in its green murky depths and dots of violet light flashed.

"It looks strange," Smolin muttered.

"And how." Yurkov laughed. "Go on."

"How?"

"Very simple. Choose a site. Uneven terrain, weak slope, it doesn't matter. Stand where you think the house should be. Just watch that there are at least ten meters to the nearest tree or bush. That's it!"

Smolin took a few uncertain steps.

"How about here?" he asked, looking around.

"Wonderful! Throw the egg."

Smolin carefully lowered the crystal to the ground. The bright edge of a cloud, glowing blindingly, touched the sun. The meadow grew dark.

"Now stand back."

From the same bag Yurkov extracted a funnel with a prismatic reflector on the end. Stepping back toward the jetcar, he unwound a cord.

"Get back, back, it'll knock you down."

"What?"

"It's going to get a bit windy. Take off your bracelet—it might get broken." Yurkov unbuckled his wrist videophone and tossed it on the jetcar seat. "Put yours there, it will be protected by the windshield. There, now everything's in order."

Leaning over the fender, Yurkov plugged in the cord and, stepping back from the jetcar, casually pointed the funnel in the direction of the egg. Something buzzed in it. Yurkov's hand froze.

Nothing happened. The crickets chirped drily, and the greenish oval of the crystal lay peacefully among the daisies. It had gotten dull in the grass and looked like an ordinary stone, except for its regular shape.

Then something changed. The surface of the crystal grew cloudy, as though spinning fast. What had been a rock a minute ago was now melting, running, puffing up in an orange blob.

"Aha!" said Yurkov. "You see?"

The blob, spreading and growing, took on a mushroom shape. Smoky streams spun wildly and silently. It looked like a miniaturized atomic blast.

A hard wind hit their backs, bent the tops of the nearest birches, and roared through the glade. Smolin spread his legs to steady himself. The wind pushed dry leaves, litter, grass, and they disappeared without a trace in the dark mushroom whirlwind.

Now resting on a thin stem, the brownish mass hung over the meadow. It whirled, gradually becoming rectangular. Yellow and reddish spots, quickly changing, appeared in it. The air trembled, breaking the outline of the bent trees.

Four branches separated themselves from the mass and touched the ground: smoke rose.

"The rooting phase," Yurkov commented. "The air gives our baby nitrogen, oxygen, carbon. The rest of the materials it needs it gets from the earth, as becomes as well-behaved plant. My raygun plays the part of the sun. Of course, I wouldn't recommend trying to get a tan under a sun like that . . . There, the segmentary phase has begun."

The wind had died down a bit. About a meter and a half from the ground the shapeless mass had formed a smooth bottom with five supports going into the ground—one in each corner and a fifth, thicker one, right in the middle. The grass around it was covered with hoarfrost. The mass itself took up a solid expanse of space. It was obviously turning to glass, even though the inner agitation did not quiet down. Semispheres took shape—one, two, three. Quickly, as in a kaleidoscope, the pattern of the surface changed. Inside, voluminous shapes formed. Some passed out the outside, others went deep inside. One of the semispheres suddenly melted. It was as if someone had waved a chisel and now it was a wall and in it—the most natural, transparent, slightly convex window.

The wind stopped completely. The house continued taking shape. It looked as if someone's sneaky fingers were constructing it from inside.

The cloud finally crept down from the sun, and the first bright ray was reflected in the crystal sails of the windows, warmed up the convex walls, deepened the shadows, added the finishing touches.

"There!" Yurkov looked at his watch. "And it only took seventeen and a half minutes. Congratulations on your new house!"

"Yes," Smolin drawled. "Embryotechnology, I see, has made significant strides. How fast and accurate!"

"We do our best," Yurkov said and smiled with restraint. "Oh course, speed is not the important thing here. In general, classical embryotechnology is a finished phase."

"Finished?"

"Well, the basic principle of course, is the same," Yurkov explained with condescension. "Do everything like nature does, do it better than nature does. And the basic methods of construction coincide, too. Embryo or seed, or cell, in which lies the entire genetic program of the development, the way the oak lies in the acorn. Feeding, growth at the expense, so to speak, of local materials—air, earth, water, solar energy . . . Of the raygun, but that's not the point. Basically the analogy is complete except for the speed—this is millions of times faster. Man speeds up whatever he touches, isn't that so?"

"Everything, including himself?" Smolin shook his head suspiciously. "However you haven't answered my question."

"Patience, patience. You won't just hear, you'll see an answer."

"See?"

"Like this house."

"Then why not do it now?"

"First of all, I have to show you the house first, and we can't cross the threshold until there is thermodynamic equilibrium. Secondly, my ancestors were salesmen—I like to show off my wares! You wanted to live alone and work in a beautiful setting. Right? Right. You approved of the place, and here's the house. Do you like it?"

Smolin nodded. The house resembled an exquisite

shell surrounded by birches. Even though it was raised above the ground and the supports looked shaky, it did not create the impression of instability. Smolin couldn't tell how that was achieved.

The house wasn't pretentious, either. It fit well into the landscape. It had the naturalness of a creation of mother nature. Yes, its creator knew how to work with scope and taste.

"I feel funny," Smolin muttered. "All this, and for just one person. I mean, I understand that the house wasn't built just for me, when I leave, other people will live in it. But . . . What's that!"

The underpinnings of the house were suddenly bathed in a soft, diffused glow.

"Come on!"

Grabbing his bag, Yurkov trotted to the house.

"That light," he said over his shoulder, "means that the house is ready to welcome its owners. By the way, look under the floor."

Smolin bent down. The entire bottom of the house emitted a warm, sunny light. Under the house and around it thick dew glistened in rainbow drops. If you didn't count that, the grass was just the same, except for the dried blades that surrounded the central support.

"It will repair itself there, too," Yurkov said, waving his hand. "You must agree that our house doesn't harm the environment at all."

"You mean that light replaces the sun for the grass under . . ."

"Exactly right. Come in, come in! I have to introduce you to the house."

"What do you mean?"

"Well, familiarize you with it, don't nitpick. After all these aren't simply walls, roof, and so on. Before you, if you will, is a quasicreature. It grew, fed, it's breathing, it's alive in a way."

Yurkov halted in the entryway.

"The last operation, just a minute . . . Do you see that red circle in the wall? The latch is here. We push back the cover. This is the nest for the battery. We take it . . ."

He took out a knurled cylinder from his bag and removed the cap from the face. The blue-gray sockets were revealed.

"There! We attach the battery in the nest—watch!—like so, there . . . Everything's fine! For a month, or maybe more, the house is guaranteed energy. The length of time without recharging depends on your usage and sky conditions. Absolutely correct: the house accumulates solar light, it shouldn't be wasted . . . At first the house also has a reserve of activational energy, which is stored during construction. But it's a piffle, as is the solar energy. The real heart of the house is here! Let's look at the rooms. After you."

There were two rooms—a smaller one for the study and a larger bedroom. In the bedroom a huge stereo screen showed the swaying shadows of the birches.

And there was nothing else in the rooms. Smolin lifted his eyebrows.

"Thought furniture?"

"The very same."

Yurkov gracefully waved his hand. The floor swayed, crested, formed a back and armrests.

Yurkov, without a glance, sank into the already formed armchair.

"What's wrong with it?"

Smolin shrugged.

"I'm not saying anything's wrong with it. I just don't understand this new fashion. Why build the mental image of chair, bed, table every time, why invent more and more complex receptors for their creation, when it would be a lot simpler, I think, to just put in ordinary furniture. We economize on muscular energy and strain our brain."

"You exaggerate." Yurkov instantly changed the armchair into a swing and leaned back. "It's not that complicated or difficult. Is it better to drag your furniture around with you? Two moves equal one fire, as they used to say in the olden days. By the way, don't you find this light just a little harsh? We didn't bring shades, but . . ."

Yurkov squinted petulantly. The crystal of the windows, remaining transparent, grew darker, and a pleasant, diffused light filled the rooms.

"Nice work," Smolin said respectfully.

"That's nothing!" Yurkov had jumped up with the look of a magician who had a fluttering pigeon up his sleeve. "Come over here, at the edge of the window you can see the thickness of the glass biolyte. A petal, right? One hard hit and . . . and what if there are children? The little fellow plays hard, runs and trips . . . He'd fall a meter or two. Let's re-create the situation! I weigh more than a child, I take a running leap . . . Don't watch me, watch the window! One, two . . ."

Yurkov leaped. The biolyte of the window was so transparent and thin that it seemed that Yurkov would shoot through like a cannon ball. Smolin lurched forward involuntarily to help him. And in vain. The wall seemed to blink; the window narrowed and thickened and the biolyte bounced Yurkov back, like a rubber ball.

Smolin gasped. The window slowly melted and went back to its original form.

"There you go!" Yurkov said, rubbing his shoulder.

"It would have been easier to make the biolyte thicker in the first place," Smolin said in confusion.

"That remains to be seen," Yurkov said with a slight laugh. "The water, by the way, is supplied by the house itself; no matter how low the water table is, the central support reaches it as efficiently as a tree root."

Yurkov gabbed on, "Do you smell any odors? Staleness?"

"What? No, the air is fresh."

"It's forest air, notice, all the rooms are filled with fresh forest air! Even though constant metabolic reactions are taking place. Even brick has a smell, and as for a living creature . . . But try to find the ventilation. Or find a crack anywhere. It's solid! Total hermetic seal everywhere. There's no ventilation in the usual sense of the word, no vents, no drafts, yet the air is marvelous. Have you ever seen anything like it?"

"I have to admit that I haven't."

"Can you guess how it's done?"

Smolin shook his head.

"It's the whole house," Yurkov said, lowering his voice in awe. "The windows breathe and ventilate. Millions of invisible apertures and without any diminution of transparency—what do you think of that? That's why the membrane is so thin. Once upon a time they used to call a house a 'machine for living.' It should have been called a tin can . . . Everything is different here. Functionally, our house is an organism. Like any organism, it tries to maintain an optimum internal environment. The principle of homeostatis! But . . . there is another, very important difference. The optimum for the house is you and me. We set it. *We* do!"

Yurkov had his finger in the air. His eyes shone with rapture and naturally, Smolin should have made some appropriate comment, expressed some awe, but he couldn't manage it.

"Interesting," he said shortly. "We are the house's optimum. What does that mean?"

"But it's clear!" Yurkov shouted. "No house is capable of supporting itself and certainly not of protecting man. Only our house can protect itself, the way it did with the window, and protect man. A plant with its reactions speeded up a million times! Come what may—storm, earthquake, Attila with his cannons—you can sleep peacefully . . ."

"Excuse me! Attila didn't have cannons."

"Does that matter? The important thing is that the house will set down extra roots, instantly shore up its walls, it will adjust. I'm sure that's the way it would be in nature if not for the paltry amount of energy. But we aren't limited by that."

"Well, it's a wonderful house for inclement planets . . ."

"It's ideal! The most important difference between our house and all creations of nature and technology is this. Plants exist for themselves. Machines belong to us completely, but they are inert physical bodies, alas. We crossed both types of evolution, taking the best of both and deleting the drawbacks. The entire basic program of life activity of the house consists in satisfying human needs as if they were its own. If the house had even a glimmer of intelligence it would acknowledge us as its most important part, its soul, if you will. Air—for us, water—for us warmth, pliancy, flexibility—all, everything just for us!"

"That's genius!" Smolin exclaimed.

"And believe me, it is worthy of pride and astonishment! That's not an empty compliment. When I think that all this—the walls, the faucets, the breathing, protective windows, the floor that creates furniture—that all this inconceivable complexity was a crystal, a code inside it, just a few minutes ago—a shiver comes over me! Yes, you've surpassed nature, I congratulate you with all my heart."

"Thank you. But it's not complex . . ." Yurkov waved his hand feebly. "You feel pride but when you remember that we ourselves, our eyes that are capable of weeping, our tireless hearts, our brains that learn about the universe, it all came from a clump of tiny molecules, was merely a notation, a code inside them . . . We're so far behind nature. But there's something about our new creation that you really don't like. What is it?"

"You see," Smolin began, choosing his words carefully and pacing. "The point is . . . No, first, this question. Why did you offer your experimental house to me—why me!? My tastes, preferences . . .''

"That's what determined the choice."

"Another riddle?"

"On the contrary. I spent too much time impressing you, mystifying you, and I deserve the rebuke. The house is experimental, but not technologically, everything is proven in that area. It promises a revolution in the way of life for all of humanity. That's why we had to know ahead of time which people would react to it. In relation to progress you can always find those who welcome anything new, simply because it's new, and those who are hostile to any innovation. Everything is clear with those two small groups. We are more interested in the reaction of that large part of humanity that is in no hurry to trust innovation. You are a typical representative of it.''

"Thank you very much," Smolin said drily. "It's so flattering to find out you're considered a typical conservative.''

"Moderate, moderate!" Yurkov smiled.

"All right, we've exchanged pleasantries, now we're quits. I'm all for honest, businesslike relations. What do you need from me, concretely?"

"For now, a preliminary critique of the house, based on your first impressions.''

"You'll have it, don't worry."

Smolin created a chair for himself with great effort and seated himself opposite Yurkov.

"I don't want to dwell on details. The windows that are so perfected that you can't open them, even though it's sometimes nice to have the wind travel around the room!"

"I agree," Yurkov nodded. "The house is overly concerned with maintaining its integrity. We hope in future models to . . . ."

"Trifles! But have you realized what you're doing? You've removed the last obstacle that keeps man from settling wherever he wants. And the results? Houses that arise with the ease of mushrooms instantly fill up the earth. Except for the preserves, soon there will be no untouched corner left. Not one! Hasn't the history of the automobile taught us anything? At least, they rusted quickly. But billions of your houses! What will we turn the planet into?"

"You're right!" Yurkov slapped his knee. That's your main objection? You don't have any others?"

Smolin hesitated. There was something else important, some feeling, but he couldn't verbalize it.

"That's it for now," he said slowly. "What makes you so happy about that?"

"I'll explain. Billions of new houses, you say? In every corner of the earth? What about hundreds of billions? Trillions? You're convinced that you'll be in this house temporarily and that it's meant for everyone. A mistake! As soon as we finish our testing, every person will have the opportunity to grow his own house to his own taste. Everyone! And as many as he wants. There are the true prospects. Don't look at me like that! I'll show you something. Come on."

Yurkov caught Smolin in his turbulent wake and carried him out to the foyer.

"Here," and Yurkov's finger triumphantly pressed into the battery nest, "is hidden the most important aspect of the house. What, I ask you, is the basic flaw in construction? Man needs housing in the most varied parts of the planet, many houses—for work, rest, travel—and he can't live in all of them simultaneously. That's why there are so many empty and half-empty houses, necessary from time to time, taking up space and material. Therefore, what should the ideal house be? A house that exists when it's necessary and does not exist when it is no longer necessary. We are standing in just such a house."

"You don't mean to say . . ."

"Yes!!! We push back the cover—one! Here, as you see, there is the most banal switch. We remove the safety, without touching the battery—two! Push."

"And . . . and then what?"

"The house disappears."

Smolin's hand froze on the switch.

"Will we have time to get out?"

"As long as a person has at least one foot inside the house, the house remains a house. Come on! There, that's right . . . And now, outside. Don't rush, there's no rush, there's a three-minute delay, like the best mines. That's just insurance. Get comfortable on the grass and watch."

Yurkov immediately followed his own advice, but Smolin's legs had turned to wood. The house was melting, softening, right before his eyes. It was melting, billowing smoke. A pale rainbow hung in the shimmering air. A stiff breeze hit his face, the birch branches moved in the air. A dangerous smell of ozone came from the darkness and whirlwind.

Yurkov slowly looked at his watch.

"Exactly sixteen minutes." He got up and

stretched. "What do you say?"

"Genius." Smolin looked around in confusion at the spot where the house had stood and was now empty. "I never even dreamed of such a thing!"

With a springy tread, Yurkov walked around the spot where the darkness had swirled. "A clean field! No house, it disappeared, disintegrated, it gave back to nature everything it took. Dust thou art and . . . A completely closed cycle! How about that?"

Smolin walked around, looking for traces of damage. Five flattened spots where the supports had been. The dried grass showed red in the sun's rays. And that was all that was left of the house.

Not, not all. By a flattened hole stood the cylinder of the energy cell, and next to it lay a greenish egg with angled facets.

"There!" Yurkov said triumphantly. "You can pick it up, carry it anywhere you want, use it again and again, millions of times. And if you think that the energy used in construction is lost, you're wrong. With the disintegration of the house it accumulates in the battery, with an insignificant unavoidable loss. There cannot be any less expensive form of construction."

"And the embryo . . . is it the same one?" Smolin asked in a whisper.

"Yes and no," Yurkov answered merrily. "A tree bears fruit, and so does the house. From this 'acorn' will grow another house, no worse than the one before. Which we shall see right now."

He carelessly rolled away the battery, whistling under his breath, and went to the jetcar for the raygun. Smolin heavily sank to the ground. His head was spinning. High in the sky, just as in prehistoric times, fluffy white clouds floated. Smolin shut his eyes. "It's time I was accustomed to these things. Just what I needed! Another technological revolution, another upheaval, there have been so many . . ."

The cold wind hit his back again. Lying on his side and squinting, Smolin watched the house grow. His house. The house that appeared and disappeared with the ease of a magic trick, which could be carried away in a bag, moved to the other side of the world, grown there, and then put back in your pocket. A house that takes everything from nature and returns everything to nature, like a tree, a daisy, a mushroom.

"Let's go to your housewarming!" Yurkov called.

Smolin walked around the house. The building was slightly different from the previous one. A tiny bit. The main characteristics had been preserved, the proportions, sizes, and the differences in a few niggling details were sensed rather than seen.

"Right," Yurkov said, beating him to the question. "The descendant is never exactly like the ancestor. But monotony gets boring, so it's for the best."

Smolin brought his hand close to the wall and felt a current of raw warmth, as though it were a house's croup.

Yurkov winked. "Now you're in charge."

Smolin said nothing. He went into the house, plugged in the battery himself, without hurrying, looked over the premises. Yurkov walked behind him, maintaining his indifference. The air everywhere was fresh and pleasant, the water in the faucets flowed freely, the stereo screen readily switched from channel to channel, the thought furniture, obediently pliant, took the right forms. The forest showed green beyond the windows, the bend of the river glinted with gold sparkles, and the deep evening shadows had begun to creep out from the folds of the hills.

"Your storehouse of miracles is empty, I hope?" Smolin asked.

"Alas!" Yurkov replied, spreading his hands contritely.

"The house won't turn into a windmill or a dragon?"

Yurkov smiled sneakily.

"Well, if you insist . . ."

"What?"

"I was just joking. The work on remote hybridization is still in the theoretical stage."

"Oof!" Smolin sank into a chair.

"I'll bring your things in," said Yurkov.

"Why? I can do it."

"No, let me. It's my responsibility to get you settled."

Passing Smolin, he slipped out the door. Shrugging, Smolin stayed in his armchair.

He was astonished by the quiet of the house. It filled it like water. Not a sound, not a stirring, like in an enchanted castle.

Not totally, of course. The slanting rays of the sun showed dust motes and you could see the walls attracting the light dancing hordes. The house let you know it was there, it was in front, behind, everywhere, an invisible, impassive, obsequious servant.

87

Smolin's shoulder and neck muscles tensed. It was only then that he realized that he was not simply within walls, but inside an organism that was breathing, watching, living its secret life.

Jumping up harshly, Smolin approached the window. The mountain peaks looked like sugar in the distance. In parts of the meadow the shadows of the birches touched the shadows of the forest, but the golden green slices of light still predominated. The world was peaceful, quiet, and customary. Smolin's tension left. He turned. Nothing was watching, observing, breathing down his back, the rooms were like any rooms—spacious, cozy. "What a conservative you are," Smolin accused himself. "You really are. It's just a question of getting used to it."

Nearby he could smell an odor, vague and redolent, the smell that sometimes overwhelms you in a forest glade. Smolin touched the wall. The material felt like wood, like smooth pine planks. His fingers felt coolness, but it wasn't the coolness of stone or plastoconcrete; this was the coolness of alder bark in the cozy shade of midafternoon.

He wanted to continue the sensation, but it was interrupted by a muffled noise beyond the closed door of the foyer.

"Can I help you?" Smolin called out.

"It's nothing," he heard in reply. "Just a tiny moment . . ."

There was a thud.

"Yurkov?"

"Just a minute . . . don't worry . . ."

Smolin rushed to the foyer and froze in shock. A

frazzled Yurkov, angrily muttering to himself, was struggling with the closed front door. There was no sign of the things he was supposed to have brought.

"What's the matter?"

"Nothing, absolutely nothing, just a slight malfunction . . . I'll fix it in a flash . . ."

Looking away, Yurkov struck the door with his shoulder, but it didn't budge.

"It's locked!" Smolin said in amazement.

"Nonsense," Yurkov muttered. "It's not locked at all, who puts in locks nowadays? . . . It's just stuck! Come on, we'll try together . . ."

Not believing it, Smolin rushed to help. The door bent slightly from their joint attack.

"Aha! A little more . . ."

"Yurkov!" Smolin grabbed his arm in horror. "Look!"

"What?"

"The wall and door are growing together!"

"You're crazy . . ."

"The clearance is disappearing! Look!"

Yurkov's face, purple with exertion, turned white.

"Quick! Let's take a flying leap! One, two . . ." The blow made the door bend again.

"It's giving!"

Nothing of the sort. They might have been breaking down a cliff.

"Listen!" Smolin said, gasping. "What does this mean? I don't like it."

"Me neither," Yurkov admitted in a low voice. "This simply can't be happening . . . It can't!"

"But it's a fact! How will we get out of here?"

Yurkov looked around in fear.

"We'll try again."

"That won't work, we've tried."

"Damn it! Maybe it will get thinner. Another try won't kill us."

"All right, all right . . ."

They stepped back to the far end of the foyer and ran. Smolin saw stars from the blow.

"A fine pastime," he hissed, grimacing with pain. "You didn't mix up the embryos, did you? Maybe this is a blind, a prison for, say, lovers of antiquity?"

"Go ahead and laugh," Yurkov said grimly, rubbing his shoulder. "It's improbable, but it looks like the house has trapped us."

"So call in technical help!"

Yurkov gave Smolin a dirty look.

"There won't be any help."

"And why not?"

"We left our videophones outside. In the jetcar, if you recall."

"But this is impossible!" Smolin shouted. "This is . . . Where are you going!"

But Yurkov had left the foyer. He ran into the living room, picked up a stool, and hit the window as hard as he could.

The stool bent.

"That's what I thought. It had time to thicken," Yurkov said, tossing away the stool, and ran around the room. "Well, why don't you say something?! Curse me, damn me, I don't understand. There's a door and no exit!"

Smolin was silent and confused.

"All right," Yurkov said angrily. "Enough ratlike attacks. Let's be logical . . ."

He ran around the room again.

"Calm down," Smolin said softly. "What's the problem? People have lost their keys since time immemorial. I remember reading an old book with a funny story about a naked man who accidentally locked himself out . . . I'll, no, you'll certainly be missed if not today, then tomorrow."

"Make it a month, why don't you! What a coincidence! I was planning to fly to Mars tonight, to see my wife, and everyone knows I'll be away for a while."

"But your report . . ."

"No one needs the preliminary one, and the final one . . . You were planning to seclude yourself for a month, weren't you?"

Smolin laughed softly.

"You find our situation amusing?" Yurkov grumbled.

"In part, yes. Forgive me . . . I forget that this isn't simply an adventure for you. But, it's really not your fault."

"That's not the point," Yurkov said, sinking into a chair. "I don't have the foggiest idea what happened to the house, and that worries me the most. What does it have in mind?"

"In mind? But you said that it didn't . . ."

"It's no more rational than a birch tree. But nevertheless, it behaved independently. The program has been violated, which is impossible!"

"Hm." Smolin sat down too. An orange ray of the setting sun crossed his knees. "Of course, I'm no embryotechnologist, but in my free time I like to garden. The program, independence, or freedom of will ... We have to think about this without hurrying.''

"There's nothing else we can do," Yurkov observed acidly. "I don't see a way out, even though there should be one, and shame on us if we can't find it!"

He struck a windowsill with his fist.

"Yes, it is stupid," Smolin agreed. "It's so wild! You say the program was violated. Which one? Everything the plant does, it does for self-preservation. Of itself, its progeny, its species ... Actually, every creature behaves that way. This program, as I understand it, is characteristic of the house, as well.''

"Naturally! But its basic program is preserving its inhabitants. Us, that is. And it's been violated.''

"Is it? The house's action—it can be called an action, can't it?—as I see it, doesn't contradict either program.''

Yurkov shook his head in despair.

"No, you don't understand! The house stopped obeying. The second program clearly rules that out.''

"It has a clear, specific command to that effect?''

"No, not exactly. Dealing with genetics, you don't have to regulate everything down to the last dot. You just give the basic principle.''

"Ah, the basic principle!" Smolin smiled sourly. "Once, digging around in literature, I came across an ancient legal case. Two broad-shouldered men, meeting lone women on a dark, unpeopled street very politely asked them to lend them some money. The men did not threaten, their weapon was the situation of the times, the fear of possible violence.

But formally, they did not break the law, because it would be silly to prohibit people from asking for a loan, even from strangers. After these robbers were caught, they had to add to the laws."

"You're comparing the house to an intelligent creature again," Yurkov said, grimacing. "It's been tested hundreds of times and it never . . ."

"Could the house have mutated?"

"Mutated?"

"Yes. Or isn't it subject to mutations? The genetics are similar."

Yurkov stared uncomprehending at Smolin.

"Wait a minute! The theoretical probability of such a mutation . . . And anyway, why should it suddenly mutate . . ."

"Well, who knows . . . Cosmic radiation, elements in the soil . . ."

"Don't think the creators were fools," Yurkov replied. "Of course they took the possibility of mutation into account. All known factors were foreseen and . . ."

Yurkov froze with his mouth open.

"Idiot!" he shouted, jumping up. "No, you really have to be a metaphysician! Damn us all . . . Listen, you have a marvelous mind!"

"Then I guessed right?"

"That's not what we're talking about!" Yurkov gesticulated and ran around the room. "Instant adaptability, another quality of evolution, another type, forget our pathetic mutations, no, this will overturn the theory, no, it'll create a new one! Do you understand, do you?! Biological evolution is mutation and selection. And in the new, hybrid type of evolution should there or should there not be special instances of mutation and selection? And how! We're brainless dialecticians! What is the first, basic aim of the house! Right, self-preservation. Does our order to destroy itself countermand it? And how! But the house is no more capable of stopping its death than a tree stopping being chopped down. But . . . But, I ask you, under which conditions is the 'death program' not realized, even if the button has been pushed? Aha, you've guessed! It will not be completed if and only if there is a person in the house. There you are! The house died hundreds of times in experiments, and that is evolution, selection. And the house learned how to get around the order without disobeying. By keeping us inside, it has achieved immortality, we made it eternal as long as the sun shines!"

"What about the second program?" Smolin exclaimed.

"That's it precisely!" Yurkov rubbed his hands together. "Its actions are derived from both programs. After all the house can only take care of a person as it does itself when there is a person in it. Only then! No, this is simply astounding. Hit wood with an ax and the cut will heal over. And why isn't an open door a wound? It all makes sense! Listen, this is fantastic . . . We created a special type of evolution and had thought that it was ideally adapted for us. But it made an adjustment and ideally adapted us to it. It is a genius house, isn't it?"

"Wonderful," Smolin said drily. "I'm overjoyed to have become the object of the optimal adaptation of my dwelling to my person. But what are we going to do about our incarceration?''

"Hmmm." Yurkov grew downcast. "In future models we planned to teach the houses to grow all foods, but in this cabin . . ." He scratched his head. "I'm afraid for all its genius this house won't be able to manage a steak for us. But it's all right, now that we've figured out the reason, we know that the house hasn't gone mad. We'll think and figure out a way to outsmart it, we have time."

Lowering his head, Yurkov paced around the room. Smolin watched him in confusion. Ten minutes passed in silence. Twenty. A half hour. Evening shadows completely drowned the meadow. In the distance over the smoky blue hills the snow peaks of the mountains turned pink. Swifts swooped in the still-light sky. Smolin looked that way. The jetcar with its lowered wings was so close to the window that the thought of its inaccessibility could not be accommodated by his mind. Smolin had never appreciated his ability since childhood to move wherever he wanted at any time, like breathing, and what was happening to him now did not seem real. He tried to rid himself of the feeling, but he couldn't.

Locked in! Did the house feel anything? No, of course not. If it did, then every time a person left the house it would suffer the loss of the most precious thing, the reason for its life on earth. It would be wracked with pain. But it did sense it all somehow, it did.

"Couldn't we enter into negotiations with it?" Smolin suddenly spoke. "There is contact on the thought furniture level."

"It's dumb, but I've already tried to convince it of a thing or two," Yurkov replied. "No, the abilities of the house to comprehend are similar to the abilities of a mushroom spawn to grow mushrooms under the action of the sun. It's more complicated, but the level of communication is the same."

"It's a shame that the house is brainless."

"I suppose. The progress of evolution is also the progress of consciousness, and mentally addressing the house, I had hoped for a few things. In vain! But we do have plans . . ."

"You can still think of future houses? After a lesson like this?"

"Why not! New qualities are new opportunities. Lesson? Well, fire burns, and radiation kills, but there would be no civilization without them. Don't worry, we'll manage. You wouldn't know any signal codes, would you?"

"No!"

"Neither do I. Too bad. In the darkness we could have signalled with the lights."

"We could just turn them on and off."

"Of course. But the area is remote and even if someone did notice . . . Personally, I would think it was a game of some sort. Danger? Not realistic. Don't they have a videophone? And the jetcar right outside the door. And just to stick my nose in for no good reason, uninvited—this isn't the last century, you know."

"By the second or third night of blinking, however, someone will put his scruples aside, I hope."

Without turning, Yurkov waved his hand in despair. His profile fluttered against the background of the graying windows, and the movement was an unconscious reproach. Smolin sighed quietly. What did he care, it wasn't his responsibility. How many days can a man go without food? Ah, if he only knew embryotechnology . . . What good was a know-nothing like him? What?

"Give a signal, a signal . . ." Yurkov muttered. "Something has to escape from the house . . . Let's say light—that's clear enough; sound—won't work. Water? Open all the faucets, fill in the cracks, drown the house. Then, then . . . Say, what do you think?"

"I don't understand what good it will do."

"The optimum will be violated, the house will have to . . . It will probably make new openings."

"The size of a mouse hole?"

"You're right. Maybe . . ." Yurkov looked out the window. "No, that's nonsense too."

"What precisely? Let out a stream and float a bottle with a note on it?"

"Just imagine!" Yurkov laughed bitterly. "Think what we've been reduced to . . . I'm beginning to have my doubts about which of us is stupider—me or the house. That's it. Period. Let's use the scientific method. I'll outsmart you, you brainless bastard!"

Yurkov brandished his fist, and that incongruous action seemed natural to Smolin. He caught himself seeing the house, contrary to all reason, as an animate being, perhaps even malevolent. He was very hungry, not like he used to be as a child when he would miss supper because he was busy playing, but with a gnawing, shameful, violent hunger.

The last reflection of the sunset died on the peaks. In the dark zenith the violet pulse of a distant cosmic

97

flight exploded and burned. "Take-off on orbit seven," Smolin thought automatically. The sparkling amethyst trembled quietly in the night sky. Yurkov sank into a chair with a sigh. A black flash—Smolin jumped—flew past the window—a bat.

An indistinct muttering came from the corner. Then it stopped. Then . . .

"Just as I thought, it's very simple." Yurkov jumped up noisily. "Our exit is in an elementary syllogism: for the house we are part of itself, while the opposite is not true. Therefore it follows that we can and must kill the house."

"How?" Smolin jumped up. "In what way?"

"The most banal," Yurkov said, gently caressing the back of his armchair. "What a wonderful invention—thought furniture . . . I always thought that man had only one serious enemy—his own stupidity. After all, we're inside the organism now, aren't we? Just like bacteria."

"What a comparison!"

"But it's true, isn't it? In any case, there's nothing to keep us from turning from peaceful inhabitants to virulent ones."

"I don't understand . . ."

"The house is required to fulfill all its functions, all of them. It must! A man won't obey an order to do sit ups until he has a heart attack, but the house can't distinguish between stupid orders and reasonable ones. And that will give us our freedom."

"Riddles again?"

"I'm sorry, I must be incorrigible. The idea is so simple as to be primitive. What is stopping us from breaking the window? The ability of the material to thicken on its own. Under which conditions will the material not thicken automatically? When there is no energy in the house. It hasn't made an adequate reserve of solar energy yet, and as for the battery . . . we'll unplug it.''

"Ah-ha!"

"There you are! The uncomprehensible only seems difficult! Let's get on with it and I may still make my flight to Mars.''

"Wait! And what if we don't manage to get out before the house stops breathing?''

"We'll put the battery back, that's all. But we'll get out.''

Yurkov raced over to the foyer and returned a minute later with the cylinder in his hands.

"Finally,'' Smolin, said. "It's crazy, but while I was waiting for you, I imagined that the house had guessed our plans.''

"And blocked the battery," Yurkov said merrily. "You know, I had a similar thought. Primordial fears are so strong! Now, let's get to work.''

"What do we have to do?"

"Everything. Turn on the water—let it pump. Hot, very hot, so it expends more energy. . . . We'll put on the lights, turn on the stereo, let the house blaze! Tune in on something bravura. There, the lunar station, ice skating to the Turkish March . . . that's appropriate for us . . . Look at those jumps! Now pile on the furniture. More, hurry, tons of it! We're off.''

Smolin couldn't remember anything more bizarre. The music roared, the walls glowed, steam poured from the sauna, the skaters whirled like ghosts, water

99

hissed in the sinks, and he and Yurkov dashed around in the chaos, piling on tables, chairs, couches, armchairs, everything as wild and misshapen as their fleeting mental images. The floor was shaking and he also had to avoid benches, stools, and sofas that appeared at the most inappropriate times on Yurkov's whim, and the forgotten battery cylinder lay underfoot, but they didn't have time to think about it now, it wasn't the time for details, Smolin was caught up in the frenzy. Night darkened grimly outside the steamy windows.

"Come on, come on!" Yurkov shouted, leaping like a devil.

The frenzy confused his thoughts, his heart thumped, and the house was feeling it, too—the furniture formed more and more wanly, the water didn't rush as triumphantly, the light no longer blinded his eyes, and even the skaters seemed to be moving more slowly.

With a screech, the music stopped in mid-beat.

"Just a little more . . . not much left," Yurkov said, gasping. "Come on, give it what you've got!"

Suddenly his eyes grew big. With a howl he fell to the floor, grabbing the cylinder which had lost its cap from the shaking. Something pale, like underground roots, was moving near the contacts, looping around the battery.

"Hold it!!! The house found it!!!"

Stunned, Smolin watched Yurkov crouch, trying to pull away the cylinder and the floor throw out new creeping growths.

"Help me!"

The cry brought Smolin out of his stupor. They

pulled at it together. Manic efforts lifted one end of the cylinder, but the other seemed to have grown into the floor.

"It's not important," Yurkov whispered heavily. "As long as the house doesn't reach the contacts . . . Careful, don't touch them yourself."

With an agile movement, Yurkov slipped his hand under the free end and embraced it.

"No, you don't . . . Where's the cap?!"

But they couldn't find it, it was lost in the chaos of furniture.

"Pull, pull!"

Smolin almost screamed when an outgrowth appeared from the side and touched his hand. Yurkov was trying to shield the contacts with his elbow. The feelers, it seemed, were confused. They didn't let go of the cylinder, but the free feelers moved randomly. Their movements reminded him of the agitated swaying of the cilia of the sundew, blindly and stubbornly trying to feel out nearby prey.

For a minute or two, nothing could be heard except the rasping breathing of the people and the hoarse hissing of the faucets. The light in the room was clearly and quickly turning yellow.

"The important thing is to hold on to it," Yurkov said hoarsely. "Save your strength, everything will be over soon. But it's terrific, isn't it?"

"What?"

"The house, what else! The petal reaches for the sun, the root for water, and it went straight . . . What a marvelous reaction! Lightning-fast restructuring of tissue . . . Even in its death throes!"

"The feelers have stopped. Should we let go?"

"Not on your life! We're lucky that the house was weakened before the contacts accidentally touched the floor and gave the house a source of energy. But it's still looking for it—look! Just one of them has to touch it . . . Bend that one back over there . . ."

"The light's going out . . ."

"Too soon, too soon! Remember how a drowning person behaves and hold on tight! If the house gets the battery we can kiss our freedom good-bye."

"I'm holding it . . ."

The light flickered a few times, as though the house wanted to get a better look at something, and went out. In the gray patches of the windows the pattern of the constellations slowly became visible.

With a last rattle, the faucets stopped.

"It really does resemble death agony," Smolin whispered.

"Life is still burning in the house. Something slid across my fingers."

"Do you think it will keep up to the very end?"

"What else is there for it?"

Smolin shuddered.

"Air! Maybe it would be better if . . ."

"We let it go and bury ourselves? Don't worry, asphyxiation is never instantaneous—we'll have time."

"Can you guarantee that the window will give right away?"

"Yes, if we hit it hard enough."

The floor seemed covered with sweat from its exertion—it gave off that kind of smell. Overcoming his disgust, Smolin felt around in the dark until he came across a feeler. It moved weakly. It was like a warm sensing tip of a pinkie that passed across his palm. It was unbearable—Smolin jerked his hand away. The deathly silence of the house wouldn't fool him any more. There was a tense struggle going on, horrible in its wordlessness. He vividly pictured how the tissues were rebuilding themselves, in agonizing pain, how signals raced throughout the whole mass of the house feverishly, how currents connecting the organism coursed, weakening, going out, and how the house with the instincts of its last strength sought a flow of saving energy, sought it wildly, blindly, constantly, without ever feeling it, like a huge sliced-off mushroom . . . Or an unconscious man, one on one with approaching death.

Smolin felt that he was suffocating. Was it his imagination? He gasped for air and the new intake, instead of bringing relief, filled his throat with a heavy, suffocating smell, so unexpected and nauseating that his heart began throbbing in a panic and a sharp pain pierced his temples.

"Listen, Yurkov . . ."

A convulsive movement instead of an answer. The ventilation was off . . . So soon?! Impossible! . . ."

"I'm suffocating . . ."

"Easy! I've got a feeler . . . It almost got it, the viper . . ."

"Air . . . Give the house energy, give it to it!"

"Don't panic! That's the smell of the house, the product of its disintegration, it sinks and collects below . . I'll hold on, and you throw! Right at the window, hear me?"

Smolin wanted to jump up but his legs gave out under him. His eyes swam and red spots pulsed before

his eyes. There seemed to be no air at all. His throat
and lungs were stuffed with something viscid, sticky,
suffocating.

"The house . . . Everything is speeded up . . . It's
dead and it's decaying . . . I have . . . to hurry . . ."

He held on to something and stood up shakily. The
pain in his head overcame the horror, the shock,
everything. As though from another world, he heard
rasping breaths.

"Is it the faucets hissing? . . . No, it's Yurkov . . .
We miscalculated. The house's environment is a trap
. . . Come on, another step . . ."

His hands grabbed onto something heavy. They
pulled it from the floor. In the window, painful to
behold, a constellation burned bright.

"There, into the constellation . . . Don't you dare
fall, you bastard!"

His hands and body threw the weight right into the
center of the fiery constellation. It shot up and
Smolin felt himself topple, falling, and the horrible
pain in his brain blissfully stopped.

Everything went out.

. . . An instant, an eternity? Darkness, the needles
of starlight, something wet dropping down his
face . . .

"Are you conscious?"

Someone's hands carefully lifted him, cold air
cooled his wet face, a familiar voice by his ear.
Yurkov?

"Did I . . . break the window?"

"Everything's fine. No, you didn't break it."

"You mean, you gave it back . . ."

A short laugh.

"It's dark, see? I didn't give it back."

"But the air . . . how? Did you . . ."

"The house. Look closer."

Smolin lifted his head—he could do it without any effort. There was no deafening pain. The window was in front of his eyes. It was covered with thousands of tiny lines, and the stars were lost in that diamond-brilliant blackness.

"With its last, very last effort," Yurkov whispered, "the house opened, tore open all its apertures. After all, breathing is most important of all."

"For whom?" Smolin squeezed Yurkov's hand. "For whom?"

"For us, of course." Yurkov's voice revealed surprise. "Everything the house did, it did only for us. Even before its death it worried about . . . our safety. We were its soul, after all."

Yurkov gave another short laugh. Smolin, awkwardly leaning on his shoulder, stood.

"Can you walk?" Yurkov asked.

"As you can see . . ."

"Then let's not waste any time. Press on, press on! We'll break the window and hurry off. Ah, it all went so badly! Now I'm sure you won't even come near our house, no matter how carefully and strictly we program it."

"You don't understand at all," Smolin grumbled, unexpectedly for himself. "We have to live with the house, but the house has to live with us, too. We have to find a common language, and that is work for those who are not impatient . . ."

THE MAN WHO MET PICASSO

By Michael Swanwick

In another time, another place, the shop could have been a magician's lair. A gargoyle crouched, stone wings spread, above the shabby brownstone's doorway. Submerged within dark windows were cracked Tiffany shades and statuettes of Greek gods, lacking here an arm, there a head, that on the originals had survived into modern times. Weathered gilt lettering on the panes read FRANZ WEIL—RESTORATIONS.

Half a block away a gas station stood at the corner of an expressway feeder. Beyond it, air shimmered over the pavement. It mingled with exhaust fumes, was blasted apart by loud cars bright with hot chrome. Somewhere a burglar alarm warbled.

But inside, the shop was quiet, the traffic muted. Shadowed shelving reared over a nondescript desk and a few square yards of carpet. The vases and platters, cracked goblets, and broken figurines might have been the slow limestone growths of a cave. An air conditioner in some distant part of the house took the edge off the heat, making it possible to keep the windows closed.

The old man positioned himself by the desk, reached a gnarled hand to the side, closed it about a circle of glass. He shuffled to the nearest window, where a solitary sunbeam pierced the interior gloom. It caught his white hair and suffused it with holy light.

The glass plate flashed purple fire as he held it up, turning it over and over again in his hands. "The fragments had to be baked together, or else, with the first little touch of tension, they would snap again." His voice was gentle and contemplative. "It's no great trick if you have the clamps to hold the pieces together perfectly. But they don't sell such things; there's not the market. You have to build them yourself, you see?"

The customer nodded respectfully.

Weil put the glass down and started to turn, then stopped to pick up a Hummel figurine. It was a fat boy with rouged cheeks; he was playing an accordion. "Look at this," he said with mild disgust. "People collect these things, you know. Tell me. Would *you* waste your time repairing a thing like this?"

The man smiled and shook his head.

"That's good. Time is precious. It's the one limitation you can't ignore. When I was young, I spent a *month* building a single set of clamps—imagine that! There was a statue with a broken bit of base—a nose—that I had to set perfectly. But just as I finished the clamps, I saw some children playing in the mud. I looked at them and put my work aside. And I held that nose in place with a piece of putty.

"Well, at least I had the skill. I was a sculptor then. Yes, I was." He straightened slightly, to stare off into some nonexistent distance, and his voice grew reminiscent. "How I wasted my youth! When I think of all I had—and I spent my life working on trash like this!"

Still the customer said nothing, but it was an encouraging sort of silence, and after a quick glance through his shaggy eyebrows, Weil gestured the man to a chair.

"It was so very long ago," he mused.

It was an early autumn evening. Paris was wet and miserable, and I was on my way to the Opera. This was a ridiculous expense for an art student—there were days when all I had to eat was one lousy apple—but my friend Marissa had received the tickets from her parents and had invited me along. I remember that I had been working in granite that day, and my hands were slightly red and tingled pleasantly.

We were just chums, Marissa and I, not lovers, and she was not a good-looking woman. No, I lie—she was extremely beautiful. But it was all internal; to the eye, she was quite ugly.

We were walking along a drab and weary street—quickly, for our coats were light—and the buildings were all huddled together and soaked with *tristesse*. I was making some laughing comment when

Marissa grabbed my arm and pointed across the street.

"Le Boeuf!" she hissed. We'd nicknamed Picasso the Bull because at that time he was painting all those pictures of minotaurs. I looked, and there he was. Seated at a café table by the curb, hunched over a drink, with that little black beret of his slouched across his head.

I shrugged. "So?"

"This is your chance," she whispered urgently. "Go up and ask him about the navel our teacher was telling us about."

"You want me—a student, a nobody—to go up to *Le Boeuf* and ask him about one of his paintings?" I snorted. "He wouldn't give me the time of day."

"You must go up and ask," she insisted fiercely.

"No, no, I couldn't."

"Well, if you won't, then I *will.*" And looking into those blazing green eyes, I knew that she meant it. My heart sank.

"No, don't do that. He would only be rude to you." He had a reputation for that kind of behavior. "Better that I go."

"Then go!"

I waited a beat by the curb, then darted between the cars to the other side. Taking a deep breath, I approached Picasso's table and stood across from him, not daring to speak before he noticed me.

Slowly he raised his head, lifted those baleful eyes to mine. They glared with a malevolent light, and his mouth moved like that of a camel.

"Idiote!" he spat.

I bowed politely and said in a low voice, *"Oui,*

Maître.'' If the Master told me I was an idiot, who was I to disagree?

"Maître?'' he asked. "You are one of us then? An artist?''

"Un élève,'' I said. "Only a student.''

"Sit!'' He pointed imperiously at the wire chair opposite him, and I obeyed. He glanced at my rough, callused hands. "A sculptor, eh?''

I admitted this was so, and he looked pleased. "You will have a drink with me.''

"Thank you, *Maître,* but I—''

"Garçon!'' He snapped his fingers and a waiter materialized. He pointed at his glass. "Another for my companion.''

The waiter brought anisette, a drink I had always loathed. I took a sip, trying not to grimace.

For a moment he studied me silently. A leaf fell to the table, and he glanced at it, deemed it unworthy, and swept it away. "You have a girlfriend across the street?'' he asked suddenly.

Marissa was indeed standing where I'd left her, clutching her light cloth coat about her and peering anxiously at us. But Picasso was facing away from her; he must have seen my glances. "She is not exactly my girlfriend,'' I began.

"Bring her over!''

Back across the street I ran, to where Marissa stood shivering. I took her hand and led her back. She stood humbly before the great man, and he looked her up and down with those basilisk eyes. "You know,'' he said, "you are a remarkably ugly woman.''

"Oui, Maître.''

111

"Sit down!"

Picasso snapped his fingers for the waiter, then pointed to his glass again. The man darted away. "And yet—there is something about that chin. Come by my studio next week, and I will paint you."

"Merci, Maître."

"Bah!" he snorted in disgust. Marissa's anisette arrived, and she drank it with apparent pleasure. Picasso turned to me again.

"So. Obviously you have a question, or you would not have dared approach me. Out with it!"

I stared into the milky liquid in my glass. "You did a painting," I said hesitantly, "some ten years ago of a woman—a nude. It was called *La Belle*—"

"Bah! Do you have any idea how many women I have painted in my life? Hundreds! Thousands! And out of all these years you expect me to remember *one* painting?"

"She had an orange navel," I said. The principal of our school had lectured us for a full day on that one painting.

"Ahhh," Picasso said. "I know the one you speak of. What about it?"

"Our teacher, the dean of our school, he said that the navel should not have been orange—that it should have been green."

Picasso's attention was absolute. A truck smashed through a nearby puddle, throwing up a rooster-tail of water that almost sprayed the table, and he did not notice. "And what did he say about my painting it orange?"

"He said that you were a fool."

"Das Scheisskopf!" The Master's face turned red,

and he began swearing in German, an endless stream of truly foul words. I wriggled in my chair in embarrassment.

He noticed my reaction and stopped in mid-curse. "So," he said. *Sie sprechen das deutsch.*"

"Ein klein plattdeutsch," I admitted. I was by no means fluent, but I knew enough German to follow his outburst.

"Well, then, you go back to your teacher, and tell him he plays with himself."

"What!" I cried in astonishment. Marissa's hand flew up to her mouth, tried unsuccessfully to stifle a giggle.

"Tell this pig that he plays with himself. Tell him that *Picasso* says so."

I shook my head politely but firmly. "You want me to tell the dean of my school this? No, I am afraid not."

"Ahhh," he said. "You are one of *those.*" I had managed to choke down my anisette, and he noticed that the glasses were empty, gestured for refills. I winced inwardly. Picasso glared at me. "And what do *you* think, eh?"

"I do not know why you painted it thus," I said hesitantly. "But I know that Picasso had a reason."

"Oh? And how do you know that?" There was something dangerous, something very animal, about the way he hunched forward over the table, and I found myself tongue-tied, unable to reply.

Marissa, silent until now, said, "The painting has become almost an obsession with Franz; we have discussed it again and again. And he told me that you must have had a reason because, he said, Picasso is a wizard!"

Picasso rocked back in his chair, bellowing with laughter. "A wizard! That's good! So you think I am a wizard, eh, my little sculptor?"

"Oui, Maître," I said humbly.

"Then, my young sorcerer's apprentice, I must *be* your wizard, eh?" His eyes filled with dark, demonic mirth. "But understand first of all that I do not speak about my work. The paintings themselves must do the talking, or else it is only words."

He was silent for a moment, but it was a compelling silence. He was in control of it.

"But," he said at last, "if you really wish to learn, then I will tell you what to do. Are you familiar with the works of El Greco?"

"Yes, certainly, in reproductions."

"Reproductions—bah! Reproductions are nothing. You cannot know a work until you have seen it. But I'll tell you what. You must go to the Prado."

"Me? Go to Madrid?" I was astonished all over again.

"Yes. To the Prado. On the second floor you will find an El Greco called *Rooftops of Toledo*. You go there and stand before it. Look at it. There is a vast spread of roofs, all the city laid out under either a sunrise or a sunset. Just off the center is one orange roof, the only orange one among all the others. Hold your thumb so that it covers that roof and no more. You must study the painting, see it as a whole. Then *pull* your thumb away, and you will have your answer."

"And for this I have only to go to the Prado?" It was so ludicrous a suggestion that I had to struggle not to laugh aloud.

"Yes, that is your quest; your wizard is sending you there."

I shrugged. "I know you can tell by my accent that I am an American. But you must understand that my family is poor and I am here on a scholarship. Where would I come up with that kind of money?"

He stared at me for a moment. Then he took out a leather wallet, ran a thumb through its contents, calmly counted out five hundred francs, and gave them to me! "Take this," he said, "and go. Take her"—he jerked his head at Marissa—"your girlfriend, with you. Both of you do as I have directed." The night was beginning to fall, the street going dark. We had missed the beginning of our opera.

"Now I am not giving this to you. If you go to Madrid and spend your time foolishly, *you owe me this back*. But if you do as I have instructed, and return with the answer, then you owe me nothing. The money is yours. And I will tell you why I painted the woman's navel orange."

I sat there, his money in my hand, not knowing what to say or do. I opened my mouth, shut it again.

Picasso grew suddenly angry. "Go away!" he snapped. "You are disturbing me—get out of here!"

So we went.

It was an interesting trip. Marissa costumed herself as an *haute-bourgeoise* and with a constant stream of demands and complaints made life miserable for the staff. It got so that the porter would hunch his shoulders and try to bull his way past our compartment. To no avail. Marissa darted out, fox stole swinging, and seized the man's arm with her long red nails. "My pillows!" she shrilled. "They are *flat!*"

The man threw up his hands in dismay. His little mustache drew in on itself. "Madame—"

"And the sandwiches in the luncheon car—the lettuce is quite definitely wilted!"

The porter could not edge away, for Marissa still clung to his arm. She leaned quite close to the poor man and, with an air of final triumph, added, "And my lover—this morose young artist here—he is *lousy* in bed!" Then she released him.

The porter fled down the corridor. As soon as he was out of sight, Marissa collapsed across her seat in laughter.

I sat cracking my knuckles, thinking of Picasso, of all the money I owed.

The Prado was all smooth marble floors and cold echoes. We arrived early—I had not even allowed us time to freshen up—and the galleries were virtually deserted. Now and then we'd hear twinned sets of heels click-click by, or a scattered fragment of light conversation. It did not take us long to find *The Rooftops of Toledo*.

Humbly, like supplicants, we stood before the work. It was a grandiose sweep of roofs caught in the rich, low-lying Spanish sun. I could have eaten an apple in the time we stood there, core, seeds, and all. Then slowly, hesitantly, I raised my thumb at arm's length until it just covered the orange roof near the center of the painting.

Agonized minutes crept by. My thumb wavered slightly, but I held it stationary until my entire arm ached with fatigue poisons. Cold sweat beaded on my forehead. Still I didn't move. And finally I *pulled* my thumb away triumphantly.

And I saw—nothing.

I almost collapsed. The painting floated before me, flat, daubed with colors, the speck of orange enigmatic and mocking. Sweaty and pale, I turned to Marissa to ask had *she* seen it.

She shrugged—no. Whatever this great secret was, she had not seen it, nor did she especially care.

That was Marissa. She had shrewd intelligence, verve, and self-confidence and a cool, discerning eye. But she was only a *dilettante,* a dabbler. She had enrolled in the school because it was fashionable, the thing to do. There is no discredit to her in this—only she was not an artist. She didn't care.

But I had to care, because to fail this test would be to admit that I also was no artist. So again I tried, only this time differently.

You cannot actually see a painting unless it fills you. I had been thinking of Picasso, feeling the weight of his money and the fear of his disapproval. All of this I forced myself to forget. I stood and simply let the painting grow, until it was all I saw and all I thought of. Instead of seeking answers, I waited.

Marissa wandered away to look at other works, but I did not notice. Only dimly, distantly, was I aware of the slow passage of time, of the still air, the quiet. Moving like a somnambulist, I raised my thumb, held it steadily before me. I studied the painting, without demands or expectations.

117

I snapped my thumb away. And I *saw*.

I could have sobbed in relief. The museum gallery seemed to swim about me. I turned to Marissa, saw that she was not there, that she was several paintings away, and hurried to her side.

"Do you want to try again? Look harder this time," I said.

"No," she said. She looked at me oddly. "You have the most idiotic grin on your face."

I realized suddenly that my cheeks hurt. But what did I care? I grabbed Marissa, swung her around, kissed her right there in the middle of the Prado!

Events kept me from reporting back to Picasso immediately on my return. But one bright October morning found me on the Rue des Grands-Augustins, where his studio was. The seventeenth-century mansion houses along the street had been subdivided into offices and businesses, a little worn but not quite shabby. Balzac had lumbered ponderously down this very way, a walrus touched by divine fire, and I followed in his footsteps. The day was unseasonably warm, so bright and fine that I almost forgot my troubles.

At number 7, I plunged within and hurried up a gloomy spiral stairway. I took the steps two and three at a time, past a process server's office, up to a simple door on which was tacked a hand-written note. *"C'est ici,"* it said: Here it is. I knocked.

For a moment, nothing. Then the door flew open, and Picasso stood before me, wearing a striped sailor shirt and white duck pants. He carried a mop under one arm, and in the hand of that same arm held a galvanized steel bucket of whitewash.

"Herr Weil," he said threateningly. I was flattered that he had remembered my name. "Come in!"

Flooded with cool, northern light, the studio was a vast and colorful pigsty. Frayed chairs were half-buried under piles of tin cans, pegboards, burlap, and steel rods. Canvas flats leaned against walls brightened by here a Matisse, there a Rousseau. And everywhere, of course, were his own canvases, but they were placed facing walls, not to be seen.

"You have interrupted me in the middle of my work," Picasso said, steering me around a pile of newspapers and paintpots, out of which poked an old, rusting bicycle. "Stand *there*—and do not make a sound until I am done."

He planted me beside a broken-seated cane chair on which rested several canvases, a Modigliani peeking out from the rear. I almost caught my ankle in a snarl of wire when I realized that I was standing on one of the Master's sketches, and frantically I hopped away. I steadied myself with one hand on a paint-flecked ladder and watched him work.

One wall of the studio was all plate glass, with clear autumn light streaming through. Beyond, I could see the tail end of a line of brick rowhouses, with tiny, walled-in yards, and a cemetery. The sky was as flatly blue as that of any Miró, and the graveyard, with its orchardlike lines of small white tombstones, was all grass gone brown.

Picasso was painting goats on the window. He dipped the mop into the bucket of whitewash, then smoothly, surely, painted directly onto the glass, as if

119

the mop were a gigantic brush. I stood entranced.

Those goats! The man had an uncanny, a perfect knowledge of animal anatomy. The goats gamboled joyfully on the glass, and though they were drawn with broad strokes, almost as cartoons, every detail was perfect. In a continuous sweep he drew a head, continuing the line to include the bump on the back, the upswelling behind the cranium.

The mop danced across the glass, creating ritual, making these creatures of the spring into something sacred, something that could not be expressed in words alone.

Finally he was done. He stepped back to study the work and without looking at me, said, "What do you think?"

I kissed my fingertips. *"C'est magnifique!* You are truly a great artist."

"No," he snarled. "I want your honest opinion. Don't try to flatter me."

There was some small movement in the cemetery beyond the glass, but I could not look past those luminous, spritely goats. "No opinion was ever more honest," I said, "You are magnificent, a great artist—truly a wizard!"

Grasping a large sponge, he advanced menacingly on the window. "It is not good enough for *Picasso*," he said and wiped it all clean.

I could have cried to see first one goat, then another, disappear in ugly white smears. The Master worked vigorously, attacking the glass, until it was all clean. I could look beyond now and see the tiny figures on the dying grass, gathered about a small hole in the ground, a funeral.

Picasso threw the sponge away and turned on me. "You have been to the Prado; otherwise you would not dare show your stupid face before me. And now you *think* you have seen what I instructed you to see, eh? Well—I am waiting."

I faced him squarely. He could not bully me; I knew what I had seen. "I have done as you told me, *Maître,* and I have two observations."

"Eh! I send you to see one thing, and you come back with *two,"* he sneered.

"The first thing I saw was that it was not a sunrise, but a sunset."

"That is so," he said impatiently. "And the other?"

"The second thing I saw was that the orange roof spreads the color of the setting sun about the roof-tops, so that the eye sees its warmth on them all, even though there is not a touch of orange paint on any of the others."

"Exactly!" he cried. *"That* was what I sent you to see. El Greco had set himself a problem: He wanted to show the rich glow of sunset on the roofs, but without daubing pigment on each and every roof. He wanted to do it in the most economical fashion possible. It is a *trompe l'oeil,* a trick of the eye. The orange roof spreads its glow, but only in the eye of the viewer—not on the canvas itself. It supports the others without touching them.

"And *that* is why I painted the woman's navel orange. That painting had given me a lot of trouble, the stomach and limbs were too angular, too flat, and I wanted them to be rounded—soft. But I did not want to ring in the third dimension. That is *your* province, my young sculptor. It is not the painter's.

"Painting is merely design. It is flat. To bring in the third dimension is to cheat. But still I wanted that illusion of roundness.

"It was a problem that I thought about for weeks—at the easel, in the cafés, on the crapper. Until I finally remembered El Greco, and painted her navel not green, but orange.

"The orange, you see, spreads its glow across her belly and breasts, her arms and legs—and the eye is tricked into seeing them as rounded and soft. *Yes,* I broke the rules—but knowingly. For that is the artist's chore—to first master the rules, and then overcome them. The rules exist, but they can all be circumvented."

He fixed those cold eyes on me. "And there is the gist of it. The actual painting is nothing, it is dead. It is only the working out of problems that the artist sets for himself that matters. The learning." Behind him, the coffin was being lowered into the cold earth.

"You—you will be an artist. You have the eye for it. But you must learn to never stop learning. Discipline—sure you need discipline; you must work constantly, every minute of every day. But that is something you pick up along the way. Even you already have that kind of discipline, eh?"

I reddened and muttered, "Oui, *Maître.*" It was true.

"You have called me a great artist—I do not believe there is such a thing. You have called me a wizard. Well," he smiled oddly, "perhaps I am. But first and foremost—pay attention to me now—I am a Student, now and for the rest of my life."

I fell back a pace from the intensity of his harangue. The Master came after me, grabbed my collar, and said, "Now recite back to me what you have learned, my apprentice sorcerer."

"First, about the roof," I said. "It supports without touching."

Picasso released his grip. "Hah! Good—your artist's eye sees right to the core of it. Yes, it is very much like the artist in that sense, aloof yet supporting all, lending color and meaning to the world. Go on."

"Next, that the rules exist to be learned, and then overcome." Outside, the prayers were done, and dirt was being shoveled into the grave.

He almost smiled. "One more."

"That one never ceases to learn."

"That an *artist* never ceases to learn," he corrected. "All very good. But you came back with only two observations, and I have given you three answers. How shall we correct this imbalance, eh?"

"I—"

"I have it! You will go out now—today! You will make a bust of your girlfriend, the ugly one, and you will return with it to me within a week. If it is good, I will see that it is sold. If not—" He made a gesture with his hands, as if balling up and discarding a scrap of paper.

The joy I had been feeling all died at once. Rather than face the Master, I stared out at the funeral, which was slowly beginning to break up. "I am sorry, *Maître,* but I cannot."

Picasso was outraged. "You say no to *me?*" He

123

grabbed the mop from the floor, hurled it away to crash noisily against a stack of corrugated iron sheeting.

"I am sorrier than words can say, *Maître*. But I have just received a telegram from home, and—" I fished the piece of paper from my pocket, and he snatched it out of my hand.

His face sour, Picasso read the telegram aloud. " 'Come home. Your father is dying.' " He threw it on the floor in disgust.

"All the preparations have been made," I said. "I leave in the morning."

"Shall I tell you what will happen?" he asked. He took me by the shoulders, turned me to face the funeral party. "First of all you will go home and your father will die. Never doubt it—fathers die."

He pointed at the small black figures. "That woman—*there*—the one apart from the others, like an old carrion crow. She is your mother. She will take you aside as soon as the funeral is over."

The woman was joined by another small speck; from this distance it could as well have been me as anyone else.

"She will say to you, 'There's me, and the five children. And there's you. While he was alive, your father took care of us. Now it's your turn.' "

Perhaps the two were talking; it was impossible to tell. I saw the woman place an arm around the other's shoulder.

"And you will say, 'You mean—my career? It's over?' " His voice became mocking, whiny, and he shook me ferociously as he predicted these words.

"And do you know what she will say then, this

mother of yours? She will say, 'It's a tough world.' " He flung me away from him. His eyes were savage. "Haven't you heard a single God-damned *word* of what I've told you?"

Turning my back on the funeral, I gave him a small bow and headed for the door. "I'm sorry, *Maître.*"

"Then go!" he screamed. "Pass by your chance to be a sorcerer. What do I care? But you have wasted my time, and in the final reckoning that sin will weigh heaviest against you!"

He slammed the door behind me.

The old man sighed. "Ah, well," he said, "what did I know? The Master was a prophet. The conversation went almost word for word as he said it would. And then came the war, and then I married and raised a family. They are all gone now, vanished like smoke. I tell myself that when I retire, I will return to sculpting. But I know that I won't. I'll never retire."

The man said nothing.

"Picasso said that I would be an artist! I could laugh, if it weren't so sad. For the greatest artist of our times to be wrong on a matter of art!"

Midway through his story, weariness had forced Weil to sit down. Now he grasped the arms of his chair, still staring down at the desktop. "I could have been an artist—once. No more. An artist needs to have an enormous ego in order to create, and I don't have it now. Not after the life I've had. It was all kicked out of me."

Slowly, painfully, he stood. Holding the plate up into the light, he watched it flash and sparkle. "There is a lesson in this for you. I tried to support everyone with my work—my mother, my family, my country, and then my other family. Now all the people I loved are dead, and I realize that this was wrong. I should have been like that little orange roof. Supporting from a distance."

He glanced up. "Eh? What do you think?"

But the customer was no longer there. His chair contained nothing but shadows, and save for the old man the shop was empty. Weil shook his head in chagrined puzzlement. If his maunderings had driven a customer away, he could understand. But the man had left without his plate.

Then, too, he should have *heard* the man leave. No matter how deeply sunk in his reveries he had been, he should at least have heard the bell over the door. Only the deaf or the senile fail to notice when people leave.

"I truly am growing old," he said sadly.

Mocking laughter burst out of nowhere and filled the room. Dark and sardonic, it roared and reverberated.

Weil spun about fearfully and saw nothing. Only a solid wall separating the shop from the rest of the house. The laughter must have come from beyond, he decided, and took a step backward.

And Picasso walked jauntily through the wall as if it weren't there.

"So, my sorcerer's apprentice—not so young now, eh? Not so spry around the knees and elbows. I tell you there were times I thought you would *never* get the lesson."

The old man leaned heavily against his desk. *"Maître!"* he gasped. "But you—you are dead."

The Master laughed scornfully. "Death. Bah! Death is just another God-damned limitation. How many times do I have to tell you? The artist's job is to go beyond these limits" His manner was so quick and alert that by his very presence he made the shop a dreary and confining place.

Weil gingerly stretched out a hand, not daring to touch. His heart was pounding wildly. "You . . . *look* like him. But perhaps I am going mad."

Picasso's voice was almost gentle as he took Weil's hand. "My poor little apprentice! The first lesson, though, is always the roughest. Come, we have unfinished business back in Paris."

But the old man hung back. "Can it be?" he murmured to himself. Then, "No, I am too old."

"Old!" Picasso sneered. Weil shivered as if touched by a crisp autumn breeze. "Age is just another limitation—move *around* it." He looked stern. "In time you must learn to do this yourself. I am not your Daddy, to look after you every instant of every day. But this once I am at your disposal. I can return to you your youth, your will, the years you have wasted. Only tell me what you want."

"I—" He stopped and swallowed. "I want to be an artist! I want to sculpt again! I want to form stone and clay and bronze into shapes that have never been seen before, that no one but I could create!"

"All this you shall have," Picasso promised. He seized Weil's shoulders, turned him toward the wall. "Come, it is time for your next lesson."

And as the wizard shoved him through the wall, through the cold decades and vast distances and weary regrets that were, after all, only limitations, he snarled, "But from now on let's get it right the *first* time!"

THE VACUUM-PACKED PICNIC

By Rick Gauger

As she approached my table across the pilots'
crowded ready room with her teacup in her hand, I
felt an urge coming over me. I had an urge to bite
her—on the smooth, ivory neck, which emerged
from the heavy aluminum collar ring of her close-
fitting pilot's vacuum suit. Maybe it was the way she
jangled all those pockets, tubes, clipboards, and
electronic terminals as she made her way through the
mob toward me. The typical space pilot's
swagger—but female. Maybe it was the merry brown
eyes and the humorous twist of her lips as she sat
down in front of me.

"You're Captain Suarez, aren't you?"

"Yeah. My friends call me—"

"Pancho. Right?"

"Right. I hope you're one of my friends," I said,
my figurative tail wagging furiously. Worst case of
vibes I'd ever had. It seemed to be mutual. She

studied me amusedly while her tea cooled.

I said, "Surely we've never met before. I know I'm pretty absent-minded, but . . ."

"Your friend Arunis Pittman told me about you. I met him on the polar sky station. He thought I should look you up when I got to West Limb. He said you would probably offer to keep me amused. You were highly recommended."

"Old Arunis! Damn! How is he?"

"He's fine. He said I should ask you whether you're still keeping the CO_2 high in your spacecraft life-support system, instead of doing the regulation aerobic exercises, the way you're supposed to."

"Damn again! How could he know about that? I'll bet he's trying to warn me that the agency is monitoring my life-support system again. I appreciate that. Thanks, Captain . . . er . . . "

"Cramblitt. I prefer Stacy, however." After a pause she asked, "Well, are you?"

"Not anymore. I don't want to be grounded again. I'll do my exercises like a good boy—"

"I don't mean that," she said. "I mean, are you going to amuse me? This is the first time I've been on the moon. I don't have anything to do until the passenger shuttle begins its preflight countdown tomorrow night."

An opening big enough to drive a truck into. I had to think of something, immediately, that would capture her imagination. She tucked an errant strand of glossy black hair into her chignon as my mind raced.

"A picnic. How would you like to go on a picnic? With me," I said, blurting out the first idiocy that came into my mind. "If you like, I'll take you to one of my favorite spots. It's not far, just a short walk from the base."

Her reaction was everything I could have hoped for. Her delicate mouth dropped open a little. "You're kidding. An *outdoor* picnic?"

"Why, sure," I lied. "It's a new recreation we have come up with here on the moon. Gets us away from the madding crowd. A great view, the hills, some nice rock colors. Perfect time of the month for it, too." Bridges were flaming behind me. *Why do I do these things?* "Of course you'd probably rather not go to the trouble. You're probably too tired, right?"

Her excitement showed on her face. Her eyes began to twinkle. "Oh, no! I wouldn't miss this for anything!" she exclaimed. "A picnic on the moon! That's fantastic! Arunis was right about you, Pancho."

"Aw," I mumbled, standing up and giving her my boyish grin. "Just leave it all to me. Meet me at Hatch Seven-Charlie—anyone can tell you where it is—at ten hours tomorrow. Put on your vacuum suit and bring a fully charged backpack. I'll take care of the rest. I have to make a hopper run now. See you then."

Her smile followed me across the ready room as I made my way to the hopper dock. I waved goodbye before turning into the corridor. Male residents of the base who happened to be in the ready room watched all this enviously. They didn't see the grimace that appeared on my face as soon as I was out of sight. I had really jumped into it with both feet this time.

Well, the business I had handed her about a picnic wasn't one-hundred-percent baloney. No one had ever really been on a picnic on the moon before, but the West Limb intellectual elite (my pals and I) had been discussing the idea for quite a while. We regarded our project as a noble pioneering effort, an expansion of man's capability in the space environment, but, mainly, as a way to get some privacy with our female colleagues. The base at West Limb hadn't yet become the luxurious suburb that it is today. In those days it was more like a big locker room on the moon, a crowded, noisy set of tunnels and domes, which reeked of old socks and new paint. We all lived in this warren like so many rats in a hole. The transients among us, from months of isolation, were nearly barbarians, while the permanent residents were antagonistic from never being able to get away from one another. Life on the old high frontier was rough, yes, sir!

Unfortunately, plans for outings *à deux* hadn't gotten past the speculative stage yet. One of my friends had analyzed the problem of picnic-site selection. Using lots of stolen computer time, he had determined which areas on the lunar surface around West Limb could be inhabited by a man—and a woman—for a reasonable length of time in a standard vacuum-survival tent. Of course, the idea was to obtain a comfortable shirt-sleeves-or-less habitat.

You know what survival tents are. They're what's inside those emergency boxes you see everywhere on the moon. Buggies have to carry one per passenger; so do the rocket hoppers. You've undoubtedly got several small ones under the bed in your hotel room. Solo prospectors and other outdoor workers use them regularly when they can't get to any other pressurized shelter. They climb into a tent, seal the opening, and inflate it with their reserve air. The tents blow up into a transparent plastic dome. Once the dome is pressurized, you can take off your vacuum suit and relax a bit. The old-timers say they're for leaks, whether you get one or have to take one. That's a joke.

Anyway, the most important element of my friend's analysis was the temperature inside the tent. Sunshine was everything. Anyone exposing his ass to the direct rays coming through the plastic would be rapidly rump-roasted. Complete lunar nighttime would be a glacial and gloomy experience, to say the least. No, what we wanted was a cheerful, sunshiny, picnicky sort of experience, with lots of scenery, close to, but not in sight of, the base or any of the main trails. A flat, shady spot on a slope facing a sunlit landscape, with an illuminated boulder nearby to reflect warmth toward the picnickers, would be ideal.

The computer in my friend's office, properly (and illegally) stroked, coughed up a number of map overlays, one for each standard day in the lunar month, showing where such sites might be looked for in the area around West Limb. It was a brilliant piece of applied astronomy.

That afternoon my rocket hopper was scheduled to haul a load of hung-over engineers back to Polar Solar from their monthly spree at Grimaldi, and we had to make a lot of local trips, too. I let my copilot do all the flying while I studied one of those maps. Each time we boosted out of the West Limb hopper pad, I compared the map with the territory (or it is lunitory?) round about. By quitting time, I had selected a promising rock field a short distance north of the base. It all seemed so safe and easy.

That night I cashed in on the accumulated favors that people on the base owed me. I got the next day off and a free recharge of my vacuum-suit backpack, and I borrowed two one-man vacuum-survival tents. I arranged for an airtight case packed with cold chicken, potato salad, cole slaw, some vegetables, a fresh loaf of French bread with real butter, lemon-ade, and two bottles of Boordy Vineyards' *vin gris*. West Limb may have been a real sty in those days, but the pigs ate and drank well.

The cafeteria manager had heard rumors. He drew me into a corner of the kitchen, looked around carefully, and leered at me.

"Suarez," he said confidentially, "What are you up to? I mean, really?"

"Porkner," I said, "a gentleman, who is entrusted—"

"No, I mean, really. No kidding. Is it—"

"You got it. It's a technical operation. Something new," I said, leering back at him.

I made my escape while he was oh-ho-ho-ing at me. It doesn't do to antagonize the cafeteria manager, or to tell him anything, either. I went to bed early that evening. Lucky for me, it was my turn in the shower.

Stacy Cramblitt was waiting for me at the hatch when I got there at ten hours. All the running around and plotting I had done had seemed a little sordid to me, I guess. But the way she looked, standing there, cool and amused, in her tailor-made, fluorescent-pink pilot's vacuum suit, made my conscience clear up right away.

"Everything set?" she asked.

"Not quite yet," I said, putting my load of survival tents, blankets, and the food case into the airlock. For once there wasn't anyone in the corridor near the hatch. I held her by the arms and drew her close to me.

"I'm setting your suit radio on my private channel," I said. She looked at my face as I clicked the knob on her chest module. A delicate perfume rose from her collar ring.

"You have nice eyes," she said. "Now you're blushing."

"Nonsense. After you."

We stepped into the airlock and went through the rest of the suit-checkout procedure. I locked us through to the outside. The sun was glaring in the west. The structures scattered on the surface extended inky shadows across the rutted, pock-marked ground. As we walked, Stacy's helmet swiveled. She was taking in the torn-up ground, the glinting litter of aluminum scraps and shards, the awkward tangle of antenna towers and guy wires, and the humped and ugly buildings.

"It's not very pretty," I said.

"The human race takes its mess with it everywhere it goes," she said.

"Better here than on the earth," I said. "Besides, it's not all like this. This is a little zit on the face of a whole world. We're just a short walk from the real moon, where no one has ever set foot. Give it a chance." I took hold of one of her gloved hands.

"Okay," she said, looking at me. I couldn't see her face through her mirrored sun visor, but I felt her squeeze my hand.

We must have been an odd sight as we hiked out of view over the first ridge north of the base. There were undoubtedly a hundred people peeking at us from the windows of the base buildings. I was lugging the rolled-up tents and the food case. Stacy had a blanket over each shoulder. One of the blankets was a garish plaid; the other was white with green and orange stripes and the words *FUERZAS ARMADAS DE MEXICO* printed on it.

An hour later we were crossing the vast, boulder-strewn slopes of Hevelius Crater, overlooking the flat Oceanus to our right. I noted that our feet were in the shade, but the tallest boulders reflected a lot of sunlight onto the ground. We could see well enough to pick our way along, and my blackbody thermometer registered in the middle teens. The map supplied by my computer-pushing pal was proving remarkably reliable.

"You know, it's not just all gray, black, and white," Stacy said. "I can see all kinds of subtle colors. Look at that greenish streak in the rocks over there. See it?"

"I sure do. You've really got good eyes. Most people can't see these things until they've been on the moon for a year or more. Most don't care. There's a lot of beauty here. It just doesn't smack you in the eye the way it does back on Earth. God didn't make this scenery for clods. You have to have some talent and sensitivity.'' I was laying it on a bit thick, but it wasn't *all* crap.

Stacy was having a good time in the low gravity, bouncing around me as I went striding along. She kicked up a big cloud of dust in front of us.

"Look at that," she said. "That dust settled so quickly that I could almost hear the thump it made on the ground. I've logged a lot of hours in space, but this is the first time I've ever been on my feet like this on another world. Do you ever get used to the strangeness?"

"Not really," I answered. "I never really get completely used to it. I'm always finding new things to look at." I stopped suddenly and stooped to look at the ground. "Look here."

As she bent over, I pointed out a circular pattern in the dust. In the center of the circle was a tiny grain of shiny glass. Hairlike lines radiated from the center of the pattern. The lines looked as if someone had drawn them in the dust with a fine needle. The entire formation was about the size of a dime. There were also concentric arcs in the pattern I had discovered.

"What *is* it?" Stacy asked.

"I call them dust flowers," I said. "Don't touch it; it'll fall apart if you do. A friend of mine thinks they're micrometeorite craters. Where the glass is in the middle is where the micrometeorite struck, and the pattern around it was formed by shock waves traveling in the dust. My friend says they can form only on this kind of fine-dust surface. He's writing a paper about it."

"What do *you* think they are?"

"I think they're dust flowers. We'll probably find more of them if we look around carefully."

"I'd hate to step on something that's maybe been waiting here for millions of years."

"Let's keep our eyes open."

We started off again, passing among shattered heaps of rocks and skirting around the lesser craters.

Stacy said, "You know, it seems odd to me that there should be so much fine dust on the ground around here. I thought the lunar soil wasn't supposed to be differentiated—no wind or water to sort it out into particles of varying sizes, and so forth."

"That's right," I said. "Somebody's not following the rules."

We marched along in silence. I kept looking for an open spot to pitch the tents in. After a while Stacy and I emerged, so to speak, from a forest of boulders into a clearing. The scene was extraordinary, really. It was like a natural Stonehenge, with a circle of rough columns surrounding a sort of terrace in the hillside. The circle was open to the east, and we could see far out over the flatlands. A nearly full Earth hung low over the razor horizon. I almost expected to see a sail on that dappled, oceanlike expanse and surf rolling in on the beach several kilometers below us.

Stacy was superimpressed. She just stood there and said, "Glorious. Glorious. It really is." She turned to me. "No one else has ever been here, have they?"

"Don't see any footprints, do you? I've been saving it for someone special." *Someday God is going to punish me,* I thought.

"Let's get out of these suits and have some lunch," I said. "I'm starving."

I untied the roll of survival tents and laid them out on the ground, arranging them so that their door openings faced each other. The openings in tents of the kind I had are round, surrounded by a complicated, flexible gasket. You can seal up a single tent with its own door, or double up two tents by pressing their door gaskets together. The gaskets are supposed to interlock tightly when the tents are filled with air.

I held up the entrance of one of the tents to allow Stacy to crawl in, dragging the food case and the blankets. Then I crawled into it. Crouching on my knees, I carefully sealed the two tents together.

"That looks airtight," I said. "Let's see what happens when I let the air out of one of these reserve bottles. If it doesn't hold, we'll have to call it off and go back to the base."

"That would be miserable," Stacy said, poking me playfully in the backside.

I opened the valve on the air bottle. The tents stirred like living things, then ballooned into a pair of dome shapes.

"It's like being inside a waterbed mattress," Stacy remarked.

"Or two jellyfish kissing," I answered, watching the other tent through the transparent plastic walls of our tent.

Stacy began to spread the blankets on the tent floor. "Why did we bring two tents?" she asked.

"For storage. When we take our suits off, it'll be like having two extra people in here."

"So long as they don't want any lunch. Did you notice what's happening to the blankets?" she asked, holding up a ripped-off handful. "Looks like vacuum and sunlight aren't good for wool."

"They were getting pretty worn out anyway."

"How's the inflation going?" she said.

"Looks okay so far," I answered. The two tents, joined at their doorways, had become rigid. The air temperature had leveled off at twenty-five degrees centigrade, and the air pressure was holding steady at an alpine two hundred thirteen millibars.

"Can we take off our suits now?"

"Let me go first," I said. Cautiously I rotated the locking ring on my suit collar. Nothing happened. So I removed my helmet. The air in the tent felt fine. On my cheeks I could feel the cheery warmth of the nearest boulders.

"It's great," I said, disconnecting my backpack hoses. Soon we were both shucking ourselves out of our vacuum suits.

In her long johns, Stacy looked like a tax-free million. She removed her inner gloves and socks and sat, twiddling her toes at me and smiling. I gathered up our suits, helmets, and boots and passed them through the now-rigid doorway into the other tent. That made enough room in our tent for us to spread out the blankets. I kept my backpack with us and shoved Stacy's through the doorway into the other tent with the rest of our gear.

"All righty," I said, unlatching the food container, "luncheon is served at noon, under the stars. We have chicken, cold, and French bread, hot. We have slaw, tomatoes, and chilis. Have a glass of this good rosé, my dear Captain Cramblitt." I poured some wine into our glasses. Then I dished up big platefuls of everything. We lay down together on the blankets, resting our backs on my backpack.

"Pancho, this is delicious," Stacy mumbled through a mouthful of Porkner's warm bread.

"Yep. My compliments to Cookie, and I'm so glad he's not here now," I joked.

After two hours I was feeling pleasantly tight around the middle. Stacy was pouring refills for us from our second bottle. The atmosphere in the tent was tropical. The brilliant earth, blazing cobalt, turquoise, and white, shone down on us. We lay, hips touching, Stacy's head on my shoulder.

I raised my glass to the home planet. "Here's to everybody who happens to be looking at us right now. Here's looking at them." My speech was only a little slurred.

"They can't see us," Stacy whispered, finishing her wine. "We're in the new-moon phase right now."

I turned to her and said, "Well, here's looking at you, anyway," and what the hell, I kissed her on the mouth. She kissed me back, clutching at my neck.

"Guess what we're having for dessert," she whispered into my ear, sending goose bumps along my arms and down my back.

Well, I never kiss and tell, but I will say that Stacy and I peeled each other out of our remaining clothing. I threw the food box and our long johns into the other tent with the other stuff. Infrared from the ground and the surrounding boulders shone on our naked bodies, but it was nothing compared to the glow that was in the tent already. Her breasts flushing dark rose, Stacy spread herself on the blankets and held her arms out to me.

Now you're not going to believe this, but I hesitated at this point. I was, after all, an old space hand, and the open doorway leading to the other tent had been troubling me. There was no reason to worry about it, but open hatches of any kind hover in my mind's eye until I get up and close them. Most of us out here are like that.

"Don't go away," I said, rising to my knees. I found the tent's door, a flat disk of flexible, transparent plastic, rolled up in a corner. I unrolled it and pressed its gasket into place around the circumference of the doorway between the two tents.

"Now I can give you the attention you deserve," I said, and I embraced her. Stacy snuggled in my arms and gave me a kiss. I really was enjoying every moment of this.

While Stacy was tickling the lobes of my ears, we were interrupted by a strange noise. It sounded like a sudden release of steam. The total silence of the lunar mountainside had seeped into our unconscious during the afternoon, and this uncanny sound made us leap off the floor. There was one second of panicky thrashing as we disentangled our arms and legs. I crouched like a cornered alley cat, glaring around at the motionless landscape outside the tent. I didn't see anything. Then I noticed Stacy was staring goggle-eyed at the entrance of our tent.

"Holy Mother of God," I moaned. The other tent, the one with our stuff in it, had become detached from the tent we were in. The two door gaskets had separated, the air had escaped, and now the other tent was lying collapsed over our suits, our helmets, our boots, our underwear, the food

142

container, Stacy's backpack, the dirty dishes. All of it was out there in the clean, fresh vacuum I had been talking about. We were left buck-naked in the tent, with nothing but the blankets and my backpack.

Stacy gulped for several seconds. "Well," she finally said in a small voice, "now we won't have to wash the dishes."

There was only one reason we weren't already dead of explosive decompression: I had sealed the door of our tent after getting rid of the last of our clothes. I could see my vacuum suit and helmet less than a meter away through the transparent plastic of the tent. I studied Stacy's backpack. A little red tag was sticking out of the air-regulator compartment. For some reason, the safety on her air bottle had blown, allowing the bottle to vent freely in the sealed tent. The excess pressure had blown the door gaskets of the two tents apart. The storage tent lost its pressure suddenly; if it hadn't had all our equipment in it, it probably would have flown away like a released balloon. Our own tent was holding air just fine, although the plastic door was bulging outward unnervingly.

I dragged my backpack toward me and looked at the readouts. Four hours, at the most, of reserve air and CO_2 absorption. The arm's length of vacuum that separated us from the radios in our helmets might as well have been millions of kilometers. Our ass was really in a sling, and my face must've shown it as I looked up from the backpack.

Stacy covered my hand with hers. As calm and beautiful as an angel, she said to me, "Don't be afraid, Pancho."

Guilt replaced terror in my wretched soul. "N-no," I said. "We're not dead yet, eh, Stacy."

"Although we might as well disregard the chances of anybody finding us out here by accident," she said firmly.

Oh, yes. And my own stupid fault, too.

"Well, I shouldn't have pressured you into bringing me out here," she said.

"Don't say that, Stacy. I always think I know what I'm doing." *Don't I ever!* By this time she was holding me, stroking me. There I was, lower than a crater's bottom, and *she* was trying to comfort *me*.

The sky over our heads was black. The stars were waiting to see what I could come up with. "Whatever we do, we'll have to do it soon," I quavered. "Any suggestions?"

"Only two. The first one is, we say the hell with it, hope for rescue, and have a good, but short, time."

"I'm not up to it."

"Forget it. The other idea is to open the entrance of our tent and try to grab one of the helmets before the decompression kills us."

"Now I'm *really* not up to it."

"Nothing to it. You get the helmet and reseal the door. I let out all the air from your backpack reserve bottle to repressurize our tent. One, two, three. Then we radio for help."

"I could never reclose the door gasket fast enough."

"We could wrap ourselves in strips of blanket, mummy-style, really tight, to prevent embolism."

"Darling, it sounds like a brave way to commit suicide. If we can't think of anything else, we'll try it, all right?"

"Okay," she said, crestfallen.

"Besides, the blankets are falling apart," I said, holding one up. The blankets had become so dried out and flimsy that they were turning to shreds as we moved around in the tent.

There was a long silence. We sat huddled, arms around each other, like a pair of monkeys in a thunderstorm. Stacy had been doing her best to encourage me. Her proposal, to chance letting the air out of our tent, was a long shot, but it was basically practical. Definitely worth a try. But I couldn't face it right away. She was a better man than I was.

Stacy started to droop a little. I hugged her more tightly, and she straightened up again. Damn it! I visualized the path we had walked from West Limb. Just a short walk, if we didn't stop for sightseeing and fooling around. Between the rocks, the ground was smoother than usual for the moon, like a beach made of fine ash instead of sand. We could do it bare-footed. I was beginning to have a thought.

"Stacy—"

She responded with a loud sniff. Then she said, "I'm sorry. I thought I was being brave. It's just such a damn rotten break—"

"I should be shot for getting you into this," I said. "When we get back to the base, you should turn me in for disciplinary action."

"I d-definitely will. Corrupting my morals—" By this time tears were running down my face, too.

"Listen, Stacy, there's another thing we can do. We can try to walk back to the base. We could stand the tent on its edge and roll it along from the inside. We'll just leave all our stuff here. There's enough air in my backpack for us to make it if we start now."

She thought about it for a moment. "Why not?" she said, finally. "Even if the tent rips and we depressurize, we won't be any worse off than we are now, will we?"

"Nope."

"Let's do it," she said, jumping up and pulling me to my feet.

I lifted up my backpack and hung it on my back, tucking the dangling air and coolant hoses under one of the shoulder straps. Stacy helped me adjust the harness to fit my naked torso.

Stooping, we both pushed against the wall on one side of the tent, trying to tip it over. The plastic felt icy cold against my hands.

"Try to shuffle your feet toward the edge of the floor," I said. The tent slowly rolled onto its side, the scraps of blanket sliding downward as the tent floor tilted upward. The rim of the tent flattened on the ground. It was like standing inside a huge flat tire. The floor of the tent was now a wall to my right. Since it was no longer resting on the ground, it was building outward almost as much as the dome roof on my left side. The floor was made of the same kind of transparent plastic as the dome was. I tapped on it to knock off the dust that stuck to its outside surface. Very little dust actually fell off, but at least we could see through the material.

"Okay," I said. "Luckily, we're already facing the way we want to go. Stacy, stay close behind me. The idea is to step along carefully and make the tent roll like a wheel on its edge."

"I hope we don't have to make any sharp turns."

We took a tentative step. As I put my weight on the plastic that curved up in front of me, it stretched until my foot was on the ground. Alarming stress wrinkles developed in the dome and floor. Abruptly the tent lurched forward. Stacy fell against me from behind. We both staggered, but we managed to keep the tent upright.

"What happened?" I asked Stacy over my shoulder.

"When I picked up my foot, the tent rolled forward and pushed me into you," she said. "If we want the tent to roll smoothly, I've got to take my trailing foot off the ground at the same time you put your leading foot down on the plastic. We'll have to march in step. I'll have to hold on to your backpack."

"Jesus Christ! All right, forward, march. Left, right, left, right, left, right . . ."

And so it went. The tent rolled along like a big wheel, wobbling this way and that, but never quite falling over. Whenever we came to one of the huge boulders, we would walk a little to one side of the edge of the dome, forcing the tent to curve its path in that direction. Occasionally we had stop and put the tent into reverse. Generally, I followed the footprints we had made on our way to the picnic site, but, as we came to more open country, I started taking shortcuts. I carefully avoided the rims of any craters more than a few meters across; I didn't care to find out whether we could develop enough traction to climb up out of one of them.

Things went better than I'd hoped. We moved steadily downhill, with me still counting cadence until

Stacy yelled at me to shut up.

On and on we trundled the tent, my arches flattening in little craters, sharp little rocks jabbing my soles. As we tramped out of the dust area into coarser soil, I started worrying about puncturing the tent. There wasn't a single damn thing I could do about it at all. Stacy was cussing under her breath with pain as she marched behind me.

The blankets had turned to scraps and fuzz by this time, sliding down to the lowest part of the tent as it rotated. I attempted to walk on the stuff, but the effort threw Stacy and me out of step.

"Even if we had our boots with us," I said, "we probably couldn't wear them in this tent. The cleats would hurt the tent worse than the ground outside does."

"Yeah," said Stacy. "Let's keep moving."

I didn't have a watch, but we must have gone on that way about three hours. We left the boulders behind us, and the air grew chilly in the tent. If the ground hadn't been warm, we would have had trouble with frostbite. The pocked fields of the moon were around us. It seemed as if we were making our way down the sides of an endless ash heap. My bare skin cringed from the sharp stars overhead.

"At least it's a nice cloudy day," Stacy said.

"What?"

"On Earth. We can see where we're going."

"Oh."

I wondered whether we could jump the tent over an obstacle if we had to. I was taking bigger chances, leading us into unfamiliar ground, trying to make our return to West Limb along a more nearly straight line than the route we had taken to reach the place where we had our picnic.

As we got closer to the base, the sloping side of Hevelius trended more to the west. The sun began to peep among the undulating hills on our right horizon. When we came to the first long strip of sunlight shining directly on the ground, it was like stepping on a hot griddle.

"Yow! Back up, quick!"

"Is your foot burnt?" Stacy asked.

"No, thank God."

"Will the tent plastic be able to stand the heat?"

"Oh, sure. It's designed for use on hotter surfaces than this. But we'll need to protect our feet with something."

We allowed the tent to topple over. Then we sat down for a breather.

"How far do we still have to go?" Stacy asked me as we bound our bruised and blistered feet with strips of disintegrating blanket.

"Less than a kilometer. The base is right around the corner of that ridge." Good thing, too. I had taken advantage of our halt to inspect the condition of our tent. The plastic was frosty and scratched and was obviously starting to wear out.

After tying up our makeshift booties, we got the tent up and rolling again. The remaining distance had to be covered more slowly than we had been proceeding. We were forced to go from one patch of shade to another. Crossing the strips of sunlight was hell. I felt as if I was being roasted in a bonfire. At each stopping place in the shade I tried to plan the next sunlight crossing so we could as much as possible avoid running over rocks. The tent plastic was beginning to make little crackling noises with each step we took. I kept slogging away on my throbbing feet. Whatever was bad for me was worse for Stacy, I knew.

At last, the base buildings came in sight. I never thought I could be so happy to see that dump as I was just then. "Stacy!" I cried. "You see that? We're almost there!"

I couldn't see her behind me, but I could feel her leaning heavily on my backpack.

"Don't stop now, honey. We're getting there," I said, doggedly pacing on. There were no more sunlit places to cross. I had to consider the problem of how to get inside the buildings. The quickest thing to do would be to head for the buggy hatch, the only airlock big enough to allow us to roll the tent inside without collapsing it first.

I explained all this to Stacy while we approached the buildings. "Fortunately, it'll be easy to get somebody to cycle the airlock for us," I said. "The trail to the buggy hatch runs right under the picture window of the staff bar and lounge. My instincts tell me it must be about Happy Hour now. The bar will be full of people. It'll be easy to attract their attention—"

Stacy came to an abrupt halt, jerking on my backpack so hard that I almost fell.

"What did you say?" she said thickly.

"Huh?"

"You expect me to walk in front of the West Limb Base staff bar and lounge during Happy Hour on Friday night *stark-naked?*"

"Stacy," I said, turning to face her, "we're lucky to be *alive,* and—"

She burst into tears. "I can't. I won't."

She had been carrying me through an ordeal so harrowing that it still gives me the creeps just thinking about it. We were sunburned salmon-pink; our feet were bleeding; we were in deadly danger just standing there. She had bolstered my morale and kept me from despair. This was the first crack in her bravery and her sense of humor I had seen during the whole terrible thing. Some other short-tempered son of a bitch might have raised his voice at that point, but not I.

I held her close, then looked her up and down. My hands ran up her back, caressed her hair, fondled her breasts, rubbed against her downy belly. I almost wasn't aware of what I was doing.

"Stacy, Stacy, darling," I choked. "You'll be the most beautiful thing any of them has ever seen, you know." Just then my left ear popped. It had always been the sensitive one. The air pressure in the tent was falling. We had finally sprung the dreaded leak!

Stacy felt it, too. She grabbed the straps of my backpack and whirled me around.

I stifled the impulse to bolt. "Double time!" I barked. "Leftrightleftrightleftright!"

We were lucky again. Though fog was forming in the tent, I could see that the buggy hatch stood wide open. This was in violation of base safety directives, but I'll be eternally grateful to whoever was responsible. With me in front and Stacy clinging behind, we bustled across the open space in front of the window.

I caught a glimpse of round eyes, open mouths, and hands holding drinks in suspended animation. Porkner just happened to be tending the bar that night. He later told me that it was the only dead silence he had ever heard in that place.

Stacy and I ran into the airlock so fast that I got a black eye colliding with the inside door. Icepicks in my ears, heart slamming, I pounded at the airlock controls through the tent plastic. I managed to hit the EMERGENCY CLOSE button; the outer door clanged down. The tent folded around us as the airlock roared itself full of that wonderful air.

I staggered against the wall, fighting the tent. Stacy sat down hard on the floor. We were both gasping for air. I was about to say we had made it, or words to that effect, when I became aware of the sound of trampling feet and the murmur of voices from behind the inner door. The Happy Hour stampede had arrived. Stacy ripped the plastic door off the entrance of the tent and stepped out. She said through clenched teeth, "I'll kill the first bastard who—"

"Hey! Suarez! You all right?" It was Porkner's voice, coming over the airlock speaker. He had won the footrace down the corridor from the bar to the buggy hatch. I jumped out of the tent and palmed the lens of the TV camera that surveilled the airlock.

"We're all right," I said into the intercom grille. "We, uh, we need some clothes."

"Already taken care of," Parkner's voice answered. "We've got a red light on the airlock panel out here. We'll have to open the hatch by hand. Stand by."

Stacy and I stood to one side. After much talk and clanking, the hatch opened a crack, and Porkner's arm came through proffering a couple of white tablecloths. Blessed be the name of Porkner, and I'll never malign his spaghetti again.

Stacy and I emerged discreetly togaed, to the plaudits of the multitude, and entered the dusty buggy bay. Stacy was escorted into her quarters, and I had to answer a lot of questions. There were some sly remarks about my, ah, alleged physical state, which had not gone unnoticed as we sprinted past the picture window. I always say that it's up to us pioneers to point the way forward, as it were.

As for my relationship with Captain Cramblitt, her goodbye kiss at the shuttle pad the next day seemed promising. The next time I saw her, she asked me whether I wanted to go skiing. We were on the north polar icecap of Mars at the time, but that's another story.

BLIND SPOT

By Jayge Carr

Some of a doctor's duties are hard—and some even harder. "You're blind." Lip unconsciously caught between his teeth, he faced the mirror. "You're blind. Totally, incurably, and permanently blind." His holo image stared back at him: hairless, pale skin over neatly muscled bones, a sensitive mouth, cruelly jutting cheekbones, and E-norm ears flat to the narrow skull. And the eyes: jewel-faceted like an insect's, glittering silver. The prosthetic eyes that could see macroscopic or microscopic, in a range of wavelengths much broader than human norm, in a full three-hundred-sixty-degree scan, as if his head and body weren't there or were transparent.

He ordered the holo mirror to show him in the latest fashion in reflective body paint: a splashy chrome-and-vermilion-distorted houndstooth check.

"You're blind, and there's nothing medical science can do." He replaced the houndstooth with an

155

intricate pattern of paisley tears in gold/orange/turquoise/scarlet, his own natural skin color, a shadowy blue-gray, showing between.

"There's nothing medical science can do, but there are prosthetics that we can use."

He ordered his eyes to "see" in infrared, decided he didn't like the pattern in that mode, and replaced two of the colors with heat paints. To normal vision, the heat paints were merely a subtle haze; in infrared a transparent color unlike anything "seen" in normal range. He made a few minor adjustments to the pattern and shut his eyes. Holding his breath, he ordered the autovalet to spray, and he felt the warmth envelop him. Very good! The pattern had been faithfully transferred. Only . . . it looked a little . . . incomplete.

"Prosthetics," he repeated aloud, his mind still with his Very Important Patient.

At his mental command, the holo image added a long scarf in a complementary color. He experimented with various drapes, added a few hundred angstroms to the shade, and nodded to himself. The autovalet obediently dispensed a long strip of cloth. He held it up against himself, approved the shade, and arranged it carefully, with the neat movements of a man who splices living nerves. Some preferred to have the autovalet do it all, but he felt the results, when it came to actual synthetic materials, were a little artificial.

He ordered true image again and stiffened his spine. He was ready.

The patient was sitting in the solarium, as she always was when she was free of testing or therapy, her face turned toward the sun she could no longer see except as the palest blur—and not even that for much longer.

She turned toward him as he approached, the rippling floor carrying him along with a barely perceptible hum. And despite the fine, downy white hair that covered her face (and her body, too) he knew that she knew what he was going to say. Her soft "Well, Doctor," was anticlimactic.

He ordered a seat, and the floor formed one. He sat down before answering. "I have the results of the latest test."

"How much longer?"

"Before the deterioration of the optic nerve is complete and total? Between twenty and thirty days."

"Ah!" A deep, shuddering sigh. She took the blow well; he had to admire her gallant spirit. He wondered whether she looked as ugly to her own people as she did to him, or was her ugliness merely the product of a different world, a different culture? She was short and round, totally covered with the velvety, milk-white fur. She never used any kind of body paint. Her nose was broad, lying against her flat cheeks; the inside of her nostrils, the lips, and the naked tips of the huge furred ears were black like an animal's.

"And the other possibilities?" she asked.

"We'll try autotransplants first," he told her patiently, as if she hadn't heard it all a dozen times before. "We'll control-clone new nerves and try to graft them in. It's a tricky procedure all around. It can succeed. I've used it successfully myself many times." *You're the problem,* he was thinking. Many high-T worlds had low-T enclaves, peopled with those who rejected the technology for religious or other reasons or who had been isolated and had never developed it. And the records showed in an amazing number of cases that when those low-T people were exposed to high-T procedures, especially delicate medical procedures, those procedures failed. The mind rejected or disbelieved, and the body followed. Her preliminary tests had not been promising. But he was the best; he'd never failed a patient before. And he wouldn't fail this supremely important one.

"What if the grafts fail to—take?" she asked, her ugly face, with the visual augmenters that made it even uglier, turned toward him.

"We've discussed that," he replied. "We'll have to go to the prosthetics, with a direct mind interface."

Her hands clenched. He saw the effort she needed to unclench them. "Yes." Her voice was calm, but it was the calmness of a thin net holding back an avalanche. "We've discussed it. Do you really think your artificial eyes will be usable? Do you imagine that I will be able to continue my work, using dead. . . ?" She left the sentence unfinished.

She was ugly, but she was a genius—a genius whose works were revered, almost worshiped, throughout the inhabited galaxy. It was his responsibility to restore that genius so that it could continue those deathless creations of sublime art. He gritted his teeth. "I assure you, if it comes to that, you won't even be able to tell the difference."

"I will." That utter assurance that geniuses need to have now turned against him—and her own future. "I will."

"Treat the patient as well as the problem," one of his professors had been fond of saying. But how was he to treat this strange off-worlder whose precious eyes were deteriorating daily? This primitive from a culture so degenerate that, had it not been for luck and some determined missionaries, she would have spent her entire life in the wild, grubbing for roots, speaking in grunts, fighting with every other member of her species she met except, of course, during the rutting season.

Now—a genius. Unique. Honored and adored. And facing the worst of all fates, the loss of what made her what she was.

"I have a reproduction of one of your works. Did I tell you that?"

"Yes." she said, nodding. "You mentioned it. *Mayflight in the Morning*. One of my earliest and best. What size is it?"

"I hold it in my hand."

He remembered his surromother bringing in the program, crooning. She had said that the artist would be recognized as a genius, and she had been right. He remembered her inserting the program, waiting that fraction of a second while the machine constructed the artifact. The children had surged forward, irresistibly drawn toward the strange concatenations of subtle curves and infinite inter-plays of color and texture. But the first child to touch it had jerked back as the piece sang with the gentlest tinkling voice.

"It's a multisense piece," the surromother had told them. "You feel it, you look at it, and when you touch it, it sings. Here—'' She programmed for two more copies and passed them around so that there was a chorus of fairy voices. "I understand the original had scent and taste, too. You could lick it, but since it was made by an off-worlder, whose sensory judgments might be different from ours, those have been suppressed.''

"An off-worlder?'' he had asked, reluctantly passing the piece along (share-and-share) to his neighbor. One day, he had promised himself, he would have one of those for his very own. And he had kept that promise.

"Yes, the artist was discovered by a group of missionaries and was brought here, to be properly trained and to have her works disseminated through our simultaneity projector. And quite right, too. Such talent belongs to all worlds. Ironically, though, thanks to the relativistic effects on the voyage—you do know about relativistic time effects at almost the speed of light, don't you, children?—while she was traveling from her world to ours, her own world was able to acquire both a simultaneity projector of its own and technicians to service it. But their loss is our gain.''

"It sings soprano in that size,'' the genius who created it told him, as if he hadn't heard the song a thousand times. "And do you like what it sings?''

"Yes . . . no,'' he admitted. "It makes me sad sometimes. I don't know why, and yet I can't keep my fingers off it, even though I know its song is likely to make me sad.''

She smiled, and her almost blind eyes looked at

him and saw something else. "When you understand the song, you'll understand what the difference is, and why it's so important."

"We'll try the grafts first," he said firmly.

Three times he painstakingly inserted and spliced the fragile nerves, then supervised the slow recovery. And three times something in her rejected them. A normal person would be satisfied with the sight they gave her. But she was not normal. She was a genius. She demanded perfection, or perhaps something beyond, something that made her subtle creations possible. She would not be satisfied with anything less, and three times the implanted nerves withered and died.

They tried the prosthetics next. He did the delicate work, the implanting of the organically neutral interfaces, the almost unnoticeable (because he was sure that this was what she wanted) exterior scanners. And though it wasn't his personal responsibility, he watched over her therapy, his face twisted into a frown as again and again she lurched through the obstacle course. A genuinely blind subject would have done better. And this from a mind that could curve shapes together into the subtlest of relationships, an artist whose works were balanced to within a microgram, a millimeter.

"It's not seeing. I can't *see,*" she insisted over and over. Often her control would fail, and she would pound on the nearest objects with her hard, bony fists, bruising those fingers that had worked miracles.

He had carefully adjusted her prosthetics to normal vision. He tested them repeatedly, showing her how the graphs matched up, how the prosthetics were well within the tolerances.

And still she fought—or wept. "I can't *see.*"

He tried to comfort her, but she only turned away. No one else in the giant hospital complex had any better luck. He thought of getting her foster parents to help, but they were missionaries of a rootless sect on whose homeworld religion had died centuries before, and they had already moved on, not wanting to linger in a world that denied the need for what they offered. Now they were on another endless voyage to another primitive world. Wombships traveled more slowly than light, but they were fast enough that their voyages involved relativistic time contraction. People aboard the ships lived months while decades passed on the worlds they visited. Only simultaneity projectors could exceed the speed of light, and they were limited to transmitting knowledge, programs, and nonmaterial information.

"Don't keep showing me your machine-made charts. They're wrong, they're all wrong. I can't *see!*"

He searched for others on this world who might help—teachers, lovers, friends. But she had so surpassed her teachers, and so quickly, that she had formed no lasting relationships with any of them. As for lovers or friends, she was an alien, an off-worlder, obsessed with her work. She had none. Her life had been her art, and her art her life, and now she had lost it.

There were a dozen rehabilitation centers in the giant medical complex. Physical therapy, occupational therapy (the cruelest failure of all), many varieties of mental gymnastics—and she tried every one of them unsuccessfully.

"I can't see."

Failure. *His* failure. His *first* failure.

He should have been glad when she announced, "I'm going home."

But in his own way he was as fanatical about his work as she was about hers. First he ordered no, as her doctor. When she laughed in his face, he threatened, cajoled, begged, tried to have her declared mentally incompetent, sulked when that failed, and always, always argued. Usually she ignored him. Once, when he accused her of deliberately denying her art to the worlds, she answered wearily. "My world has simultaneity projectors now, like any *civilized* world. Or at least the cresters do." It was the first time he realized that her world was populated by two separate races.

"I'm a trog," she asserted matter-of-factly. "But the cresters aren't fools. They've enjoyed the prestige of my work for years, simply because I come from their world. If I ever manage to work again, they'll trip over themselves rushing to program duplicates through the simultaneity projectors for other worlds to admire."

"I'm going with you," he declared.

"What?" She was incredulous. Then, "Why? Love? It's physically impossible, you know."

"I'm a doctor," he reminded her.

"Then you'd know better than I. But it hasn't stopped—the infatuates, the worshipers, those who tried to translate artistic admiration into something more physical."

163

"I'm a doctor," he repeated stubbornly. "You're my patient."

She shook her head. "You don't know the 'floor.' You can't imagine. . .believe me, there's nothing, *nothing* you can do."

For once immovable object met irresistible force. "Your world is primitive, except for a few high-T enclaves. I know that. All right. I'll just have to be careful to bring everything I might need with me, that's all."

"Doctor—" She took a deep breath, for the first time moving those unseeing eyes away from him. "It isn't just the primitiveness. My world is far away. We couldn't get a direct route. We'll be lucky if we have to change wombships only once. In real time that's fifty years, a hundred, or more, for the trip. If you ever returned here, all your friends, children, family—all will be dead or changed almost beyond recognition. And your profession—"

"If I ever return, I'll catch up, professionally and personally. But if it's such a bad trip, why are you taking it?"

"I'm going home," she muttered. And he told himself he didn't hear two more unsaid words: to die.

He consulted a reference library about her world and found out why she didn't want him to go. Her world was even more primitive than he had thought. The trogs lived on the forest floor, in an eternal night produced by the shadows of the giant leaves in the crests of immense trees, animals among animals, without language, clothing, tools, or society.

The cresters were a different race entirely; they lived in the sunlight, in the tops of the huge trees.

Not much was known about them except that they were bioengineers with the highest skills. Crester plants, for food or cloth or simply exotic beauty, were valuable exports that had paid for the simultaneity projector that was installed and for the technicians willing to exile themselves from their homeworlds to keep the device running.

Some of the other information about them was confusing or simply unbelievable. (Cultivating on giant leaves? Irrigating *leaves?*) Most physical trading was done through the wombships. And the simultaneity projector disseminated all kinds of art and information, but the cresters were not so foolish as to pass on the secrets of their skills.

The doctor absorbed all the information he could, and when his patient boarded the wombship, he was right behind her.

The wombers refused payment. (They revered the artist and her work.) And the doctor agreed to spend time and skills on patients aboard the ship. He even trained as many healers as possible in whatever skills he could pass on.

He never asked what the wombshippers thought of her, as a person, or what they thought of him for that matter, but he was fascinated by them.

For thousands of years wombshippers had been pariahs. But they were also the only thread that held the human worlds together, that is, the worlds colonized by humans, or what had been humans before they adapted to their new environments. Each isolated world thought of itself as the norm, its people as human, and anyone different—and the wombship pariahs were invariably different—as not human.

Then the simultaneity projector was developed, linking the worlds together with pictures. World after world realized that *all* of their thousands of brother and sister worlds held intelligent beings who were different yet "human."

Some worlds reacted by raising their barriers higher, rejecting projectors and wombships alike.

Some rejected only the projectors, grudgingly allowing the alien pariah wombshippers to trade.

And some transcended their insularity, their prejudices, and recognized that it was the soul, not the body or the culture, that was important.

And the pariahs, too, were a culture—a culture formed by countless years of rejection and by the radiation they couldn't shield against entirely, that killed many of them in their physiological teens and twenties. It was a cosmic irony that one of the reasons why they were rejected was that they seemed immortal, possessing the immortality that relativistic time contraction at almost light velocities gave them so that they would return after fifty planetary years and seem only a few months older. The truth was that their actual life spans were much shorter than those of most planet-bounds.

The wombship itself was a spaghetti tangle of corridors and living spaces. The doctor's guide was a tall, thin, but prepubescent female, bald and radiation scarred, whose vocabulary consisted of "Essr" and "Nossr" and whose jaw continually worked on something. He preferred not to speculate on what it was. The first time she took his hand and they were, with no transition he could detect, someplace else, he nearly had a heart attack. Eventually he learned to appreciate the speed of travel and to be thankful that his hosts had assigned him a guide capable of taking him as well as herself "through." He did what research he could on psionics, another gift of radiation, but his results were contradictory, and with a sigh he simply accepted.

There were plenty of medical problems to occupy his time, and doing what he could for the wombers helped keep his mind off the continued deterioration of his prime patient. Over the months he became friendly with many of the wombers, mostly the medical staff, and especially their chief, a wizened gremlin of a woman with the unlikely sobriquet of Camel. But when he told her his pet theory regarding his patient, she only threw back her head and laughed.

"This is the wrong place to talk about back to the womb, you know." She sobered. "But it's certainly one of our major problems. If that's her trouble, you needn't worry. She'll decide to stay here, and we've developed a few"—a toothless grin—"techniques that might prove effective. Anyway, once a diagnosis is confirmed, you're more than halfway to a cure. But I think you're off the mark. Way off. I've talked to her myself, and I think she's just following instinct. Sometimes following one's instinct is the smartest thing to do."

"Even if it means going back to a primitive, scratch-for-a-living world?"

Camel shrugged. "You see it that way. But she wants to go *home*"—all the longing of a people denied a permanent home for generations contained in that one word. "Sometimes that's the best—and only—medicine."

He grew to like the wombshippers, to find in their

company a relief from the continual frustration of his primary task. He was almost sorry when the voyage ended.

But nothing on the tapes had prepared him for the frantic vitality of the world called (not by its own people) Sequoia Upper.

It was hard to remember he was in the crest of a giant tree. He seemed to be walking on a thick, resilient carpet, muddy aqua (the basic plant color here). The gently moving, ever-changing "walls" were like a holo abstract; actually they were leaves, vines, stalks, growths, saprophytes, tendrils, some close, some far away, the whole blurring into a panorama of relentless growth.

"It's as if the very air were alive and growing," he told his guide, a short, prehensile-tailed male whose costume revealed no fewer than six apparently functional nipples as well as indisputable evidence of masculinity (The doctor learned later that the costumes—all the "clothes" in fact—were plants, stem and hair roots concealed somewhere in the fur or manes, the rest growing in a controlled pattern around the Sequoian wearing them.)

"Rainforest, I believe it's called," the guide commented, politely. "Though I understand on other worlds what they call rainforest would be a strand of sprouts not yet ready to be transplanted here. Now this tree, called baldcypress"—he waved his hand, and the doctor, who hadn't seen any trace of structure or point of division, wondered whether everything he saw wasn't part of a single organism—"has sprouted an ancient and honorable family; I

168

myself"—a deprecating gesture, but a smug grin over it—"am proud to be an acknowledged branch of the hundred ninety-seventh generation nurtured within its leaves." He obviously expected a reaction. When it didn't come, he made a disappointed moue and went on. "So this entire tree is quite well cultivated and most tame. If you wish to visit one of the wilder trees, it can be arranged."

The doctor heard his patient mutter something under her breath.

"And of course"—the guide was obviously working up to an oration—"if there's anything you need, for any reason, we'll be pleased, and proud, and honored, to be allowed to serve, in however minor a fashion—"

The doctor tuned out the rest; he'd sat through banquets before.

It was then that a fluff of silver tendrils drifted against his patient's cheek. Automatically he reached over to pluck it off, but her hand was quicker. With a facile gesture that spoke of long habit, she grasped it, slid it into her mouth, and sucked on the arsenic-green roundness below the pale parachute.

He opened his mouth to protest, but she had already spit the thing out, not a gesture of distaste, but rather an absent-minded expulsion of something sucked dry of interest. It tumbled along the surface until he couldn't see it any longer.

She didn't drop dead, and before he could lick his dry lips and *ask,* his guide interrupted his monologue long enough to repeat the gesture, this time with a thing like two gray wings run together but no bigger than his finger.

This time he did ask, and the guide laughed and

caught something from the air and put it to his lips. Five minutes later the doctor was still mulling over the multiple subtleties of his first taste of sequoia.

There was so much to assimilate, so many flavors and smells and customs and whatnot, that adapting to life on the wombship had been like preform play, while this was final specialization residency. But he was enjoying it—part of him even wallowed in the VIP treatment—until his parent told him the truth.

"We're both pariahs, you know."

He didn't believe her. He'd been escorted through some of their finest research strands of planting (though he still wasn't sure whether the sprouts were merely being nurtured on their leaf fields or whether they were products of the leaves themselves), wined and dined and deferred to and flattered and listened to and even entertained in an ancient but still appreciated fashion.

She interrupted his protests by reaching over and tapping the wall of the room they were in, one of several that was "theirs" for the duration. "Dead," she said simply. "Dead wood." She tapped again, and it was a dull sound. "The ultimate insult in their language is 'Go live in deadwood.' " She spat, and he watched the green-tinged liquid disappear into the floor. "Or is it merely the penultimate insult?" she mused aloud. "Go live with the trogs. Yes, I think that is the ultimate. And I wonder which of us they despise more, me, the trog, or you, the trog lover." A breath. "Doctor."

"Yes?" He wondered about something himself: what the penalty was here for a doctor strangling his patient?

"Take my advice. Take the next wombship away

from here, no matter where it's going. Just *go*. Get away. This isn't your world, and ultimately it will reject you.''

"You're my patient, and I'm going to cure you. I promise."

"Blind, blind," she murmured. "But which of us is it that will not see?"

Three days later she was gone.

"Once a trog, always a trog," said the incredible old woman coldly.

"And that's it. Throw her and her potential away." He had bulled his way up to this Sequoian Ultimate Authority in a barely controlled rage.

"She's a trog," the woman muttered. Something fluttered through the air and landed against her cheek. Her fingers went up in a caressing gesture, and—he blinked—had those fingers somehow flicked the airborne wisp away, or had it been absorbed into the crepey, powdery old skin?

"And that covers it," he heard himself snarling. Some of the leaves from the plant he'd been forced to wear fluttered away from his mouth, and he saw her flinch. That plant had driven home his patient's point, about his being a pariah. It clung to and covered every inch of skin and gave off a rank odor. Even the windbornes kept away from him, and he knew it for what it was: this world's equivalent of a contamination suit. Nothing of him must infect their happy lives. "Just throw her away. She's a trog, a worthless, useless animal of a trog. All right, all right then. But don't be surprised at how other worlds react to what you've done. Other worlds have values

171

different from yours. They might see your actions in an unflattering light. On other worlds racial prejudice is considered—"

"Prejudice!" She was slight and slender, antique and fragile. "Off-worlder, you came here, *knowing* you knew all there was to know about us. You look and you do not see. You are a—a dissonance, a flaw in our lives, a wrongness we cannot right. Yet we have made you welcome. And in return you would tell other worlds about the sins that we committed only in your mind." She stood, one hand against a leaf that formed the "wall" of this cozy nook, and tiny tendrils twined around her arm. He had a sudden vision of a woman and tree, unity, a single living organism.

"Your prejudice," he said, but more calmly, "drove her off this world in the first place. And now it has driven her down to her death."

"*Our* prejudice? Prejudice means prejudging, doesn't it? Were we given a chance, or were we prejudged, off-worlder? Some people see only what they want to see, and perhaps the motives of those so-called selfless missionaries ought to be examined more closely." He caught his lip, remembering a news holo of an awards ceremony; there had been several off-worlders with the artist then, all of them radiating a complacent, almost arrogant pride. "The trog was spirited away from here. Did you know that? Because my predecessors protested at the very thought. And after, when we warned that she would be damaged away from her home, when we asked that she be returned, we were sneered at, accused of wanting to keep her treasures selfishly to ourselves, accused—it was sickening. And no one believed us,

as you don't believe us now.'' She shrugged. ''We
could prove all we have said, but you, outlander,
with your closed mind, have already determined our
guilt. Would you believe the truth if it were right in
front of you?''

''Try me.''

''It will be dangerous.''

''For you or for me?'' He couldn't help sneering.

''So be it.'' Her pale lips were tight, and the very
wall of living plant seemed to shudder with her
restrained anger.

The only way down, short of the dangerous climb
down the clifflike trunk, was by being lowered, at
dizzying speed, on immensely long vines.

The others were armed with a variety of weapons,
only some of them recognizable. His companions
were all grim, their prehensile tails stiffly erect, and
he knew that if looks could kill, he wouldn't survive
to reach the floor.

The floor. It wasn't as totally dark as he'd
imagined, because many of the plants—and animals,
too—phosphoresced. A phrase he'd heard once long
ago kept echoing through his head. The caves of
night. He was wandering lost through the caves of
night. Above was a leafy canopy of solid darkness.
And beneath . . .

The trunks of the giant trees were tens, some even
hundreds, of meters in diameter, and girding their
lower reaches were living buttresses, great knees of
wood larger than most of the trees he was accustomed
to. And in and around and on and under and through
was all living forest, a veritable ocean solid with life,

competing, eating, growing, dying, layer on layer, predator on predator. A normal rainforest (he had consulted the records he had brought) was actually scant of life on its floor, because the canopy above shut out too much light. But here, even without light, there was enough organic material raining down from the giants above to provide the basis for an ecology. And what an ecology! What a competitive, fetid, voracious ecology! And so complex!

He saw vines climbing up a treeling a mere ten meters or so high. He blinked, and the vines swarmed upward and spread out, sending in tendrils to tap the tree's life fluids, round and round, leaves unfurling and sending spines into the treeling until between one breath and the next what had been a tree was a mound of pulsing leaves.

"Stranglervine," one of the guides (guards) answered to his stammered question. "By tomorrow it'll have sucked the infant dead and dry. Then it'll curl up in a ball and tumble away, until leaf-breath wind brings it to another vine."

"Will it . . ."

She snorted, her swishing tail imperiously contemptuous.

"You wouldn't taste right. But there are threats here, plant and animal, that make the stranglervine seem like Anna Sweetteat."

He glared. But in minutes he knew she had spoken the simple truth. The floor was a pesthole, a hothouse and breeding ground for desperate appetites. Animal, plant—and trog.

Two strong cresters were at point, hacking with off-world metal machetes at the living mass. Hacked and headless corpses of small animals were trampled underfoot along with the severed plants. The cresters' progress was measured in meters. He could still see the doomed tree under its mound of stranglervine when a shapeless, many-legged horror dropped onto the shoulder of a crester walking not two paces in front of him. The victim dropped without as much as a gasp, but another guide reached over and touched the wetly glistening horror with a vine wrapped around her wrist, and, with a teeth-tearing keen, legs convulsing, the horror shriveled and fell off, to be kicked away into the dimness. Its victim was loaded onto a sling and carried by his fellows.

The attacks were almost continuous. From above, behind, the side, the front. Things even slithered up out of the crushed-down matter they were walking on. Big things, little things, all bristling with every natural weapon he'd ever heard of, and a few he wouldn't have dreamed existed. Things crisped by lasers, hacked by machetes, destroyed by the symbiotic plants. Still, dying, they came on, claws grasping, tendrils reaching, teeth slavering, spitting acids, dribbling caustics, limbs flailing, tentacles reaching—reaching—reaching—

Despite all their efforts, there was soon a second casualty and, even before that victim could be settled in a sling to be carried, a third one.

The trogs, his guide informed him between attacks, are among the most dangerous of the floor dwellers, thanks to their claws and teeth, their cunning and ferocity; they glide through the growth like sunbeams through broken clouds. They kill and eat and breed prolifically, a dozen or more to the litter, and so survive. They're marsupial, and if the mother's killed, the tough pouch convulses shut, protecting the litter against all but the worst of tooth and claw and acid. The newborn are tiny, and the pouch is small; often the killer swallows it whole. But inside the stomach, the dissolvents act on the pouch in a curious way. The pouch has a simple nervous system of its own: it attaches itself to the stomach wall and absorbs nutrients from its surroundings to feed the litter. The litter grows until it completely blocks off the stomach, and the killer starves. Then the litter eats its way out of the pouch, fast, before the floor dwellers can devour corpse, pouch, litter, and all.

"But would you have believed this?" she finished with a grim nod to the voracity around them. "Any of this if you hadn't seen it with your own eyes, actually experienced—the floor?"

Around him birth and death alike exploded in the green-white light.

"How long do you think a blind trog would survive?"

"Seconds," he admitted, "minutes, no more. But can't *you* understand? I have to *try!*" Despite the protective clothing he'd been given, things had burrowed under it. He could feel the skittering legs—or were they tendrils?—in a dozen places. He jumped abruptly as a white-hot needle bored in just below the point of his left shoulderblade.

And then a trog attacked. It had the cunning to go for one of the back points, but the troops were all watching one another, and a loud voice gave the alarm before the victim hit the ground. The trog tore off a great chunk of its victim with its teeth and ran, the bleeding strip dangling from its mouth. One of the guards made a throwing motion with her arm, and the trog went down, its booty still clamped tightly between its teeth. By the time they ran up to it, both the trog and its gruesome treasure were being swarmed over by hundreds of tiny crawling and flying things.

He watched, gulping and unable to speak. Dead eyes, yellow-green like hers, stared up at him; the white fur was slimed with dark blood, the teeth glistened with it. As he watched, the body disintegrated, and the swarm ate it, bite by bite. It was no longer a body; it had become nothing but a heap of crawling, fighting—

Fascinated, he continued to watch until he was staring at a scatter of yellow bones, polished, gleaming, clean. Something no bigger than his hand, a cuddly gray ball of living velvet, ambled over, snapped off a rib, and chewed it with gusto. The rib went down in seconds, and the ball cracked off a second and began chewing, but an odd, growled rumble made it freeze and then scurry hastily away.

The dead guard was being attended to by one of the troops. The doctor was embarrassed, professionally shamed. It was his duty, after all, to tend the wounded. He had seen the bright arterial blood spurting from the torn throat, but the trog had been the greater compulsion. Even so, he told himself, what could he have done with the few supplies he'd brought with him? He was about to ask why the corpse hadn't been attacked by the crawling things when the "corpse" fluttered her eyelids.

"An even chance for her, if we turn back now," the chief of the guard said.

"But how? It would have taken a high-T machine to have stopped the bleeding in time. I don't understand."

She shrugged. "What you do with machines, we do with life." Impatiently, "How many of us must die before you are convinced?"

His head flicked back the way they'd come, then again forward, drawn by the inexorable compulsion, drawn to the floor, the hotbed of life, knowing he was a fool, knowing it was failure. His failure he couldn't face, and yet—He licked his lips and said, "As long as there's a chance, any chance that—"

He didn't see the chief make a gesture to a guard standing directly behind him; he didn't see that guard move. Then he didn't see anything at all, not even the guard's rueful mixture of regret and admiration as she gazed down at his limp body.

He opened his eyes to an almost perfect replica of his room back at Continental General. It wasn't until he reached out his hand to the intercom that he realized it was a clever fake. Everything was plant growth. But even as intellect recognized falsity, his instincts were relaxing, so that he was already smiling muzzily when the crester bustled in, "clothed" in the traditional blue of surgery service.

"Don't tell me, plants," he murmured, a man, purged temporarily at least of every emotion but a sort of languid curiosity. "But how did you get them the right shade of blue?"

She twinkled at him, her tail curling and uncurling joyously. "Oh, you're feeling better at last. Wouldn't a little sun be nice, eh? Easy over now—"

He had a lot of time to think, sitting in the warm sunlight, shaded by a friendly leaf. "I can teach you as much as you can teach me," he told them. And it was true. He never found their secret, how they grew the plants they did, but he isolated a dozen useful ones and helped them develop a dozen more, from the little saprophyte that could be clamped on an open wound and would seal in seconds, reducing blood loss immeasurably, to a seed that when swallowed went directly to an ulcer and grew over it, protecting all the delicate tissues. He taught them new medical techniques: how to set a bone pin, how to treat the stump of a limb so, that when it healed, it could be fitted with a (hand-carved) prosthetic, how to transplant organs, and how to do a bypass.

And then the wombship came. When it left, he went with it, taking supplies of all the plants he thought would be useful on other primitive worlds, as well as the Agrippa seeds he had learned to love chewing.

His patient had been right; as much as he loved his work, this wasn't his world, and it was better that he leave it.

He knew that he could never go back to his own world. Too many years, too many changes, had alienated him as much as any of the wombers.

And the years passed. Few for him, many for the worlds spinning warm and smug around their suns, and he discovered that, thanks to relativistic time contraction and the simultaneity projector (were *people* really going through the projector now?), he was becoming a legend. Whole worlds were grateful to Johnny Healerseed.

Even the wombers took to calling him that, at first in gentle derision, later just from habit, and he gradually forgot he had once been called by any other name.

It was on a world called Getchergoat that he found the last piece of his personal puzzle. Getchergoat had projectors, and a fairly high level of technology, so that he was learning as well as teaching. When he learned and taught as much as he could, and knew that his ship would be orbiting for several standard weeks yet, he asked, as he had on many other worlds, what sights his colleagues recommended he see.

Everyone agreed that the one thing he mustn't miss was the Pan-Art Exhibition in the Sept-millennial Memorial Audisseum. The Audisseum was multilevel, a freeform hugeness in transparent weather sheathing. He hesitated in the dilating entrance, a radiation-scarred old man, and an ovoid shimmer materialized at his elbow. "May I direct you to any specific exhibit?" the ovoid inquired.

"Have you anything here by the Sequoian troglodyte Inanna Kantanitanki?"

"A man of taste," the ovoid purred. "Do you prefer Early, Mature, or Final period?"

"All three," he said.

In the Early display, he was pleased to see a copy of *Mayflight in the Morning,* enlarged so that it sang baritone instead of soprano. When he tried to arrange some sort of credit, so he could have another copy to replace the one left behind somewhere long ago, he was embarrassed because they refused any exchange. A middle-aged man, attired only in Mercury's winged shoes, came sailing out on a striped orange-and-lime flying disc. He was holding a large-sized copy in his arms, and he refused to take anything. The artwork would be the smallest possible appreciation to Johnny

Healerseed from the grateful world of Getchergoat.

It was this man—"My current label is Drifting-through-Anomie," he said—who insisted on guiding him through the rest of the display, which ended in a series of untitled pieces. "Why untitled?" he wondered aloud, his hands caressing a piece that curved subtly around and through itself.

His guide shrugged. "It's the custom here, with pieces untitled by the artist, or where the title is unknown or has been lost."

"Solipsism," he said, still playing with the piece.

"Good, good, very good," Drifting-through-Anomie beamed. "Should I add it to the list of suggested titles?"

"No." He continued to turn the pieces, shaking his head. "So many pieces I don't recognize, and I thought I knew most of her work. I must be getting senile."

"Idegosuper forfend!" Drifting-through-Anomie was appalled. "No, these would be the pieces discovered on Sequoia after you left there to begin your pilgrimage, I'm sure!"

"Discovered *after*—" His mouth dropped open. "You mean, she was alive after all! *She was alive, and I left her!*"

"I'm sure not." Drifting-through-Anomie cocked his head to one side, as if listening to unheard silent voices, as he undoubtedly was. "No, the first work of her final period was discovered in Stanyear 809, at least two hundred years after she returned to her native world. The next three—"

"Two hundred!"

"Oh dear! How mannerless of me! You'd like to see it *in situ,* wouldn't you?" Between them a tiny sphere appeared, and the doctor realized it was a holo, taken from the crests. "It was a womber who spotted it—" The view descended, hovered over the treetops, and focused on the oddly convoluted crest of one particular tree.

"Aesculapius!"

"The style is unmistakable, of course. The original is about seventy meters high and about twenty-five meters in diameter, and its song has been recorded"—a deep rumble of triumph filled the air around them—"though how that great genius managed to shape the growth of the trees, we don't know—"

The doctor thought of a hand putting a seed into a mouth, the mouth spitting it out again—of chemical signals of amazing complexity that make a body grow and change—of a world where plants and animals had grown so interrelated that he had often thought of it as one, immense, complex, single living organism, a living world that isolated outside contaminants in deadness—and he knew how his once-hosts grew their medical and other miracles and why the trog had *had* to return. He smiled gently at Drifting-through-Anomie.

"They ate her soul with her bones," he said.

A SEPULCHER OF SONGS

By Orson Scott Card

She was losing her mind during the rain. For four weeks it came down nearly every day, and the people at the Millard County Rest Home didn't take any of the patients outside. It bothered them all, of course, and made life especially hellish for the nurses, everyone complaining to them constantly and demanding to be entertained.

Elaine didn't demand entertainment, however. She never seemed to demand much of anything. But the rain hurt her worse than anyone. Perhaps because she was only fifteen, the only child in an institution devoted to adult misery. More likely because she depended more than most on the hours spent outside; certainly she took more pleasure from them. They would lift her into her chair, prop her up with pillows so her body would stay straight, and then race down the corridor to the glass doors. Elaine calling, "Faster, faster," as they pushed her until finally they were outside. They told me she never really said anything out there. Just sat quietly in her chair on the lawn, watching everything. And then later in the day they would wheel her back in.

I often saw her being wheeled in—early, because I was there, though she never complained about my visits' cutting into her hours outside. As I watched her being pushed toward the rest home, she would smile at me so exuberantly that my mind invented arms for her, waving madly to match her childishly delighted face; I imagined legs pumping, imagined her running across the grass breasting the air like great waves. But there were the pillows where arms should be, keeping her from falling to the side, and the belt around her middle kept her from pitching forward, since she had no legs to balance with.

It rained four weeks, and I nearly lost her.

My job was one of the worst in the state, touring six rest homes in as many counties, visiting each of them every week. I "did therapy" wherever the rest home administrators thought therapy was needed. I never figured out how they decided—all the patients were mad to one degree or another, most with the helpless insanity of age, the rest with the anguish of the invalid and the crippled.

You don't end up as a state-employed therapist if you had much ability in college. I sometimes pretend that I didn't distinguish myself in graduate school because I marched to a different drummer. But I didn't. As one kind professor gently and brutally told me, I wasn't cut out for science. But I was sure I *was* cut out for the art of therapy. Ever since I comforted my mother during her final year of cancer I had believed I had a knack for helping people get straight in their minds. I was everybody's confidant.

Somehow I had never supposed, though, that I would end up trying to help the hopeless in a part of the state where even the healthy didn't have much to live for. Yet that's all I had the credentials for, and when I (so maturely) told myself I was over the initial disappointment, I made the best of it.

Elaine was the best of it.

"Raining raining raining," was the greeting I got when I visited her on the third day of the wet spell.

"Don't I know it?" I said. "My hair's soaking wet."

"Wish mine was," Elaine answered.

"No, you don't. You'd get sick."

"Not me," she said.

"Well, Mr. Woodbury told me you're depressed. I'm supposed to make you happy."

"Make it stop raining."

"Do I look like God?"

"I thought maybe you were in disguise. *I'm* in disguise," she said. It was one of our regular games. "I'm really a large Texas armadillo who was granted one wish. I wished to be a human being. But there wasn't enough of the armadillo to make a full human being; so here I am." She smiled. I smiled back.

Actually, she had been five years old when an oil truck exploded right in front of her parents' car, killing both of them and blowing her arms and legs right off. That she survived was a miracle. That she had to keep on living was unimaginable cruelty. That she managed to be a reasonably happy person, a favorite of the nurses—that I don't understand in the least. Maybe it was because she had nothing else to do. There aren't many ways that a person with no arms or legs can kill herself.

"I want to go outside," she said, turning her head away from me to look out the window.

Outside wasn't much. A few trees, a lawn, and beyond that a fence, not to keep the inmates in but to keep out the seamier residents of a rather seamy town. But there were low hills in the distance, and the birds usually seemed cheerful. Now, of course, the rain had driven both birds and hills into hiding. There was no wind, and so the trees didn't even sway. The rain just came straight down.

"Outer space is like the rain," she said. "It sounds like that out there, just a low drizzling sound in the background of everything."

"Not really," I said. "There's no sound out there at all."

"How do *you* know?" she asked.

"There's no air. Can't be any sound without air."

She looked at me scornfully. "Just as I thought. You don't *really* know. You've never *been* there, have you?"

"Are you trying to pick a fight?"

She started to answer, caught herself, and nodded. "Damned rain."

"At least you don't have to drive in it," I said. But her eyes got wistful, and I knew I had taken the banter too far. "Hey," I said. "First clear day I'll take you out driving."

"It's hormones," she said.

"What's hormones?"

"I'm fifteen. It always bothered me when I had to stay in. But I want to scream. My muscles are all bunched up, my stomach is all tight, I want to go outside and *scream*. It's hormones.''

"What about your friends?" I asked.

"Are you kidding? They're all out there, playing in the rain.''

"All of them?''

"Except Grunty, of course. He'd dissolve.''

"And where's Grunty?''

"In the freezer, of course.''

"Someday the nurses are going to mistake him for ice cream and serve him to the guests.''

She didn't smile. She just nodded, and I knew that I wasn't getting anywhere. She really was depressed.

I asked her whether she wanted something.

"No pills," she said. "They make me sleep all the time.''

"If I gave you uppers, it would make you climb the walls.''

"Neat trick," she said.

"It's that strong. So do you want something to take your mind off the rain and these four ugly yellow walls?''

She shook her head. "I'm trying not to sleep.''

"Why not?''

She just shook her head again. "Can't sleep. Can't let myself sleep too much.''

I asked again.

"Because," she said, "I might not wake up." She said it rather sternly, and I knew I shouldn't ask anymore. She didn't often get impatient with me, but I knew this time I was coming perilously close to overstaying my welcome.

"Got to go," I said. "You *will* wake up." And

then I left, and I didn't see her for a week, and to tell the truth I didn't think of her much that week, what with the rain and a suicide in Ford County that really got to me, since she was fairly young and had a lot to live for, in my opinion. She disagreed and won the argument the hard way.

Weekends I live in a trailer in Piedmont. I live alone. The place is spotlessly clean because cleaning is something I do religiously. Besides, I tell myself, I might want to bring a woman home with me one night. Some nights I even do, and some nights I even enjoy it, but I always get restless and irritable when they start trying to get me to change my work schedule or take them along to the motels I live in or, once only, get the trailer-park manager to let them into my trailer when I'm gone. To keep things cozy for me. I'm not interested in "cozy." This is probably because of my mother's death; her cancer and my responsibilities as housekeeper for my father probably explain why I am a neat housekeeper. Therapist, therap thyself. The days passed in rain and highways and depressing people depressed out of their minds; the nights passed in television and sandwiches and motel bedsheets at state expense; and then it was time to go to the Millard County Rest Home again, where Elaine was waiting. It was then that I thought of her and realized that the rain had been going on for more than a week, and the poor girl must be almost out of her mind. I bought a cassette of Copland conducting Copland. She insisted on cassettes, because they stopped. Eight-tracks went on and on until she couldn't think.

"Where have you been?" she demanded.

"Locked in a cage by a cruel duke in Transylvania. It was only four feet high, suspended over a pond filled with crocodiles. I got out by picking the lock with my teeth. Luckily, the crocodiles weren't hungry. Where have *you* been?"

"I mean it. Don't you keep a schedule?"

"I'm right on my schedule, Elaine. This is Wednesday. I was here last Wednesday. This year Christmas falls on a Wednesday, and I'll be here on Christmas."

"It feels like a year."

"Only ten months. Till Christmas. Elaine, you aren't being any fun."

She wasn't in the mood for fun. There were tears in her eyes. "I can't stand much more," she said.

"I'm sorry."

"I'm afraid."

And she *was* afraid. Her voice trembled.

"At night, and in the daytime, whenever I sleep. I'm just the right size."

"For what?"

"What do you mean?"

"You said you were just the right size."

"I did? Oh, I don't know what I meant. I'm going crazy. That's what you're here for, isn't it? To keep me sane. It's the rain. I can't do anything, I can't see anything, and all I can hear most of the time is the hissing of the rain."

"Like outer space," I said, remembering what she had said the last time.

She apparently didn't remember our discussion. She looked startled. "How did you know?" she asked.

"You told me."

"There isn't any sound in outer space," she said.

"Oh," I answered.

"There's no air out there."

"I knew that."

"Then why did you say, 'Oh, of course'? The engines. You can hear them all over the ship. It's a drone, all the time. That's just like the rain. Only after a while you can't hear it anymore. It becomes like silence. Anansa told me."

Another imaginary friend. Her file said that she had kept her imaginary friends long after most children give them up. That was why I had first been assigned to see her, to get rid of the friends. Grunty, the ice pig; Howard, the boy who beat up everybody; Sue Ann, who would bring her dolls and play with them for her, making them do what Elaine said for them to do; Fuchsia, who lived among the flowers and was only inches high. There were others. After a few sessions with her I saw that she knew that they weren't real. But they passed time for her. They stepped outside her body and did things she could never do. I felt they did her no harm at all, and destroying that imaginary world for her would only make her lonelier and more unhappy. She was sane, that was certain. And yet I kept seeing her, not entirely because I liked her so much. Partly because I wondered whether she had been pretending when she told me she knew her friends weren't real. Anansa was a new one.

"Who's Anansa?"

"Oh, you don't want to know." She didn't want to talk about her; that was obvious.

"I want to know."

She turned away. "I can't make you go away, but I wish you would. When you get nosy."

190

"It's my job."

"Job!" She sounded contemptuous. "I see all of you, running around on your healthy legs, doing all your *jobs.*"

What could I say to her? "It's how we stay alive," I said. "I do my best."

Then she got a strange look on her face; *I've got a secret,* she seemed to say, *and I want you to pry it out of me.* "Maybe I can get a job, too."

"Maybe," I said. I tried to think of something she could do.

"There's always music," she said.

I misunderstood. "There aren't many instruments you can play. That's the way it is." Dose of reality and all that.

"Don't be stupid."

"Okay. Never again."

"I meant that there's always the music. On my job."

"And what job is this?"

"Wouldn't you like to know?" she said, rolling her eyes mysteriously and turning toward the window. I imagined her as a normal fifteen-year-old girl. Ordinarily I would have interpreted this as flirting. But there was something else under all this. A feeling of desperation. She was right. I really would like to know. I made a rather logical guess. I put together the two secrets she was trying to get me to figure out today.

"What kind of job is Anansa going to give you?"

She looked at me, startled. "So it's true then."

"What's true?"

"It's so frightening. I keep telling myself it's a dream. But it isn't, is it?"

191

"What, Anansa?"

"You think she's just one of my friends, don't you. But they're not in my dreams, not like this. Anansa—"

"What about Anansa?"

"She sings to me. In my sleep."

My trained psychologist's mind immediately conjured up mother figures. "Of course," I said.

"She's in space, and she sings to me. You wouldn't believe the songs."

It reminded me. I pulled out the cassette I had bought for her.

"Thank you," she said.

"You're welcome. Want to hear it?"

She nodded. I put it on the cassette player. *Appalachian Spring*. She moved her head to the music. I imagined her as a dancer. She felt the music very well.

But after a few minutes she stopped moving and started to cry.

"It's not the same," she said.

"You've heard it before?"

"Turn it off. Turn it *off!*"

I turned it off. "Sorry," I said. "Thought you'd like it."

"Guilt, nothing but guilt," she said. "You always feel guilty, don't you?"

"Pretty nearly always," I admitted cheerfully. A lot of my patients threw psychological jargon in my face. Or soap-opera language.

"*I'm* sorry," she said. "It's just—it's just not the music. Not *the music*. Now that I've heard it, everything is so dark compared to it. Like the rain, all gray and heavy and dim, as if the composer is trying to see the hills but the rain is always in the way. For a few minutes I thought he was getting it right.''

''Anansa's music?''

She nodded. ''I know you don't believe me. But I hear her when I'm asleep. She tells me that's the only time she can communicate with me. It's not talking. It's all her songs. She's out there, in her starship, singing. And at night I hear her.''

''Why you?''

''You mean, Why only me?'' She laughed. ''Because of what I am. You told me yourself. Because I can't run around, I live in my imagination. She says that the threads between minds are very thin and hard to hold. But mine she can hold, because I live completely in my mind. She holds on to me. When I go to sleep, I can't escape her now anymore at all.''

''Escape? I thought you liked her.''

''I don't know what I like. I like—I like the music. But Anansa wants me. She wants to have me—she wants to give me a job.''

''What's the singing like?'' When she said *job,* she trembled and closed up; I referred back to something that she had been willing to talk about, to keep the floundering conversation going.

''It's not like anything. She's there in space, and it's black, just the humming of the engines like the sound of rain, and she reaches into the dust out there and draws in the songs. She reaches out her—out her fingers, or her ears, I don't know; it isn't clear. She reaches out and draws in the dust and the songs and turns them into the music that I hear. It's powerful. She says it's her songs that drive her between the stars.''

193

"Is she alone?"

Elaine nodded. "She wants me."

"Wants you. How can she have you, with you here and her out there?"

Elaine licked her lips. "I don't want to talk about it," she said in a way that told me she was on the verge of telling me.

"I wish you would. I really wish you'd tell me."

"She says—she says that she can take me. She says that if I can learn the songs, she can pull me out of my body and take me there and give me arms and legs and fingers and I can run and dance and—"

She broke down, crying.

"I patted her on the only place that she permitted, her soft little belly. She refused to be hugged. I had tried it years before, and she had screamed at me to stop it. One of the nurses told me it was because her mother had always hugged her, and Elaine wanted to hug back. And couldn't.

"It's a lovely dream, Elaine."

"It's a terrible dream. Don't you see? I'll be like *her*."

"And what's she like?"

"She's the ship. She's the starship. And she wants me with her, to be the starship with her. And sing our way through space together for thousands and thousands of years."

"It's just a dream, Elaine. You don't have to be afraid of it."

"They did it to her. They cut off her arms and legs and put her into the machines."

"But no one's going to put you into a machine."

"I want to go outside," she said.

"You can't. It's raining."

"Damn the rain."

"I do, every day."

"I'm not joking! She pulls me all the time now, even when I'm awake. She keeps pulling at me and making me fall asleep, and she sings to me, and I feel her pulling and pulling. If I could just go outside, I could hold on. I feel like I could hold on, if I could just—"

"Hey, relax. Let me give you a—"

"No! I don't want to sleep!"

"Listen, Elaine. It's just a dream. You can't let it get to you like this. It's just the rain keeping you here. It makes you sleepy, and so you keep dreaming this. But don't fight it. It's a beautiful dream in a way. Why not go with it?"

She looked at me with terror in her eyes.

"You don't mean that. You don't want me to go."

"No. Of course I don't want you to go anywhere. But you won't, don't you see? It's a dream, floating out there between the stars—"

"She's not floating. She's ramming her way through space so fast it makes me dizzy whenever she shows me."

"Then be dizzy. Think of it as your mind finding a way for you to run."

"You don't understand, Mr. Therapist. I thought you'd understand."

"I'm trying to."

"If I go with her, then I'll be dead."

I asked her nurse, "Who's been reading to her?"

"We all do, and volunteers from town. They like her. She always has someone to read to her."

"You'd better supervise them more carefully.

Somebody's been putting ideas in her head. About spaceships and dust and singing between the stars. It's scared her pretty bad.''

The nurse frowned. ''We approve everything they read. She's been reading that kind of thing for years. It's never done her any harm before. Why now?''

''The rain, I guess. Cooped up in here, she's losing touch with reality.''

The nurse nodded sympathetically and said, ''I know. When she's asleep, she's doing the strangest things now.''

''Like what? What kind of things?''

''Oh, singing these horrible songs.''

''What are the words?''

''There aren't any words. She just sort of hums. Only the melodies are awful. Not even like music. And her voice gets funny and raspy. She's completely asleep. She sleeps a lot now. Mercifully, I think. She's always gotten impatient when she can't go outside.''

The nurse obviously liked Elaine. It would be hard not to feel sorry for her, but Elaine insisted on being liked, and people liked her, those that could get over the horrible flatness of the sheets all around her trunk. ''Listen,'' I said. ''Can we bundle her up or something? Get her outside in spite of the rain?''

The nurse shook her head. ''It isn't just the rain. It's cold out there. And the explosion that made her like she is—it messed her up inside. She isn't put together right. She doesn't have the strength to fight off any kind of disease at all. You understand— there's a good chance that exposure to that kind of weather would kill her eventually. And I won't take a chance on that.''

''I'm going to be visiting her more often, then,'' I

said. "As often as I can. She's got something going on in her head that's scaring her half to death. She thinks she's going to die."

"Oh, the poor darling," the nurse said. "Why would she think that?"

"Doesn't matter. One of her imaginary friends may be getting out of hand."

"I thought you said they were harmless."

"They were."

When I left the Millard County Rest Home that night, I stopped back in Elaine's room. She was asleep, and I heard her song. It was eerie. I could hear, now and then, themes from the bit of Copland music she had listened to. But it was distorted, and most of the music was unrecognizable—wasn't even music. Her voice was high and strange, and then suddenly it would change, would become low and raspy, and for a moment I clearly heard in her voice the sound of a vast engine coming through walls of metal, carried on slender metal rods, the sound of a great roar being swallowed up by a vast cushion of nothing. I pictured Elaine with wires coming out of her shoulders and hips, with her head encased in metal and her eyes closed in sleep, like her imaginary Anansa, piloting the starship as if it were her own body. I could see that this would be attractive to Elaine, in a way. After all, she hadn't been born this way. She had memories of running and playing, memories of feeding herself and dressing herself, perhaps even of learning to read, of sounding out the words as her fingers touched each letter. Even the false arms of a spaceship would be something to fill the great void.

Children's centers are not inside their bodies; their

centers are outside, at the point where the fingers of the left hand and the fingers of the right hand meet. What they touch is where they live; what they see is their self. And Elaine had lost herself in an explosion before she had the chance to move inside. With this strange dream of Anansa she was getting a self back.

But a repellent self, for all that. I walked and sat by Elaine's bed, listening to her sing. Her body moved slightly, her back arching a little with the melody. High and light; low and rasping. The sounds alternated, and I wondered what they meant. What was going on inside her to make this music come out?

If I go with her, then I'll be dead.

Of course she was afraid. I looked at the lump of flesh that filled the bed shapelessly below where her head emerged from the covers. I tried to change my perspective, to see her body as she saw it, from above. It almost disappeared then, with the foreshortening and the height of her ribs making her stomach and hint of hips vanish into insignificance. Yet this was all she had, and if she believed—and certainly she seemed to—that surrendering to the fantasy of Anansa would mean the death of this pitiful body, is death any less frightening to those who have not been able to fully live? I doubt it. At least for Elaine, what life she had lived had been joyful. She would not willingly trade it for a life of music and metal arms, locked in her own mind.

Except for the rain. Except that nothing was so real to her as the outside, as the trees and birds and distant hills, and as the breeze touching her with a violence she permitted to no living person. And with that reality, the good part of her life, cut off from her by the rain, how long could she hold out against the incessant pulling of Anansa and her promise of arms and legs and eternal song?

I reached up, on a whim, and very gently lifted her eyelids.

Her eyes remained open, staring at the ceiling, not blinking.

I closed her eyes, and they remained closed.

I turned her head, and it stayed turned. She did not wake up. Just kept singing as if I had done nothing to her at all.

Catatonia, or the beginning of catalepsy. *She's losing her mind,* I thought, *and if I don't bring her back, keep her here somehow, Anansa will win, and the rest home will be caring for a lump of mindless flesh for the next however many years they can keep this remnant of Elaine alive.*

"I'll be back on Saturday," I told the administrator.

"Why so soon?"

"Elaine is going through a crisis of some kind," I explained. An imaginary woman from space wants to carry her off—that I didn't say. "Have the nurses keep her awake as much as they can. Read to her, play with her, talk to her. Her normal hours at night are enough. Avoid naps."

"Why?"

"I'm afraid for her, that's all. She could go catatonic on us at any time, I think. Her sleeping isn't normal. I want to have her watched all the time."

"This is really serious?"

"This is really serious."

On Friday it looked as if the clouds were breaking, but after only a few minutes of sunshine a huge new bank of clouds swept down from the northwest, and it was worse than before. I finished my work rather carelessly, stopping a sentence in the middle several times. One of my patients was annoyed with me. She squinted at me. "You're not paid to think about your woman troubles when you're talking to me." I apologized and tried to pay attention. She was a talker; my attention always wandered. But she was right in a way. I couldn't stop thinking of Elaine. And my patients saying that about woman troubles must have triggered something in my mind. After all, my relationship with Elaine was the longest and closest I had had with a woman in many years. If you could think of Elaine as a woman.

On Saturday I drove back to Millard County and found the nurses rather distraught. They didn't realize how much she was sleeping until they tried to stop her, they all said. She was dozing off for two or three naps in the mornings, even more in the afternoons. She went to sleep at night at seven-thirty and slept at least twelve hours. "Singing all the time. It's awful. Even at night she keeps it up. Singing and singing."

But she was awake when I went in to see her.

"I stayed awake for you."

"Thanks," I said.

"A Saturday visit. I must really be going bonkers."

"Actually, no. But I don't like how sleepy you are."

She smiled wanly. "It isn't my idea."

I think my smile was more cheerful than hers. "And I think it's all in your head."

"Think what you like, Doctor."

"I'm not a doctor. My degree says I'm a master."

"How deep is the water outside?"

"Deep?"

"All this rain. Surely it's enough to keep a few dozen arks afloat. Is God destroying the world?"

"Unfortunately, no. Though He has killed the engines on a few cars that went a little fast through the puddles."

"How long would it have to rain to fill up the world?"

"The world is round. It would all drip off the bottom."

She laughed. It was good to hear her laugh, but it ended too abruptly, and she looked at me fearfully. "I'm going, you know."

"You are?"

"I'm just the right size. She's measured me, and I'll fit perfectly. She has just the place for me. It's a good place, where I can hear the music of the dust for myself, and learn to sing it. I'd have the directional engines."

I shook my head. "Grunty the ice pig was cute. This isn't cute, Elaine."

"Did I ever say I thought Anansa was cute? Grunty the ice pig was real, you know. My father made him out of crushed ice for a luau. He melted before they got the pig out of the ground. I don't make my friends up."

"Fuchsia the flower girl?"

"My mother would pinch blossoms off the fuchsia by our front door. We played with them like dolls in the grass."

"But not Anansa."

"Anansa came into my mind when I was asleep. She found me. I didn't make her up."

"Don't you see, Elaine, that's how the real hallucinations come? They feel like reality."

She shook her head. "I know all that. I've had the nurses read me psychology books. Anansa is—Anansa is other. She couldn't come out of my head. She's something else. She's real. I've heard her music. It isn't plain, like Copland. It isn't false."

"Elaine, when you were asleep on Wednesday, you were becoming catatonic."

"I know."

"You know?"

"I felt you touch me. I felt you turn my head. I wanted to speak to you, to say good-bye. But she was singing, don't you see? She was singing. And now she lets me sing along. When I sing with her, I can feel myself travel out, like a spider along a single thread, out into the place where she is. Into the darkness. It's lonely there, and black, and cold, but I know that at the end of the thread there she'll be, a friend for me forever."

"You're frightening me, Elaine."

"There aren't any trees on her starship, you know. That's how I stay here. I think of the trees and the hills and the birds and the grass and the wind, and how I'd lose all of that. She gets angry at me, and a little hurt. But it keeps me here. Except now I can hardly remember the trees at all. I try to remember, and it's like trying to remember the face of my mother. I can remember her dress and her hair, but her face is gone forever. Even when I look at a picture, it's a stranger. The trees are strangers to me now."

I stroked her forehead. At first she pulled her head away, then slid it back.

"I'm sorry," she said. "I usually don't like people to touch me there."

"I won't," I said.

"No, go ahead. I don't mind."

So I stroked her forehead again. It was cool and dry, and she lifted her head almost imperceptibly, to receive my touch. Involuntarily I thought of what the old woman had said the day before. *Woman troubles.* I was touching Elaine, and I thought of making love to her. I immediately put the thought out of my mind.

"Hold me here," she said. "Don't let me go. I want to go so badly. But I'm not meant for that. I'm just the right size, but not the right shape. Those aren't my arms. I know what my arms felt like."

"I'll hold you if I can. But you have to help."

"No drugs. The drugs pull my mind away from my body. If you give me drugs, I'll die."

"Then what can I do?"

"Just keep me here, any way you can."

Then we talked about nonsense, because we had been so serious, and it was as if she weren't having any problems at all. We got on to the subject of the church meetings.

"I didn't know you were religious," I said.

"I'm not. But what else is there to do on Sunday? They sing hymns, and I sing with them. Last Sunday there was a sermon that really got to me. The preacher talked about Christ in the sepulcher. About Him being there three days before the angel came to let Him go. I've been thinking about that, what it must have been like for Him, locked in a cave in the darkness, completely alone."

"Depressing."

"Not really. It must have been exhilarating for

Him, in a way. If it was true, you know. To lie there on that stone bed, saying to Himself, 'They thought I was dead, but I'm here. I'm not dead.' "

"You make Him sound smug."

"Sure. Why not? I wonder if I'd feel like that, if I were with Anansa."

Anansa again.

"I can see what you're thinking. You're thinking, 'Anansa again.' "

"Yeah," I said. "I wish you'd erase her and go back to some more harmless friends."

Suddenly her face went angry and fierce.

"You can believe what you like. Just leave me alone."

I tried to apologize, but she wouldn't have any of it. She insisted on believing in this star woman. Finally I left, redoubling my cautions against letting her sleep. The nurses looked worried, too. They could see the change as easily as I could.

That night, because I was in Millard on a weekend, I called up Belinda. She wasn't married or anything at the moment. She came to my motel. We had dinner, made love, and watched television. She watched television, that is. I lay on the bed, thinking. And so when the test pattern came on and Belinda at last got up, beery and passionate, my mind was still on Elaine. As Belinda kissed and tickled me and whispered stupidity in my ear, I imagined myself without arms and legs. I lay there, moving only my head.

"What's the matter, you don't want to?"

I shook off the mood. No need to disappoint Belinda—I was the one who had called *her*. I had a responsibility. Not much of one, though. That was what was nagging at me. I made love to Belinda slowly and carefully, but with my eyes closed. I kept superimposing Elaine's face on Belinda's. Woman troubles. Even though Belinda's fingers played up and down my back, I thought I was making love to Elaine. And the stumps of arms and legs didn't revolt me as much as I would have thought. Instead, I only felt sad. A deep sense of tragedy, of loss, as if Elaine were dead and I could have saved her, like the prince in all the fairy tales; a kiss, so symbolic, and the princess awakens and lives happily ever after. And I hadn't done it. I had failed her. When we were finished, I cried.

"Oh, you poor sweetheart," Belinda said, her voice rich with sympathy. "What's wrong—you don't have to tell me." She cradled me for a while, and at last I went to sleep with my head pressed against her breasts. She thought I needed her. I suppose that, briefly, I did.

I did not go back to Elaine on Sunday as I had planned. I spent the entire day almost going. Instead of walking out the door, I sat and watched the incredible array of terrible Sunday morning television. And when I finally did go out, fully intending to go to the rest home and see how she was doing, I ended up driving, luggage in the back of the car, to my trailer, where I went inside and again sat down and watched television.

Why couldn't I go to her?

Just keep me here, she had said. Anyway you can, she had said.

And I thought I knew the way. That was the problem. In the back of my mind all this was much too real, and the fairy tales were wrong. The prince didn't wake her with a kiss. He wakened the princess with a promise: In his arms she would be safe forever. She awoke for the happily ever after. If she hadn't known it to be true, the princess would have preferred to sleep forever.

What was Elaine asking of me?

Why was I afraid of it?

Not my job. Unprofessional to get emotionally involved with a patient.

But then, when had I ever been a professional? I finally went to bed, wishing I had Belinda with me again, for whatever comfort she could bring. Why weren't all women like Belinda, soft and loving and undemanding?

Yet as I drifted off to sleep, it was Elaine I remembered, Elaine's face and hideous, reproachful stump of a body that followed me through all my dreams.

And she followed me when I was awake, through my regular rounds on Monday and Tuesday, and at last it was Wednesday, and still I was afraid to go to the Millard County Rest Home. I didn't get there until afternoon. Late afternoon, and the rain was coming down as hard as ever, and there were lakes of standing water in the fields, torrents rushing through the unprepared gutters of the town.

"You're late," the administrator said.

"Rain," I answered, and he nodded. But he looked worried.

"We hoped you'd come yesterday, but we couldn't reach you anywhere. It's Elaine."

And I knew that my delay had served its damnable purpose, exactly as I expected.

"She hasn't woken up since Monday morning. She

206

just lies there, singing. We've got her on an IV. She's asleep.''

She was indeed asleep. I sent the others out of the room.

"Elaine," I said.

Nothing.

I called her name again, several times. I touched her, rocked her head back and forth. Her head stayed wherever I placed it. And the song went on, softly, high and then low, pure and then gravelly. I covered her mouth. She sang on, even with her mouth closed, as if nothing were the matter.

I pulled down her sheet and pushed a pin into her belly, then into the thin flesh at her collarbone. No response. I slapped her face. No response. She was gone. I saw her again, connected to a starship, only this time I understood better. It wasn't her body that was the right size; it was her mind. And it was her mind that had followed the slender spider's thread out to Anansa, who waited to give her a body.

A job.

Shock therapy? I imagined her already-deformed body leaping and arching as the electricity coursed through her. It would accomplish nothing, except to torture unthinking flesh. Drugs? I couldn't think of any that could bring her back from where she had gone. In a way, I think, I even believed in Anansa, for the moment. I called her name. "Anansa, let her go. Let her come back to me. Please. I need her."

Why had I cried in Belinda's arms? Oh, yes. Because I had seen the princess and let her lie there unawakened, because the happily ever after was so damnably much work.

I did not do it in the fever of the first realization

that I had lost her. It was no act of passion or sudden fear or grief. I sat beside her bed for hours, looking at her weak and helpless body, now so empty. I wished for her eyes to open on their own, for her to wake up and say, "Hey, would you believe the dream *I* had!" For her to say, "Fooled you, didn't I? It was really hard when you poked me with pins, but I fooled you."

But she hadn't fooled me.

And so, finally, not with passion but in despair, I stood up and leaned over her, leaned my hands on either side of her and pressed my cheek against hers and whispered in her ear. I promised her everything I could think of, I promised her no more rain forever. I promised her trees and flowers and hills and birds and the wind for as long as she liked. I promised to take her away from the rest home, to take her to see things she could only have dreamed of before.

And then at last, with my voice harsh from pleading with her, with her hair wet with my tears, I promised her the only thing that might bring her back. I promised her me. I promised her love forever, stronger than any songs Anansa could sing.

And it was then that the monstrous song fell silent. She did not awaken, but the song ended, and she moved on her own; her head rocked to the side, and she seemed to sleep normally, not catatonically. I waited by her bedside all night. I fell asleep in the chair, and one of the nurses covered me. I was still there when I was awakened in the morning by Elaine's voice.

"What a liar you are! It's still raining."

It was a feeling of power, to know that I had called

someone back from places far darker than death. Her life was painful, and yet my promise of devotion was enough, apparently, to compensate. This was how I understood it, at least. This was what made me feel exhilarated, what kept me blind and deaf to what had really happened.

I was not the only one rejoicing. The nurses made a great fuss over her, and the administrator promised to write up a glowing report. "Publish," he said.

"It's too personal," I said. But in the back of my mind I was already trying to figure out a way to get the case into print, to gain something for my career. I was ashamed of myself for twisting what had been an honest, heartfelt commitment into personal advancement. But I couldn't ignore the sudden respect I was receiving from people to whom, only hours before, I had been merely ordinary.

"It's too personal," I repeated firmly. "I have no intention of publishing."

And to my disgust I found myself relishing the administrator's respect for that decision. There was no escape from my swelling self-satisfaction. Not as long as I stayed around those determined to give me cheap payoffs. Ever the wise psychologist, I returned to the only person who would give me gratitude instead of admiration. *The gratitude I had earned,* I thought. I went back to Elaine.

"Hi," she said. "I wondered where you had gone."

"Not far," I said. "Just visiting with the Nobel Prize committee."

"They want to reward you for bringing me here?"

"Oh, no. They had been planning to give me the award for having contacted a genuine alien being from outer space. Instead, I blew it and brought you back. They're quite upset."

She looked flustered. It wasn't like her to look flustered—usually she came back with another quip. "But what will they do to you?"

"Probably boil me in oil. That's the usual thing. Though, maybe they've found a way to boil me in solar energy. It's cheaper." A feeble joke. But she didn't get it.

"This isn't the way she said it was—she said it was—"

She. I tried to ignore the dull fear that suddenly churned in my stomach. *Be analytical,* I thought. *She could be anyone.*

"She said? Who said?" I asked.

Elaine fell silent. I reached out and touched her forehead. She was perspiring.

"What's wrong?" I asked. "You're upset."

"I should have known."

"Known what?"

She shook her head and turned away from me.

I knew what it was, I thought. I knew what it was, but we could surely cope. "Elaine," I said, "you aren't completely cured, are you? You haven't got rid of Anansa, have you? You don't have to hide it from me. Sure, I would have loved to think you'd been completely cured, but that would have been too much of a miracle. Do I look like a miracle worker? We've just made progress, that's all. Brought you back from catalepsy. We'll free you of Anansa eventually."

Still she was silent, staring at the rain-gray window.

"You don't have to be embarrassed about pretending to be completely cured. It was very kind of you. It made me feel very good for a little while. But

I'm a grown-up. I can cope with a little disappointment. Besides, you're awake, you're back, and that's all that matters." Grown-up, hell! I was terribly disappointed, and ashamed that I wasn't more sincere in what I was saying. No cure after all. No hero. No magic. No great achievement. Just a psychologist who was, after all, not extraordinary.

But I refused to pay too much attention to those feelings. Be a professional, I told myself. She needs your help.

"So don't go feeling guilty about it."

She turned back to face me, her eyes full. "Guilty?" She almost smiled. "Guilty." Her eyes did not leave my face, though I doubted she could see me well through the tears brimming her lashes.

"You tried to do the right thing," I said.

"Did I? Did I really?" She smiled bitterly. It was a strange smile for her, and for a terrible moment she no longer looked like my Elaine, my bright young patient. "I meant to stay with her," she said. "I wanted her with me, she was so alive, and when she finally joined herself to the ship, she sang and danced and swung her arms, and I said, 'This is what I've needed; this is what I've craved all my centuries lost in the songs.' But then I hear *you.*"

"Anansa," I said, realizing at that moment who was with me.

"I heard *you,* crying out to her. Do you think I made up my mind quickly? She heard you, but she wouldn't come. She wouldn't trade her new arms and legs for anything. They were so new. But I'd had them for long enough. What I'd never had was—you."

"Where is she?" I asked.

"Out there," she said. "She sings better than I ever did." She looked wistful for a moment, then smiled ruefully. "And I'm here. Only I made a bad bargain, didn't I? Because I didn't fool you. You won't want me, now. It's Elaine you want, and she's gone. I left her alone out there. She won't mind, not for a long time. But then—then she will. Then she'll know I cheated her."

The voice was Elaine's voice, the tragic little body her body. But now I knew I had not succeeded at all. Elaine was gone, in the infinite outer space where the mind hides to escape from itself. And in her place—Anansa. A stranger.

"You cheated her?" I said. "How did you cheat her?"

"It never changes. In a while you learn all the songs, and they never change. Nothing moves. You go on forever until all the stars fail, and yet nothing ever moves."

I moved my hand to put it to my hair. I was startled at my own trembling touch on my head.

"Oh, God," I said. They were just words, not a supplication.

"You hate me," she said.

Hate her? Hate my little, mad Elaine? Oh, no. I had another object for my hate. I hated the rain that had cut her off from all that kept her sane. I hated her parents for not leaving her home the day they let their car drive them on to death. But most of all I remember my days of hiding from Elaine, my days of resisting her need, of pretending that I didn't remember her or think of her or need her, too. She must have wondered why I was so long in coming. Wondered and finally given up hope, finally realized that there was no one who would hold her. And so she left, and when I finally came, the only person waiting inside her body was Anansa, the imaginary friend who had come, terrifyingly, to life. I knew whom to hate. I thought I would cry. I even buried my face in the sheet where her leg would have been. But I did not cry. I just sat there, the sheet harsh against my face, hating myself.

Her voice was like a gentle hand, a pleading hand touching me. "I'd undo it if I could," she said. "But I can't. She's gone, and I'm here. I came because of you. I came to see the trees and the grass and the birds and your smile. The happily ever after. That was what she had lived for, you know, all she lived for. Please smile at me."

I felt warmth on my hair. I lifted my head. There was no rain in the window. Sunlight rose and fell on the wrinkles of the sheet.

"Let's go outside," I said.

"It stopped raining," she said.

"A bit late, isn't it?" I answered. But I smiled at her.

"You can call me Elaine," she said. "You won't tell, will you?"

I shook my head No, I wouldn't tell. She was safe enough. I wouldn't tell because then they would take her away, to a place where psychiatrists reigned but did not know enough to rule. I imagined her confined among others who had also made their escape from reality, and I knew that I couldn't tell anyone. I also knew I couldn't confess failure, not now.

Besides, I hadn't really completely failed. There was still hope. Elaine wasn't really gone. She was still there, hidden in her own mind, looking out through this imaginary person she had created to take her place. Someday I would find her and bring her home. After all, even Grunty the ice pig had melted.

I noticed that she was shaking her head. "You won't find her," she said. "You won't bring her home. I won't melt and disappear. She *is* gone, and you couldn't have prevented it."

I smiled. "Elaine," I said.

And then I realized that she had answered thoughts I hadn't put into words.

"That's right," she said. "Let's be honest with each other. You might as well. You can't lie to me."

I shook my head. For a moment, in my confusion and despair, I had believed it all, believed that Anansa was real. But that was nonsense. Of course Elaine knew what I was thinking. She knew me better than I knew myself. "Let's go outside," I said. A failure and a cripple, out to enjoy the sunlight, which fell equally on the just and the unjustifiable.

"I don't mind," she said. "Whatever you want to believe. Elaine or Anansa. Maybe it's better if you still look for Elaine. Maybe it's better if you let me fool you after all."

The worst thing about the fantasies of the mentally ill is that they're so damned consistent. They never let up. They never give you any rest.

"I'm Elaine," she said, smiling. "I'm Elaine, pretending to be Anansa. You love me. That's what I came for. You promised to bring me home, and you did. Take me outside. You made it stop raining for me. You did everything you promised, and I'm home again, and I promise I'll never leave you."

She hasn't left me. I come to see her every Wednesday as part of my work, and every Saturday and

214

Sunday as the best part of my life. I take her driving with me sometimes, and we talk constantly, and I read to her and bring her books for the nurses to read to her. None of them know that she is still unwell—to them she's Elaine, happier than ever, pathetically delighted at every sight and sound and smell and taste and every texture that they touch against her cheek. Only *I* know that she believes she is not Elaine. Only *I* know that I have made no progress at all since then, that in moments of terrible honesty I call her Anansa, and she sadly answers me.

But in a way I'm content. Very little has changed between us, really. And after a few weeks I realized, with certainty, that she was happier now than she had ever been before. After all, she had the best of all possible worlds, for her. She could tell herself that the real Elaine was off in space somewhere, dancing and singing and hearing songs, with arms and legs at last, while the poor girl who was confined to the limbless body at the Millard County Rest Home was really an alien who was very, very happy to have even that limited body.

And as for me, I kept my commitment to her, and I'm happier for it. I'm still human—I still take another woman into my bed from time to time. But Anansa doesn't mind. She even suggested it, only a few days after she woke up. "Go back to Belinda sometimes," she said. "Belinda loves you, too, you know. I won't mind at all." I still can't remember when I spoke to her of Belinda, but at least she didn't mind, and so there aren't really any discontentments in my life. Except.

Except that I'm not God. I would like to be God. I would make some changes.

When I go to the Millard County Rest Home, I never enter the building first. She is never in the building. I walk around the outside and look across the lawn by the trees. The wheelchair is always there; I can tell it from the others by the pillows, which glare white in the sunlight. I never call out. In a few moments she always sees me, and the nurses wheel her around and push the chair across the lawn.

She comes as she has come hundreds of times before. She plunges toward me, and I concentrate on watching her, so that my mind will not see my Elaine surrounded by blackness, plunging through space, gathering dust, gathering songs, leaping and dancing with her new arms and legs that she loves better than me. Instead I watch the wheelchair, watch the smile on her face. She is happy to see me, so delighted with the world outside that her body cannot contain her. And when my imagination will not be restrained, I am God for a moment. I see her running toward me, her arms waving. I give her a left hand, a right hand, delicate and strong; I put a long and girlish left leg on her, and one just as sturdy on the right.

And then, one by one, I take them all away.

COLONEL STONESTEEL'S GENUINE HOME-MADE TRULY EGYPTIAN MUMMY

By Ray Bradbury

That was the autumn they found the genuine Egyptian mummy out past Loon Lake.

How the mummy got there, and how long it had been there, no one knew. But there it was, all wrapped up in its creosote rags, looking a bit spoiled by time, and just waiting to be found by someone.

The day before, it had been just another autumn day with the trees blazing and dropping down their burnt-looking leaves when Charlie Flagstaff, aged twelve, stepped to the middle of a pretty empty street, stared at the sky, the horizon, the whole world, and shouted, "Okay! I'm waiting. Come on!"

Nothing happened. So Charlie kicked the leaves ahead of him across town until he came to the tallest house on the greatest street, the house where everyone in Green Town came with his troubles. Charlie scowled, shut his eyes, and yelled at the big house windows. "Colonel Stonesteel!"

The front door burst open, as if the old man had been waiting there, like Charlie, for something incredible to happen in Green Town, Illinois.

"Charlie," Colonel Stonesteel called. "You're old enough to knock. What's there about boys makes them shout around houses?"

The door slammed shut.

Charlie sighed, walked up, and knocked softly.

"Why, Charlie Flagstaff, is that you?" The door opened a squint for the Colonel. "Good gravy, look at that weather!"

The old man strode forth to hone his fine hatchet nose on the sharp wind. "Don't you just love autumn, son? Just smell that air."

He remembered to glance down at the boy's pale face.

"Why, son, you look as if your last friend drowned and your dog died. What's wrong? School starts next week? On top of which, Halloween's not coming fast enough?"

"Still eight long weeks off. Might as well be ten years," the boy sighed, staring out at the autumn town. "You ever notice, Colonel, not much ever happens around here?"

"Why, hell's bell's son, it's Labor Day tomorrow, big parade, seven almost-brand-new cars, mayor in his next-best suit, fireworks, maybe—er . . ."

The Colonel stopped, not impressed with his own grocery list. "How old are you, Charlie?"

"Thirteen. Almost."

"Things do tend to run down, come thirteen. Meanwhile, Charlie, what do we do to survive until noon today?"

"If anyone knows, it's you, Colonel."

"Charlie . . ." The old man flinched from the boy's clear-water stare. "I can move politicians big as prize hogs, shake town hall skeletons, make locomotives run back uphill. But small boys on long, dry autumn weekends, suffering from a bad attack of the desperate empties? Well . . ."

Colonel Stonesteel eyed the future in the clouds.

"Charlie," he said at last, "I am touched and moved by the circumstance of your lying there on the damn railway tracks, waiting for a murderous train that will never come. So, listen. I'll bet you six Baby Ruth candy bars that Green Town, upper Illinois, population one thousand dogs, will be changed forever, changed for the best, by God, sometime in the next twenty-four miraculous hours! Bet?"

"A bet!" Charlie seized and pumped the old man's hand. "Colonel, I knew you could do it!"

"Ain't done yet, but look. This town's the Red Sea. I herewith order it to part. Gangway!"

The Colonel marched (Charlie ran) into the house, where the Colonel sniffed a vast door leading up to a dry-timber attic. "Listen, Charlie. Hear. The attic storms."

The Colonel yanked the door wide on autumn whispers, high winds trapped and shuddering in the beams.

"What's it say?"

Just then a gust of wind hurled the Colonel, like so much flimsy chaff, up the dark stairs. He was philosophical along the way: "Time, it says, mostly. Oldness. Memory. Dust. Pain. Listen to those beams. When the weather cracks a roof's skeleton on a fine fall day, you truly got time-talk, Bombay snuffs, tombyard flowers gone to ghost—"

"Boy, Colonel," Charlie gasped, climbing, "you oughta write for *Top Notch Magazine*!"

"Did once. Got rejected. Here we are!"

And there they were indeed, in a place with no calendar, no days, no months, no years, but only vast spider shadows and glints of light from collapsed chandeliers lying about like shed tears in the dust.

"Boy!" Charlie cried, scared, and glad of it.

"Charles," the Colonel said, "you ready for me to birth you a real live, half-dead, sockdolager, on-the-spot mystery?"

"Ready!"

"Now!"

The Colonel swept charts, maps, agate marbles, glass eyes, and sneezes of dust off a table, then rolled up his sleeves.

"Great thing about midwifing mysteries is you don't have to boil water or wash up. Hand me that papyrus scroll there, boy, that darning needle just beyond, that old rickshaw blueprint on the wall, that plug of fired cannonball-cotton underfoot. Jump!"

"I'm jumping!" Charlie ran and fetched, fetched and ran.

"Here, here, and here! There, there, and there!"

Bindles of dry twigs, clutches of pussy willow, and cattails flew. The Colonel's sixteen hands were wild in the air, flashing sixteen bright suture needles, flakes of meadow grass, flickers of owl feather, glares of bright yellow fox eye.

"There, by God. Half-done!"

The Colonel pointed with a chop of his nose.

"Peel an eye, son. What's it commence to start to resemble?"

Charlie circled the table, eyes stretched so wide his mouth gaped.

"Why . . . why—" he sputtered. And then: "A mummy! Can't be!"

"Is, boy! Is!"

Wrist-deep in his creation, the Colonel listened to its reeds and thistles, its dry-flower whispers.

"Now, why did I build this mummy? You, you inspired it, Charlie. Go look out the attic window."

Charlie spat on the dusty pane, wiped a clear viewing spot, and peered out.

"What do you see out there in the damn town?" the Colonel asked. "Any murders being transacted?"

"Heck, no—"

"Anyone falling off church steeples or being run down by maniac lawn mowers?"

"Nope."

"Any *Monitors* or *Merrimacks* sailing up the dry lake, dirigibles falling on the Masonic Temple and squashing six thousand Masons flat?"

"Heck, there's only five thousand folks in Green Town!"

"Don't unhinge me with facts. Stare, boy. Spry. Report!"

"No dirigibles." Charlie stared. "No squashed Masonic temples."

"Right you are, boy."

The Colonel trotted over to join Charlie, surveying the dire territory. He pointed with his great hound nose.

"In all Green Town, in all your life, not one

murder, not one orphanage fire, not one mad fiend carving his initials on librarian ladies' wooden legs. Face it, son, Green Town, upper Illinois, is the most common, mean, ordinary, plain old bore of a graveyard in the eternal history of the Roman, Greek, Russian, Anglo-American empires. If Napoleon had been born here, he'd have committed hari-kari by the age of nine. Boredom. If Caesar had been raised here, he'd have raced to the Forum at the age of ten, shoved in his *own* dagger—"

"Boredom," said Charlie.

"Kee-rect!" Colonel Stonesteel ran back to flailing and pushing and cramming a strange lumpish shape around on the groaning table. "Boredom by the pound and ton. Boredom by the doomsday yard and the funeral mile. Lawns, homes, dog fur, men's haircuts, cheap suits in dark store windows, all cut from the same cloth—"

"Boredom," said Charlie, on cue.

"And what do you do when you're bored, son?"

"Er . . . break a window in a haunted house?"

"We got no haunted houses in Green Town!"

"Used to be. Old Higley's place. Torn down."

"See my point?! What else should we try? Quick!"

"Hold a massacre?"

"No massacre here in dogs' years. Lord, even our police chief's honest. Mayor? Not corrupt. Madness. Whole damn town faced with stark-raving ennuis and lulls. Last chance, Charlie. What's our salvation?"

Charlie smiled. "Build a mummy?"

"Bulldogs in the belfry! Yes! Lend a hand. Help me to finish, boy!"

While the old man cackled and sewed and swooped, Charlie seized and snatched and grabbed and hauled more lizard tails, old nicotine bandages left from a skiing accident that had busted the Colonel's ankle and broken a romance in 1895, some patches from a 1922 Kissel Kar inner tube, a few burned-out sparklers from the last peaceful summer of 1913, and a collection of gypsy moths and death's-head beetles that once had labels and now flew nameless as Charlie and the old man kneaded and wove, shuttled and tapped and molded a brittle, dry wicker shape.

"*Voilà,* Charlie! Finished. Done."

"Oh, Colonel!" The boy stared and gasped with love. "Can I make him a crown?"

"Make him a crown, boy. Make him a crown."

The sun was setting when the Colonel and Charlie and their Egyptian friend came down the dusky backstairs of the old man's house. Two of them were walking iron-heavy, the third was floating light as toasted cornflakes on the September air.

"Colonel," Charlie wondered aloud. "What we going to do with this pharaoh, now we got him? It ain't as if he could talk much, or run around doing things—"

"No need. Let folks talk, let folks run. Peek out."

They cracked the door and peered out at a town smothered in peace and ruined by nothing to do.

"All right, son, now you have recovered from your almost-fatal seizure of desperate empties. But that whole blasted population out there lies up to its elbows in glum and despond, fearful to rise each morn and find it's always and forever Sunday!

Who'll save 'em, boy?''

"Amon Bubastis Rameses Ra the Third, just arrived on the Four O'Clock Limited?''

"God love your sprightly tongue, Charles. What we got here is a giant seed. Seed's no good unless we—''

"Plant it?'' Charles asked.

"Plant. Then watch it grow. Then what? Harvest time. Harvest! Come on, boy. Er . . . bring your friend.''

The Colonel crept out into the first nightfall.

The mummy came soon after, helped by Charlie.

Labor Day at high noon, Osiris Bubastis Amon-Ra-Tut arrived from the Land of the Dead.

An autumn wind stirred the land and flapped doors wide, not with the sound of the usual Labor Day parade, seven touring cars, a fife-and-drum corps, and the mayor, but with a mob that grew as it flowed through the streets and fell in a tide to inundate the lawn in front of Colonel Stonesteel's house. The Colonel and Charlie were sitting on the front porch; they had been sitting there for some hours, waiting for the conniption fits to arrive, the storming of the Bastille to occur. Now with dogs going mad and biting boys' ankles and boys dancing around the fringes of the mob, the Colonel gazed down upon the Creation (his and Charlie's) and gave his secret smile.

"Well, Charlie. Do I win my bet?''

"You sure do, Colonel!''

"Come on.''

Phones rang all across town and lunches burned on stoves as the Colonel strode forth to give the annual Labor Day parade his papal blessing.

At the center of the mob was a horse-drawn wagon. On top of the wagon, his eyes wild with discovery, was Tom Tuppen, owner of a half-dead farm just beyond town. Tom was babbling, and the crowd was babbling, because in the back of the wagon was the special harvest delivered out of four thousand lost years of time.

"Well, flood the Nile and plant the Delta," the Colonel gasped, eyes wide, staring. "Is or is it not that a genuine old Egyptian mummy lying there in its original papyrus and coat-tar wrappings?"

"Sure is!" Charlie cried.

"Sure is!" everyone yelled.

"I was plowing the field this morning," said Tom Tuppen. "Plowing, just plowing and—bang! Plow turned this up, right before me! Like to have had a stroke! Think! The Egyptians must've marched through Illinois three thousand years ago, and no one knew! Revelations, I call it! Outa the way, kids! I'm taking this find to the post office lobby. Setting it up on display! Giddap, now, git!"

The horse, the wagon, the mummy, the crowd moved away, leaving the Colonel behind, his eyes still pretend-wide, his mouth open.

"Hot dog," the Colonel whispered, "we did it, Charles. This uproar, babble, talk, and hysterical gossip will last for a thousand days or Armageddon, whichever comes first!"

"Yes, *sir,* Colonel!"

"Michelangelo couldn't've done better. Boy David's a castaway, lost and forgotten wonder compared to our Egyptian surprise and—"

The Colonel stopped as the mayor rushed by.

"Colonel, Charlie, howdy! Just phoned Chicago. Newsfolks here tomorrow breakfast! Museum folks by lunch! Glory Hallelujah for the Green Town Chamber of Commerce!"

The mayor ran off after the mob.

An autumn cloud crossed the Colonel's face and settled around his mouth.

"End of Act One, Charlie. Start thinking fast. Act Two coming up. We *do* want this commotion to last forever, don't we?"

"Yes, sir—"

"Crack your brain, boy. What does Uncle Wiggily say?"

"Uncle Wiggily says—ah—go back two hops?"

"Give the boy an A-plus, a gold star, and a brownie! The Lord giveth and the Lord taketh away, eh?"

Charlie looked into the old man's face and saw visitations of plagues there. "Yes, sir."

The Colonel watched the mob milling around the post office, two blocks away. The fife-and-drum corps arrived and played some tune vaguely inclined toward the Egyptian.

"Sundown, Charlie," the Colonel murmured, his eyes shut. "We make our final move."

What a day it was! Years later people said, "That was a day!" The mayor went home and got dressed up and came back and made three speeches and held two parades, one going up Main Street toward the end of the trolley line, the other coming back, and Osiris Bubastis Amon-Ra-Tut was at the center of both, smiling now to the right as gravity shifted his flimsy weight and then to the left as they rounded a

226

corner. The fife-and-drum corps, now heavily augmented by accumulated brass, had spent an hour drinking beer and learning the Triumphal March from *Aida,* and this they played so many times that mothers took their screaming babies into the house and men retired to bars to soothe their nerves. There was talk of a third parade and a fourth speech, but sunset took the town unawares, and everyone, including Charlie, went home to a dinner mostly talk and short on eats.

By eight o'clock Charlie and the Colonel were driving along the leafy streets in the fine darkness, taking the air in the old man's 1924 Moon, a car that took up trembling where the Colonel left off.

"Where we going, Colonel?"

"Well," the Colonel mused, steering at ten philosophical miles per hour, nice and easy, "everyone including your folks, is out at Grossett's Meadow right now, right? Final Labor Day speeches. Someone'll light the gasbag mayor, and he'll go up about forty feet, kee-rect? Fire Department'll be setting off the big skyrockets. Which means the post office, plus the mummy, plus the sheriff sitting there with him, will be empty and vulnerable. Then the miracle will happen, Charlie. It *has* to. Now ask me why the miracle will happen."

"Why?"

"Glad you asked. Well, boy, folks from Chicago'll be jumping off the train steps tomorrow, hot and fresh as pancakes, with their pointy noses and glass eyes and microscopes. Those museum snoopers, plus the Associated Press, will rummage our Egyptian pharaoh seven ways from Christmas and blow their fuse boxes. That being so, Charles—"

"We're on our way to mess around with the evidence."

"You put it indelicately, boy, but truth is at the core. Look at it this way, child. Life is a magic show, or *should* be if people didn't go to sleep on each other. Always leave folks with a bit of mystery, son. Now, before people get used to our ancient friend, before he wears out the wrong bath towel, like any smart weekend guest, he should grab the next scheduled camel west and hightail it out of town. There!"

The post office stood silent, with one light shining in the foyer. Through the great window they could see the sheriff seated alongside the mummy on display, neither of them talking, abandoned at last by the attentive mobs that had gone for suppers and fireworks.

The Colonel brought forth a brown bag, in which a mysterious liquid gurgled. "Give me thirty-five minutes to mellow the sheriff down, Charlie. Then you creep in, listen, follow my cues, and work the miracle. Here goes nothing!"

And the Colonel stole away.

Beyond town, the mayor sat down and the fireworks went up.

Charlie stood on top of the Moon and watched them for half an hour. Then, figuring the mellowing time was over, he dogtrotted across the street and moused himself into the post office to stand in the shadows.

"Well, now," the Colonel was saying, seated between the Egyptian pharaoh and the sheriff, "why don't you just finish that bottle, sir?"

"It's finished," said the sheriff, obeying without hesitation.

The Colonel leaned forward in the half-light and peered at the gold amulet on the mummy's breast.

"You believe them old sayings?"

"What old sayings?" the sheriff inquired.

"If you read them hieroglyphics out loud, the mummy comes alive and walks."

"Horseradish," said the sheriff.

"Just look at all those fancy Egyptian symbols!" the Colonel pursued.

"Someone stole my glasses," the sheriff blurted. "You read that stuff to me. Make the fool mummy walk."

Charlie took this as a signal to move, and he sidled around through the shadows, closer to the Egyptian king.

"Here goes." The Colonel bent even closer to the pharaoh's amulet, meanwhile slipping the sheriff's glasses out of his cupped hand into his side pocket. "First symbol on here is a hawk. Second one's a jackal. That third's an owl. Fourth's a yellow fox eye—"

"Continue," the sheriff commanded.

The Colonel did so, and his voice rose and fell, and the sheriff's head nodded, and all the ancient Egyptian pictures and words flowed and touched around the mummy until at last the Colonel gave a great gasp and pointed.

"Good grief, Sheriff. Look!"

The sheriff blinked both eyes wide.

"The mummy," said the Colonel. "It's going for a walk!"

"Can't be!" the sheriff cried. "Can't be!"

"Is," said a voice, somewhere. Maybe the pharaoh under his breath.

And the mummy lifted up, suspended, and drifted toward the door.

"Why," the sheriff suggested, tears in his eyes, "I think he might just *fly!*"

"I'd better follow and bring him back," the Colonel said.

"*Do* that!" the sheriff replied.

The mummy was gone. The Colonel ran. The door slammed.

"Oh, dear." The sheriff lifted the bottle and shook it. "Empty."

They drove through avenues of autumn leaves that were suddenly the temples of dusting Egypt and the lily-sculpted pillars of time. Charlie let the car motor hum in his soul while over his shoulder, in the backseat, taking the ancient air, enjoying the warm river of wind, the mummy leaned this way and that as the car swerved.

"Say it, Colonel," said Charlie at last.

"What?" asked the old man.

"I love to hear you talk. Say what I want to hear. About the mummy. What he truly is. What he's really made of. Where he comes from—"

"Why, boy, you were there, you helped make, you saw—"

But the boy was looking at him steadily with bright autumn eyes. The mummy, their ancient harvest-tobacco dried-up Nile River bottom old-time masterpiece, leaned in the wind over their shoulder, waiting as much as the boy for the talk to come.

"You want to know who he truly was, once upon a time?"

The Colonel gathered a handful of dust in his lungs

and softly filtered it out before he answered.

"He was everyone, no one, someone. You. Me."

"Go on," Charlie whispered.

Continue, said the lapis-lazuli gleam in the mummy's eyes.

"He was, he is," the Colonel murmured, "a bundle of old Sunday comic pages stashed in the attic to spontaneously combust from all those forgotten notions and stuffs. He's a stand of papyrus left in an autumn field long before Moses, a papier-mâché tumbleweed blown out of time, this way long-gone dusk, that way come-again dawn . . . a chart map of Siam, Blue River Nile source, hot desert dustdevil . . . all the confetti from lost trolley transfers, dried-up yellow cross-country road maps petering off in sand dunes . . . dry crushed flowers from wedding memory books . . . funeral wreaths . . . ticker tapes unraveled from gone-off-forever parades to Far Rockaway . . . lost scrolls from the great burned library at Alexandria . . . smell the chars? His rib cage, covered with what?! Posters torn off seed barns in North Storm, Ohio, shuttled south toward Fulfilment, Texas . . . dead gold-mine certificates, wedding and birth announcements . . . all the things that were once need, hope, dream . . . first nickel in the pocket, dollar on the wall . . . wrapped and ribboned yellow-skinned letters from failed old men, time-orphaned women saying Tomorrow and Tomorrow . . . there'll be a ship in the harbor, horse on the road, knock on the door. . . . He's . . . he's telegrams you're afraid to open . . . poems you wrote and threw away . . . all the dumb, strange shadows you ever grew, boy, or I ever inked out inside my head at three A.M., crushed, stashed, and now shaped in one form under our hands and here in our gaze. That, that, that is what old King Pharaoh Seventh Dynasty Holy Dust *is!*''

"Wow," Charlie sighed.

As they drove up and parked in front of his house, Colonel Stonesteel peered out cautiously.

"Your folks ever go up in your attic, boy?"

"Too small. They poke me up to rummage."

"Good. Hoist our ancient Egyptian friend out of the backseat there. Don't weigh much, twenty pounds at the most. You carried him fine, Charlie. Oh, that was a sight. You running out of the post office, making the mummy walk. You shoulda seen the sheriff's face!"

"I hope he don't get in trouble because of this."

"Oh, he'll bump his head and make up a fine story. Can't very well admit he saw the mummy go for a walk, can he? He'll think of something—organize a posse. You'll see. But right now, son, get our ancient friend here up, hide him good, visit him weekly. Feed him night talk. Then thirty, forty years from now—"

"What?" Charlie asked.

"In a bad year so brimmed up with boredom it drips out your ears, when the town has long forgotten this first arrival and departure, on a morning, I say, when you lie in bed and don't want to get up, don't even want to twitch your ears or blink, you're so damned bored . . . well, on *that* morning, Charlie, you just climb up in your rummage-sale attic and shake this mummy out of bed, toss him in a cornfield, and watch new hellfire mobs break loose. Life starts over that hour, that day, for you, the town, everyone. Now grab git, and hide, boy! Hop to it!"

"I hate for the night to be over," Charlie said very quietly. "Can't we circle a few more blocks and then finish off some lemonade on your porch, and *him* along, too?"

"Lemonade!" Colonel Stonesteel banged his heel on the car floor. The car exploded and surged. "For the Lost and Found King, and the Pharaoh's Illinois Son!"

It was late on Labor Day evening, the two of them seated on the Colonel's front porch again, rocking up a fair breeze, lemonades in hand, ice in mouth, sucking the sweet savor of the night's incredible adventures. A wind blew. The mummy, behind Charlie's rocker, propped against the porch wall, almost seemed to be listening.

"Boy!" Charlie exclaimed. "I can see tomorrow's *Clarion* headlines: PRICELESS MUMMY KIDNAPPED. RAMESES-TUT VANISHES. GREAT FIND GONE. REWARD OFFERED. SHERIFF NONPLUSSED. BLACKMAIL EXPECTED."

"Talk on, boy. Like I taught you."

The last Labor Day fireworks were dying in the sky. Their light faded in the lapis-lazuli eyes of boy and man and their withered friend, all fixed in shadow.

"Colonel." Charlie gazed into the future. "What if, even in my old age, I don't ever *need* my own particular mummy?"

"Eh?"

"What if I have a life chock-full of things, never bored, find what I want to do, *do* it, make every day count, every night swell, sleep tight, wake up yelling, laugh lots, grow old, still running fast, what *then,* Colonel?"

"Why then, boy, you'll be one of God's luckiest people!"

"For you see, Colonel," Charlie said, looking at him with pure round, unblinking eyes, "I made up my mind. I'm going to be the greatest writer that ever lived."

The Colonel braked his rocker and searched the innocent fire in that small face.

"Lord, I see it. Yes. You *will*. Well, then, Charles, when you are very old, you must find some lad, not as lucky as you, to give Osiris-Ra to. Your life may be full, but others, lost on the road, will need our Egyptian friend. Agreed? Agreed."

The last skyrockets soared and fell, the last fire balloons went sailing out among the gentle stars. Cars and people were driving or walking home, some fathers or mothers carrying their tired and already-sleeping children. As the quiet parade passed Colonel Stonesteel's porch, some folks glanced in and waved at the old man and the boy and the tall, dim-shadowed servant who stood between. The night was over forever.

Charlie said, "Say some more, Colonel."

"No. I'm shut. Listen to what *he* has to say now. Let *him* tell your future, Charlie. Let him start you on stories. Ready?"

A wind came up and blew in the dry papyrus and sifted the ancient wrappings and trembled the curious hands and softly twitched the lips of their old/new four-thousand year nighttime visitor, whispering.

"What's he saying, Charles?"

Charlie shut his eyes, waited, listened, nodded, let a single tear slide down his cheek, and at last said, "Everything . . . Everything I always wanted to hear."

234

TRIGGERING

By John Shirley

It was one of those protectiplated Manhattan brown-stones, rewired in the Nineties, every square inch evenly coated with a thin, flexible preserving plastic. The old building was a jarring sight, snugged between the glassy highrises. It was the distant past all neatly wrapped up and embalmed. It seemed appropriate, considering the job I'd been sent there to do.

I went up the slippery hall stairs, one hand on the plastic-coated wooden railing, wondering what un-protected wood felt like. They'd even preserved the quaint twentieth-century graffiti spraypainted in bright crimson on the faded walls: NUKE REAGAN BEFORE HE NUKES YOU and DEATH TO THE COMPROMISE SOCIALISTS.

I pressed 2-D's doorbell. An eye goggled through the old-fashioned glass peephole. The place apparently had no inspection cameras. The door opened—on real hinges—and I was looking down at a four-year-old boy. Behind him was the chair he'd been standing on. He pushed it aside.

He glanced at my clingsuit, at the department's suit-and-tie stenciled sharply on the front (the painting of the white hankie and the tie clip were beginning to fade), and chuckled grimly. He noticed my dark eyes, my short black hair, my duskiness, and his recognition of me as an Americanized East Indian showed in his face: a flicker of suspicion. It was a very adult expression.

I stared. They hadn't told me what the Tangle was. I had a feeling it began here. With the boy. The boy had curly brown hair, big blue eyes, a pug nose, and pursed lips. He wore a formal spiral-leg suit. It was an adult's suit, in miniature. In his mouth was clamped a black cigarette holder containing a Sherman's Real Tobacco burnt nearly to the butt. Smoke geysered at intervals from his nostrils.

A midget? But he wasn't. He was a four-year-old boy.

"You're staring at me," he said abruptly, his voice high-pitched but carefully articulated, accented almost aristocratically. "Is there some specific reason for this intrusive scrutiny, or are you simply a man who practices his penetrating glance on any unsuspecting citizen he encounters?"

"I'm Ramja," I said, nodding politely. "I'm from the Department of Transmigratology. And your name?" I covered my astonishment well.

He frowned at his cigarette, which had gone out. "Care for a smoke?"

"I don't smoke, thanks."

"Self-righteous, the way you say that. But you

federal men are always self-righteous bastards. There was another here, fellow named Hextupper or something. You're the follow-up. Very orderly. You can go and dance with Dante for all I care, friend. But if you must know"—he gestured me inside and moved to close the door behind me—"my name's Conrad Frampton. How-do-you-do, salutations, and et cetera."

"You're overcompensating your self-consciousness about being a little boy," I said, returning his hostility.

He shrugged. "Could be. If you were a forty-one-year-old man trapped in a four-year-old body, you'd feel like overcompensating, too. You'd feel like leaping out the window now and then. Believe me." He led me to a couch, and I sat beside him.

"When did you die?" I asked, watching him. He made me nervous.

"I died in 1982," he said, not even blinking. "Care for a drink?"

"No, thanks. You go ahead."

"Damned right I will." There was a low yellow table beside the couch. He punched for a cocktail on the table's programmer.

I looked around. The room wasn't antique; it seemed like a broken promise after the outside of the building. It was a standard decorbubble, done in various shades of pastel yellow, the curved walls blending in cornerlessly into the concave ceiling; the floor was more or less flat but of the same spongy synthetic. The walls, floor, ceiling, and furniture were all of a piece, shaped by the inhabitants. The room spoke to me about those inhabitants.

"Who else lives here?" I asked. The department

had told me nothing about the people involved in the Tangle, except the address. It's better that way.

Conrad took a silvery cigarette case from a table, his infant fingers struggling for smooth movements; he lit a thin Sherman sulkily with a thumbnail lighter. "A couple of degenerates live here," he said, blowing smoke rings, "who call themselves my parents. *Fawther* is a musician. George Marvell, snooty concert guitarist. Plays one of those hideous flesh guitars. They're both flesh-machine fetishists. Mother works at the genvats, helping make more genetic-manipulation horrors. She's not so bad, really, though it nauseates me when she looks at me with her big brown eyes welling, hoping I'll turn into her widdoo Ahmed again. Her name's Senya. They named me Ahmed, but I make them call me by my real name," he said defensively.

"I take it you don't approve of flesh machines." I sensed there was a flesh machine near at hand. A big one.

He made a something-smells bad face. "Soulless things. Ugly. I don't know which is worse, the flesh guitar or that living *pit* they call a bedroom. They *are* soulless, aren't they? You're from the Department of Transmigratology. So you're allegedly an expert on souls. What's your stand on flesh machines, old boy?"

"Depends on what you mean by *soul*. We don't use the word. We say *plasma field composed of tightly interwoven subatomic particles, capable of recording its host's sensory input*. And capable of traveling from body to body, evolving psychically so that species survival is more likely. It's not religion. It's a function of the first law of thermodynamics,

238

but we use certain *mystical* techniques to work with it. Training for seeing life patterns, that sort of thing. Karma-buildup release. But if we use words like *karma* and *soul* in our reports to the National Academy of Sciences, we'll lose our funding. It took us twelve years of regressing people, and tracing facts, to get them to admit it was a bona fide science."

"I don't know about science. But in my current circumstances. . ." He made a bitter face. "I'm forced to believe in reincarnation." He looked at me. "Why the hell are you here? Level with me."

"We had a report of a rather nasty Tangle here. The lines of spiritual evolution tangled. Sometimes a gross emotional trauma from one life surfaces in the next. The people involved in the trauma are reborn in close circumstances in the next life, and the next, until the thing's cleared up."

I considered telling him more. I might have said I came because a Tangle needs a Triggering. And they sent me, Ramja, specifically, because I'm part of the Tangle. Not sure how yet. But I'm one of the few department staffers who can't remember his last life. Part of it's repressed irretrievably. The computer model connected me with this tangle. They sent me, though they know that there's a big probability that someone involved will die.

But I didn't say that. Instead: "As for flesh machines, I don't know how much so-called soul they have. Or even how much awareness. The department believes that they're part of the evolution of the lower orders. Animal minds, animal souls." I shook my head. "I'm not sure. Conrad, what do you remember of your death?"

239

He shakily relit his cigarette. "I . . . I drowned. Scuba . . . uh, scuba-diving. Sickening circumstances. Trapped underwater. My air ran out. Big pain in my chest. Gigantic buzzing in my ears. And a white rush. Next thing I remember is hearing this sad guitar song. Only it was a flesh guitar; so it sounded like they do—like a guitar crossed with a human voice. I looked around, and there was Senya looming over me, her arms outstretched, and I was staggering toward her. It must have looked like toddling. And then the guitar *screamed*. That's what brought me to myself. I remembered who I was . . . My *real* parents are Laura and Marvin Frampton. Were. They died together in a nursing-home fire, I'm told."

He crossed his small legs and propped an elbow on one knee, his cigarette holder poised continentally between thumb and forefinger. "George would like to have me adopted. He doesn't like me, and neither does his room. But then the room is rude to George, too. It shakes when he strokes it. Unpleasantly. I'll show you the damn thing."

We got up. I followed him to a doorway on the right and into the bedroom.

The room was in pain.

The cavelike walls were all rosy membranes, touched with blue, pulsing. Across the room and near the living floor was a blue-black bruise, swollen and pustulent, a half-meter across. Conrad carefully didn't look at it.

"You're just full of hostility, Conrad," I said softly. "You've been kicking the wall there. Or hitting it with something."

He turned to me with a very adult look of outrage.

240

"If I have, it's in self-defense. I sleep in the next room, but I can feel this thing *radiating* at me even in there. It won't let me sleep! It wants something from me. I'm half-crazy living in this kid's body anyway, and this thing makes it worse. I can feel it nagging at me."

"And you kicked it to make it stop. In the same spot. Repeatedly."

"What do you know about it?" Conrad muttered, turning away.

I felt uncomfortable in the room, too. It wasn't hostility that I felt from the walls. It was the shock of recognition.

The moist ceiling was not far over my head, curvingly soft, and damp. It wasn't much like a womb. It was more like a boneless head turned inside out. The wall at the narrower end, to my left, contained the outlines of a huge unfinished face. The nose was there, but flattened, broad as my chest. The eyes were forever closed, milky oblongs locked behind translucent lids.

The room was a genvat creation, a recombinant-DNA organism expanded to fill an ordinary bedroom. The old bedroom's windows were behind the eyes. The light from the windows shone through the eyes, as if through lampshades, defining the outsize capillaries in the lids. The face's lips were on the floor, puckered toward the ceiling. The lips were the room's bed, disproportionately wide. They were soft-looking, about the size of a single bed; they would open out for two. There would be no opening beneath them, no teeth.

"It was grown from Senya's cells, you know," Conrad said. "From her fingers." He deliberately ground out his still-smoldering cigarette on the room's floor. The fleshy walls quivered.

I controlled the impulse to box Conrad's ears as he continued, "There's a tank of nutrifluid outside the window. Personally, I think the creature is disgusting. I can hear it breathe. I can smell it. You should see the lips move when Senya stretches out on them. Ugh!"

The room's odor was briny, smelling faintly of Woman. It breathed through its nose with a gentle sigh.

Returning to the main room, Conrad said, "Sure you won't have a drink?"

"This time I will have one, thanks." The womb-room had shaken me.

I stood on a secret brink. My heart was beating quickly and irregularly. Spasmodic waves of fear swept through me. I focused on them, brought them to a peak, shuddered, and let the fear vaporize in the light of internal self-awareness. Calmness temporarily wrapped the restlessness in me.

I sipped my plastic cup of martini, for the moment relaxing. Sitting beside Conrad, I said, "You said something about George's guitar being sick."

Conrad smirked. "George is hoping his guitar will be better today. But it won't sing for him. I know it won't. It'll start screaming again as soon as he plays it. It sounds vicious—the most awful screams you can imagine. He may have to go back to playing electric guitar."

"It's screaming of its own volition? Maybe it's allergic to him."

"Possibly. It doesn't scream when Senya plays it."

I felt my trance level deepening. The outlines of the furniture seemed hallucinogenically to expand, softly strobing. I glimpsed ghostly human figures on flickering paths; the apartment's inhabitants had left their life patterns on the room's electric field. In those subtly glowing lines I could see the Triggering foreshadowed.

"Conrad," I said carefully, trying not to show my excitement, "tell me about your life just before transition. Give me details of the death itself." I waited, breathless.

Conrad was pleased. He lit another cigarette and watched the smoke curl up as he spoke. "I was a copy editor for a book publisher. I was a good one, but I was becoming bored with the work. I'd accumulated a lot of vacation time; so I accepted Billy Lilac's invitation to go on a cruise with him and his friends. I felt sort of funny about it, because I was having an affair with his wife. But she insisted that it would be good because we would remain casual for the duration of the trip—four days—and that would cool Billy's suspicions about us. Billy was rolling in the Right Stuff. He owned a lucrative chain of fast-food restaurants.

"His yacht had what he called a mousetrap aquarium built into it. The boat had a deep draft, and by pressing a button, he opened a chamber in the hull. Water would be sucked into it, along with little fish and sometimes squid or even a small shark. Then the gates at the bottom would close, temporarily trapping the creatures in there, and we would watch them through a glass pane in the deck of the hold.

"There were five of us on the cruise. Lana Lilac, Billy's teen-aged wife, thirty years younger than Billy; his secretary, Lucille Winchester; Lucille's son Lancer—"

"Who? Who did you say? The last two?" My interruption was too eager.

Conrad looked at me strangely. "Lucille and Lancer Winchester," he said impatiently. "*Any*way, Billy asked a bunch of us to go down and scare some octopuses into the aquarium. We were over a certain Jamaican reef where they were quite common. So we went down in scuba gear. There were me and Lana and—"

"And Lucille. You three went down," I interrupted. My head contained a whirlpool. *Calm. Perceive objectively. Perceive in the perspective of time. Evolutionary patterns.*

The mummified hurt. Tonight I would resolve the hurt.

"You three went down," I repeated, "and when you approached the gate where the hull opened, good old Billy pressed the button that opens the gate and makes the current that pulls things in, and all three of you were sucked into the mousetrap aquarium. He closed the gate behind you, and then he stood in the hold, over your heads, watching, chuckling quietly now and then. As you ran out of air."

For a few minutes I couldn't talk. I felt as if I were choking, though it hadn't been me who'd drowned on that occasion. I'd drowned later, choking to death on my own vomit: drug overdose. Years later.

Conrad's irritation visibly became astonishment.

But I was only peripherally aware of him. I was seeing myself, as fifteen-year-old Lancer Winchester, hands cuffed behind me, lying facedown on the glass floor, watching as my mother drowned. My gasping and my tears misted the glass, blurring the scene for me. But somehow the blur emphasized their frantic movements as they tried to pry the gate. Their frenzied hand signals. Their fingers clawing at the glass.

While Billy Lilac stood with his hands in his pocket beside me, like a man mildly amused by a zoo, chuckling occasionally and sweetly chatting to me, politely explaining that he'd killed Conrad because Conrad had been having an affair with Lana. And he'd killed my mother because she helped them keep the secret and had permitted Lana and Conrad to use her apartment.

I'd expected him to kill me. But he simply uncuffed me and put me ashore. He knew that my history of emotional disturbance destroyed my credibility. No one would believe me when there were three others testifying differently. He'd bribed his two crewpeople handsomely. They claimed a mechanical failure had caused the gate to open prematurely, and Billy had been on deck and hadn't seen it. They'd been with him the whole time. Craig and Judy Lormer, husband and wife, were his crew. Only, after a while, Judy began to have nightmares about the people drowning in the hold. Judy had threatened to go to the police. Craig told Billy, asking for more money to help keep her quiet. Billy had Judy kidnapped. Craig took another bribe and left. I knew this, because Billy came to me in the asylum and told me in the visitors room.

He enjoyed talking about it. Billy was the quintessential son of a bitch. "I drowned Judy in the aquarium in my house, Lancer," he'd said, his voice mild and pleasant. Like a taxidermist talking shop.

"You want to explain yourself, friend, hmm?" Conrad said, in the present.

I was thinking about my own death. I'd been in and out of institutions for the four years after my mother drowned. Treated for paranoid dementia and drug abuse—the drug abuse, heroin, was real—till I wondered whether I *had* hallucinated Billy's quiet enjoyment as he stood on the glass, watching the bubbles, forced from exhausted lungs, shatter on the pane between his feet.

I died of an overdose in 1987.

"No coincidences, Conrad," I said suddenly. "I'm here because I knew you in your last life. I was Lancer Winchester. I watched you die. You and Lana Lilac and Mother. Strangling under glass." I paused to clear my throat. I tranced to calmness. "Really, Conrad," I said distantly, gazing down the corridors of time, "you ought to slow down on the drinking."

Ignoring my advice, he gulped another cocktail, swearing softly.

I turned my eyes toward the doors, first the front door and then the door to the bedroom. The orifice in the womb-room had contracted a little, twitching, so that its blue-pink flesh showed at the open door's corners.

I felt its excitement subliminally, and I shared its half-slumbering yearning. Conrad felt it, too, and glanced at it, irritated.

But only the womb-room and I were aware that George and Senya Marvell were climbing the plastic-coated steps to the apartment. Now I felt them stopping on the landing to rest, and to quarrel. I felt the Trigger near. I hadn't quite located it.

"Conrad," I began. "Senya is—"

The door opened. Senya came in, toting something behind her. She and the man I took to be George were carrying a large transparent plasglass case between them. Within the case's thick liquids, something wallowed like a pink sea animal. A flesh guitar. An expensive one, too.

But I could hardly take my eyes from Senya. She was lovely. I had a disquietingly powerful sense of *déjà vu,* taking in her strong, willowy shape; an anomalously campy Old Glory flag pattern was worked into the thick spill of flaxen hair flipped to fall onto her right shoulder. Something in the gauntness of her face excited me. There was both curiosity and empathy in her expression, seeming out of place with her black, clinging Addams Family Revival gown and her transparent spike heels.

"Who the hell is *he?*" George puffed, looking me over as they carried the flesh guitar's case into the bedroom.

"He'd be the man from the Department of Transmigratology, George," she replied off-handedly. "I had them send someone over about, umm, about Conrad."

The *déjà vu* resurged when I listened to her voice. The tone of it wasn't familiar. The familiarity was in the way she used it.

George and Senya returned from the bedroom. In contrast to Senya, George was stocky and pallid, his hair permaset into a solid yellow block over his head. His smoky-blue eyes swept over me, then flicked angrily at Conrad. "The kid's drunk again." His voice, when he spoke to me, was a distillation of condescension: "So you think you can clear the garbage from the kid's head here?"

"If there is any garbage to be cleared in this room," Conrad interrupted, "it spills from your mouth, George."

As George bent to punch for a drink, his motions set off reverberations containing within them, coded, all the actions of his lifetime. And implications of earlier lifetimes.

"Actually, I'm not here to 'clear' anything from Conrad in particular," I said, crossing my legs and leaning back against the couch. Watching Senya, I went on, "In this lifetime my name's Ramja; in the last it was Lancer." Her eyes met mine. She was puzzled. I hadn't hit the Trigger yet. I smiled at her, felt a flush of pleasure run through me when she smiled back.

"No, George, I'm here," I continued, trying to keep the fervor from my voice, "to deal with a rather complex transmigrational entanglement. It results from a past-life trauma shared by everyone here. A memory that brought us back together. For Triggering. And the funny thing is, George, I don't really have to *do* much of anything. My being here completes the karmic equation. I'm not sure how it's going to trigger." I sipped my drink and asked, "How did your guitar perform today, George?"

George just shook his head at me. He was close to throwing me out.

Senya answered for him. "It screamed. As usual! Every time George touched it." She looked at George as if she could understand perfectly why *anyone* would scream if George touched them.

"I rather suspected that," I said. "And I suspect, too, that there's a growing alienation between you and George lately, Senya. Since the day the guitar started screaming—and Conrad appeared in your son."

"What the bad-credit do *you* know about it?"

George blurted. He was tense with fear. He, too, could feel the Triggering coming.

"The man's right, George," Conrad put in, grinding his cigarette out on the table, his little-boy fingers trembling. "The guitar's screaming and my, ah, my *coming out* came close together. And then the tension between you and Senya got nasty. I saw it. But it's not like it's *my* fault. The damn guitar may not have more than the brains of a squirrel, but it knows a creep when it senses one. George was playing it, and this scream came out of it. It finally got fed up with the creep."

George said suddenly, "If you think there's some link between *him*"—he jabbed a thumb at Conrad without looking at him—"and what's wrong with my guitar, then maybe you can—I dunno, uh—clear it away so the guitar works again?"

"Maybe," I said, smiling. "Let's go into the bedroom. And—clear it away."

A moment later we were standing around the plasglass case, beside the bed-sized, upthrust lips at one end of the womb-room. Senya opened the case and lifted the guitar free as the floor's lips quivered and the room's walls twitched. The guitar dried almost immediately. It was the approximate shape of an acoustic guitar, but composed of human flesh, covered in pink-white skin, showing blue veins. The neck of the guitar was actually fashioned after a human arm, with the elbow fused so that it was always outstretched. The tendonlike strings were stretched from the truncated fingers, which served as string pegs. But the guitar's small brain kept the strings always in tune. Its lines were soft, feminine, its lower end suggesting a woman's hips. Where the sound hole would be on an acoustic guitar was a woman's mouth, permanently wide open, its lips thin and pearly-pink; toothless, but with a small tongue and throat. There were no eyes, no other physical suggestions of humanity.

Senya held it in her arms, leaning its lower end on her lifted knee, her right foot propped on the brim of the open guitar case. She played an E chord, her fingers lightly brushing the tendonlike strings. The strings vibrated, and the guitar's mouth sang the note. The tone was hauntingly human, melancholy, sympathetic. An odd look came over Senya's face. She glanced up at me, and then at Conrad, who reeled, drunk, to one side. And back at me.

"Well?" George said.

"You play the guitar, George," I said. "Go on. I think all the integers of the equation are here, in place. You play it."

"No, thanks," he said, looking at the pink, infantlike guitar in his wife's arms.

I could feel the lines of karmic influence tightening the room. Unconsciously we'd moved into symmetrical formation around the glass case: myself, Conrad, Senya, George, and the guitar, which Senya held over the case, her arms trembling with its weight. We were the five points of a pentacle, encircled by the waiting, brooding presence of the womb-room.

"Go on, George," said Conrad, slurring his words. "Don't be a simpering coward. Play the guitar." Like a defiant midget, he sneered up at George.

George snorted and took the guitar from Senya. Its strings contracted with a faint whine when he touched it. He strummed a chord and relaxed as the notes came out normally. He strummed again, shrugged, and glanced nervously at the living blue-pink ceiling and the bruise low on the ceiling walls.

The guitar's scream shattered the glass of the window hidden behind the flesh wall and made me clap my hands over my ears. The walls rippled and from somewhere gave a long sigh. Blood ran from the lower edge of the closed eyelids, like crimson tears. An ugly, ripping sound made me look up; the ceiling had ruptured. Blood rained on us in fine droplets. Conrad began to laugh hysterically, his voice piping manically. His eyes rolled back, into his head.

George flung the guitar down furiously. I had to look away as the flesh guitar struck the edge of its case. It howled again as something vital within it snapped. It rolled onto the floor, facedown, moaning. The room moaned with it. Panic enlarging his eyes, George looked at each of us. He looked as if we'd suddenly become strange to him. He was seeing us differently now, all his self-assurance gone.

I said, loudly, staring hard at George, "Yours was the sort of crime that required a major effort at karmic justice, Billy."

"You call him Billy . . ." Conrad said, staring at George.

"Billy Lilac," I said, smiling at Senya. "By now you should be remembering. And wondering, maybe, why a man should be punished for things he did in another life. Was Billy the same man as George, really? He is the same man, at the root. Remember what he did? That sort of crime, Billy . . . ah! The womb-room remembers, on some level. The guitar remembers. Their brains are small, but their memories are long. You drowned three people, and, perhaps worse, you chuckled while you watched. You destroyed my life. Me? I was Lancer Winchester." I waited for the full impact of my words to hit the others.

The red mist sifted down on us. The floor's lips snapped open and shut soundlessly. Senya and Conrad listened raptly, their eyes strange. "You killed my mother, Billy. But she's here with us. Everyone you killed is here. It's going to be a big shock to the genvat industry when I tell them we've got evidence that human spirit-plasma fields can incarnate into flesh machines. It will shake up my department, too. My mother? She incarnated into the room that surrounds us, Billy. And Lana is here in Senya. The guitar woke up in your arms one day and remembered what you had done. So it screamed. The guitar is Judy Lormer. Remember Judy? The crew-woman you drowned when she threatened to talk?"

I didn't mention the fact that young Lancer had been genuinely in love with Lana Lilac.

George aka Billy Lilac wasn't listening. He was backing into a corner, making odd, subhuman sounds and swiping at his eyes. Overwhelmed by the sudden remembrance I'd triggered. Realization: who he was and what he'd done and how it had always been a shaping influence on his life.

The room's walls were closing in around us. The room itself was undergoing contractions, squeezing us. We felt waves of air pressuring us, slapping us toward the door. We staggered.

Howling, his voice almost lost in the room's keening and the dis-chording of the dying guitar, Conrad struggled on all fours after us. He looked like a frightened child.

Senya and I stumbled out into the main room, both

of us fighting panic, shuddering with identity disorientation.

Gasping, I turned and looked through the shrinking entranceway. The aperture was irising shut. I glimpsed George standing over the guitar case. The bleeding flesh guitar yowled at his feet. George swayed toward us as the room got smaller around him, his arms outstretched plaintively, face white, his expression alternating terror and confusion, mouth open in a scream lost in the room's own clamor. Behind him, the fused lower edges of the lids over the room's eyes tore free; the lids snapped abruptly open. The eyes glared, pupils brimmed with blood. The room contracted again, and George tripped. He fell against the open plasglass guitar case, facedown over churning liquids. The aperture closed.

"Ahmed!" Senya shouted, recovering herself, "Ahmed's trapped!"

She was calling Conrad by the name she'd given him. The doorway was blocked by a convex wall of tense, damp human tissue; it was puckered into a sort of closed cervix at the middle. But slowly the "cervix" dilated. The top of a head poked through. Conrad's head. His eyes were closed, his face blank. Gradually the room pressed him out. He was unconscious but breathing. Senya held him in her arms. His clothing was badly torn and slick-wet with the room's blood. When he opened his eyes a minute later, he said nothing, but gazed up at her, all trace of Conrad gone. Conrad had withdrawn to whatever closet of the human brain it is that erstwhile personalities are kept in.

The womb-room had shrunk to a bruised, agonized ball of flesh less than two meters across, clamped rigidly around the plasglass case. It died, mangled by the corners of the big glass case, and inwardly burst from its own convulsions.

George, Billy Lilac, died within it. He'd been forced by the shrinking enclosure into the glass case, into its glutinous, transparent fluids. He died under glass. He died by drowning.

OUT OF LUCK

By Walter Tevis

It was only three months after he had left his wife and children and moved in with Janet that Janet decided she had to go to Washington for a week. Harold was devastated. He tried not to let her see it. The fiction between them was that he had left Gwen so he could grow up, change his life, and learn to paint again. But all he was certain was that he had left Gwen to have Janet as his mistress. There were other reasons: his recovery from alcoholism, the years he had wasted his talent as an art professor, and Gwen's refusal to move to New York with him. But none of these would have been sufficient to uproot him and cause him to take a year's leave from his job if Janet had not worn peach-colored bikini panties that stretched tightly across her lovely bottom.

He spent the morning after she left cleaning up the kitchen and washing the big pot with burnt zucchini in it. Janet had made him three quarts of zucchini soup before leaving on the shuttle, along with two jars of chutney, veal stew in a blue casserole dish, and two loaves of Irish soda bread. It was very international. The mess in the tiny kitchen of her apartment took him two hours to clean up. Then he cooked himself a breakfast of scrambled eggs and last night's mashed potatoes, fried with onions. He drank two cups of coffee from Janet's Chemex. Drinking the coffee, he walked several times into the living room, where his easel stood, and looked at the quarter-done painting. Each time he looked at it his heart sank. He did not want to finish the painting —not *that* painting, that dumb, academic abstraction. But there was no other painting for him to paint right now. What he wanted was Janet.

Janet was a very successful folk-art dealer. They had met at a museum party. She was in Washington now as a consultant to the National Gallery. She had said to him, "No, I don't think you should come to Washington with me. We need to be apart from each other for a while. I'm beginning to feel suffocated." He had nodded sagely while his heart sank.

One problem was that he distrusted folk art and Janet's interest in it, the way he distrusted Janet's fondness for her cats. Janet talked to her cats a lot. He was neutral about cats themselves, but he felt people who talked to them were trivial. And being interested in badly painted nineteenth-century portraits also seemed trivial to him now.

He looked at the two gold-framed American primitives above Janet's sofa, said, "Horseshit!" and drew back his mug in a fantasy of throwing coffee on them both.

Across from the apartment on Sixty-third Street workmen were renovating an old mansion; they had been at it three months before, when Harold moved in. He watched them for a minute now, mixing cement in a wheelbarrow and bringing sacks of it from a truck at the corner of Madison Avenue. Three workmen in the white undershirts held sunlit discourse on the plywood ramp that had replaced the building's front steps. Behind windows devoid of glass he could see men moving back and forth. But nothing happened; nothing seemed to change in the building. It was the same mess it had been before, like his own spiritual growth: lots of noise and movement and no change.

He looked at his watch, relieved. It was ten-thirty. The morning was half over, and he needed to go to the bank. He put on a light jacket and left.

As he was waiting in a crowd at the Third Avenue light, he heard a voice shout, "Taxi!" and a man pushed roughly past him, right arm high and waving, onto the avenue. The man was about thirty, in faded blue jeans and a sleeveless sweater. A taxi squealed to a stop at the corner, and the man conferred with the driver for a moment before getting in. He seemed to be quietly arrogant, preoccupied with something. Harold could have kicked him in the ass. He did not like the man's look of confidence. He did not like his sandy, uncombed hair. The light changed, and the cab took off fast, up Third Avenue.

Harold crossed and went into the bank. He went to a table, quickly wrote out a "Cash" check for a hundred, then walked over toward the line. Halfway across the lobby, he stopped cold. The man in the sleeveless sweater was standing in line, holding a checkbook. His lips were pursed in silent whistling. He was wearing the same faded blue jeans and—Harold now noticed—Adidas.

He was looking idly in Harold's direction. Harold averted his eyes. There were at least ten other people waiting behind the man. He had to have been here awhile. An identical twin? A mild hallucination, making two similar people look exactly alike? Harold got in line. After a while the man finished his business and left. Harold cashed his check and left, stuffing five twenties into his billfold. Another drain on the seven thousand he had left Michigan with. He had seven thousand to live on for a year in New York, with Janet, while he learned to paint again, to be the self-supporting artist his whiskey dreams had been filled with. Whiskey had left him unable to answer the telephone or open the door. That had been two years ago in Michigan. Whiskey had left him sitting behind closed suburban blinds at two in the afternoon, reading the J. C. Penney catalog and waiting for Gwen to come home from work. Well, he had been free of whiskey for a year and a half now. First the hospital, then A.A., now New York and Janet.

He walked back toward her apartment, thinking of how his entire bankroll of seven thousand could not pay Janet's rent for three months. And she had taken this big New York place after two years of living in an even larger apartment in Paris. On a marble-topped lingerie chest in one of the bathrooms was a snapshot of her, astride a gleaming Honda, on the Boulevard des Capucines by the ironwork doorway of that apartment. When that photograph was taken, Harold was living in a ranch house in

Michigan and was driving a Chevrolet.

He glanced down Park Avenue while crossing it and saw a sleeveless sweater and faded jeans, from the back, disappearing into one of the tall apartment buildings. He shuddered and quickened his pace. He shifted his billfold from a rear to a front pocket, picturing those pickpockets who bump you from behind and rob you while apologizing on the streets of New York. His mother—his very protective mother—had told him about that twenty years before. Part of him loved New York, loved its action and its anonymity, along with the food and clothes and bookstores. Another part of him feared it. The sight of triple locks on apartment doors tended to frighten him, or of surly Puerto Ricans with well-muscled arms, carrying their big, noisy, arrogant radios. Their Kill-the-Anglo radios. The slim-hipped black men frightened him, with long, tight-assed trousers in pale colors, half-covering expensive shoes—Italian killer shoes. And there were drunks everywhere. In doorways. Poking studiously through garbage bins for the odd half-eaten pizza slice, the usable worn shirt. Possibly for emeralds and diamonds. Part of him wanted to scrub up a drunk or two, with a Brillo pad, like the zucchini pot. Something satisfying in that.

The man in the sweater had been white, clean, nonmenacing. Possibly European. Yet Harold, crossing Madison now, felt chilled by the thought of him. Under the chill was anger. That spoiled, arrogant face! That sandy hair! He hurried back to Janet's apartment building, walked briskly up the stairs to the third floor, let himself in. There in the living room stood the painting. He suddenly saw that

259

it could use a sort of rectangle of pale green, like a distant field of grass, right there. He picked up a brush, very happy to do so. Outside the window the sun was shining brightly. The workmen on the building across the street were busy. Harold was busy.

He worked for three solid hours and felt wonderful. It was good work, too, and the painting was coming along. At last.

For lunch he made himself a bacon-and-tomato sandwich on toast. It was simple midwestern fare, and he loved it.

When he had finished eating, he went back into the living room, sat in the black director's chair in front of the window, and looked at the painting by afternoon light. It looked good—just a tad spooky, the way he wanted it to be. It would be a good painting after all. It was really working. He decided to go see a movie.

The movie he wanted to see was called *Out of Luck*. It was a comedy from France, advertised as "a hilarious sex farce," with subtitles. It sounded fine for a sunny fall afternoon. He walked down Madison toward the theater.

There were an awful lot of youthful, well-dressed people on Madison Avenue. They all probably spoke French. He looked in the windows of places with names like Le Relais, La Bagagerie, Le Bijou. He would have given ten dollars to see a J. C. Penney's or a plain barber shop with a red-and-white barber's pole.

As he was crossing Park Avenue, trafic snarled as usual, there was suddenly the loud *harrumphing* of a pair of outrageously noisy motorcycles, and with a rush of hot air two black Hondas zoomed past him. From the back the riders appeared to be a man and a woman, although the sexual difference was hard to detect. Each wore a spherical helmet that reflected the sun; the man's helmet was red; the other, green. Science-fiction helmets, they hurt the eyes with reflected and dazzling sunlight. There was a smell of exhaust. Each of the riders, man and woman, was wearing a brown sleeveless sweater and blue jeans. Each wore Adidas over white socks. Their shirts were short-sleeved, blue. So had been the shirts of the man in the taxi and the man in line at Chemical Bank. Harold's stomach twisted. He wanted to scream.

The cyclists disappeared in traffic, darting into it with insouciance, tilting their black bikes first this way and then that, as though merely leaning their way through the congestion of taxis and limousines and sanitation trucks.

Maybe it was a fad in dress. Maybe coincidence. He had never noticed before how many people wore brown sleeveless sweaters. Who counted such things? And everyone wore jeans. He was wearing jeans himself.

The movie was at Fifty-seventh and Third. There was only a scattering of people in the theater, since it was the middle of the afternoon. The story was about a woman who was haunted by the gravelly voice of her dead lover—a younger man who had been killed in a motorcycle accident. She was a gorgeous woman and went through a sequence of affairs, breaking up with each new lover after the voice of her old, dead one pointed out their flaws to her, or distracted her while making love. It really was funny. Sometimes, though, it made Harold edgy when he thought of the young lover Janet had had before him, who had disappeared from her life in some way Harold did not know about. But several times he laughed loudly.

And then, toward the end of the movie, her lover reappeared, apparently not dead at all. It was on a quiet Paris street. She was out walking with an older man she had just slept with, going to buy some coffee, when a black Honda pulled up to the curb beside her. She stopped. The driver pulled off his helmet. Harold's heart almost stopped beating, and he stared crazily. There in front of him, on the Cinemascope movie screen, was the huge image of a youngish man with sandy hair, a brown sleeveless sweater, blue shirt, Adidas. The man smiled at the woman. She collapsed in a dead faint.

When the man on the motorcycle spoke, his voice was as it had been when it was haunting her: gravelly and bland. Harold wanted to throw something at the screen, wanted to scream at the image, "Get out of here, you arrogant fucker!" But he did nothing and said nothing. He stayed in his seat, waiting for the movie to end. It ended with the woman getting on the dead lover's motorcycle and riding off with him. He wouldn't tell her where he lived now. He was going to show her.

Harold watched the credits closely, wanting to find the actor who had played the old lover. His name in the film had been Paul. But no actor was listed for the name of Paul. The others were there, but not Paul. *What in God's name is happening?* Harold thought. He left the theater and, hardly daring to look around himself on the bright street, flagged down a cab and went home. Could a person hallucinate a character into a movie? Was the man at the bank in fact a French movie actor? Twelve years of drinking could mess up your brain chemistry. But he hadn't even had the D.T.'s. His New York psychiatrist had told him he tended to get badly regressed at times, but his sanity had never been in question.

In the apartment he was somehow able, astonishingly, to get back into the painting for a few hours. He made a few changes, making it spookier. *He* felt spookier now, and it came out onto the canvas. The painting was nearly done. When he stopped, it was just eight o'clock in the evening. The workmen across the street had finished their day, hours before, had packed up their tools, and had gone home to Queens or wherever. The building, as always, was unchanged; its doorways and windows gaped blankly. There was a pile of rubble by the plywood entry platform where there had always been a pile of rubble.

He went into the kitchen, ignored the veal stew Janet had made for him, and lit the oven. Then he took a Hungry Man chicken pie out of the freezer, ripped off the cardboard box, stabbed the frozen top crust a few times with her Sabatier, slipped it into the oven, and set the timer for forty-five minutes.

He went back into the living room, looked again at the painting. "Maybe I needed the shit scared out of me," he said aloud. But the thought of the man in the sweater chilled him. Harold went over to the hutch in the corner, opened its left door, and flipped on the little Sony TV inside. Then he walked across the big room to the dry sink and began rummaging for candy. He kept candy in various places.

He found a couple of pieces of butterscotch and began sucking on one of them. Back in the kitchen he opened the oven door a moment, enjoying the feel of hot air. His little Hungry Man pie sat inside, waiting for him.

There had been a man's voice on television for a minute or so, reciting some kind of disaster news. A California brush fire or something. There in the kitchen Harold began to realize that the voice was familiar, gravelly. It had a slight French accent. He rushed into the living room, still holding a potholder. On the TV screen was the man in the brown sweater, saying, "... from Pasadena, California, for NBC News." Then John Chancellor came on.

Harold threw the potholder at the TV screen. "You son of a bitch!" he shouted. "You ubiquitous son of a bitch!" Then he sank into the director's chair, on the edge of tears. His eyes burned.

When his pie was ready, he ate it as if it were cardboard, forcing himself to eat every bite. To keep his strength up, as his mother would have said, for the oncoming storm. For the oncoming storm.

He kept the TV off that evening and did not go out. He finished the painting by artificial light at three in the morning, took two Sominex tablets, and went to bed, frightened. He had wanted to call Janet but hadn't. That would have been chicken. He slept without dreaming for nine hours.

It was noon when he got up from the big platform bed and stumbled into the kitchen for breakfast. He drank a cup of cold zucchini while waiting for the coffee from yesterday to heat up. He felt okay, ready for the man in the sweater whenever he might strike. The coffee boiled over, spattering the white wall with brown tears. He reached to pull the big Chemex off the burner and scalded himself. "Shit!" he said and held his burned hand under cold tapwater for half a minute.

He walked into the living room and began looking at the painting in daylight. It was really very good. Just the right feeling, the right arrangement. Scary, too. He took it from the easel, set it against a wall. Then he thought better of that. The cats might get at it. He hadn't seen the cats for a while. He looked around him. No cats. He put the painting on top of the dry sink, out of harm's way. He would put out some cat food.

From outside came the sound of a motorcycle. Or of two motorcycles. He turned, looked out the window. There was dust where the motorcycles had just been, a light cloud of it settling. On the plywood platform at the entryway to the building being renovated stood two people in brown sleeveless sweaters, blue shirts, jeans. One was holding a clipboard, and they were talking. He could not hear their voices, even though the window was open. He walked slowly to the window, placed his hands on the ledge, stared down at them. He stared at the same sandy hair, the same face. Two schoolgirls in plaid skirts walked by, on their way to lunch. Behind them was a woman in a brown sleeveless sweater and blue jeans, with sandy hair. She had the same face as the man, only slightly feminine in the way the head set on the shoulders. And she walked like a woman. She walked by the two men, her twins, ignoring them.

Harold looked at his watch. Twelve-fifteen. His heart was pounding painfully. He went to the telephone and called his psychiatrist. It was lunch hour, and he might be able to reach him.

He did—for just a minute or two. Quickly he told him that he was beginning to see the same person everywhere. Even on TV and in the movies. Sometimes two or three at a time.

"What do you think, Harold?" he said to the doctor. The psychiatrist's name also was Harold.

"It would have to be a hallucination, wouldn't it? Or maybe coincidence."

"It's not coincidence. There've been seven of them, and they are identical, Doctor. *Identical.*" His voice, he realized, was not hysterical. It might become that way, he thought, if the doctor should say, "Interesting," as they do in the movies.

"I'm sorry that you have a hallucination," Harold the psychiatrist said. "I wish I could see you this afternoon, but I can't. In fact, I have to go now. I have a patient."

"Harold!" Harold said. "I've had a dozen sessions with you. Am I the type who hallucinates?"

"No, you aren't, Harold," the psychiatrist said. "You really don't seem to me to be like that at all. It's puzzling. Just don't drink."

"I won't, Harold," he said, and hung up.

What to do? he thought. *I can stay inside until Janet comes back. I don't have to go out for anything. Maybe it will stop on its own.*

And then he thought, *But so what? They can't hurt me. What if I see a whole bunch of them today? So what? I can ignore them.* He would get dressed and go out. What the hell. Confront the thing.

When he got outdoors, the two of them were gone from in front of the building. He looked to his right, over toward Madison. One of them was just crossing the street, walking lightly on the Adidas. There were ordinary men and women around him. Hell, *he* was ordinary enough. There were just too many of him. Like a clone. Two more crossed, a man and a woman. They were holding hands. Harold decided to walk over to Fifth Avenue.

Just before the corner of Fifth there was a wastebasket with a bum poking around in it. Harold had seen this bum before, had even given him a quarter once. Fellow alcoholic. There but for the grace of God, et cetera. He fished a quarter from his pocket and gave it to the bum. "Say," Harold said, on a wild impulse, "have you noticed something funny? People in brown sweaters and jeans?" He felt foolish asking. The bum was fragrant in the afternoon sun.

"Hell, yes, buddy," the bum said. "Kind of light brown hair? And tennis shoes? Hell, yes, they're all over the place." He shook his head dazedly. "Can't get no money out of 'em. Tried 'em six, eight times. You got another one of those quarters?"

Harold gave him a dollar. "Get yourself a drink," he said.

The bum widened his eyes and took the money silently. He turned to go.

"Hey!" Harold said, calling him back. "Have a drink for me, will you? I don't drink, myself." He held out another dollar.

"That's the ticket," the bum said, carefully, as if addressing a madman. He took the bill quickly, then turned toward Fifth Avenue. "Hey," he said, "there's one of 'em," and pointed. The man in the brown sleeveless sweater went by, jogging slowly on his Adidas. The bum jammed his two dollars into a pocket and moved on.

Well, the bum had been right. Don't let them interfere with business. But it wasn't hallucination—not unless he had hallucinated the bum and the conversation along with the bum. He checked his billfold and found the two dollars were indeed gone. Where would they have gone if he had made up the bum in his unconscious? He hadn't eaten them. If he had, the game was over anyway and he was really in a straitjacket somewhere, being fed intravenously, while somebody took notes. Well.

He turned at Fifth Avenue, toward the spire of the Empire State Building, and stopped cold. Most of the foot traffic on the avenue was moving uptown toward him, and every third or fourth one of them was the person in the brown sweater and the blue short-sleeved shirt. It was like an invasion from Mars. And he saw that some of the normal people—the people like himself—were staring at them from time to time. The brown-sweatered person was always calm, whistling softly sometimes, cool. The others looked flustered. Harold jammed his hands into his pockets. He felt suddenly cold. He began walking down Fifth Avenue.

He kept going for a few blocks, then on an impulse ran across the street to the Central Park side and climbed up on a park bench that faced the avenue and then from the bench onto the stone railing near the Sixtieth Street subway station. He looked downtown, up high now so that he could see. And the farther downtown he looked, the more he saw of an array of brown sweaters, light brown in the afternoon sunlight, with pale, sandy-haired heads above them. On a crazy impulse he looked down at his own clothes and was relieved to see that he was not himself wearing a brown sleeveless sweater and that his jeans were not the pale and faded kind that the person—that the multitude—was wearing.

He got down from the bench and headed across Grand Army Plaza, past people who were now about one half sandy-haired and sweatered and the other half just random people. He realized that the repeated person hadn't seemed to crowd the city any more than usual. They weren't *new*, then. If anything, they were replacing the others.

Abruptly he decided to go into the Plaza Hotel. There were two of them in the lobby, talking quietly with each other, in French. He walked past them toward the Oak Bar; he would get a Perrier in there.

In the bar, there were three of them sitting at the bar itself and two of them were at a table near the front. He seated himself at the bar. A man in a brown sweater turned from where he was washing glasses, wiped his hands on his jeans, came over, and said, "Yes, sir?" The voice was gravelly, with a slight French accent, and the face was blank.

"Perrier with lime," Harold said. When the man brought it, Harold said, "How long have you been tending bar here?"

"About twenty minutes," the man said and smiled.

"Where were you before?"

"Oh, here and there," the man said. "You know how it is."

Harold stared at him, feeling his own face getting

269

red. *"No, I don't know how it is!"* he said, in frustration.

The man started to whistle softly. He turned away.

Harold leaned over the bar and took him by the shoulder. The sweater was soft—probably cashmere. "Where do you come from? What are you doing?"

The man smiled coldly at him. "I come from the street. I'm tending bar here." He stood completely still, waiting for Harold to let go of him.

"Why are there so many of you?"

"There's only one of me," the man said.

"Only one?"

"Just one." He waited a moment. "I have to wait on that couple." He nodded his head slightly toward the end of the bar. A couple of them had come in, a male and a female as far as Harold could see in the somewhat dim light.

Harold let go of the man, got up, and went to a pay telephone on the wall. He dialed his psychiatrist. The phone rang twice, and then a male voice said, "Doctor Morse is not in this afternoon. May I take a message?" The voice was the gravelly voice. Harold hung up. He spun around and faced the bar. The man had just returned from serving drinks to the identical couple at the far end. "What in hell is your name?" he said wildly.

The man smiled. "That's for me to know and you to find out," he said.

Harold began to cry. "What's your goddamned *name?*" he said, sobbing. "My name's Harold. For Christ's sake, what's yours?"

Now that he was crying, the man looked sympathetic. He turned for a moment to the mirrored shelves behind him, took two unopened bottles of whiskey, and then set them on the bar in front of Harold. "Why don't you just take these, Harold?" he said pleasantly. "Take them home with you. It's only a few blocks from here."

"I'm an alcoholic," Harold replied, shocked.

"Who cares?" the man said. He got a bright-orange shopping bag from somewhere under the bar and put the bottles in it. "On the house," he said.

Harold stared at him. "What is your goddamned, fucking *name?*"

"For me to know," the man said softly. "For you to find out."

Harold took the shopping bag, pushed open the door, and went into the lobby. There was no doorman at the big doorway of the hotel, but the man in the sleeveless sweater stood there like a doorman. "Have a good day now, Harold," the man said as Harold went on his way.

Now there was no one else on the street but the man. Everywhere. And now they all looked at him in recognition, since he had given his name. Their smiles were cool, distant, patronizing. Some nodded at him slightly as he made his way slowly up the avenue toward Sixty-third; some ignored him. Several passed on motorcycles, wearing red helmets. A few waved coolly to him. One slowed his motorcycle down near the curb and said, "Hi, Harold," and then sped off. Harold closed his eyes.

He got home all right, and up the stairs. When he walked into the living room, he saw that the cats had knocked his new painting to the floor and had badly smeared a corner of it. Apparently one of them had rolled on it. The cats were nowhere in sight. He had not seen them since Janet had gone.

He did not care about the painting now. Not really. He knew what he was going to do. He could see in his mind the French movie, the man on the motorcycle.

In the closet where she kept her vacuum cleaner, Janet also kept a motorcycle helmet. A red one, way up on the top shelf, behind some boxes of candles and light bulbs. She had never spoken to him before about motorcycles; he had never asked her about the helmet. He hadn't thought about it since he first noticed it when he was unpacking months before and looking for a place to put his Samsonite suitcase.

He set the bag of bottles on the ledge by the window overlooking the building where men in brown sleeveless sweaters were now working. He opened one bottle with a practiced fingernail, steadily. The cork came out with a pop. He took a glass from the sideboard and poured it half full of whiskey. For a moment he stood there motionless, looking down at the building. The work, he saw without surprise, was getting done. There was glass in the window frames now; there had been none that morning. The plywood ramp had been replaced with marble steps. Abruptly he turned and called, "Kitty! Kitty!" toward the bedroom. There was silence. "Kitty! Kitty!" he called again. No cat appeared.

In the kitchen there was a red-legged stool by the telephone. Carrying his untasted glass of whiskey in one hand, he picked up the stool with the other and headed toward the closet at the back of the apartment. He set the whiskey on a shelf, set the stool in the closet doorway. He climbed up carefully. There was the motorcycle helmet, red, with a layer of dust on top. He pulled it down. There was something inside it. He reached in, still standing on the stool, and pulled out a brown sleeveless sweater. There were stains on the sweater. They looked like bloodstains. He looked inside the helmet. There were stains there, too. And there was a little blue band with letters on it. It read PAUL BENDEL—PARIS. Once in bed, Janet had called him Paul. *Oh, you son of a bitch!* he said.

Getting down from the stool, he thought, *For him to know. For me to find out.* He stopped only to pick up the drink and take it to the bathroom, where he poured it down the toilet. Then he went into the living room and looked out the window. The light was dimming; there was no one on Sixty-third Street. He pushed the window higher, leaned out. Looking to his right, he could see the intersection with Madison. He saw several of them crossing it. One looked his way and waved. He did not wave back. What he did was take the two bottles and drop them down to the street, where they shattered. He thought of a man's body, shattering, in a motorcycle wreck. In France? Certainly in France.

A group of four of them had turned the corner at Madison and were walking toward him. All of them had their hands in their pockets. Their heads were all inclined together, and they appeared to be having an intimate conversation. *Why whisper?* Harold thought. *I can't hear you anyway.*

He pulled himself up and sat on the window ledge, letting his legs hang over. He stared down at them and forced himself to say aloud, "Paul." They were directly below him now, huddled and whispering. They seemed not to have heard him.

He took a deep breath and said it louder, *"Paul."* And then he found somewhere the strength to shout it, in a loud, clear, steady voice. "Paul," he shouted. *"Paul Bendel."*

Then the four faces looked up, shocked. "You're Paul Bendel," he said. "Go back to your grave in France, Paul."

They stood transfixed. Harold looked over toward Madison. Two of them there had stopped in their tracks in the middle of the intersection.

The four faces below were now staring up at him in mute appeal, begging for silence. His voice spoke to this appeal with strength and clarity. "Paul Bendel," he said, *"you must go back to France."*

Abruptly all four of them averted their eyes from his and from one another's. Their bodies seemed to become slack. Then they began drifting apart, walking dispiritedly away from one another and from him.

The cats appeared sleepily from an open closet, waiting to be fed. He fed them.

He was redoing a smeared place on the painting when the telephone rang. It was Janet. She was clearly in a good mood, and she asked whether the zucchini soup had been all right.

"Fine," he said. "I had it cold."

She laughed. "I'm glad it wasn't too burned. How was the *jarret de veau?"*

Immediately, at the French, his stomach tightened. Despite the present clarity of his mind, he felt the familiar pain of the old petulance and jealousy. For a moment he hugged the pain to himself, then dismissed it with a sigh.

"It's in the oven right now," he said. "I'm having it for dinner."

EYES I DARE NOT MEET IN DREAMS

By Dan Simmons

Bremen left the hospital and his dying wife and drove east to the sea. The roads were thick with Philadelphians fleeing the city for the weekend, and Bremen had to concentrate on traffic, leaving only the most tenuous of touches in his wife's mind.

Gail was sleeping. Her dreams were fitful and drug-induced. She was seeking her mother through endlessly interlinked rooms filled with Victorian furniture. As Bremen crossed the pine barrens, the images of the dreams slid between the evening shadows of reality. Gail awoke just as Bremen was leaving the parkway. For a few seconds after she awoke the pain was not with her. She opened her eyes, and the evening sunlight falling across the blue blanket made her think—for only a moment—that it was morning on the farm. Her thoughts reached out for her husband just as the pain and dizziness struck behind her left eye. Bremen grimaced and dropped the coin he was handing to the toll-booth attendant. "What's the matter, buddy?" Bremen shook his head, fumbled out a dollar, and thrust it blindly at the man. Throwing his change in the Triumph's cluttered console, he concentrated on pushing the car's speed to its limit. Gail's pain faded, but her confusion washed over him in a wave of nausea.

She quickly gained control despite the shifting curtains of fear that fluttered at the tightly held mindshield. She subvocalized, concentrating on narrowing the spectrum to a simulacrum of her voice.

"Hi, Jerry."

"Hi, yourself, kiddo." He sent the thought as he turned onto the exit for Long Beach Island. He shared the visual—the startling green of grass and pine trees overlaid with the gold of August light, the sports car's shadow leaping along the curve of asphalt. Suddenly the unmistakable salt freshness of the Atlantic came to him, and he shared that with her also.

The entrance to the seaside community was disappointing: dilapidated seafood restaurants, overpriced cinderblock motels, endless marinas. But it was reassuring in its familiarity to both of them, and Bremen concentrated on seeing all of it. Gail began to relax and appreciate the ride. Her presence was so real that Bremen caught himself turning to speak aloud to her. The pang of regret and embarrassment was sent before he could stifle it.

The island was cluttered with families unpacking station wagons and carrying late dinners to the beach. Bremen drove north to Barnegat Light. He glanced to his right and caught a glimpse of some fishermen standing along the surf, their shadows intersecting the white lines of breakers.

Monet, thought Gail, and Bremen nodded, although he had actually been thinking of Euclid.

Always the mathematician, thought Gail, and then her voice faded as the pain rose. Half-formed sentences shredded like clouds in a gale.

Bremen left the Triumph parked near the lighthouse and walked through the low dunes to the beach. He threw down the tattered blanket that they had carried so many times to just this spot. There was a group of children running along the surf. A girl of about nine, all long white legs in a suit two years too small, pranced on the wet sand in an intricate, unconscious choreography with the sea.

The light was fading between the Venetian blinds. A nurse smelling of cigarettes and stale talcum powder came in to change the IV bottle and take a pulse. The intercom in the hall continued to make loud, imperative announcements, but it was difficult to understand them through the growing haze of pain. The new doctor arrived about ten o'clock, but Gail's attention was riveted on the nurse who carried the blessed needle. The cotton swab on her arm was a delightful preliminary to the promised surcease of pain behind her eye. The doctor was saying something.

"... your husband? I thought he would be staying the night."

"Right here, doctor," said Gail. She patted the blanket and the sand.

Bremen pulled on his nylon windbreaker against the chill of the night. The stars were occluded by a high cloud layer that allowed only a few to show through. Far out to sea, an improbably long oil tanker, its lights blazing, moved along the horizon. The windows of the beach homes behind Bremen cast yellow rectangles on the dunes.

The smell of steak being grilled came to him on the breeze. Bremen tried to remember whether he had eaten that day or not. He considered going back to the convenience store near the lighthouse to get a sandwich but remembered an old Payday candy bar in his jacket pocket and contented himself with chewing on the rock-hard wedge of peanuts.

Footsteps continued to echo in the hall. It sounded as if entire armies were on the march. The rush of footsteps, clatter of trays, and vague chatter of voices reminded Gail of lying in bed as a child and listening to her parents' parties downstairs.

Remember the party where we met? thought Bremen.

Chuck Gilpen had insisted that Bremen go along. Bremen had never had much use for parties. He was lousy at small talk, and the psychic tension and neurobabble always left him with a headache from maintaining his mindshield tightly for hours. Besides, it was his first week teaching graduate tensor calculus and he knew that he should be home boning up on basic principles. But he had gone. Gilpen's nagging and the fear of being labeled a social misfit in his new academic community had brought Bremen to the Drexel Hill townhouse. The music was palpable half a block away, and had he driven there by himself, he would have gone home then. He was just inside the door—someone had pressed a drink in his hand—when suddenly he sensed another mindshield quite near him. He had put out a gentle probe, and immediately the force of Gail's thoughts swept across him like a searchlight.

Both were stunned. Their first reaction had been to raise their mindshields and roll up like frightened armadillos. Each soon found that useless against the unconscious probes of the other. Neither had ever encountered another telepath of more than primitive, untapped ability. Each had assumed that he or she was a freak—unique and unassailable. Now they stood naked before each other in an empty place. Suddenly, almost without volition, they flooded each other's mind with a torrent of images, self-images, half-memories, secrets, sensations, preferences, perceptions, hidden fears, echoes, and feelings. Nothing was held back. Every petty cruelty committed, sexual shame experienced, and prejudice harbored poured out along with thoughts of past birthday parties, ex-lovers, parents, and an endless stream of trivia. Rarely had two people known each other as well after fifty years of marriage. A few minutes later they met for the first time.

The beacon from Barnegat Light passed over Bremen's head every twenty-four seconds. There were more lights burning out at sea now than along the dark line of beach. The wind came up after midnight, and Bremen wrapped the blanket around himself tightly. Gail had refused the needle when the nurse had last made her rounds, but her mindtouch was still clouded. Bremen forced the contact through sheer strength of will. Gail had always been afraid of the dark. Many had been the times during their six years of marriage that he had reached out in the night with his mind or arm to reassure her. Now she was the frightened little girl again, left alone upstairs in the big old house on Burlingame Avenue. There were things in the darkness beneath her bed.

Bremen reached through her confusion and pain and shared the sound of the sea with her. He told her stories about the antics of Gernisavien, their calico cat. He lay in the hollow of the sand to match his body with hers. Slowly she began to relax, to surrender her thoughts to his. She even managed to doze a few times, and her dreams were the movement of stars between clouds and the sharp smell of the Atlantic. Bremen described the week's work at the farm—the subtle beauty of his Fourier equations across the chalkboard in his study and the sunlit satisfaction of planting a peach tree by the front drive. He shared memories of their ski trip to Aspen and the sudden shock of a searchlight reaching in to the beach from an unseen ship out at sea. He shared what little poetry he had memorized, but the words kept sliding into images and feelings.

The night drew on, and Bremen shared the cold clarity of it with his wife, adding to each image the warm overlay of his love. He shared trivia and hopes for the future. From seventy-five miles away he reached out and touched her hand with his. When he drifted off to sleep for only a few minutes, he sent her his dreams.

Gail died just before the false light of dawn touched the sky.

The head of the mathematics department at Haverford urged Bremen to take a leave or a full sabbatical if he needed it. Bremen thanked him and resigned.

Dorothy Parks in the psychology department spent

a long evening explaining the mechanics of grief to Bremen. "You have to understand, Jeremy," she said, "that moving is a common mistake made by people who have just suffered a serious loss. You may think that a new environment will help you forget, but it just postpones the inevitable confrontation with grief."

Bremen listened attentively and eventually nodded his agreement. The next day he put the farm up for sale, sold the Triumph to his mechanic on Conestoga Road, and took the bus to the airport. Once there, he went to the United Airlines counter and bought a ticket for the next departing flight.

For a year Bremen worked in central Florida, loading produce at a shipping center near Tampa. The next year Bremen did not work at all. He fished his way north from the Everglades to the Chattooga River in northern Georgia. In March he was arrested as a vagrant in Charleston, South Carolina. In May he spent two weeks in Washington, during which he left his room only to go to liquor stores and the Congressional Library. He was robbed and badly beaten outside of the Baltimore bus station at 2 A.M. on a June night. Leaving the hospital the next day, he returned to the bus station and headed north to visit his sister in New York. His sister and her husband insisted that he stay several weeks, but he left early on the third morning, propping a note up against the salt shaker on the kitchen table. In Philadelphia he sat in Penn Station and read the help-wanted ads. His progress was as predictable as the elegant, ellipsoid mathematics of a yo-yo's path.

Robby was sixteen, weighed one hundred seventy-five pounds, and had been blind, deaf, and retarded since birth. His mother's drug addiction during pregnancy and a placental malfunction had shut off Robby's senses as surely as a sinking ship condemns compartment after compartment to the sea by the shutting of watertight doors.

Robby's eyes were the sunken, darkened caverns of the irrevocably blind. The pupils, barely visible under drooping, mismatched lids, tracked separately in random movements. The boy's lips were loose and blubbery, his teeth gapped and carious. At sixteen, he already had the dark down of a mustache on his upper lip. His black hair stood out in violent tufts, and his eyebrows met above the bridge of his broad nose.

The child's obese body was balanced precariously on grub-white, emaciated legs. Robby had learned how to walk at age eleven but still would stagger only a few paces before toppling over. He moved in a series of pigeon-toed lurches, pudgy arms pulled as tight as broken wings, wrists cocked at an improbable angle, fingers separate and extended. Like so many of the retarded blind, his favorite motion was a perpetual rocking with his hand fanning above his sunken eyes as if to cast shadows into the pit of darkness.

He did not speak. His only sounds were occasional, meaningless giggles and a rare squeal of protest, which sounded like nothing so much as an operatic falsetto.

Robby had been coming to the Chelton Day School for the Blind for six years. His life before that was unknown. He had been discovered by a social worker visiting Robby's mother in connection with a court-ordered methadone-treatment program. The door to the apartment had been left open, and the social worker heard noises. The boy had been sealed into the bathroom by the nailing of a piece of plywood over the bottom half of the door. There were wet papers on the tile floor, but Robby was naked and smeared with his own excrement. A tap had been left on, and water filled the room to the depth of an inch or two. The boy was rolling fitfully in the mess and making mewling noises.

Robby was hospitalized for four months, spent five weeks in the county home, and was then returned to the custody of his mother. In accordance with further court orders, he was dutifully bused to Chelton Day School for five hours of treatment a day, six days a week. He made the daily trip in darkness and silence.

Robby's future was as flat and featureless as a line extending nowhere, holding no hope of intersection.

"Shit, Jer, you're going to have to watch after the kid tomorrow."

"Why me?"

"Because he won't go into the goddamn pool, that's why. You saw him today. Smitty just lowered his legs into the water, and the kid started swinging and screaming. Sounded like a bunch of cats had started up. Dr. Whilden says he stays back tomorrow. She says that the van is too hot for him to stay in. Just keep him company in the room till Jan McLellan's regular aide gets back from vacation."

"Great," said Bremen. He pulled his sweat-plastered shirt away from his skin. He had been hired to drive the school van, and now he was helping to feed, dress, and babysit the poor bastards. "Great. That's just great, Bill. What am I supposed to do with him for an hour and a half while you guys are at the pool?"

"Watch him. Try to get him to work on the zipper book. You ever see that page in there with the bra stuff—the eyes and hooks? Let him work on that. I useta practice on that with my eyes shut."

"Great," said Bremen. He closed his eyes against the glare of the sun.

Bremen sat on the front stoop and poured the last of the scotch into his glass. It was long past midnight, but the narrow street teemed with children playing. Two black teen-agers were playing the dozens while their friends urged them on. A group of little girls jumped double Dutch under the street-lamp. Insects milled in the light and seemed to dance to the girls' singing. Adults sat on the steps of identical rowhouses and watched one another dully. No one moved much. It was very hot.

It's time to move on.

Bremen knew that he had stayed too long. Seven weeks working at the day school had been too much. He was getting curious. And he was beginning to ask questions about the kids.

Boston, perhaps. Farther north. Maine.

Asking questions and getting answers. Jan McLellan had told him about Robby. She had told him about the bruises on Robby's body, about the broken arm two years before. She told him about the teddy bear that a candy striper had given the blind boy. It had been the first positive stimulus to evoke an emotion from Robby. He had kept the bear in his arms for weeks. Refused to go to X-ray without it. Then, a few days after his return home, Robby got into the van one morning, screaming and whining in his weird way. No teddy bear. Dr. Whilden called his mother only to be told that the God-damned toy was lost. "God-damned toy" were the mother's words, according to Jan McLellan. No other teddy bear would do. Robby carried on for three weeks.

So what? What can I do?

Bremen knew what he could do. He had known for weeks. He shook his head and took another drink, adding to the already thickened mindshield that separated him from the senseless, pain-giving world.

Hell, it'd be better for Robby if I didn't try it.

A breeze came up. Bremen could hear the screams from a lot down the street where two allied gangs played a fierce game of pick-up ball. Curtains billowed out open windows. Somewhere a siren sounded, faded. The breeze lifted papers from the gutter and ruffled the dresses of the girls jumping rope.

Bremen tried to imagine a lifetime with no sight, no sound.

Fuck it! He picked up the empty bottle and went upstairs despondently.

The van pulled up the circular drive of the day school, and Bremen helped unload the children with a slow care born of practice, affection, and a throbbing headache.

Scotty emerged, smiling, hands extended to the unseen adult he trusted to be waiting. Tommy Pierson lurched out with knees together and hands pulled up to his chest. Bremen had to catch him or the frail boy would have fallen face first into the pavement. Teresa jumped down with her usual gleeful cries, imparting inexact but slobberingly enthusiastic kisses on everyone who touched her.

Robby remained seated after the others had exited. It took both Bremen and Smitty to get the boy out of the van. Robby did not resist; he was simply a mass of pliable but unresponsive fat. The boy's head tilted back in a disturbing way. His tongue lolled first from one corner of the slack mouth and then from the other. The short, pigeon-toed steps had to be coaxed out of him one at a time. Only the familiarity of the short walk to the classroom kept Robby moving at all.

The morning seemed to last forever. It rained before lunch, and for a while it looked as if the swimming would be canceled. Then the sun came out and illuminated the flowerbeds on the front lawn. Bremen watched sunlight dance off the moistened petals of Turk's prize roses and listened to the roar of the lawnmower. He realized that it was going to happen.

After lunch he helped them prepare for departure. The boys needed help getting into their suits, and it saddened Bremen to see pubic hair and a man's penis on the body of someone with a seven-year-old's mind. Tommy would always start masturbating idly until Bremen touched his arm and helped him with the elastic of the suit.

Then they were gone, and the hall, which had been filled with squealing children and laughing adults, was silent. Bremen watched the blue-and-white van disappear slowly down the drive. Then he turned back to the classroom.

Robby showed no awareness that Bremen had entered the room. The boy looked absurd dressed in a striped, green top and orange shorts that were too tight to button. Bremen thought of a broken, bronze Buddha he had seen once near Osaka. What if this child harbored some deep wisdom born of his long seclusion from the world?

Robby stirred, farted loudly, and resumed his slumped position.

Bremen sighed and pulled up a chair. It was too small. His knees stuck into the air, and he felt ridiculous. He grinned to himself. He would leave that night. Take a bus north. Hitchhike. It would be cooler in the country.

This would not take long. He need not even establish full contact. A one-way mindtouch. It was possible. A few minutes. He could look out the window for Robby, look at a picture book, perhaps put a record on and share the music. What would the boy make of these new impressions? A gift before leaving. Anonymous. Share nothing else. Better not to send any images for Robby, either. All right.

Bremen lowered his mindshield. Immediately he flinched and raised it again. It had been a long time since he had allowed himself to be so vulnerable. The thick, woolly blanket of the mindshield, thickened even further by alcohol, had become natural to him. The sudden surge of background babble—he thought of it as white noise—was abrasive. It was like coming into a glaringly bright room after spending months in a cave. He directed his attention to Robby and lowered his barriers again. He tuned out the neurobabble and looked deeply into Robby's mind.

Nothing.

For a confused second Bremen thought that he had lost the focus of his power. Then he concentrated and was able to pick out the dull, sexual broodings of Turk out in the garden and the preoccupied fragments of Dr. Whilden's thoughts as she settled herself into her Mercedes and checked her stockings for runs. The receptionist was reading a novel—*The Plague Dogs*. Bremen read a few lines with her. It frustrated him that her eyes scanned so slowly. His mouth filled with the syrupy taste of her cherry coughdrop.

Bremen stared intensely at Robby. The boy was breathing asthmatically. His tongue was visible and heavily coated. Stray bits of food remained on his lips and cheeks. Bremen narrowed his probe, strengthened it, focused it like a beam of coherent light.

Nothing.

No. Wait. There was—what?—an *absence* of something. There was a hole in the field of mind-babble where Robby's thoughts should have been. Bremen realized that he was confronting the strongest mindshield he had ever encountered. Even Gail had not been able to concentrate a barrier of that incredible tightness. For a second Bremen was deeply impressed, even shaken, and then he realized the cause of it. Robby's mind was damaged. Entire segments were probably inactive. With so few senses to rely on and such limited awareness, it was little wonder that the boy's consciousness—what there was of it—had turned inward. What at first seemed to

Bremen to be a powerful mindshield was nothing more than a tight ball of introspection going beyond autism. Robby was truly alone.

Bremen was still shaken enough to pause a minute and take a few deep breaths. When he resumed, it was with even more care, feeling along the negative boundaries of the mindshield like a man groping along a rough wall in the dark. Somewhere there had to be an opening.

There was. Not an opening so much as a soft spot—a resilience set amidst the stone. Bremen half-perceived the flutter of underlying thoughts, much as a pedestrian senses the movement of trains in a subway under the pavement. He concentrated on building the strength of the probe until he felt his shirt beginning to soak with sweat. His vision and hearing were beginning to dim in the singleminded exertion of his effort. No matter. Once initial contact was made, he would relax and slowly open the channels of sight and sound.

He felt the shield give a bit, still elastic but sinking slightly under his unrelenting pressure. He concentrated until the veins stood out in his temples. Unknown to himself, he was grimacing, neck muscles knotting with the strain. The shield bent, Bremen's probe was a solid ram battering a tight, gelatinous doorway. It bent further. He concentrated with enough force to move objects, to pulverize bricks, to halt birds in their flight.

The shield continued to bend. Bremen leaned forward as into a strong wind. There was only the concentrated force of his will. Suddenly there was a ripping, a rush of warmth, a falling forward. Bremen lost his balance, flailed his arms, opened his mouth to yell.

His mouth was gone.

He was falling. Tumbling. He had a distant, confused glimpse of his own body writhing in the grip of an epileptic seizure. Then he was falling again. Falling into silence. Falling into nothing.

Nothing.

Bremen was inside. Beyond. Was diving through layers of slow thermals. Colorless pinwheels tumbled in three dimensions. Spheres of black collapsed outward. Blinded him. There were waterfalls of touch, rivulets of scent, a thin line of balance blowing in a silent wind.

Supported by a thousand hands—touching, exploring, fingers in the mouth, palms along the chest, sliding along the belly, cupping the penis, moving on.

He was buried. He was underwater. Rising in the blackness. But he could not breathe. His arms began to move. Palms flailed against the viscous current. Up. He was buried in sand. He flailed and kicked. He moved upwards, pulled on by a vacuum that gripped his head in a vise. The substance shifted. Compacted, pressed in by a thousand unseen hands, he was propelled through the constricting aperture. His head broke the surface. He opened his mouth to scream, and the air rushed into his chest like water filling a drowning man. The scream went on and on.

ME!

Bremen awoke on a broad plain. There was no sky. Pale, peach-colored light diffused everything. The ground was hard and scaled into separate orange segments, which receded to infinity. There was no horizon. The land was cracked and serrated like a floodplain during a drought. Above him were levels of peachlit crystal. Bremen felt that it was like being in the basement of a clear plastic skyscraper. An empty one. He lay on his back and looked up through endless stories of crystallized emptiness.

He sat up. His skin felt as if it had been toweled with sandpaper. He was naked. He rubbed his hand across his stomach, touched his pubic hair, found the scar on his knee from the motorcycle accident when he was seventeen. A wave of dizziness rolled through him when he stood upright.

He walked. His bare feet found the smooth plates warm. He had no direction and no destination. Once he had walked a mile on the Bonneville Salt Flats just before sunset. It was like that. Bremen walked. *Step on a crack, break your mother's back.*

When he finally stopped, it was in a place no different from any other. His head hurt. He lay back and imagined himself as a bottom-dwelling sea creature looking up through layers of shifting currents. The peach-colored light bathed him in warmth. His body was radiant. He shut his eyes against the light and slept.

He sat up suddenly, with nostrils flaring, ears actually twitching with the strain of trying to pinpoint a half-heard sound. Darkness was total.

Something was moving in the night.

Bremen crouched in the blackness and tried to filter out the sound of his own ragged breathing. His glandular system reverted to programming a million years old. His fists clenched, his eyes rolled uselessly in their sockets, and his heart raced.

Something was moving in the night.

He felt it nearby. He felt the power of it. It was

huge, and it had no trouble finding its way in the darkness. The thing was near him, above him. Bremen felt the force of its blind gaze. He kneeled on the cold ground and hugged himself into a ball.

Something touched him.

Bremen fought down the impulse to scream. He was caught in a giant's hand—something rough and huge and not a hand at all. It lifted him. Bremen felt the power of it through the pressure, the pain in his ribs. The thing could crush him easily. Again he felt the sense of being viewed, inspected, weighed on some unseen balance. He had the naked, helpless, but somehow reassuring feeling one has while lying on the X-ray table, knowing that invisible beams are passing through you, searching for any malignancy, probing.

Something set him down.

Bremen heard no sound but sensed great footsteps receding. A weight lifted from him. He sobbed. Eventually he uncurled and stood up. He called into the blackness, but the sound of his voice was tiny and lost and he was not even sure whether he had heard it at all.

The sun rose. Bremen's eyes fluttered open, stared into the distant brilliance, and then closed again before the fact registered fully in his mind. *The sun rose.*

He was sitting on grass. A prairie of soft, knee-high grass went off to the horizon in all directions. Bremen pulled a strand, stripped it, and sucked on the sweet marrow. It reminded him of childhood afternoons. He began walking.

The breeze was warm. It stirred the grass and set up a soft sighing, which helped to ease the headache that still throbbed behind his eyes. The walking pleased him. He contented himself with the feel of grass bending under his bare feet and the play of sunlight and wind on his body.

By early afternoon he realized that he was walking toward a smudge on the horizon. By late afternoon the smudge had resolved itself into a line of trees. Shortly before sunset he entered the edge of the forest. The trees were the stately elms and oaks of his Pennsylvania boyhood. Bremen's long shadow moved ahead of him as he moved deeper into the forest.

For the first time he felt fatigue and thirst begin to work on him. His tongue was heavy, swollen with dryness. He moved leadenly through the lengthening shadows, occasionally checking the visible patches of sky for any sign of clouds. It was while he was looking up that he almost stumbled into the pond. Inside a protective ring of weeds and reeds lay the circle of water. A heavily laden cherry tree sent roots down the bank. Bremen took the last few steps forward, expecting the water to disappear as he threw himself into it.

It was waist-deep and cold as ice.

It was just after sunrise that she came. He spotted the movement immediately on awakening. Not believing, he stood still, just another shadow in the shade of the trees. She moved hesitantly with the tentative step of the meek or the barefoot. The tasseled sawgrass brushed at her thighs. Bremen watched with a clarity amplified by the rich, horizontal sweeps of morning light. Her body seemed to glow. Her breasts, the left ever so slightly fuller than the right, bobbed gently with each high step. Her black hair was cut short.

She paused in the light. Moved forward again. Bremen's eyes dropped to her strong thighs, and he watched as her legs parted and closed with the heart-stopping intimacy of the unobserved. She was much closer now, and Bremen could make out the delicate shadows along her fine ribcage, the pale, pink circles of areolae, and the spreading bruise along the inside of one arm.

Bremen stepped out into the light. She stopped, arms rising across her upper body in a second's instinctive movement, then moved toward him quickly. She opened her arms to him. He was filled with the clean scent of her hair. Skin slid across skin. Their hands moved across muscle, skin, the familiar terrain of vertebrae. Both were sobbing, speaking incoherently. Bremen dropped to one knee and buried his face between her breasts. She bent slightly and cradled his head with her fingers. Not for a second did they relax the pressure binding them together.

"Why did you leave me?" he muttered against her skin. "Why did you go away?"

Gail said nothing. Her tears fell into his hair and her hands tightened against his back. Wordlessly she kneeled with him in the high grass.

Together they passed out of the forest just as the morning mists were burning away. In the early light the grass-covered hills gave the impression of being part of a tanned, velvety human torso, which they could reach out and touch.

They spoke, softly, occasionally intertwining

fingers. Each had discovered that to attempt tele-
pathic contact meant inviting the blinding headaches
that had plagued both of them at first. So they
talked. And they touched. And twice before the day
was over, they made love in the high, soft grass with
only the golden eye of the sun looking down on them.

Late in the afternoon they crossed a rise and looked
past a small orchard at a vertical glare of white.

"It's the farm!" cried Gail, with wonder in her
voice. "How can that be?"

Bremen felt no surprise. His equilibrium remained
as they approached the tall old building. The saggy
barn they had used as a garage was also there. The
driveway still needed new gravel, but now it went
nowhere, for there was no highway at the end of it. A
hundred yards of rusted wire fence that used to
border the road now terminated in the high grass.

Gail stepped up on the front porch and peered in
the window. Bremen felt like a trespasser or a
weekend house browser who had found a home that
might or might not still be lived in. Habit brought
them around to the back door. Gail gingerly opened
the outer screen door and jumped a bit as the hinge
squeaked.

"Sorry," Bremen said. "I know I promised to oil
that."

It was cool inside and dark. The rooms were as they
had left them. Bremen poked his head into his study
long enough to see his papers still lying on the oak
desk and a long-forgotten transform still chalked on
the blackboard. Upstairs, afternoon sunlight was falling from the skylight he had wrestled to install that
distant September. Gail went from room to room,
making small noises of appreciation, more often just

touching things gently. The bedroom was as orderly as ever, with the blue blanket pulled tight and tucked under the mattress and her grandmother's patchwork quilt folded across the foot of the bed.

They fell asleep on the cool sheets. Occasionally a wisp of a breeze would billow the curtains. Gail mumbled in her sleep, reaching out to touch him frequently. When Bremen awoke, it was almost dark, that late, lingering twilight of early summer.

There was a sound downstairs.

He lay without moving for a long while. The air was thick and still, the silence tangible. Then came another sound.

Bremen left the bed without waking Gail. She was curled on her side with one hand lifted to her cheek, the pillow moist against her lips. Bremen walked barefoot down the wooden stairs. He slipped into his study and carefully opened the lower-right-hand drawer. It was there under the empty folders he had laid atop it. He removed the rags from the drawer.

The thirty-eight Smith and Wesson smelled of oil and looked as new as the day his brother-in-law had given it to him. Bremen checked the chambers. The bullets lay fat and heavy, like eggs in a nest. The roughened grip was firm in his hand, the metal cool. Bremen smiled ruefully at the absurdity of what he was doing, but kept the weapon in his grip when the kitchen screen door slammed again.

He made no sound as he stepped from the hallway to the kitchen door. It was very dim, but his eyes had adapted. From where he stood he could make out the pale white phantom of the refrigerator. Its recycling pump chunked on while he stood there. Holding the revolver down at his side, Bremen stepped onto the cool tile of the kitchen floor.

The movement startled him, and the gun rose an inch or so before he relaxed. Gernisavien, the tough-minded little calico, crossed the floor to brush against his legs, paced back to the refrigerator, looked up at him meaningfully, then crossed back to brush against him. Bremen kneeled to rub her neck absently. The pistol looked idiotic in his clenched hand. He loosened his grip.

The moon was rising by the time they had a late dinner. The steaks had come from the freezer in the basement, the ice-cold beers from the refrigerator, and there had been several bags of charcoal left in the garage. They sat out back near the old pump while the steaks sizzled on the grill. Gernisavien had been well fed earlier but crouched expectantly at the foot of one of the big, old wooden lawn chairs.

Both of them had slipped into clothes—Bremen into his favorite pair of cotton slacks and his light blue workshirt and Gail into the loose, white cotton dress she often wore on trips. The sounds were the same they had heard from this backyard so many times before: crickets, night birds from the orchard, the variations of frog sounds from the distant stream, an occasional flutter of sparrows in the outbuildings.

Bremen served the steaks on paper plates. Their knives made criss-cross patterns on the white. They had just the steaks and a simple salad from the garden, fresh radishes and onions on the side.

Even with the three-quarter moon rising, the stars were incredibly clear. Bremen remembered the night they had lain out in the hammock and waited for *Skylab* to float across the sky like a windblown ember. He realized that the stars were even clearer tonight because there were no reflected lights from Philadelphia or the tollway to dim their glory.

Gail sat back before the meal was finished. *Where are we, Jerry?* The mindtouch was gentle. It did not bring on the blinding headaches.

Bremen took a sip of Budweiser. "What's wrong with just being home, kiddo?"

There's nothing wrong with being home. But where are we?

Bremen concentrated on turning a radish in his fingers. It had tasted salty, sharp, and cool.

What is this place? Gail looked toward the dark line of trees at the edge of the orchard. Fireflies winked against the blackness.

Gail, what is the last thing you can remember?

"I remember dying." The words hit Bremen squarely in the solar plexus. For a moment he could not speak or frame his thoughts.

Gail went on. "We've never believed in an after-life, Jerry." *Hypocritical fundamentalist parents. Mother's drunken sessions of weeping over the Bible.* "I mean . . . I don't . . . How can we be . . ."

"No," said Bremen, putting his dish on the arm of the chair and leaning forward. "There may be an explanation."

Where to begin? The lost years, Florida, the hot streets of the city, the day school for retarded blind children. Gail's eyes widened as she looked directly at this period of his life. She sensed his mindshield, but did not press to see the things he withheld. *Robby. A moment's contact. Perhaps playing a record. Falling.*

He paused to take a long swallow of beer. Insects chorused. The house glowed pale in the moonlight.

Where are we, Jerry?

"What do you remember about awakening here, Gail?"

They had already shared images, but trying to put them into words sharpened the memories. "Darkness," she said. "Then a soft light. Rocking. *Being rocked. Holding and being held.* Walking. Finding you."

Bremen nodded. He lifted the last piece of steak and savored the burnt charcoal taste of it. *It's obvious we're with Robby.* He shared images for which there were no adequate words. Waterfalls of touch. Entire landscapes of scent. A movement of power in the dark.

With Robby, Gail's thought echoed.????????? *In his mind.* "How?"

The cat had jumped into his lap. He stroked it idly and set it down. Gernisavien immediately raised her tail and turned her back on him. "You've read a lot of stories about telepaths. Have you ever read a completely satisfying explanation of how telepathy works? Why some people have it and others don't? Why some people's thoughts are loud as bullhorns and others' almost imperceptible?"

Gail paused to think. The cat allowed herself to be rubbed behind the ears. "Well, there was a really good book—no, that only came close to describing what it *felt* like. No. They usually describe it as some sort of radio or TV broadcast. *You* know that, Jerry. We've talked about it enough."

"Yeah," Bremen said. Despite himself he was already trying to describe it to Gail. His mindtouch interfered with the words. Images cascaded like printouts from an overworked terminal. Endless

Schrödinger curves, their plots speaking in a language purer than speech. The collapse of probability curves in binomial progression.

"Talk," Gail said. He marveled that after all the years of sharing his thoughts she still did not always see through his eyes.

"Do you remember my last grant project?" he asked.

"The wavefront stuff," she said.

"Yeah. Do you remember what it was about?"

"Holograms. You showed me Goldmann's work at the university," she said. She seemed a soft, white blur in the dim light. "I didn't understand most of it, and I got sick shortly after that."

"It was based on holographic research," Bremen interrupted quickly, "but Goldmann's research group was working up an analog of human consciousness . . . of thought."

"What does that have to do with . . . with *this?*" Gail asked. Her hand made a graceful movement that encompassed the yard, the night, and the bright bowl of stars above them.

"It might help," Bremen said. "The old theories of mental activity didn't explain things like stroke effects, generalized learning, and memory function, not to mention the act of thinking itself."

"And Goldmann's theory does?"

"It's not really a theory yet. Gail. It was a new approach, using both recent work with holograms and a line of analysis developed in the Thirties by a Russian mathematician. That's where I was called in. It was pretty simple, really. Goldmann's group was doing all sorts of complicated EEG studies and scans. I'd take their data, do a Fourier analysis of them, and then plug it all into various modifications of Schrödinger's wave equation to see whether it worked as a standing wave.''

"Jerry, I don't see how this helps."

"God damn it, Gail, it *did* work. Human thought *can* be described as a standing wavefront. Sort of a superhologram. Or, maybe more precisely, a hologram containing a few million smaller holograms.''

Gail was leaning forward. Even in the darkness Breman could make out the frown lines of attention that appeared whenever he spoke to her of his work. Her voice came very softly. "Where does that leave the mind, Jerry . . . the brain?''

It was his turn to frown slightly. "I guess the best answer is that the Greeks and the religious nuts were right to separate the two," he said. "The brain could be viewed as kind of a . . . well, electrochemical generator and interferometer all in one. But the mind . . . ah, the *mind* is something a lot more beautiful than that lump of gray matter.'' He was thinking in terms of equations, sine waves dancing to Schrödinger's elegant tune.

"So there *is* a soul that can survive death?'' Gail asked. Her voice had taken on the slightly defensive, slightly querulous tone that always entered in when she discussed religious ideas.

"Hell, no," said Bremen. He was a little irritated at having to think in words once again. "If Goldmann was right and the personality is a complex wavefront, sort of a series of low-energy holograms interpreting reality, then the personality certainly couldn't survive brain death. The template would be destroyed as well as the holographic generator.''

"So where does that leave us?'' Gail's voice was almost inaudible.

Bremen leaned forward and took her hand. It was cold.

"Don't you see why I got interested in this whole line of research? I thought it might offer a way of describing our . . . uh . . . ability."

Gail moved over and sat next to him in the broad, wooden chair. His arm went around her, and he could feel the cool skin of her upper arm. Suddenly a meteorite lanced from the zenith to the south, leaving the briefest of retinal echoes.

"And?" Gail's voice was very soft.

"It's simple enough," said Bremen. "When you visualize human thought as a series of standing wavefronts creating interference patterns that can be stored and propagated in holographic analogs, it begins to make sense."

"Uh-huh."

"It *does*. It means that for some reason our minds are resonant not only to wave patterns that we initiate but to transforms that others generate."

"Yes," said Gail, excited now, gripping his hand tightly. "Remember when we shared impressions of the talent just after we met? We both decided that it would be impossible to explain mindtouch to anyone who hadn't experienced it. It would be like describing colors to a blind person . . ." She halted and looked around her.

"Okay," said Bremen. "Robby. When I contacted him, I tapped into a closed system. The poor kid had almost no data to use in constructing a model of the real world. What little information he did have was mostly painful. So for sixteen years he had happily gone about building his own universe. My mistake was in underestimating, hell, never even *thinking* about, the power he might have in that world. He grabbed me, Gail. And with me, you.''

The wind came up a bit and moved the leaves of the orchard. The soft rustling had a sad, end-of-summer sound to it.

"All right," she said after a while, "that explains how *you* got here. How about me? Am I a figment of your imagination, Jerry?

Bremen felt her shiver. Her skin was like ice. He took her hand and roughly rubbed some warmth back into it. "Come on, Gail, *think*. You weren't just a memory to me. For over six years we were essentially one person with two bodies. That's why when . . . that's why I went a little crazy, tried to shut my mind down completely for a couple of years. You *were* in my mind. But my ego sense, or whatever the hell keeps us sane and separate from the babble of all those minds, kept telling me that it was only the *memory* of you. You were a figment of my imagination . . . the way we all are. Jesus, we were both dead until a blind, deaf, retarded kid, a goddamn vegetable, ripped us out of one world and offered us another one in its place.''

They sat for a minute. It was Gail who broke the silence. "But how can it seem so real?"

Bremen stirred and accidentally knocked his paper plate off the arm of the chair. Gernisavien jumped to one side and stared reproachfully at them. Gail nudged the cat's fur with the toe of her sandal. Bremen squeezed his beer can until it dented in, popped back out.

"You remember Chuck Gilpen, the guy who dragged me to that party in Drexel Hill. The last I heard he was working with the Fundamental Physics

Group out at the Lawrence Berkeley Labs.''

"So?"

"So for the past few years they've been hunting down all those smaller and smaller particles to get a hook on what's real. And when they get a glimpse of reality on its most basic and pervasive level, you know what they get?" Bremen took one last swig from the beer can. "They get a series of equations that show standing wavefronts, not too different from the squiggles and jiggles Goldmann used to send me."

Gail took a deep breath, let it out. Her question was almost lost as the wind rose again and stirred the tree branches. "Where is Robby? When do we see his world?"

"I don't know," Bremen replied. He was frowning without knowing it. "He seems to be allowing us to define what should be real. Don't ask me why. Maybe he's enjoying a peek at a new universe. Maybe he can't do anything about it."

They sat still for a few more minutes. Gernisavien brushed up against them, irritated that they insisted on sitting out in the cold and dark. Bremen kept his mindshield raised sufficiently to keep from sharing the information that his sister had written a year ago to say that the little calico had been run over and killed in New York. Or that a family of Vietnamese had bought the farmhouse and had already added new rooms. Or that he had carried the thirty-eight police special around for two years, waiting to use it on himself.

"What do we do now, Jerry?"

We go to bed. Bremen took her hand and led her into their home.

* * *

Bremen dreamed of fingernails across velvet, cold tile along one cheek, and wool blankets against sunburned skin. He watched with growing curiosity as two people made love on a golden hillside. He floated through a white room where white figures moved in a silence broken only by the heartbeat of a machine. He was swimming and could feel the tug of inexorable planetary forces in the pull of the riptide. He was just able to resist the deadly current by using all of his energy, but he could feel himself tiring, could feel the tide pulling him out to deeper water. Just as the waved closed over him he vented a final shout of despair and loss.

He cried out his own name.

He awoke with the shout still echoing in his mind. The details of the dream fractured and fled before he could grasp them. He sat up quickly in bed. Gail was gone.

He had taken two steps toward the stairway before he heard her voice calling to him from the side yard. He returned to the window.

She was dressed in a blue sundress and was waving her arms at him. By the time he was downstairs she had thrown half a dozen items into the picnic basket and was boiling water to make iced tea.

"Come on, sleepyhead. I have a surprise for you!"

"I'm not sure we need any more surprises," Bremen mumbled.

"*This* one we do," she said, and she was upstairs, humming and thrashing around in the closet.

She led them, Gernisavien following reluctantly, to a trail that led off in the same general direction as the highway that had once been in front of the house. It led up through pasture land to the east and over the rise. They carried the picnic basket between them. Bremen repeatedly asking for clues, Gail repeatedly denying him any.

They crossed the rise and looked down to where the path ended. Bremen dropped the basket into the grass. In the valley where the Pennsylvania Turnpike once had been was an ocean.

"Holy shit!" Bremen exclaimed softly.

It was not the Atlantic. At least not the New Jersey Atlantic that Bremen knew. The seacoast looked more like the area near Mendocino where he had taken Gail on their honeymoon. Far to the north and south stretched broad beaches and high cliffs. Tall breakers broke against black rock and white sand. Far out to sea the gulls wheeled and pivoted.

"Holy shit!" Bremen repeated.

They picnicked on the beach. Gernisavien stayed behind to hunt insects in the dune grass. The air smelled of salt and sea and summer breezes. It seemed they had a thousand miles of shoreline to themselves.

Gail stood and kicked off her dress. She was wearing a one-piece suit underneath. Bremen threw his head back and laughed. "Is that why you came back? To get a suit? Afraid the lifeguards would throw you out?"

She kicked sand at him and ran to the water. Three strides in and she was swimming. Bremen could see from the way her shoulders hunched that the water was freezing.

"Come on in!" she called, laughing. "The water's fine!"

He began walking toward her.

The blast came from the sky, the earth, the sea. It knocked Bremen down and thrust Gail's head underwater. She flailed and splashed to make the shallows, crawled gasping from the receding surf.

NO!!!

Wind roared around them and threw sand a hundred feet in the air. The sky twisted, wrinkled like a tangled sheet on the line, changed from blue to lemon-yellow to gray. The sea rolled out in a giant slack tide and left dry, dead land where it receded. The earth pitched and shifted around them. Lightning flashed along the horizon.

When the buckling stopped, Bremen ran to where Gail lay on the sand, lifted her, calmed her with a few stern words.

The dunes were gone, the cliffs were gone, the sea had disappeared. Where it had been now stretched a dull expanse of salt flat. The sky continued to shift colors down through darker and darker grays. The sun seemed to be rising again in the eastern desert. No. The light was moving. Something was crossing the wasteland. Something was coming to them.

Gail started to break away, but Bremen held her tight. The light moved across the dead land. The radiance grew, shifted, sent out streamers that made both of them shield their eyes. The air smelled of ozone and the hair on their arms stood out.

Bremen found himself clutching tightly to Gail and leaning toward the apparition as toward a strong wind. Their shadows leaped out behind them. The light struck at their bodies like the shock wave of a bomb blast. Through their fingers, they watched while the radiant figure approached. A double form became visible through the blaze of corona. It was a human figure astride a huge beast. If a god had truly come to Earth, this then was the form he would have chosen. The beast he rode was featureless, but besides light it gave off a sense of . . . warmth? Softness?

Robby was before them, high on the back of his teddy bear.

TOO STRONG CANNOT KEEP

He was not used to language but was making the effort. The thoughts struck them like electrical surges to the brain. Gail dropped to her knees, but Bremen lifted her to her feet.

Bremen tried to reach out with his mind. It was no use. Once at Haverford he had gone with a promising student to the coliseum, where they were setting up for a rock concert. He had been standing in front of a scaffolded bank of speakers when the amplifiers were tested. It was a bit like that.

They were standing on a flat, reticulated plain. There were no horizons. White banks of curling fog were approaching from all directions. The only light came from the Apollo-like figure before them. Bremen turned his head to watch the fog advance. What it touched, it erased.

"Jerry, what . . ." Gail's voice was close to hysteria.

Robby's thoughts struck them again with physical force. He had given up an attempt at language, and the images cascaded over them. The visual images were vaguely distorted, miscolored, and tinged with an aura of wonder and newness. Bremen and his wife reeled from their impact.

A WHITE ROOM WHITE
THE HEARTBEAT OF A MACHINE
SUNLIGHT ON SHEETS
THE STING OF A NEEDLE
VOICES   WHITE SHAPES MOVING
A GREAT WIND BLOWING
A CURRENT PULLING, PULLING,
PULLING

With the images came the emotional overlay, almost unbearable in its knife-sharp intensity: discovery, loneliness, wonder, fatigue, love, sadness, sadness, sadness.

Both Bremen and Gail were on their knees. Both were sobbing without being aware of it. In the sudden stillness after the onslaught, Gail's thoughts came loudly. *Why is he doing this? Why won't he leave us alone?*

Bremen took her by the shoulders. Her face was so pale that her freckles stood out in bold relief.

Don't you understand, Gail? It's not him doing it.
Not??? Who . . .?????

Gail's thoughts rolled in confusion. Splintered images and fragmented questions leaped between them as she struggled to control herself.

It's me, Gail. Me. Bremen had meant to speak aloud, but there was no sound now, only the crystalline edges of their thoughts. *He's been fighting to keep us together all along. I'm the one. I don't belong. He's been hanging on for me, trying to help me to stay, but he can't resist the pull any longer.*

Gail looked around in terror. The fog boiled and reached for them in tendrils. It was closing around the god figure on his mount. Even as they watched, his radiance dimmed.

Touch him, thought Bremen.

Gail closed her eyes. Bremen could feel the wings of her thought brushing by him. He heard her gasp.

My God, Jerry. He's just a baby. A frightened child!

If I stay any longer, I'll destroy us all. With that thought Bremen conveyed a range of emotions too complex for words. Gail saw what was in his mind and began to protest, but before she could pattern her thoughts, he had pulled her close and hugged her fiercely. His mindtouch amplified the embrace, added to it all the shades of feeling that neither language nor touch could communicate in full. Then he pushed her away from him, turned, and ran toward the wall of fog. Robby was visible as only a faint glow in the white mist, clutching the neck of his teddy bear. Bremen touched him as he passed. Five paces into the cold mist and he could see nothing, not even his own body. Three more paces and the ground disappeared. Then he was falling.

The room was white, the bed was white, the windows where white. Tubes ran from the suspended bottles into his arm. His body was a vast ache. A green plastic bracelet on his wrist said BREMEN, JEREMY H. The doctors wore white. A cardiac monitor echoed his heartbeat.

"You gave us all quite a scare," said the woman in white.

"It's a miracle," said the man to her left. There was a faint note of belligerence in his voice. "The EEG scans were flat for five days, but you came out of it. A miracle."

"We've never seen a case of simultaneous seizures

like this," said the woman. "Do you have a history of epilepsy?"

"The school had no family information," said the man. "Is there anyone we could contact for you?"

Bremen groaned and closed his eyes. There was distant conversation, the cool touch of a needle, and the noises of leave-taking. Bremen said something, cleared his throat as they turned, tried again.

"What room?"

They stared, glanced at each other.

"Robby," said Bremen in a hoarse whisper. "What room is Robby in?"

"Seven twenty-six," said the woman. "The intensive care ward."

Bremen nodded and closed his eyes.

He made his short voyage in the early hours of the morning when the halls were dark and silent except for the occasional swish of a nurse's skirt or the low, fitful groans of the patients. He moved slowly down the hallway, sometimes clutching the wall for support. Twice he stepped into darkened rooms as the soft, rubber tread of quickly moving nurses came his way. On the stairway he had to stop repeatedly, hanging over the hard, metal railing to catch his breath, his heart pounding.

Finally he entered the room. Robby was there in the far bed. A tiny light burned on the monitor panel above his head. The fat, faintly odorous body was curled up in a tight fetal position. Wrists and ankles were cocked at stiff angles. Fingers splayed out against the tousled sheets. Robby's head was turned to the side, and his eyes were open, staring blindly. His lips fluttered slightly as he breathed, and a small circle of drool had moistened the sheets.

He was dying.

Bremen sat on the edge of the bed. The thickness of the night was palpable around him. A distant chime sounded once and someone moaned. Bremen reached his hand out and laid a palm gently on Robby's cheek. He could feel the soft down there. The boy continued his labored, asthmatic snoring. Bremen touched the top of the misshapen head tenderly, almost reverently. The straight, black hair stuck up through his fingers.

Bremen stood and left the room.

The suspension on the borrowed Fiat rattled over the rough bricks as Bremen swerved to avoid the streetcars. It was quite early, and the eastbound lane on the Benjamin Franklin Bridge was almost empty. The double strip of highway across New Jersey was quiet. Bremen cautiously lowered his mindshield a bit and flinched as the surge of mindbabble pushed against his bruised mind. He quickly raised his shield. Not yet. The pain throbbed behind his eyes as he concentrated on driving. There had not been the slightest hint of a familiar voice.

Bremen glanced toward the glove compartment, thought of the rag-covered bundle there. Once, long ago, he had fantasized about the gun. He had half-convinced himself that it was some sort of magic wand—an instrument of release. Now he knew better. He recognized it for what it was—a killing instrument. It would never free him. It would not allow his consciousness to fly. It would only slam a projectile through his skull and end once and for all the mathematically perfect dance within.

Bremen thought of the weakening, quiet figure he had left in the hospital that morning. He drove on.

He parked near the lighthouse, packed the revolver in a brown bag, and locked the car. The sand was very hot when it lopped over the tops of his sandals. The beach was almost deserted as Bremen sat in the meager shade of a dune and looked out to sea. The morning glare made him squint.

He took off his shirt, set it carefully on the sand behind him, and removed the bundle from the bag. The metal felt cool, and it was lighter than he remembered. It smelled faintly of oil.

You'll have to help me. If there's another way, you'll have to help me find it.

Bremen dropped his mindshield. The pain of a million aimless thoughts stabbed at his brain like an icepick. His mindshield rose automatically to blunt the noise, but Bremen pushed down the barrier. For the first time in his life Bremen opened himself fully to the pain, to the world that inflicted it, to the million voices calling in their isolation and loneliness. He accepted it. He willed it. The great chorus struck at him like a giant wind. Bremen sought a single voice.

Bremen's hearing dimmed to nothing. The hot sand failed to register; the sunlight on his body became a distant, forgotten thing. He concentrated with enough force to move objects, to pulverize bricks, to halt birds in their flight. The gun fell unheeded to the sand.

From down the beach came a young girl in a dark suit two seasons too small. Her attention was on the sea as it teased the land with its sliding strokes and then withdrew. She danced on the dark strips of wet

313

sand. Her sunburned legs carried her to the very edge of the world's ocean and then back again in a silent ballet. Suddenly she was distracted by the screaming of gulls. Startled, she halted her dance, and the waves broke over her ankles with a sound of triumph.

The gulls dived, rose again, wheeled away to the north. Bremen walked to the top of the dune. Salt spray blew in from the waves. Sunlight glared on water.

The girl resumed her waltz with the sea while behind her, squinting slightly in the clean, sharp light of morning the three of them watched through Bremen's eyes.

VOX OLYMPICA

By Michael Bishop

My father had been tuning the volcano for the past year. His work was in preparation for the decennial Day of Diapason, when we who have made a home of the once-desolate mojaves and himalayas of Mars salute the long-dead planet where our species was born.

I had just turned eight, but our patriot population observes a double year, counting by the six hundred eighty-seven-day period in which Mars revolves around the sun. A colonist on Titan or Ganymede, harking back to Earth-style dating, would say I was fifteen and a half.

Though fast approaching adulthood, I had never heard my father or anyone else play the mountain. The Vox Olympica (as devout Krystic Harmonists generally call it) is not truly duplicable to any human-scale recording system, and I was eager for firsthand experience of the ancient volcano's voice. I was also eager to see my father again.

While supervising the tuning of the several hundred painstakingly cored-out calderas and vents of Olympus Mons, my father had come home for only brief visits. These obligatory "rests," mandated by the church, he had spent poring over computer diagrams of the great mountain's bowels, collating and memorizing the chromatic readouts of its glassy flues. As a result, he had made no real fuss over my improving grades in history and hydraulic science; he had shown only polite interest in my collection of preadapted insects from the Tharsis Steppe; and, although he had listened dutifully to three of my melodeon compositions (at my mother's dogged bidding), afterwards he had dispensed rote praise rather than incisive criticism. His mind had been elsewhere.

Vanora, my mother, resented the Day of Diapason as much as Theon, my father, revered it. To her it represented not only a disaster for the continuity of our family life but also a perverse wallowing in the fabled destruction of Earth. Why must we carry on so about what was lost forever? Beginning only a year after their bond-covenant, my father's first stint as Memorialist had almost destroyed their marriage. Somehow, though, they had survived the separations, the misunderstandings, the arguments. Finally my birth in Spaulding, West Tithonia, where Vanora headed one of the Northern Hemisphere's ground-based divisions of OSAS (Orbital Solar Amplification System), had confirmed their faith in the benefits of reconciliation. I was the tie that binds.

Seven years later the church had again selected my

father to oversee the preparations at Olympus Mons, and Theon, despite his many intervening promises to my mother, had accepted the commission.

I was on my father's side, and I told Vanora so.

To me Theon's selection by the Harmonists seemed a signal honor, and I was prepared to forgive him a hundred humiliating slights if only I could sit beside him in the mountain organ room on the day he made even distant Hellas ring. When he played, the whole planet was supposed to teeter in its orbit. I wanted to be with him, booming out a diapasonal lament for long-dead Earth. He had hinted that this might be possible. Perhaps he would even let the volcano give prodigious voice to one of my melodeon sonatinas. I had written an especially good one since his last visit to Spaulding.

"Gayle," my mother said, after listening to this feverish recitation of my hopes, "you shame yourself with every word."

"Why do you say that?"

"Because you're older now, child, but scarcely any wiser."

I was sitting at my melodeon, a gift from Theon on my seventh birthday. I had been filling our bunker with frisky runs and grace notes. Now I turned the melodeon off and covered its keyboard.

"Listen, Gayle, the ceremony's tradition-bound. The Memorialist plays what every other Memorialist since Zivu, the first, has played. Zivu established the program. Your father isn't going to squeeze in a little Gaylean ditty as a sop to your vanity."

"I know that, Mother. I was only talking."

"Well, your talk of joining him under the mountain is nonsense, too."

"He said I might."

"Gayle, he probably wasn't even listening." Vanora's voice conveyed her concern as well as her exasperation. "Did you know that the Memorialist hears only the ghost of his own performance?"

"The ghost?"

"It's true. The keyboard room is sound-proofed. Everyone entering it—traditionally, the Memorialist and a single technician—must wear absorbent plugs and a pair of padded earphones. Zivu went deaf hymning Earth's lost glory. Knowing full well what the result would be, he performed the entire day's program without protection."

"Father's not deaf."

"No, but his hearing's impaired. Sometimes I think he accepted this second commission not for the honor of it but because he wants to be able to hear music again in the only way he really can—through his bones."

"Then why do you begrudge him?"

Stung, Vanora leveled an appraising glance at me. Then her expression softened. "First, because he told me this would never happen again. And, second, Gayle, because the Day of Diapason's a Harmonist anachronism. It's disruptive of the new order we've established, and it's morbid in its celebration of the poisoning and death of our home world."

"It doesn't celebrate, Mother. It memorializes."

Vanora dismissed my view of the matter by picking a thread from her tunic and dropping it to the floor. I was lucky that she was talking at all. Ordinarily, except when arguing with Theon and allowing her feelings to run away with her, she avoided discussing the topic in my presence. That she had *initiated* a conversation about the Day of Diapason with me—well, that was a breakthrough akin to faster-than-light travel. I tried to press my advantage before it fled at that speed.

"What was Father's first performance like?"

My mother looked at me, then let her gaze swing past the redwood statue of Ares guarding the corridor to her night chamber. "I'm afraid I didn't hear it, Gayle. I didn't want to hear it."

"You didn't hear it?"

"I *felt* it," Vanora said, intercepting my stare. "Or at least I think I did. OSAS held a training program for executive candidates in Stanleyville, Northwest Hellas, two weeks before the Day, and I stayed there, using my leave time, even after our training sessions were over. I was in the bunker of a government hospice in the Southern Hemisphere when your father played the mountain. I felt the music he was making, and an officer at the nearby OSAS facility recorded it on a seismograph."

"You could have got back in time to hear him, and you didn't even make the effort?"

"That's right."

I shook my head. "That's astonishing, Mother." Vanora did not reply. "Are you going to listen to him this time?"

"Spaulding's much closer to Olympus than Stanleyville is. I suppose I'll hear your father's performance. I'm going to spend the day down here, though, with our sound units turned up and my ears plugged."

"That's spiteful, Mother! Sheer, irreligious spite!"

"Your father's the religionist in this family, Gayle, though he's pulled you that way, too. I just don't have any desire to hear the music he makes for a foolish memorial ceremony."

Controlling my outrage, I said, "I do."

"I know you do. Step aboveground on the Day of Diapason and you'll hear it everywhere—hour upon hour of merciless, unending bombast. But legislation in the Parliament at Chryse promises to make this year's ceremony the Harmonists' swan song, at least so far as that ogreish mountain is concerned. So listen well, Gayle, and remember what you hear."

"Goodnight, Vanora." I stood up, brushed the wrinkles from my clothes, and strode past the tutelary statue of Ares to my tiny room. My own mother was a skeptic and an enemy.

"Goodnight, child," she said, resigned to my sharpness. "Sleep well."

A week before the Day of Diapason I ran away from home. I carried with me an Isidian silver harmonica, a printout of my sonatina "If I Forget Thee, O Elysian Earth of Yore," an enameled box in which to house captured insects, and a satchel for my clothes. I left at night, when the OSAS veils throw a bronze dusk over Tithonia's giant redwood groves, for then a brown-clad figure among the trees blends with the antique shadows like an otter or a deer.

As for Spaulding, a government town where the door to every buried house resembles an upright marble grave marker—well, no one there saw me take my leave.

My destination, of course, was Olympus Mons, the enormous shield volcano in the Martian province informally known as Blackshale. The mountain's chief city is a well-to-do vacation community, incongruously called Hardscrabble, on the eastern flank, high above the Olympus Palisades, which front the Tharsis Steppe. My father received mail and occasionally slept in Hardscrabble, which lay more than twenty-one hundred kilometers northwest of our home in Spaulding.

To get there, I was going to have to pass through several government redwood groves, dairy farms, winter-wheat collectives, and mining hamlets. My course pointed me straight through the famous Wilder Plains, separating the two northernmost volcanoes of the Tharsis Ridge, Ascra and Pavo. If I made it through that pass by my second day of travel, I would be doing well. Everything depended on my catching rides. In only a week not even a towering, three-legged war machine could walk to Olympus.

That first night, though, I deliberately avoided people. I ran through the oxygen-exhaling redwoods like a two-year-old, my heart bursting with unwritten melodeon music. I was free. If anyone stopped me, I could show him my birth card, which showed me to be old enough for freelancing, and explain that I was a Harmonist novitiate on my first solo pilgrimage to the Holy Mountain. That was true, pretty much. It fell short of total truthfulness only in that I had not registered my intentions with the church.

Toward dawn I sat down beneath a redwood, emptied my pockets, and played "If I Forget Thee" on my harmonica. It sounded tinny and pitiful there in the woods, despite the sterling quality of my instrument, another gift from Theon, and I stopped before finishing the sonatina and returned both the mouth organ and my clumsy score to my satchel. I ate a dried beef cake and a seedless tangerine from Coprates, then stretched out to sleep. Around noon I was awakened by cricket song.

Instantly alert, I searched for my self-appointed alarm clock. Most crickets do not chirp during the day, but perpetual dusk has superseded night on Mars and a few cricket species have so far accommodated to this pattern that even full daylight does not inhibit them. I found my minstrel in a patch of white moss on the south side of a nearby redwood, caught in between my cupped palms, and eased it into my perforated box. It was white, my cricket—not a pink-eyed albino but an emerald-eyed mutant of a species I had never seen before. I took it with me.

Early that afternoon I left the forest and labored to a hilltop overlooking the Wilder Valley. Beneath me was a kilometer-wide tributary of the Canal Irrigation System (CIS), carrying water from the northern polar cap to Blackshale, Tithonia, Isidis, and other equatorial regions. This particular canal was the Wilder Interprovincial Tributary: CIS-WIT, to acronym lovers.

Gazing down, I was stunned by the amount of activity, both mercantile and recreational, along the broad concrete aprons of the locks. Like an immense liquid python, a strip of silver water curled away to the northwest and into a forest of dark green conifers. Up and down the middle of the canal moved colorful barges, while bathers and holiday anglers made use of the peripheral areas specifically set aside for them. Dock workers and freight vehicles labored noisily on the quays, and hundreds of gaily dressed people from nearby townships mingled among the wooden booths and striped canvas tents of the canalside markets. Spaulding, by comparison, was a drowsy memorial garden. I ran down the hill. It seemed unlikely that anyone in this busy, festive place would know or care that I was a runaway.

After buying a cup of milk and a shell sandwich with some of last year's emergency scrip (it was worthless at home, but negotiable on the canals), I sauntered along the quays, looking for up-channel transportation. No one paid me any mind. I spilled most of the granulated beef from my shell sandwich, but a black dog and a pair of cheeky fulmars cleaned up after me. No reprimand from angry authority figures.

But no advice about how to catch a ride into Blackshale, either. It seemed that three quarters of the water traffic was coming *down* the canal. I despaired of reaching my father before D-Day. Surely, though, there had to be other pilgrims journeying up the CIS-WIT to hear the Holy Mountain hymn the planet of our origins. I would join them.

Unfortunately, I could not find them. Everyone along this lock of the Wilder Tributary was pursuing secular matters—trade, water games, day labor, holiday courtships, and eating. A haggard veteran of the expedition against the Argyre Separatist Army was hawking tickets for the Recompense Lottery from her powered wheelchair. I bought a ticket with five pieces of my tattered scrip.

"Isn't there any way to get up-channel, Sergeant?"

She folded the scrip into a deerskin sporran in her lap, then pointed into the crowd north of me. "Go to

Quay Number Twelve, ask for Harbin, and tell him old Oona's calling in a favor.''

"I don't need a favor. I need a ride."

"If all you have is scrip, child, you need a favor. Go on. Find Harbin and tell him what I've said."

Backing away, I thanked the crippled sergeant repeatedly. She waved me on. I reoriented myself among the streaming pedestrians and counted off every quay until I had found Number Twelve. There, beside a ladder, sat a short, burly man in a dirty blue pea jacket. Older than my father, he was also wearing stained coveralls and boots. I approached and told him what the sergeant had instructed me to tell him. Out of the corner of my eye I saw a dilapidated airboat gently breasting the swells that broke against the canal wall.

"I'll give you a ride," Harbin said. "What's for pay?"

"Wait a minute. Oona said she was calling in a favor, remember?"

"The favor's letting you aboard, upstart. What's for pay?"

My heart sinking, I showed Harbin the last of my scrip.

"That won't do. What else have you got?"

I searched my pockets. My harmonica came into my hand. I turned it out so that the airboat owner could see it.

"Silver?"

"From Isidis," I boasted. "The best."

"It's small, though." He took the harmonica from me and examined it closely. "All right, Gayle, here's your fare. I'm assuming you play this thing. You do? Good. All right, then. You play for me whenever I

ask you to, and when we get to WIT's End—you
know, the beginning of the Blackshale Tributary—you give up the harmonica and go your own
way. Agreed?''

Although I thought about it for a minute, I finally
agreed.

Harbin's airboat sprinted northwest on a cushion
of downblasting air. Water spewed up beside us from
the vessel's sculpted hydrofoils, and the battery-
powered fans roared like miniature cyclones. So long
as we were on the move, there was no question of my
playing the mouth organ, nor could we really talk.

Holding the sides of my chair, I watched the lethar-
gic barges and canal tugs flash by us in the glitter of
the airboat's ceaseless spray. Harbin slowed down
only when we had arrived at another lock level.

Here, as if piloting a helicraft rather than a water
vessel, he would adjust the controls to power us up
and over the wall. This stunning maneuver, he later
told me, would have been impossible on Earth, where
gravity had exerted a significantly stronger force.

The sky turned bronze, and the lights of the other
mercantile craft looked like gems floating in amber
syrup. We continued to skim along. In fact, we
traveled for nearly ten hours, with only two brief
breaks, neither of which gave me enough time to
serenade Harbin on the harmonica. The conifer
forests on our left gave way to the sprawling irrigated
pastures of government dairy farms as we passed
through the Wilder Plains. On the far horizon the
peak of Olympus Mons, where even native Martians
dare not venture without oxygen gear, grew dimly
visible.

The peak was naked, wavery brown in the twilight, for several weeks ago the Harmonists had paid OSAS to melt the summit snow. The runoff, I knew, would have turned the mountain's lower skirts a stunning, deep green and replenished most of the minor tributaries of the local canal system. But we were still not close enough to see below the mountain's timberline.

Around midnight we docked at an outpost called Parkhill, a trading center built of logs and sod, with latex calking in the chinks and prefabricated plastic shutters on the double-paned windows.

The owner, who knew Harbin, gave us a late supper of beer and fried squirrel, which we consumed on a wooded hillside overlooking both the trading post and the canal. My body was vibrating from the long, noisy ride, and I ate greedily to overcome my fatigue. When I had finished, Harbin demanded that I play. Willingly enough, my hands shaking, I complied. Bittersweet ballads, lively jigs, and familiar Harmonist hymns—music that I accurately surmised would appeal to an uneducated but independent soul like my airboat pilot.

"Not too shoddy for an upstart," he commented afterward.

"My father's Theon the Memorialist."

"Ah, so *that's* why you're heading for the mountain." (It had not occurred to him to doubt my story.) "Well, maybe you'd better not tell *every* traveler along the way who your daddy is."

"Why not?"

"Harmonists—mouthy ones, anyhow—are none too popular in Blackshale this year. The hospice keepers in Hardscrabble would like to send Theon on a half-round trip to the bottom of the CIS-BIT.''

''Why?''

''Because the government's ordered a three-day evacuation of the communities around the volcano. Everyone's got to withdraw at least two hundred kilometers from the Olympus Palisades. Some have already started pulling out. That's a dandy fuss for those folks, just so the church can turn the tallest mountain in the solar system into a wind-spittin' calliope. Me, I'm rapstatic this is probably the last decennial it's ever gonna blow.''

Bitterly, I pointed out that Harbin would not be alive for the next Day of Diapason, anyway.

''Don't be so sure. My mother, without genetic reconditioning or the usual butt-minded immortalist diets—my mother lived to be sixty-one. Why, on Earth, she would have been well over a century old. These days lots of folks get older than she did.''

''Most of the ones who do are Harmonists.''

''Maybe.''

I nodded at the trading post below us. ''Ask Parkhill's terminal for an actuarial readout. What I say is true, Harbin.''

''Well, upstart, I've never understood that.''

''*Whosoever is harmonically composed delights in harmony,*'' I quoted.

''Nor that, either.''

I explained that the basic ordering of the physical universe is essentially crystalline. Because music also has a crystalline structure, it constitutes an important *seam* between the spiritual and the material worlds. Spiritually hungry human beings (I lectured the old man) have a deep-seated urge to bridge the two realities through music, and talented adepts like my father must mediate between these realms for the many people who lack his gift. Through either their own devout efforts or the salvific talent of the mediator like Theon, a longer or a more vital life comes to those who search for and find the crystalline harmonies undergirding the *whole* of Nature. Such is my credo, and I outlined it enthusiastically.

"You talk even fancier than you play," Harbin noted.

I was not finished yet. "The volcanoes surrounding us—Olympus ahead, Ascra behind, Pavo and Ars to the south—they're *frozen music,* Harbin. The entire physical universe is God's dream of creation inscribed as a secret crystalline music. You and I are parts of the dream that have awakened. We must awaken the rest. We must draw the music of God's thought out of the physical substances embodying it. That's what the colonizing—the warming, the watering, the seeding—of half-frozen planets like precolonial Mars is all about, Pilot. That's why we're here."

"Theology's never been my strong suit, upstart. I'm here because after the Punitive Expedition to the Argyre I saved enough to buy an airboat. Beats doing butt work in a government bunker, wouldn't you say?"

"Operating an airboat is what you do to accommodate to physical reality, Harbin. Too often we let that side of Nature get the upper hand. Earth was blooming, unfreezing, awakening, but people unaware or uncaring that the implicit harmonies of God's thought were finally manifesting themselves killed the planet before its music was fully audible. We betrayed ourselves. The result was not simply death for our world but a lingering"—I searched for a word—"a lingering *dissonance* in the lives of those who escaped the catastrophe. At all costs, we must save Mars from that kind of betrayal, in order to save ourselves, too."

I was preaching. Although the look on Harbin's face conveyed a wry regard for my precocious eloquence, he obviously thought it both misplaced and haughty. I promptly shut up.

The pilot reached over and rumpled my hair. "Go ahead. Get it all out, upstart. I've got plenty of time. Just don't expect a contribution when you've wound down for good."

Pulling away, I drained a last drop of beer from my stein.

"Surely you must have a *moral*, upstart. Most preachers—Harmonists, Syncretists, whatever other mouthy kind—most of 'em end up with a moral."

I stared at the pilot defiantly. "Just this, Harbin: The entire universe, the whole staff of God's harmonic thought, sings through the consciousness of every human being, but few of us train ourselves to hear the melodies. And some of us," I added pointedly, "are more deaf than others."

"Well, I'm not deaf to that singing in your pocket. What have you got there, upstart?"

Stunned, I realized that the cricket in my box had begun, quite faintly, to chirp. I had forgotten about the creature. Folding back my pocket, I turned the perforated box out onto the hillside. Then I picked it up and began stuffing grass blades and sprigs of clover through the tiny holes. It was a wonder the insect had not suffocated. As soon as the box had fallen from my pocket, of course, the cricket had stopped singing, but it appeared little the worse for close confinement, and I was relieved.

"You're not planning to keep it, are you?"

"Well, I found it this morning when—"

"Let it go."

I looked uncertainly at the airboat pilot.

"Let it go," he repeated more forcibly. "What do you want to keep the little fiddler for, anyway?"

"I collect singing insects. Cicadas, crickets, grasshoppers. It's a hobby of mine. I've been doing it since—"

"*Collect 'em!* Caterwauling Krystos, upstart, *what for?* Are you afraid you're missing a note or two of God's great hidden symphony? Do you think you have to pick 'em up secondhand? Where's your faith, upstart? *Where's your faith?*"

"Listen, it's not—"

"If you want a ride to WIT's End with me, upstart, you're going to have to let that pale little fiddler loose."

I tried to stare Harbin down, but that was impossible. Finally I pulled the top from the capture box and bumped the white cricket gently into a patch of clover, where it was conspicuous against the green.

"Now give me the box," Harbin said.

"What for?"

"To pay for your ride."

"I thought you wanted the harmonica."

"I do. I want the box, too. I always charge more for well-tuned hypocrites than for live-and-let-live folks with tin ears."

"Oh, I see. You've found out my father's Theon the Memorialist, and you're going to gouge me for having a well-known father."

"You don't see anything. And you don't hear so

good, either, even if it's not because you're deaf.''

He strode down the slope to Parkhill's trading post, to surrender his stein and wooden bowl and to scribble a farewell to the owner on the slate hanging beside the door. After seeing to our provisioning, Parkhill had gone back to bed. I followed Harbin around like a puppy, for without his airboat I would never reach Olympus.

We reached the end of the Wilder Interprovincial Tributary a little before dawn. Traffic here was non-existent; we had the canal locks and the countryside all to ourselves.

Harbin made me disembark on a lock apron from which the volcanic surface of the ancient Tharsis Steppe was visible. Unredeemed basalt and jumbled rocks rich in iron oxide. A primeval desert in the midst of irrigated pastures and lovely evergreen groves. In fact, the naked area—known today as the Tharsis Precolonial Preserve—had been set aside by the government as a commemorative park. Because few latter-day Martians care to remember what our world looked like before the Warming, however, no one was about to give me transportation farther west into Blackshale Province. I saw no prospect of continuing my journey other than by foot.

''What am I supposed to do now?'' I asked Harbin.

''Take a hike through the park''—the desert, he meant—''and if you keep bearing toward the mountain, you'll soon run up on Volcano Flats. It's too big to miss. You should be able to get help there. Just don't tell 'em you're a caterwauling Harmonist.''

Harbin had dry goods from New Tithonia to

deliver to a crater community called Lower Alba. He saluted me, leaped his airboat over the lock wall, and sprinted off north over the water. His was still the only vessel on the canal, and I stood on the vast, blank apron of the automated lock and watched it go cycloning out of my life.

Then I turned and walked westward into the antique desolation of the Tharsis Precolonial Preserve.

Lizards, birds, and rodents live among the rocks of this prehistoric landscape. They do not contribute to the precolonial authenticity of the park, but they made my passage through its barrens less lonely and therefore more endurable.

I hiked for nearly six hours along a well-marked trail and at last emerged into the stony sprawl of Volcano Flats, a lively city with an aerodrome, dozens of wide pedestrian thoroughfares, and a host of carven-looking beige buildings whose windows winked in the sunlight like murals of hammered copper. The city was full of people. Many of them, it became clear, were affluent evacuees from Olympus Mons, tourists who had come out well ahead of D-Day.

I told no one on the streets that my father was Theon the Memorialist. Nor did I say that I was a pilgrim to the Holy Mountain. Instead, after asking directions to the aerodrome, I swung along past the Volcano Flats Carnival Grounds and the Blackshale Livestock Emporia as if frivolity and commerce were my birthrights and I a native of this boisterous frontier town. No one looked at me twice.

At the aerodrome I engaged in some imaginative haggling and suffered several discouraging setbacks.

However, I finally connived my way aboard one of the skyliner dirigibles that cruised back and forth between Volcano Flats and the East Olympus Palisades. My story was that my parents, trade representatives from Epur, on the Jovian satellite Ganymede, had left me in town in order to take a three-day holiday by themselves in Hardscrabble. But they had been gone a week now, the money they had given me to get by in Volcano Flats had run out, and I feared that some terrible mishap had befallen them. The manager at the hospice where they had planned to stay had recently told me by tellaser transmission that they had never even arrived. Frantic, almost weeping, I begged the agents of the dirigible service to give me passage to Olympus Mons to find out what had happened. Although these people tried to refer me to local government authorities for help, a woman going back to Hardscrabble for an entertainment contractor overheard my pitiful tale and bought me a ticket for the next flight.

The woman's name was Ardath. She sat beside me in the dirigible's passenger gondola and plied me with questions that made me stammer, blush, and finally, full of remorse, confess my true identity. The surprising upshot of my confession was that Ardath found the truth harder to swallow than the lie I had told at the aerodrome. Disappointed, she patted my knee and folded several pieces of planetary currency into my hand, not scrip but money, nearly a hundred legitimate marsnotes.

"Gayle, maybe you won't feel compelled to counterfeit identities for yourself if you have a little money ready to hand."

"Please, Elder, it's not—"

"I don't know what it is, Gayle. Never mind, though. I think I understand. I was young once, too."

Ardath rose and went aft into the dirigible's library. Miserable, I looked out the window at the deep green landscape rolling by beneath us. Because of the impending Diapason, the gondola was virtually empty, and Ardath did not return to her seat beside me.

At dusk we tethered at an aerodrome below the Olympus Palisades, above which lighter-than-air craft may not venture without special permit. I disembarked on a marshy pasture below the great volcano. The iodine of twilight bronzed the entire world. Beneath the cliffs, two kilometers high, you could see neither the mountain's cloud-ringed summit nor its lava-coated skirts, but the distant din of running water attested to the success of the snowcap's carefully channeled melt.

While the other dirigible passengers straggled across the landing field to a village of A-frame lodges, I made for the coglift depot. There I used a little of Ardath's money to purchase a ride to the top of the Palisades.

An hour later I was in Hardscrabble, a ghost town of glass chalets and pueblo-style apartments built of rock and extruded foam. I sought out the Harmonist cloister above the village. My knowledge of *The Lore of Krystos* got me past the cenobite guards stationed outside the gate, and when I showed them my birth card, I suddenly became an honored guest.

Inside, I told a youthful cenobite named Doloro what I had come for. Like Ardath, he did not believe my father was Theon, in spite of my birth card and my facile grasp of Harmonist dogma. However, his training and his natural courtesy did not permit him to dispute my claim. He merely mentioned that most of those at the Olympus Cloister had abandoned the mountain last week. They would not return until after the Diapason. He and the other cenobites still present would depart in another three days. Meanwhile they were carrying out their traditional duties and guarding the cloister against vandalism. Theon might or might not be my father, Doloro's remarks implied, but I would not be permitted to remain on the Holy Mountain any longer than bona fide servants of the church.

"I want to hear my father play."

"Very well, but you don't warm your hands by sticking them into the fire."

Wind chimes hung in the red-glass towers of the cloister, and the quiet sawings of stringed instruments knitted its various rooms together as surely as did the crystal statues lining its corridors. In the communication center Doloro put through a tellase to my father in the keyboard room deep in the bowels of the mountain. On the third try, one of the Theon's technicians answered, and a few minutes later an image of my father's face was floating in the projection cylinder.

"Gayle!"

"You said I could come."

"Vanora was through to me yesterday. She was afraid something terrible had happened to you. Gayle, you can't stay. You just can't!"

We argued, and Doloro discreetly left the communication center. Theon adduced reasons for my returning to Spaulding, and I either countered these or attacked the general thrust of my father's argument, whichever seemed the more promising course. Finally, weary of our exchange, my father threatened to abdicate the responsibilities of Memorialist in order to discipline me. Someone else—Eldora, say, or Kiernan—could earn the glory for which he had spent the last six hundred days laying the groundwork. This threat frightened me, and even in his air-conditioned cage under the mountain he could see the cold fear in my eyes.

"I wrote a sonatina for you," I pleaded.

"For me?"

"For Earth, Father."

"Leave it with Doloro, and go back to Spaulding. Tellase your mother, and let her know you're coming. Otherwise, Gayle, I'll inform the Ecclesiarchal Council I'm resigning and take you home myself."

"In Spaulding I'll hear nothing!"

"*What is loud and cacophonous close to hand acquires, with distance, a mellow harmony.*"

I parried the epigram: "I'll retreat to Volcano Flats with the other evacuees, but I'll remain there until after the Diapason. I want to hear it, Father! I want to hear it!"

For some minutes Theon's face floated expressionless in the translucent cylinder. Then it said, "Leave your sonatina with Doloro," and it faded from view. By making a concession, I had called my father's bluff.

Doloro returned and helped me reach my mother in Spaulding. We awakened her, and she spent a few minutes trying to shake the sleep from her head. I explained what had passed between Theon and me, then told her that I would meet her not in Volcano

Flats but on an artificial hill several kilometers north of the city. This was a Harmonist retreat, where many cenobites and pilgrims, according to Doloro, would gather to hear my father's performance.

Vanora protested. She wanted me to come home at once, and she had no intention of meeting me at a Harmonist gathering place.

But I had just learned a deceitful debating technique from Theon, and I explained that if she wished to see me again, she must make the journey to Harmony Knoll and meet me there on Diapason Eve. Otherwise I would ride the canals to some faraway plain or canyon and never again set foot in West Tithonia except by a vagrant whim. Unlike my father's, this threat was one that the threatener felt capable of carrying out.

"I'll be there, Gayle, but I'll remember this."

Doloro led me to a night chamber. Later, dreaming, I heard several harsh thudding sounds, and in the morning a cenobite named Talitha told me that a small gang of adolescents from Hardscrabble had come up to the cloister and stoned its unbreakable towers of rose glass. Doloro, Risa, and two constables from the village had routed the troublemakers. The protests this decennial were mild, primarily because everyone understood that there would never be another.

The church could no longer afford to finance the attendant evacuation, and local law-enforcement units no longer wanted to organize and police the withdrawal. Those who opposed the Day of Diapason were finally inclined to be tolerant of those who cherished it. The Parliament had written their objections into law.

Two days before D-Day, I accompanied most of the Hardscrabble cenobites to Harmony Knoll. We floated back across the volcanic plains in the gondola of the same dirigible that I had boarded with Ardath. We spent the entire flight playing ceramic flutes and singing Harmonist rounds.

My reunion with Vanora was chilly. An old ecclesiarch had given us a tent in the city of tents facing Olympus Mons, and my mother and I shared this diaphanous chapel—it seemed to have been made of lavender scarves and oiled rice paper—like strangers who do not understand each other's language. I slept on one side, she on the other, and when I tried to apologize for my blackmail by bringing her tea or apples from the fellowship center, she accepted these gifts without speaking.

"Are you sure you still want me to come home with you?"

Vanora smiled, for the first time. "Of course I do. It's going to be lonely without your father."

"He'll come home, too, Mother."

"That remains to be seen."

"Whose fault will it be if he doesn't?"

"His. Mine. Who knows, Gayle?"

We did not talk about the matter again, and on Diapason Eve every cenobite and pilgrim on Harmony Knoll stood on the hillside keeping vigil with chants and musical prayer candles. Vanora and I kept vigil, too, gazing westward at the colossal blue-black silhouette of Olympus Mons. Near dawn she allowed her hand to creep into mine, and we waited together. There were more than a thousand of us waiting for the universe to sing through our individual consciousnesses, a chorus of sympathetically vibrating minds, each brain a crystal.

The sun rose at our backs, and the first deep utterance of the Vox Olympica sounded across the land.

Our feet trembled. A murmur of awe ran through our ranks like a ripple of wind over a field of wheat. A second note sounded, and the sky seemed to scintillate the way a spill of whiskey enlivens a shallow pan of water. A third, a fourth, a fifth, a dozen more notes boomed out over the plains of Blackshale, and the power of this stately melody forced people to their knees. The ground was quaking. The solar-amplification veils high above the planet seemed to ricochet sound as well as light.

It went on for twenty minutes, this first ringing hymn. The silence after the polyphonic caroling of the mountain was like a drought, a famine, an extinction. I was afraid to look up. If I did, I would find that the atmosphere of Mars had peeled back to reveal a blackness in which the crystalline arrangements of the stars shadowed forth God's primal thought. If I looked up, I would hear as well as see that thought.

So I did not look up, and no one on the hillside moved. Then my father began playing the second movement of the requiem. The sun continued to rise and our adoptive planet to stagger in its orbit.

Or so I imagined.

Later the manifold vents and calderas of the volcano gave out recognizable paraphrases of "If I Forget Thee, O Elysian Earth of Yore." Theon worked them into the various movements of Zivu's original program and played them back and forth through the laments, the paeans, and the hallelujahs.

On the winds howling so sweetly from the mountain, clouds broke apart, and like a mantle of audible fallout my sonatina traveled ever outward.

I looked at Vanora. Her face was wet, radiant. She squeezed my hand, and we stood together in the ocean of sound, listening to its cunning surges and imagining unknown or half-forgotten referents for its themes. Neither of us had ever heard the sea before, not really, but now, thanks to Theon and the Vox Olympica, we had.

Three evenings later, after Vanora and I had returned to Spaulding, a flickering of household lights indicated that visitors stood outside the upright cenotaph of our door. Expecting only the evening post or perhaps one of my mother's OSAS colleagues, I rode the entry platform to ground level and opened to our callers.

"Father!"

Supported by a young believer unfamiliar to me, Theon gave me a wan smile and touched my lower lip with a trembling finger. His face was horribly bruised. A gash in his right cheek had not reacted well to its first subcutaneous treatments, for the lips of the wound were livid.

"This is Corydon," my father said, nodding in the direction of the young man. "He's brought me home."

Too shocked to speak, I wrapped my arm about my father's waist and led him onto the platform. He was strong enough to stand without my help, but I insisted on lending my hip and shoulder. Meanwhile, wearing a half-angry, half-bereft expression, Corydon remained outside.

"A small band of anti-Harmonist fanatics met our dirigible at the Volcano Flats aerodrome," he explained, his voice deliberately loud. "Had several of us not fought back fiercely, they might have killed your father."

"The authorities intervened," Theon reminded Corydon.

"Only when they saw that we might inflict a few injuries, too. I have only contempt for the so-called authorities, Master Theon."

My father invited the young man in, urging him to rest a little before journeying back to Harmony Knoll.

"Now is a time to be with believers," Corydon said pointedly. "For an entire day, Master Theon, you knitted all the patterns together, revealed the latticework behind Creation. You did this magnificently, sir, but the deaf and the indifferent have pulled the patterns asunder again, and today—forgive me, sir—today I am unable to face even one more such person."

Before my father could reply, Corydon turned and strode off down the green hillside toward the silver tracking discs and relay towers of the OSAS facility.

Theon and I descended into the house. A moment later, in the center of the music room, he and Vanora were silently embracing. They seemed to take no notice of me.

"I thought you wouldn't come home," my mother whispered.

Theon stepped back and tugged on one earlobe to suggest that he had not really heard her, and Vanora repeated her last words aloud.

341

"Why would you think that?" he asked her, still gripping her shoulders.

"Years of argument, years of hostility, years of trying to accommodate ourselves to each other's belief." Though on the edge of tears, my mother did not ease herself back into Theon's arms. "Or lack of belief, I should probably add. Finally the connectives snap, and everything disintegrates."

Theon shook his head. "And years of loving each other, Vanora. You can't leave that out. It's unheard music—sweeter, far sweeter, than all the desperate clangor of those other things. You know that, don't you?"

This response appeared to embarrass my mother. She glanced at me, then pulled gently away from Theon's hands.

A moment later she said, "Everyone at the OSAS facility—everyone old enough to have heard the Vox Olympica two or three times before—well, they're all convinced that no performance in memory can rival this last one. They're sorry there's never going to be another. They're *genuinely* sorry, Theon and I suppose I am, too."

"After people have succeeded in murdering something important," I blurted, "it becomes fashionable to mourn what they've killed. That's the way it always is."

"Hush," my father admonished me.

"It makes me sick—angry and sick."

"Just as it does Corydon and all the other young ones," Theon replied. "Go aboveground, Gayle. Give your mother and me a chance to lay our ghosts to rest without—"

"Without my interference," I bitterly concluded.

342

But Theon merely looked me toward the entry well, and I followed his meaning look onto the platform and from there upward and into the lonely memorial gardens of the dusk. Here, cursing both my parents, I wandered about among the tombstone doorways like a spirit seeking its body's grave. Predictably I soon tired of this game and sat down in the grass bordering an orchard of flowering apple trees.

Somewhat later Theon emerged from our doorway and climbed the vast communal lawn to the orchard. He took up a sentry position only a couple of meters away. Lifting his bruised face to the sky, he surveyed the dim, almost invisible scatter of stars beyond the canted solar veils. Although I tried not to, I found myself sneaking glimpses of his dark, heavy-jowled profile.

"There's Phobos," he said presently.

I looked up and saw the inner moon come floating by. It always reminds me of a pitted hominid skull, and so of Earth, and I shuddered to see that tiny lunar death's-head passing over our township. Another emblem, it seemed that night, of our failure to deflect Martian institutions and mores from the self-destructive course taken by the majority of our home-world forebears. Another word for fear, Phobos; another word for failure.

"I'm not going to let it end this way," I told my father, loudly enough to penetrate his incipient deafness.

"Let what end this way?"

"What we believe in. I'm a Harmonist. Three days ago you played the mountain, but tonight you seem to have given up."

Theon turned toward me. "I've given up trying to

343

badger a good woman into putting on a belief system that doesn't fit her.''

"But everyone's got to—"

"Everyone's got to nothing, Gayle. For anyone past puberty intolerance is an unaffordable luxury. I'm not giving up. I'm merely passing the baton to you. If you don't try to beat everybody over the head with it, you may be able to coax some singular music from your own spiritual resources. Do you understand me? Your *own*, not this or that other poor beggar's.''

Suddenly, as if palsy-stricken, my hands were shaking.

"That's where it starts, Gayle. Do you understand what I'm telling you?''

"Yes, sir.'' A chorus of crickets had begun singing in the grass beneath the apple trees. Weeping, I went to Theon for warmth and reassurance. I was weeping, I realized, not merely in filial gratitude but in the painful knowledge that Theon could no longer hear the crickets' faint, stridulous music. My heirloom. And my charge.

FOREVER

By Damon Knight

In 1887, in Wiesbaden, Germany, Herr Doktor
Heinrich Gottlieb Essenwein discovered the elixir of
life. The elixir, distilled from pigs' bladders, was
simple to manufacture and permanent in its effects.
After taking one dose of the clear reddish liquid,
colored and flavored with cinnamon, one no longer
aged. It was as simple as that. A chicken to which the
Herr Doktor fed a dose of the elixir in January 1887
was still alive in 1983 and had laid an estimated
twenty-five thousand eight hundred eggs, of which
seven thousand had double yolks.

An unfortunate side effect of this discovery was
that Essenwein's son Gerd, to whom the good
Doktor gave a dose of the elixir in 1888, remained
twelve years old for the rest of his life. Gerd, a gifted
piccolo player, had a sunny disposition and was
loved by all, but he was pimply and shy.

Once the Herr Doktor had discovered his error, he

recommended that the elixir not be taken until one attained a suitable age, which varied according to the talents and wishes of the individual: An athlete, for instance, might take his dose at twenty-three when he was at the height of his physical powers; a financier perhaps at forty-five or so; and a philosopher at fifty.

Encouraged by Essenwein's example, the British physicist John Tyndall discovered penicillin in 1895. Three years later Louis Pasteur announced his universal bacteriophage, one injection of which would destroy any marauding germ, at the cost of making the recipient feel out of sorts for about eighteen months.

As a result, the population of the world expanded dramatically during the years 1890 to 1903, the birth rate remaining the same or even increasing a trifle, while the death rate had fallen to a negligible figure. Fortunately, in 1897 the American physician Dr. Richard Stone perfected an oral contraceptive, which worked on both men and women and also slowed down cats and dogs a great deal.

Partly because of the unbearable crankiness of children who had had their bacteriophage shots, the new contraceptive was adopted with enthusiasm all over the world, and the habit of having children fell into disrepute. Occasionally infants still came into the world, by accident or inattention, but so rarely that as early as 1953, when a one-year-old infant was displayed to Queen Victoria as a curiosity, she started in horror and exclaimed, "What is that?"

As a consequence, a number of famous people were never born. These included Yogi Berra, George Gershwin, Aldous Huxley, Leonid Brezhnev, and

Marilyn Monroe. Conversely, a number of famous people *were* born, such as McDonald Wilson Slipher, the founder of the Church of Self-Satisfaction, the songwriter Sidney Colberg ("I'll Be Good when You're Gone"), and Harriet Longworth Tubman, the first female President of the United States.

Early in the twentieth century armies all over the world were plagued by mutiny and desertion; hardly anyone was crazy enough to risk a life that might last for centuries or even, with luck and reasonable care, for thousands of years. When the Archduke Ferdinand of Austria-Hungary was killed by an assassin at Sarajevo, Emperor Franz Josef wanted to declare war on Serbia, but Conrad von Hötzendorf told him he would merely embarrass the nation by doing so. Kaiser Wilhelm of Germany consulted von Moltke and was told the same thing. Both rulers gloomily assented to an international conference to resolve the issue; war never broke out.

Thus the world entered an era of lasting peace and prosperity. A network of electric railways covered the earth; Count Zeppelin's airships, which went into service in 1898, carried freight and passengers to the farthest parts of the globe. Thomas Edison, the wizard of Menlo Park, along with Nikola Tesla, Lee De Forest, and other giants of modern invention, poured out a steady stream of scientific marvels for the enrichment of human life.

Albert Einstein, of the Kaiser Wilhelm Institute in Berlin, in 1905 published his equation $E = mc^2$, demonstrating that the release of nuclear energy was possible, but the world already had abundant electrical power, thanks to Edison and Tesla, and nobody paid any attention to Einstein.

In 1931 the astronomer Giovanni Schiaparelli persuaded Guglielmo Marconi to attempt communication with the planet Mars. Marconi built a signaling apparatus, in effect a giant spark coil, in the Piedmont, near Turin, and in 1933 he fired off electric impulses into space every night; the sounds he produced were so terrific that sheep and cattle lost their bowel control for miles around. Marconi's message, repeated over and over, was a simple one: "Two plus one is three. Two plus two is four. Two plus three is five."

At the end of six months the hopes of the two Italians were realized when they received a return message, which said, "Eight plus seven is fourteen." Critics pointed out that this was not quite right, but the achievement captured the world's imagination nevertheless.

The popular author Jules Verne, in collaboration with the German Hermann Oberth, immediately began to draw plans for a cosmobile in which to visit the Martians. The task proved difficult, and more than two decades passed before the designers were ready to test their first cosmic vehicle. Because of technical difficulties, no attempt was to be made to reach Mars at this time; the vehicle was to swing around the moon and take photographs, then return to Earth. Even so, the rocket could carry only one passenger, who must weigh no more than one hundred pounds.

Gerd Essenwein, the son of the discoverer of the elixir of life, volunteered to go, and so did a man named Brunfels, who had lost both legs in a streetcar accident in Berlin, but a midget was chosen instead. This midget was Walter Dopsch, a popular circus performer; he was a perfectly formed little fellow who stood only three feet nine inches tall and weighed seventy-five pounds. Because this was twenty-five pounds less than the allowed weight, Dopsch was able to take along on the voyage a large supply of cognac, cigars, paperbound novels, and the bonbons to which he was addicted.

The flight took place on April 23, 1956; the space vehicle was raised to a height of thirty miles by means of a balloon designed by the Piccard brothers; then it was cut free, and it ascended by rocket power. The whole world listened to Dopsch's radio transmissions as he soared through space and looped around the moon, which he described as "like a very large Swiss cheese." On the return journey, however, the parachute that was to lower the vehicle to Earth proved defective; it collapsed and Dopsch plunged flaming into the North Sea. His last radio message was: "I love you, Helga." Helga, it was later ascertained, was the fat lady in the circus in which Dopsch had been employed.

This tragedy put a damper on space exploration, and, since no further messages were received from the Martians, the whole enterprise was forgotten.

Public opinion, anyhow, was turning against such dangerous pursuits. The internal combustion engine, for example, which had enjoyed a brief vogue early in the century, was everywhere replaced by safe, quiet electric trains and interurban trolleys. The Safety Prize, instituted in 1944 by Count Alfred Nobel, was awarded every year to such inventions as no-slip shoe soles and inflatable pantaloons.

In 1958 a consortium, headed by John D. Rockefeller and John P. Morgan, constructed a graceful steel-and-glass enclosure, two hundred twenty-five feet tall, over the entire island of Manhattan. By an ingenious use of wind vanes and filters, fresh air was kept circulating inside the enclosure while smoke and grime from the industrial areas of Queens and New Jersey were kept out. Inside this enclosure, dubbed the Crystal Matterhorn by journalists, ever taller and more fanciful buildings were constructed throughout the Sixties; beginning in 1970, many were joined by spiral walkways. All vehicular travel in Manhattan was by subway and electric cars; horses, gasoline engines, and other producers of pollution were strictly banned. In the winter the enclosure was kept at a comfortable temperature by electrical heaters and by the calories generated by the island's three hundred thousand inhabitants. Thus, winter or summer, Manhattanites could stroll the pavements in perfect comfort.

In literature and the arts, unwholesome innovation was forestalled by the taste of the public, which knew what it liked, and by the survival of many of the great figures of the late nineteenth century. In 1983 the sensations of the opera season were Enrico Caruso in Puccini's *La Malavoglia* and Lillian Russell in Tchaikovsky's *Nicolas Negorev;* the best-selling novels were Mark Twain's *Life in an Iceberg,* Robert Louis Stevenson's *The Borderland,* and *The Society of Ink-Tasters,* by Sir Arthur Conan Doyle. An exhibition of new works by James McNeill Whistler, at the Metropolitan Museum, was seen by thousands.

A man in East Orange, New Jersey, found a painting by Paul Cézanne in his grandmother's attic; it was obviously old, and he took it to a dealer, who informed him regretfully that it was worthless.

Centuries passed. In 2250 it was discovered that the population was declining, but the world took little notice at first, although it mourned the increasingly frequent deaths of great men and women. The elixir and the bacteriophage, although one kept people from aging and the other made them immune to disease, could not protect them against fatal ailments such as cancer, heart failure, and hardening of the arteries, or against poison, fire, and other accidents.

By 2330, when the decline became alarming, it was too late; the youngest living women, although they were as young as nineteen in appearance, had a chronological age of more than two hundred, and they were no longer fertile.

One by one, the smaller inhabited places of the world were abandoned and their former citizens moved into the great domed cities. Eventually even these became depopulated. Forests again covered the continents, effacing the works of man; for the first time in two thousand years, there were bears in Britain and giant elk in Russia. Six centuries after the discovery of the elixir of life, there were only two human beings left on the surface of the planet.

One of these was Gerd Essenwein, who was then living in a villa overlooking Lake Lucerne, where he had collected all the sheet music for piccolo in the Lucerne and Zurich libraries. The other was a Japanese woman, Michi Yamagata, who at the time she took the elixir had been sixteen years old. The two communicated by shortwave radio. Although they could not understand each other very well because of static, they agreed to meet. Michi found a small boat in Takatsu, crossed the Sea of Japan, and made her way across Asia and Europe by bicycle, stopping frequently to rest and replenish her stocks of dried food. The trip took eleven years.

It was an emotional moment when at last she appeared on Gerd's doorstep. Neither had seen another human face, except in photographs and films, for over a century. Gerd played his piccolo for her and showed her his collection of autographs of famous musicians; he took her on a walking tour around the lake, and then they had a picnic in the country. It was a warm day, and Michi took off her dress. Speaking in German, their only common language, she said, "Essenwein-san, do you rike me?"

"I like you very much," said Gerd. "However, what you have in mind is not possible." In turn, he removed his clothing, and she saw, although he had lived for more than six centuries, his body was still that of a twelve-year-old. They looked at each other ruefully and then put their clothes back on. The next day Michi got on her bicycle and started for home. This time she was not in a hurry, and the trip lasted fifteen years.

After her return, they continued to communicate by shortwave radio on their birthdays for some years. In 2510 Michi told him that she was about to pay a visit to Fujiyama; that was her last message.

A few years later Gerd put a few prized possessions into a handcart and made his way into the mountains of Unterwalden, where he found a herd of Harz Mountain goats, a hardy and affectionate breed. When he discovered that the goats liked his piccolo playing, he built a hut on the mountainside and moved in. Besides his sheet music and his autographs, he had a small harmonium, which he also played, but not as well; also, the goats did not care for it.

It was here, one morning in the spring of 2561, that the Arcturians found him. The Arcturians had received Marconi's signals, intended for Mars, and they had also received radio transmissions of voices singing "Yes, Sir, She's My Baby," stock market reports, and *Amos 'n' Andy*.

Three of the Arcturians disembarked from their landing vehicle and approached Gerd, who was sitting beside his hut and was wearing goatskins. The Acturians were large gray worms, or, more properly, millipedes. They wore covers over their eyes to protect them from the glare of our sun and looked like bug-eyed monsters.

During their long voyage they had had plenty of time to learn Earth languages from radio and television broadcasts, but they didn't know which one Gerd spoke. "¿Es Usted el ultimo?" they asked him. "Are you the last? Etes-vous le dernier?"

Gerd looked at them and played the opening bars of the Fantasia for Unaccompanied Piccolo, by Deems Taylor.

"We come from another world," they told him in Hindi, Swedish, and Italian. Gerd went on playing.

"Do you want to come with us? Doni të vij me neve? Wollen Sie gehen mit uns?"

Gerd lowered the piccolo. "Nein, danke."

"Glück auf," said the Arcturians politely, and they went away forever.

JOHNNY MNEMONIC

By William Gibson

I put the shotgun in an Adidas bag and padded it out with four pairs of tennis socks, not my style at all, but that was what I was aiming for: If they think you're crude, go technical, if they think you're technical, go crude. I'm a very technical boy. So I decided to get as crude as possible. These days, though, you have to be pretty technical before you can even aspire to crudeness. I'd had to turn both those twelve-gauge shells from brass stock, on a lathe, and then load them myself; I'd had to dig up an old microfiche with instructions for handloading cartridges; I'd had to build a lever-action press to seat the primers—all very tricky. But I knew they'd work.

The meet was set for the Drome at twenty-three hundred, but I rode the tube three stops past the closest platform and walked back. Immaculate procedure.

I checked myself out in the chrome siding of a coffee kiosk, your basic sharp-faced Caucasoid with a ruff of stiff, dark hair. The girls at Under the Knife were big on Sony Mao, and it was getting harder to keep them from adding that chic suggestion of epicanthic folds. It probably wouldn't fool Ralfi Face, but it might get me next to his table.

The Drome is a single narrow space with a bar down one side and tables along the other, thick with pimps and handlers and an arcane array of dealers. The Magnetic Dog Sisters were on the door that night, and I didn't relish trying to get out past them if things didn't work out. They were two meters tall and thin as greyhounds. One was black and the other white, but aside from that they were as nearly identical as cosmetic surgery could make them. They'd been lovers for years and were bad news in a tussle. I was never quite sure which one had originally been male.

Ralfi was sitting at his usual table. Owing me a lot of money. I had hundreds of megabytes stashed in my head on an idiot/savant basis, information I had no conscious access to. Ralfi had left it there. He hadn't, however, come back for it. Only Ralfi could retrieve the data, with a code phrase of his own invention. I'm not cheap to begin with, but my overtime on storage is astronomical. And Ralfi had been very scarce.

Then I'd heard that Ralfi Face wanted to put out a contract on me. So I'd arranged to meet him in the Drome, but I'd arranged it as Edward Bax, clandestine importer, late of Rio and Peking.

The Drome stank of biz, a metallic tang of nervous tension. Muscleboys scattered through the crowd were flexing stock parts at one another and trying on thin, cold grins, some of them so lost under superstructures of muscle graft that their outlines weren't really human.

Pardon me. Pardon me, friends. Just Eddie Bax here, Fast Eddie the Importer, with his professionally nondescript gym bag, and please ignore this slit, just wide enough to admit his right hand.

Ralfi wasn't alone. Eighty kilos of blond California beef perched alertly in the chair next to his, martial arts written all over him.

Fast Eddie Bax was in the chair opposite them before the beef's hands were off the table. "You black belt?" I asked eagerly. He nodded, blue eyes running an automatic scanning pattern between my eyes and my hands. "Me, too," I said. "Got mine here in this bag." And I shoved my hand through the slit and thumped the safety off. Click, "Double twelve-gauge with the triggers wired together."

"That's a gun," Ralfi said, putting a plump, restraining hand on his boy's taut, blue nylon chest. "Johnny has an antique firearm in his bag." So much for Edward Bax.

I guess he'd always been Ralfi Something or Other, but he owed his acquired surname to a singular vanity. Built something like an overripe pear, he'd worn the once-famous face of Christian White for twenty years—Christian White of the Aryan Reggae Band, Sony Mao to his generation, and final champion of race rock. I'm a whiz at trivia.

Christian White: classic pop face with a singer's high-definition muscles, chiseled cheekbones. Angelic in one light, handsomely depraved in another. But Ralfi's eyes lived behind that face, and they were small and cold and black.

"Please," he said, "let's work this out like businessmen." His voice was marked by a horrible prehensile sincerity, and the corners of his beautiful Christian White mouth were always wet. "Lewis here," nodding in the beefboy's direction, "is a meatball." Lewis took this impassively, looking like something built from a kit. "You aren't a meatball, Johnny."

"Sure I am, Ralfi, a nice meatball chock-full of implants where you can store your dirty laundry while you go off shopping for people to kill me. From my end of this bag, Ralfi, it looks like you've got some explaining to do."

"It's this last batch of product, Johnny." He sighed deeply. "In my role as broker—"

"Fence," I corrected.

"As broker, I'm usually very careful as to sources."

"You buy only from those who steal the best. Got it."

He sighed again. "I try," he said wearily, "not to buy from fools. This time, I'm afraid, I've done that." The third sigh was the cue for Lewis to trigger the neural disruptor they'd taped under my side of the table.

I put everything I had into curling the index finger of my right hand, but I no longer seemed to be connected to it. I could feel the metal of the gun and the foam-padded tape I'd wrapped around the stubby grip, but my hands were cool wax, distant and inert. I was hoping Lewis was a true meatball, thick enough to go for the gym bag and snag my rigid trigger finger, but he wasn't.

"We've been very worried about you, Johnny. Very worried. You see, that's Yakuza property you have there. A fool took it from them, Johnny. A dead fool."

Lewis giggled.

It all made sense then, an ugly kind of sense, like bags of wet sand settling around my head. Killing wasn't Ralfi's style. Lewis wasn't even Ralfi's style. But he'd got himself stuck between the Sons of the Neon Chrysanthemum and something that belonged to them—or, more likely, something of theirs that belonged to someone else. Ralfi, of course, could use the code phrase to throw me into idiot/savant, and I'd spill their hot program without remembering a single quarter tone. For a fence like Ralfi, that would ordinarily have been enough. But not for the Yakuza. The Yakuza would know about Squids, for one thing, and they wouldn't want to worry about one lifting those dim and permanent traces of their program out of my head. I didn't know very much about Squids, but I'd heard stories, and I made it a point never to repeat them to my clients. No, the Yakuza wouldn't like that; it looked too much like evidence. They hadn't got where they were by leaving evidence around. Or alive.

Lewis was grinning. I think he was visualizing a point just behind my forehead and imagining how he could get there the hard way.

"Hey," said a low voice, feminine, from somewhere behind my right shoulder, "you cowboys sure aren't having too lively a time."

"Pack it, bitch," Lewis said, his tanned face very still. Ralfi looked blank.

"Lighten up. You want to buy some good free base?" She pulled up a chair and quickly sat before either of them could stop her. She was barely inside my fixed field of vision, a thin girl with mirrored glasses, her dark hair cut in a rough shag. She wore black leather, open over a T-shirt slashed diagonally with stripes of red and black. "Eight thou a gram weight."

Lewis snorted his exasperation and tried to slap her out of the chair. Somehow he didn't quite connect, and her hand came up and seemed to brush his wrist as it passed. Bright blood sprayed the table. He was clutching his wrist white-knuckle tight, blood trickling from between his fingers.

But hadn't her hand been empty?

He was going to need a tendon stapler. He stood up carefully, without bothering to push his chair back. The chair toppled backward, and he stepped out of my line of sight without a word.

"He better get a medic to look at that," she said. "That's a nasty cut."

"You have no idea," said Ralfi, suddenly sounding very tired, "the depths of shit you have just gotten yourself into."

"No kidding? Mystery. I get real excited by mysteries. Like why your friend here's so quiet. Frozen, like. Or what this thing here is for," and she held up the little control unit that she'd somehow taken from Lewis. Ralfi looked ill.

"You, ah, want maybe a quarter million to give me that and take a walk?" A fat hand came up to stroke his pale, lean face nervously.

"What I want," she said, snapping her fingers so that the unit spun and glittered, "is work. A job.

Your boy hurt his wrist. But a quarter'll do for a retainer.''

Ralfi let his breath out explosively and began to laugh, exposing teeth that hadn't been kept up to the Christian White standard. Then she turned the disruptor off.

"Two million," I said.

"My kind of man," she said and laughed. "What's in the bag?"

"A shotgun."

"Crude." It might have been a compliment.

Ralfi said nothing at all.

"Name's Millions. Molly Millions. You want to get out of here, boss? People are starting to stare." She stood up. She was wearing leather jeans the color of dried blood.

And I saw for the first time that the mirrored lenses were surgical inlays, the silver rising smoothly from her high cheekbones, sealing her eyes in their sockets. I saw my new face twinned there.

"I'm Johnny," I said. "We're taking Mr. Face with us."

He was outside, waiting. Looking like your standard tourist tech, in plastic zoris and a silly Hawaiian shirt printed with blowups of his firm's most popular microprocessor; a mild little guy, the kind most likely to wind up drunk on sake in a bar that puts out miniature rice crackers with seaweed garnish. He looked like the kind who sing the corporate anthem and cry, who shake hands endlessly with the bartender. And the pimps and the dealers would leave him alone, pegging him as innately conservative. Not up for much, and careful with his credit when he was.

The way I figured it later, they must have amputated part of his left thumb, somewhere behind the first joint, replacing it with a prosthetic tip and cored the stump, fitting it with a spool and socket molded from one of the Ono-Sendai diamond analogs. Then they'd carefully wound the spool with three meters of monomolecular filament.

Molly got into some kind of exchange with the Magnetic Dog Sisters, giving me a chance to usher Ralfi through the door with the gym bag pressed lightly against the base of his spine. She seemed to know them. I heard the black one laugh.

I glanced up, out of some passing reflex, maybe because I've never got used to it, to the soaring arcs of light and the shadows of the geodesics above them. Maybe that saved me.

Ralfi kept walking, but I don't think he was trying to escape. I think he'd already given up. Probably he already had an idea of what we were up against.

I looked back down in time to see him explode.

Playback on full recall shows Ralfi stepping forward as the little tech sidles out of nowhere, smiling. Just a suggestion of a bow, and his left thumb falls off. It's a conjuring trick: The thumb hangs suspended. Mirrors? Wires? And Ralfi stops, his back to us, dark crescents of sweat under the armpits of his pale summer suit. He knows. He must have known. And then the joke-shop thumbtip, heavy as lead, arcs out in a lightning yo-yo trick, and the invisible thread connecting it to the killer's hand passes laterally through Ralfi's skull, just above his eyebrows, whips up, and descends, slicing the pear-shaped torso diagonally from shoulder to rib cage. Cuts so fine that no blood flows until synapses misfire and the first tremors surrender the body to gravity.

Ralfi tumbled apart in a pink cloud of fluids, the three mismatched sections rolling forward onto the tiled pavement. In total silence.

I brought the gym bag up, and my hand convulsed. The recoil nearly broke my wrist.

It must have been raining; ribbons of water cascaded from a ruptured geodesic and spattered on the tile behind us. We crouched in the narrow gap between a surgical boutique and an antique shop. She'd just edged one mirrored eye around the corner to report a single Volks module in front of the Drome, red lights flashing. They were sweeping Ralfi up. Asking questions.

I was covered in scorched white fluff. The tennis socks. The gym bag was a ragged plastic cuff around my wrist. "I don't see how the hell I missed him."

"Cause he's fast, so fast." She hugged her knees and rocked back and forth on her bootheels. "His nervous system's jacked up. He's factory custom." She grinned and gave a little squeal of delight. "I'm gonna get that boy. Tonight. He's the best number one, top dollar, state of-the art."

"What you're going to get, for this boy's two million, is my ass out of here. Your boyfriend back there was mostly grown in a vat in Chiba City. He's a Yakuza assassin."

"Chiba. Yeah. See. Molly's been Chiba, too." And she showed me her hands, fingers slightly spread. Her fingers were slender, tapered, very white against the polished burgundy nails. Ten blades,

snicked straight out from their recesses beneath her
nails, each one a narrow, double-edged scalpel in pale
blue steel.

I'd never spent much time in Nighttown. Nobody
there had anything to pay me to remember, and most
of them had a lot they paid regularly to forget.
Generations of sharpshooters had chipped away at
the neon until the maintenance crews gave up. Even
at noon the arcs were soot-black against faintest
pearl.

Where do you go when the world's wealthiest
criminal order is feeling for you with calm, distant
fingers? Where do you hide from the Yakuza, so
powerful that it owns comsats and at least three
shuttles? The Yakuza is a true multinational, like ITT
and Ono-Sendai. Fifty years before I was born the
Yakuza had already absorbed the Triads, the Mafia,
the Union Corse.

Molly had an answer: You hide in the Pit, in the
lowest circle, where any outside influence generates
swift, concentric ripples of raw menace. You hide in
Nighttown. Better yet, you hide *above* Nighttown,
because the Pit's inverted, and the bottom of its bowl
touches the sky, the sky that Nighttown never sees,
sweating under its own firmament of acrylic resin, up
where the Lo Teks crouch in the dark like gargoyles,
blackmarket cigarettes dangling from their lips.

She had another answer, too.

"So you're locked up good and tight, Johnny-san?
No way to get that program without the password?"
She led me into the shadows that waited beyond the
bright tube platform. The concrete walls were overlaid with graffiti, years of them twisting into a single

metascrawl of rage and frustration.

"The stored data are fed in through a modified series of microsurgical contraautism prostheses." I reeled off a numb version of my standard sales pitch. "Client's code is stored in a special chip; barring Squids, which we in the trade don't like to talk about, there's no way to recover your phrase. Can't drug it out, cut it out, torture it. I don't *know* it, never did."

"Squids? Crawly thing with arms?" We emerged into a deserted street market. Shadowy figures watched us from across a makeshift square, littered with fish heads and rotting fruit.

"Superconducting quantum interference detectors. Used them in the war to find submarines, suss out enemy cyber systems."

"Yeah? Navy stuff? From the war? Squid'll read that chip of yours?" She'd stopped walking, and I felt her eyes on me behind those twin mirrors.

"Even the primitive models could measure a magnetic field a billionth the strength of geomagnetic force: it's like pulling a whisper out of a cheering stadium."

"Cops can do that already, with parabolic microphones and lasers."

"But your data's still secure." Pride in profession. "No government'll let their cops have Squids, not even the security heavies. Too much chance of interdepartmental funnies; they're too likely to watergate you."

"Navy stuff," she said, and her grin gleamed in the shadows. "Navy stuff. I got a friend down here who was in the Navy, name's Jones. I think you'd better meet him. He's a junkie, though. So we'll have to take him something."

"A junkie?"

"A dolphin."

He was more than a dolphin, but from another dolphin's point of view he might have seemed like something less. I watched him swirling sluggishly in his galvanized tank. Water slopped over the side, wetting my shoes. He was surplus from the last war. A cyborg.

He rose out of the water, showing us the crusted plates along his sides, a kind of visual pun, his grace nearly lost under articulated armor, clumsy and prehistoric. Twin deformities on either side of his skull had been engineered to house sensor units. Silver lesions gleamed on exposed sections of his gray-white hide.

Molly whistled. Jones thrashed his tail, and more water cascaded down the side of the tank.

"What is this place?" I peered at vague shapes in the dark, rusting chainlink and things under tarps. Above the tank hung a clumsy wooden framework, crossed and recrossed by rows of dusty Christmas lights.

"Funland. Zoo and carnival rides. 'Talk with the War Whale.' All that. Some whale Jones is . . ."

Jones reared again and fixed me with a sad and ancient eye.

"How's he talk?" Suddenly I was anxious to go.

"That's the catch. Say hi, Jones."

And all the bulbs lit simultaneously. They were flashing red, white, and blue.

RWBRWBRWB
RWBRWBRWB
RWBRWBRWB
RWBRWBRWB

RWBRWBRWB

"Good with symbols, see, but the code's restricted. In the Navy they had him wired into an audiovisual display." She drew the narrow package from a jacket pocket. "Pure shit, Jones. Want it?" He froze in the water and started to sink. I felt a strange panic, remembering that he wasn't a fish, that he could drown. "We want the key to Johnny's bank, Jones. We want it fast."

The lights flickered, died.

"Go for it, Jones!"

B
BBBBBBBBB
B
B
B

Blue bulbs, cruciform.

Darkness.

"Pure! It's *clean*. Come on Jones."

WWWWWWWWW
WWWWWWWWW
WWWWWWWWW
WWWWWWWWW
WWWWWWWWW

White sodium glare washed her features, stark monochrome, shadows cleaving from her cheekbones.

R   RRRRR
R   R
RRRRRRRRR
    R   R
RRRRR   R

The arms of the red swastika were twisted in her silver glasses. "Give it to him," I said. "We've got it."

Ralfi Face. No imagination.

Jones heaved half his armored bulk over the edge of his tank, and I thought the metal would give way. Molly stabbed him overhand with the syrette, driving the needle between two plates. Propellant hissed. Patterns of light exploded, spasming across the frame and then fading to black.

We left him drifting, rolling languorously in the dark water. Maybe he was dreaming of his war in the Pacific, of the cyber mines he'd swept, nosing gently into their circuitry with the Squid he'd used to pick Ralfi's pathetic password from the chip buried in my head.

"I can see them slipping up when he was demobbed, letting him out of the Navy with that gear intact, but how does a cybernetic dolphin get wired to smack?"

"The war," she said. "They all were. Navy did it. How else you get 'em working for you?"

"I'm not sure this profiles as good business," the pirate said, angling for better money. "Target specs on a comsat that isn't in the book—"

"Waste my time and you won't profile at all," said Molly, leaning across his scarred plastic desk to prod him with her forefinger.

"So maybe you want to buy your microwaves somewhere else?" He was a tough kid, behind his Mao-job. A Nighttowner by birth, probably.

Her hand blurred down the front of his jacket, completely severing a lapel without even rumpling the fabric.

"So we got a deal or not?"

"Deal," he said, staring at his ruined lapel with

what he must have hoped was only polite interest.
"Deal."

While I checked the two recorders we'd bought, she extended the slip of paper I'd given her from the zippered wrist pocket of her jacket. She unfolded it and read silently, moving her lips. She shrugged. "This is it?"

"Shoot," I said, punching the RECORD studs of the two decks simultaneously.

"Christian White," she recited, "and his Aryan Reggae Band."

Faithful Ralfi, a fan to his dying day.

Transition to idiot/savant mode is always less abrupt than I expect it to be. The pirate broadcaster's front was a failing travel agency in a pastel cube that boasted a desk, three chairs, and a faded poster of a Swiss orbital spa. A pair of toy birds with blown-glass bodies and tin legs were sipping monotonously from a styrofoam cup of water on a ledge beside Molly's shoulder. As I phased into mode, they accelerated gradually until their Day-Glo-feathered crowns became solid arcs of color. The LEDs that told seconds on the plastic wall clock had become meaningless pulsing grids, and Molly and the Mao-faced boy grew hazy, their arms blurring occasionally in insect-quick ghosts of gesture. And then it all faded to cool gray static and an endless tone poem in an artificial language.

I sat and sang dead Ralfi's stolen program for three hours.

The mall runs forty kilometers from end to end, a ragged overlap of Fuller domes roofing what was once a suburban artery. If they turn off the arcs on a clear day, a gray approximation of sunlight filters through layers of acrylic, a view like the prison sketches of Giovanni Piranesi. The three southernmost kilometers roof Nighttown. Nighttown pays no taxes, no utilities. The neon arcs are dead, and the geodesics have been smoked black by decades of cooking fires. In the nearly total darkness of a Nighttown noon who notices a few dozen mad children lost in the rafters?

We'd been climbing for two hours, up concrete stairs and steel ladders with perforated rungs, past abandoned gantries and dust-covered tools. We'd started in what looked like a disused maintenance yard, stacked with triangular roofing segments. Everything there had been covered with that same uniform layer of spraybomb graffiti: gang names, initials, dates back to the turn of the century. The graffiti followed us up, gradually thinning until a single name was repeated at intervals. LO TEK. In dripping black capitals.

"Who's Lo Tek?"

"Not us, boss." She climbed a shivering aluminum ladder and vanished through a hole in a sheet of corrugated plastic. " 'Low technique, low technology.' " The plastic muffled her voice. I followed her up, nursing my aching wrist. "Lo Teks, they'd think that shotgun trick of yours was effete."

An hour later I dragged myself up through another hole, this one sawn crookedly in a sagging sheet of plywood, and met my first Lo Tek.

" 'S okay," Molly said, her hand brushing my shoulder. "It's just Dog. Hey, Dog."

In the narrow beam of her taped flash, he regarded us with his one eye and slowly extruded a thick length of grayish tongue, licking huge canines. I wondered how they wrote off tooth-bud transplants from Dobermans as low technology. Immunosuppressives don't exactly grow on trees.

"Moll." Dental augmentation impeded his speech. A string of saliva dangled from his twisted lower lip. "Heard ya comin'. Long time." He might have been fifteen, but the fangs and a bright mosaic of scars combined with the gaping socket to present a mask of total bestiality. It had taken time and a certain kind of creativity to assemble that face, and his posture told me he enjoyed living behind it. He wore a pair of decaying jeans, black with grime and shiny along the creases. His chest and feet were bare. He did something with his mouth that approximated a grin. "Bein' followed, you."

Far off, down in Nighttown, a water vendor cried his trade.

"Strings jumping, Dog?" She swung her flash to the side, and I saw thin cords tied to eyebolts, cords that ran to the edge and vanished.

"Kill the fuckin' light!"

She snapped it off.

"How come the one who's followin' you's got no light?"

"Doesn't need it. That one's bad news, Dog. Your sentries give him a tumble, they'll come home in easy-to-carry sections."

"This a *friend* friend, Moll?" He sounded uneasy. I heard his feet shift on the worn plywood.

"No. But he's mine. And this one," slapping my shoulder, "he's a friend. Got that?"

"Sure," he said, without much enthusiasm, padding to the platform's edge, where the eyebolts were. He began to pluck out some kind of message on the taut cords.

Nighttown spread beneath us like a toy village for rats; tiny windows showed candlelight, with only a few harsh, bright squares lit by battery lanterns and carbide lamps. I imagined the old men at their endless games of dominoes, under warm, fat drops of water that fell from wet wash hung out on poles between the plywood shanties. Then I tried to imagine him climbing patiently up through the darkness in his zoris and ugly tourist shirt, bland and unhurried. How was he tracking us?

"Good," said Molly. "He smells us."

"Smoke?" Dog dragged a crumpled pack from his pocket and prised out a flattened cigarette. I squinted at the trademark while he lit it for me with a kitchen match. Yiheyuan filters. Beijing Cigarette Factory. I decided that the Lo Teks were black marketeers. Dog and Molly went back to their argument, which seemed to revolve around Molly's desire to use some particular piece of Lo Tek real estate.

"I've done you a lot of favors, man. I want that floor. And I want the music."

"You're not Lo Tek . . ."

This must have been going on for the better part of a twisted kilometer, Dog leading us along swaying catwalks and up rope ladders. The Lo Tek leech their webs and huddling places to the city's fabric with thick gobs of epoxy and sleep above the abyss in mesh hammocks. Their country is so attenuated that in places it consists of little more than holds for hands and feet, sawn into geodesic struts.

The Killing Floor, she called it. Scrambling after

her, my new Eddie Bax shoes slipping on worn metal and damp plywood, I wondered how it could be any more lethal than the rest of the territory. At the same time I sensed that Dog's protests were ritual and that she already expected to get whatever it was she wanted.

Somewhere beneath us Jones would be circling his tank, feeling the first twinges of junk sickness. The police would be boring the Drome regulars with questions about Ralfi. What did he do? Who was he with before he stepped outside? And the Yakuza would be settling its ghostly bulk over the city's data banks, probing for faint images of me reflected in numbered accounts, securities transactions, bills for utilities. We're an information economy. They teach you that in school. What they don't tell you is that it's impossible to move, to live, to operate at any level without leaving traces, bits, seemingly meaningless fragments of personal information. Fragments that can be retrieved, amplified . . .

But by now the pirate would have shuttled our message into line for blackbox transmission to the Yakuza comsat. A simple message: Call off the dogs or we wideband your program.

The program. I had no idea what it contained. I still don't. I only sing the song, with zero comprehension. It was probably research data, the Yakuza being given to advanced forms of industrial espionage. A genteel business, stealing from Ono-Sendai as a matter of course and politely holding their data for ransom, threatening to blunt the conglomerate's research edge by making the product public.

But why couldn't any number play? Wouldn't they

be happier with something to sell back to Ono-Sendai, happier than they'd be with one dead Johnny from Memory Lane?

Their program was on its way to an address in Sydney, to a place that held letters for clients and didn't ask questions once you'd paid a small retainer. Fourth-class surface mail. I'd erased most of the other copy and recorded our message in the resulting gap, leaving just enough of the program to identify it as the real thing.

My wrist hurt. I wanted to stop, to lie down, to sleep. I knew that I'd lose my grip and fall soon, knew that the sharp black shoes I'd bought for my evening as Eddie Bax would lose their purchase and carry me down to Nighttown. But he rose in my mind like a cheap religious hologram, glowing, the enlarged chip on his Hawaiian shirt looming like a reconnaissance shot of some doomed urban nucleus.

So I followed Dog and Molly through Lo Tek heaven, jury-rigged and jerry-built from scraps that even Nighttown didn't want.

The Killing Floor was eight meters on a side. A giant had threaded steel cable back and forth through a junkyard and drawn it all taut. It creaked when it moved, and it moved constantly, swaying and bucking as the gathering Lo Teks arranged themselves on the shelf of plywood surrounding it. The wood was silver with age, polished with long use and deeply etched with initials, threats, declarations of passion. This was suspended from a separate set of cables, which lost themselves in darkness beyond the raw white glare of the two ancient floods suspended above the Floor.

A girl with teeth like Dog's hit the Floor on all

fours. Her breasts were tattooed with indigo spirals. Then she was across the Floor, laughing, grappling with a boy who was drinking dark liquid from a liter flask.

Lo Tek fashion ran to scars and tattoos. And teeth. The electricity they were tapping to light the Killing Floor seemed to be an exception to their overall esthetic, made in the name of . . . ritual, sport, art? I didn't know, but I could see that the Floor was something special. It had the look of having been assembled over generations.

I held the useless shotgun under my jacket. Its hardness and heft were comforting, even though I had no more shells. And it came to me that I had no idea at all of what was really happening, or of what was supposed to happen. And that was the nature of my game, because I'd spent most of my life as a blind receptacle to be filled with other people's knowledge and then drained, spouting synthetic languages I'd never understand. A very technical boy. Sure.

And then I noticed just how quiet the Lo Teks had become.

He was there, at the edge of the light, taking in the Killing Floor and the gallery of silent Lo Teks with a tourist's calm. And as our eyes met for the first time with mutual recognition, a memory clicked into place for me, of Paris, and the long Mercedes electrics gliding through the rain to Notre Dame; mobile greenhouses. Japanese faces behind the glass, and a hundred Nikons rising in blind phototropism, flowers of steel and crystal. Behind his eyes, as they found me, those same shutters whirring.

I looked for Molly Millions, but she was gone.

The Lo Teks parted to let him step up onto the bench. He bowed, smiling, and stepped smoothly out of his sandals, leaving them side by side, perfectly aligned, and then he stepped down onto the Killing Floor. He came for me, across that shifting trampoline of scrap, as easily as any tourist padding across synthetic pile in any featureless hotel.

Molly hit the Floor, moving.

The Floor screamed.

It was miked and amplified, with pickups riding the four fat coil springs at the corners and contact mikes taped at random to rusting machine fragments. Somewhere the Lo Teks had an amp and a synthesizer, and now I made out the shapes of speakers overhead, above the cruel white floods.

A drumbeat began, electronic, like an amplified heart, steady as a metronome.

She'd removed her leather jacket and boots; her T-shirt was sleeveless, faint telltales of Chiba City circuitry traced along her thin arms. Her leather jeans gleamed under the floods. She began to dance.

She flexed her knees, white feet tensed on a flattened gas tank, and the Killing Floor began to heave in response. The sound it made was like a world ending, like the wires that hold heaven snapping and coiling across the sky.

He rode with it, for a few heartbeats, and then he moved, judging the movement of the Floor perfectly, like a man stepping from one flat stone to another in an ornamental garden.

He pulled the tip from his thumb with the grace of a man at ease with social gesture and flung it at her. Under the floods, the filament was a refracting thread of rainbow. She threw herself flat and rolled, jack-knifing up as the molecule whipped past, steel claws snapping into the light in what must have been an automatic rictus of defense.

The drum pulse quickened, and she bounced with it, her dark hair wild around the blank silver lenses, her mouth thin, lips taut with concentration. The Killing Floor boomed and roared, and the Lo Teks were screaming their excitement.

He retracted the filament to a whirling meter-wide circle of ghostly polychrome and spun it in front of him, thumbless hand held level with his sternum. A shield.

And Molly seemed to let something go, something inside, and that was the real start of her mad-dog dance. She jumped, twisting, lunging sideways, landing with both feet on an alloy engine block wired directly to one of the coil springs. I cupped my hands over my ears and knelt in a vertigo of sound, thinking Floor and benches were on their way down, down to Nighttown, and I saw us tearing through the shanties, the wet wash, exploding on the tiles like rotten fruit. But the cables held, and the Killing Floor rose and fell like a crazy metal sea. And Molly danced on it.

And at the end, just before he made his final cast with the filament, I saw something in his face, an expression that didn't seem to belong there. It wasn't fear and it wasn't anger. I think it was disbelief, stunned incomprehension mingled with pure aesthetic revulsion at what he was seeing, hearing—at what was happening to him. He retracted the whirling filament, the ghost disc shrinking to the size of a dinner plate as he whipped his arm above his head and brought it down, the thumbtip curving out for Molly like a live thing.

The Floor carried her down, the molecule passing just above her head; the Floor whiplashed, lifting him into the path of the taut molecule. It should have passed harmlessly over his head and been withdrawn into its diamond-hard socket. It took his hand off just behind the wrist. There was a gap in the Floor in front of him, and he went through it like a diver, with a strange deliberate grace, a defeated kamikaze on his way down to Nighttown. Partly, I think, he took that dive to buy himself a few seconds of the dignity of silence. She'd killed him with culture shock.

The Lo Teks roared, but someone shut the amplifier off, and Molly rode the Killing Floor into silence, hanging on now, her face white and blank, until the pitching slowed and there was only a faint pinging of tortured metal and the grating of rust on rust.

We searched the Floor for the severed hand, but we never found it. All we found was a graceful curve in one piece of rusted steel, where the molecule went through. Its edge was bright as new chrome.

We never learned whether the Yakuza had accepted our terms, or even whether they got our message. As far as I know, their program is still waiting for Eddie Bax on a shelf in the back room of a gift shop on the third level of Sydney Central-5. Probably they sold the original back to Ono-Sendai months ago. But maybe they did get the pirate's broadcast, because nobody's come looking for me yet, and it's been nearly a year. If they do come, they'll have a long climb up through the dark, past Dog's sentries, and I don't look much like Eddie Bax these days. I let Molly take care of that, with a local anesthetic. And my new teeth have almost grown in.

I decided to stay up here. When I looked out across the Killing Floor, before he came, I saw how hollow I was. And I knew I was sick of being a bucket. So now I climb down and visit Jones, almost every night.

We're partners now, Jones and I, and Molly Millions, too. Molly handles our business in the Drome. Jones is still in Funland, but he has a bigger tank, with fresh seawater trucked in once a week. And he has his junk, when he needs it. He still talks to the kids with his frame of lights, but he talks to me on a new display unit in a shed that I rent there, a better unit than the one he used in the Navy.

And we're all making good money, better money than I made before, because Jones's Squid can read the traces of anything that anyone ever stored in me, and he gives it to me on the display unit in languages I can understand. So we're learning a lot about all my former clients. And one day I'll have a surgeon dig all the silicon out of my amygdalae, and I'll live with my own memories and nobody else's, the way other people do. But not for a while.

In the meantime it's really okay up here, way up in the dark, smoking a Chinese filtertip and listening to the condensation that drips from the geodesics. Real quiet, up here—unless a pair of Lo Teks decide to dance on the Killing Floor.

It's educational too. With Jones to help me figure things out, I'm getting to be the most technical boy in town.

WAITING FOR THE EARTHQUAKE

By Robert Silverberg

It was eleven weeks and two days and three hours—plus or minus a little—until the earthquake that was going to devastate the planet, and suddenly Morrissey found himself doubting that the earthquake was going to happen at all. The strange notion stopped him in his tracks. He was out strolling the shore of the Ring Ocean, half a dozen kilometers from his cabin, when the idea came to him. He turned to his companion, an old fux called Dinoov, who was just entering his postsexual phase, and said in a peculiar tone, "What if the ground doesn't shake?"

"But it will," the aborigine said calmly.

"What if the predictions are *wrong?*"

The fux was a small, elegant, blue-furred creature, sleek and compact, with the cool, all-accepting demeanor that comes from having passed safely through all the storms and metamorphoses of a fux's reproductive odyssey. It raised itself on its hind legs, the only pair that remained to it now, and said, "You should cover your head when you walk in the sunlight at flare time, friend Morrissey. The brightness damages the soul."

"You think I'm crazy, Dinoov?"

"I think you are under great stress."

Morrissey nodded vaguely. He looked away and stared westward across the shining, blood-hued ocean, narrowing his eyes as if trying to see the frosty, crystalline shores of Farside beyond the curve of the horizon. Perhaps half a kilometer out to sea he detected glistening patches of bright green on the surface of the water: the spawning bloom of the balloons. High above those dazzling streaks, a dozen or so brilliant, iridescent gasbag creatures hovered, going through the early sarabands of their mating dance. The quake would not matter at all to the balloons. When the surface of Medea heaved and buckled and crumpled, they would be drifting far overhead, dreaming their transcendental dreams and paying no attention.

But maybe there will be no quake, Morrissey told himself.

He played with the thought. He had waited all his life for the vast apocalyptic event that was supposed to put an end to the thousand-year-long human occupation of Medea, and now, very close to earthquake time, he found a savage, perverse pleasure in denying the truth of what he knew to be coming. *No earthquake! No earthquake! Life will go on, and on, and on!* The thought gave him a chilling, prickling feeling. There was an odd sensation in the soles of his feet, as if he were standing with both his feet off the ground.

Morrissey imagined himself sending out a joyful message to all those who had fled the doomed world. *Come back, all is well, it didn't happen! Come live on Medea again!* And he saw the fleet of great gleaming ships swinging around, heading back, moving like mighty dolphins across the void, shimmering like needles in the purple sky, dropping down by the hundreds to unload the vanished settlers at Chong and Enrique and Pellucidar and Port Medea and Madagozar. Swarms of people rushing forth, tears, hugs, raucous laughter, old friends reunited, the cities coming alive again! Morrissey trembled. He closed his eyes and wrapped his arms tight around himself. The fantasy had almost hallucinatory power. It made him giddy, and his skin, bleached and leathery from a lifetime under the ultraviolet flares of the twin suns, grew hot and moist. *Come home, come home! The earthquake's been canceled!*

He savored the fantasy. And then he let go of it and allowed its bright glow to fade.

He said to the fux, "There are eleven weeks left. And then everything on Medea is going to be destroyed. Why are you so calm, Dinoov?"

"Why not?"

"Don't you *care?*"

"Do you?"

"I love this place," Morrissey said. "I can't bear to see it all smashed apart."

"Then why didn't you go home to Earth with the others?"

"Home? This is my home. I have Medean genes in

my body. My people have lived here for a thousand years. My great-grandparents were born on Medea, and so were *their* great-grandparents.''

"The others could say the same thing. Yet when earthquake time drew near, they went home. Why have you stayed?"

Morrissey, towering over the slender little being, was silent a moment. Then he laughed harshly and said, "I didn't evacuate for the same reason that you don't give a damn that a killer quake is coming. We're both done for anyway, right? I don't know anything about Earth. It's not my world. I'm too old to start over there. And you? You're on your last legs, aren't you? Both your wombs are gone; your male itch is gone; you're in that nice, quiet, burned-out phase, eh, Dinoov?" Morrissey chuckled. "We deserve each other. Waiting for the end together, two old hulks."

The fux studied Morrissey with glinting, unfathomable, mischievous eyes. Then he pointed downwind toward a headland maybe three hundred meters away, a sandy rise thickly furred with bladdermoss and scrubby, yellow-leaved anglepod bushes. Right at the tip of the cape, outlined sharply against the glowing sky, were a couple of fuxes. One was female, six-legged, yet to bear her first litter. Behind her, gripping her haunches and readying himself to mount, was a bipedal male, and even at this distance Morrissey could see his frantic, almost desperate movements.

"What are they doing?" Dinoov asked.

Morrissey shrugged. "Mating."

"Yes. And when will she drop her young?"

"In fifteen weeks."

"Are they burned out?" the fux asked. "Are they done for? Why do they make young if destruction is coming?"

"Because they can't help—"

Dinoov silenced Morrissey with an upraised hand. "I meant the question not to be answered. Not yet, not until you understand things better. Yes? Please?"

"I don't—"

"Understand. Exactly." The fux smiled a fuxy smile. "This walk has tired you. Come now. I'll go with you to your cabin."

They scrambled briskly up the path from the long crescent of pale blue sand that was the beach to the top of the bluff and then walked more slowly down the road, past the abandoned holiday cabins, toward Morrissey's place. Once this had been Argoview Dunes, a bustling shoreside community, but it was long ago. Morrissey in these latter days would have preferred to live in some wilder terrain where the hand of man had not weighed so heavily on the natural landscape, but he dared not risk it. Medea, even after ten centuries of colonization, was still a world of sudden perils. The unconquered places had gone unconquered for good reason. Living on alone since the evacuation, he needed to keep close to some settlement, with its stores of food and material. He could not afford the picturesque.

In any case the wilderness was rapidly reclaiming its own now that most of the intruders had departed. In the early days this steamy low-latitude tropical coast had been infested with all manner of monstrous beasts. Some had been driven off by methodical campaigns of extermination, and others, repelled by the effluvia of the human settlements, had simply disappeared. But they were beginning to return. A few weeks ago Morrissey had seen a scuttlefish come ashore, a gigantic black-scaled tubular thing, hauling itself onto land by desperate heaves of its awesome curved flippers and actually digging its fangs into the sand, biting the shore to pull itself onward. They were supposed to be extinct. By a fantastic effort the thing had dug itself into the beach, burying all twenty meters of its body in the azure sand, and a couple of hours later hundreds of young ones that had tunneled out of the mighty carcass began to emerge, slender beasts no longer than Morrissey's arm that went writhing with demonic energy down the dunes and into the rough surf. So this was becoming a sea of monsters again. Morrissey had no objections. Swimming was no longer one of his recreations.

He had lived by himself beside the Ring Ocean for two years in a little, low-roofed cabin of the old Arcan wing-structure design that so beautifully resisted the diabolical Medean winds. In the days of his marriage, when he had been a geophysicist mapping the fault lines, he and Nadia and Paul and Danielle had had a house on the outskirts of Chong, on Northcape, within view of the High Cascades, and had come here only in winter. But Nadia had gone to sing cosmic harmonies with the serene and noble and incomprehensible balloons, and Danielle had been caught in the Hotlands at double-flare time and had not returned, and Paul—tough, old, indestructible Paul—had panicked over the thought that the earthquake was only a decade away, and between Darkday and Dimday of Christmas week he packed up and boarded an Earthbound ship. All that had happened within the space of four months, and afterward Morrissey found he had lost his fondness for the chilly air of Northcape. So he had come down to Argoview Dunes to wait out the final years in the comfort of the humid tropics, and now he was the only one left in the shoreside community. He had brought persona cubes of Paul and Nadia and Danielle with him, but playing them turned out to be too painful, and it was a long time since he had talked with anyone but Dinoov. For all he knew, he was the only one left on Medea. Except, of course, the fuxes and the balloons. And the scuttlefish and the rock demons and the wingfingers and the not-turtles and all of those.

Morrissey and Dinoov stood silently for a time outside the cabin, watching the sunset begin. Through a darkening sky, mottled with the green and yellow folds and streaks of Medea's perpetual aurora, the twin suns Phrixus and Helle—mere orange-red daubs of feeble light—drifted toward the horizon. In a few hours they would be gone, off to cast their bleak glow over the dry-ice wastelands of Farside. There could never be real darkness on the inhabited side of Medea, though, for the oppressive, sullen bulk of Argo, the huge red-hot-gas giant planet whose moon Medea was, lay just a million kilometers away. Medea, locked in Argo's grip, kept the same face turned toward her enormous primary all the time. From Argo came the warmth that made life possible on Medea, and also a perpetual, dull reddish illumination.

The stars were beginning to appear as the twin suns set.

"See there," Dinoov said. "Argo has nearly eaten the white fires."

The fux had chosen deliberately archaic terms, folk astronomy, but Morrissey understood what he meant. Phrixus and Helle were not the only suns in Medea's sky. The two orange-red dwarf stars, moving as a binary unit, were themselves subject to a pair of magnificent blue-white stars, Castor A and Castor B. Though the blue-white stars were a thousand times as far from Medea as the orange-red ones were, they were plainly visible by day and by night, casting a brilliant icy glare. But now they were moving into eclipse behind great Argo, and soon—eleven weeks, two days, one hour, plus or minus a little—they would disappear entirely.

And how then could there not be an earthquake?

Morrissey was angry with himself for the pathetic softheadedness of his fantasy of an hour ago. No earthquake? A last-minute miracle? The calculations in error? Sure. Sure. If wishes were horses, beggars might ride. The earthquake was inevitable. A day would come when the configuration of the heavens was exactly *thus*. Phrixus and Helle positioned *here,* and Castor A and B *there,* and Medea's neighboring moons Jason and Theseus and Orpheus *there* and *there* and *there,* and Argo as ever exerting its inexorable pull above the Hotlands, and when the celestial vectors were properly aligned, the gravitational stresses would send a terrible shudder through the crust of Medea.

This happened every seventy-one hundred sixty years. And the time was at hand.

Centuries ago, when the persistence of certain

apocalyptic themes in fux folklore had finally led the astronomers of the Medea colony to run a few belated calculations of these matters, no one had really cared. Hearing that the world will come to an end in five or six hundred years is much like hearing that you yourself are going to die in another fifty or sixty: It makes no practical difference in the conduct of everyday life. Later, of course, as the seismic tickdown moved along, people began to think about it more seriously, and beyond doubt it had been a depressive factor in the Medean economy for the past century or so. Nevertheless, Morrissey's generation was the first that had confronted the dimensions of the impending calamity in any realistic way. And in one manner or another the thousand-year-old colony had melted away in little more than a decade.

"How quiet everything is!" Morrissey said. He glanced at the fux. "Do you think I'm the only one left, Dinoov?"

"How would I know?"

"Don't play those games with me. Your people have ways of circulating information that we were only just beginning to suspect. You know."

The fux said gravely, "The world is large. There were many human cities. Probably some others of your kind are still living here, but I have no certain knowledge. You may well be the last one."

"I suppose. Someone had to be."

"Does it give you satisfaction, knowing you are last?"

"Because it means I have more endurance, or because I think it's good that the colony has broken up?"

"Either," said the fux.

"I don't feel a thing," Morrissey said. "Either way. I'm the last, if I'm the last, because I didn't want to leave. That's all. This is my home, and here I stay. I don't feel proud or brave or noble for having stayed. I wish there weren't going to be an earthquake, but I can't do anything about that, and by now I think I don't even care."

"Really?" Dinoov asked. "That's not how it seemed a little while ago."

Morrissey smiled. "Nothing lasts. We pretend we build for the ages, but time moves and everything fades and art becomes artifacts and sand becomes sandstone, and what of it? Once there was a world here and we turned it into a colony. And now the colonists are gone, and soon the colony will be gone, and this will be a world again, as our rubble blows away. And what of it?"

"You sound very old," Dinoov interjected.

"I am very old. Older even than you."

"Only in years. Our lives move faster than yours do, but in my few years I have been through all the stages of my life, and the end would soon be coming for me even if the ground were not going to shake. But you still have time left."

Morrissey shrugged.

The fux said, "I know that there are starships standing fueled and ready at Port Medea, ready to go."

"Are you sure? Ships ready to go?"

"Many of them. They were not needed. The Ahya have seen them and told us."

"The balloons? What were they doing at Port Medea?"

"Who understands the Ahya? They wander where they please. But they have seen the ships, friend Morrissey. You could still save yourself."

"Sure," Morrissey said. "I take a flitter thousands of kilometers across Medea, and I singlehandedly give a starship the checkdown for a voyage of fifty light-years, and then I put myself into coldsleep and go home all alone and wake up on an alien planet where my remote ancestors happened to have been born. What for?"

"You will die, I think, when the ground shakes."

"I will die, I think, even if it doesn't."

"Sooner or later. But this way, later."

"If I had wanted to leave Medea," Morrissey said, "I would have gone with the others. It's too late now."

"No," said the fux. "There are ships at Port Medea. Go to Port Medea, my friend."

Morrissey was silent. In the dimming light he knelt and tugged at tough little hummocks of stickweed that were beginning to invade his garden. Once he had landscaped this place with exotic shrubs gathered from all over Medea, everything beautiful that was capable of surviving the humidity and the rainfall of the Wetlands, but now, as the end drew near, the native plants of the coast were closing in, smothering his whiptrees and dangletwines and flamestripes and the rest, and he no longer was able to check their growth. For some minutes he clawed at the sticky stoloniferous killers, baleful orange against the tawny sand, that suddenly were sprouting near his doorway.

Then he said, "I think I will take a trip, Dinoov."

The fux looked startled. "You'll go to Port Medea?"

"There, yes, and other places. It's years since I've left the Dunes. I'm going to make a farewell tour of the whole planet."

Morrissey spent the next day, Darkday, quietly planing his trip, packing, reading, wandering along the beachfront in the twilight's red glimmer. There was no sign all day of Dinoov, or indeed of any of the local fuxes, although in midafternoon a hundred or more balloons drifted past in tight formation, heading out to sea. In the darkness their shimmering colors were muted, but still they were a noble sight: huge, taut globes trailing long, coiling, ropy organs.

Toward evening he drew from his locker a dinner that he had been saving for some special occasion. Madagozar oysters and filet of vandaleur and newly ripened peeperpods. There were two bottles of golden-red Palinurus wine left; he opened one of them. He drank and ate until he started to nod off at the table; then he lurched to his cradle, programmed himself for ten hours sleep, about twice what he normally needed at his age, and closed his eyes.

When he woke, it was well along into Dimday morning, with the double sun not yet visible but already throwing pink light across the crest of the eastern hills. Morrissey, skipping breakfast altogether, went into town and ransacked the commissary. He filled a freezercase with provisions enough to last him for three months, since he had no idea what to expect by way of supplies elsewhere on Medea. At the landing strip where commuters from

Enrique and Pellucidar once had parked their flitters after flying in for the weekend, he checked out his own, an '83 model with sharply raked lines and a sophisticated moire-pattern skin, now somewhat pitted and rusted from neglect. The powerpak still indicated a full charge—ninety-year half-life; he wasn't surprised—but just to be on the safe side, he borrowed an auxiliary pak from an adjoining flitter and keyed it in as a reserve. He hadn't flown in years, but that didn't worry him much: The flitter responded to voice-actuated commands, and Morrissey doubted that he'd have to do any manual overriding.

Everything was ready by midafternoon, he slipped into the pilot's seat and told the flitter, "Give me a systems checkout for extended flight."

Lights went on and off on the control panels. It was an impressive display of technological choreography, although Morrissey had forgotten what the displays signified. He called for verbal confirmation, and the flitter told him in a no-nonsense contralto that it was ready for takeoff.

"Your course," Morrissey said, "is due west for fifty kilometers at an altitude of five hundred meters, then north-northeast as far as Jane's Town, east to Hawkman Farms, and southwest back to Argoview Dunes. Then, without landing, head due north by the shortest route to Port Kato. Got it?"

Morrissey waited for takeoff. Nothing happened.

"Well?" he queried.

"Awaiting tower clearance," the flitter responded.

"Consider all clearance programs revoked."

Still nothing happened. Morrissey wondered how to key in a program override. But the flitter evidently could find no reason to call Morrissey's bluff, and after a moment takeoff lights glowed all over the cabin, and a low humming came from aft. Smoothly the little vehicle retracted its windjacks, gliding into flight position, and spun upward into the moist, heavy, turbulent air.

Morrissey had chosen to begin his journey with a ceremonial circumnavigation of the immediate area, ostensibly to be sure that his flitter could still fly after all these years, but he suspected also that he wanted to show himself aloft to the fuxes of the district, to let them know that at least one human vehicle still traversed the skies. The flitter seemed all right. Within minutes he was at the beach, flying directly over his own cabin—it was the only one whose garden had not been overrun by jungle scrub—and then out over the dark, tide-driven ocean. Up north then to the big port of Jane's Town, where tourist cruisers lay rusting in the crescent harbor, and inland a little way to a derelict farming settlement, where the tops of mighty gattabangus trees, heavily laden with succulent scarlet fruit, were barely visible above swarming stranglervines. And then back, over sandy, scrubby hills, to the Dunes. Everything below was desolate and dismal. He saw a good many fuxes, long columns of them in some places, mainly six-legged females and some four-legged ones, with males leading the way. Oddly, they all seemed to be marching inland, toward the dry Hotlands, as if some sort of migration were under way. Perhaps so. To a fux the interior was holier than the coast, and the holiest place of all was the great jagged central peak that the colonists called Mount Olympus, directly under Argo, where the air was hot enough to make water boil and where only the most specialized of living creatures could survive. Fuxes would die in that blazing, terrible highland desert almost as quickly as humans, but maybe, Morrissey thought, they wanted to get as close as possible to the holy mountain as the time of the earthquake approached. The coming round of the earthquake cycle was the central event of fux cosmology, after all, a millennial time, a time of wonders.

He counted fifty separate bands of migrating fuxes. He wondered whether his friend Dinoov was among them. Suddenly he realized how strong was his need to find Dinoov waiting at Argoview Dunes when he returned from his journey around Medea.

The circuit of the district took less than an hour. When the Dunes came into view again, the flitter performed a dainty pirouette over the town and shot off northward along the coast.

The route Morrissey had in mind would take him up the west coast as far as Arca, across the Hotlands to Northcape, and down the other coast to tropical Madagozar before crossing back to the Dunes. Thus he would neatly touch base wherever mankind might have left an imprint on Medea.

Medea was divided into two huge hemispheres separated by the water girdle of the Ring Ocean. But Farside was a glaciated wasteland that never felt Argo's warmth, and no permanent settlements had ever been founded there, only research camps, and in the last four hundred years very few of those. The original purpose of the Medea colony had been scientific study, the painstaking exploration of a wholly alien environment. But of course, as time goes on, original purposes have a way of being forgotten. Even on the warm continent human occupation had been limited to twin arcs along the coasts from the tropics through the high temperate latitudes and timid incursions a few hundred kilometers inland. The high desert was uninhabitable, and few humans found the bordering Hotlands hospitable, although the balloons and even some tribes of fuxes seemed to like the climate there. The only other place where humans had planted themselves was on the Ring Ocean itself, where some floating raft cities had been constructed in the kelp-choked equatorial water. But during the ten centuries of Medea the widely scattered human enclaves had sent out amoeboid extensions until they were nearly continuous for thousands of kilometers.

Morrissey saw that now the iron band of urban sprawl was cut again and again by intrusions of dense underbrush. Great patches of orange and yellow foliage already had begun to smother highways, airports, commercial plazas, residential suburbs.

What the jungle had begun, he thought, the earthquake would finish.

On the third day Morrissey saw Hansonia Island ahead of him, a dark orange slash against the breast of the sea, and soon the flitter was making its approach to the airstrip at Port Kato on the big island's eastern shore. Morrissey tried to make radio contact but got only static or silence. He decided to land anyway.

Hansonia had never had much of a human population. It had been set aside from the beginning as an ecological study laboratory, because its population of strange life forms had developed in isolation from the mainland for thousands of years. And somehow it had kept its special status even in Medea's boom years.

A few groundcars were parked at the airstrip. Morrissey found one that still had a charge, and ten minutes later he was in Port Kato.

The place stank of red mildew. The buildings, wicker huts with thatched roofs, were falling apart. Angular trees of a species Morrissey did not recognize sprouted everywhere, in the streets, on rooftops, in the crowns of other trees. A cool, hard-edged wind was blowing out of Farside. Two fuxes, four-legged females herding some young six-leggers, wandered out of a tumbledown warehouse and stared at him in what was surely astonishment. Their pelts were so blue that they seemed black—the island species, different from mainlanders.

"You come back?" one asked. Local accent, too.

"Just for a visit. Are there any humans here?"

"You," said the other fux. He thought they found him amusing. "Ground shake soon. You know?"

"I know," he said.

They nuzzled their young and wandered away.

For three hours Morrissey explored Port Kato, holding himself aloof from emotion, not letting the decay get to him. It looked as if the place had been abandoned for at least fifty years. More likely only five or six, though.

Late in the day he entered a small house where the town met the forest and found a functioning persona cube setup.

The cubes were clever things. You could record

yourself in an hour or so: facial gestures, motion habits, voice, speech patterns. Scanners identified certain broad patterns of mental response and coded those into the cube, too. What the cube playback provided was a plausible imitation of a human being, the best possible memento of a loved one or friend or mentor, an electronic phantom programmed to absorb data and modify its own program, so that it could engage in conversation, ask questions, pretend to be the person who had been cubed. A soul in a box, a cunning device.

Morrissey jacked the cube into its receptor slot. The screen displayed a thin-lipped man with a high forehead and a lean, agile body. "My name is Leopold Brannum," he said at once. "My specialty is xenogenetics. What year is this?"

"It's Ninety-seven, autumn," Morrissey answered. "Ten weeks and a bit before the earthquake."

"And who are you?"

"Nobody particular. I just happen to be visiting Port Kato, and I felt like talking to someone."

"So talk," Brannum said. "What's going on in Port Kato?"

"Nothing. It's pretty damned quiet here. The place is empty."

"The whole town's been evacuated?"

"The whole planet, for all I know. Just me and the fuxes and the balloons still around. When did you leave, Brannum?"

"Summer of Ninety-two," said the man in the cube.

"I don't see why everyone ran away so early. There wasn't any chance the earthquake would come before the predicted time."

"I didn't run away." Brannum said coldly. "I left Port Kato to continue my research by other means."

"I don't understand."

"I went to join the balloons," Brannum said.

Morrissey caught his breath. The words touched his soul with wintry bleakness.

"My wife did that," he said after a moment. "Perhaps you know her now. Nadia Dutoit. She was from Chong, originally—"

The face on the screen smiled sourly. "You don't seem to realize," Brannum said, "that I'm only a recording."

"Of course. Of course."

"I don't know where your wife is now. I don't even know where *I* am now. I can only tell you that wherever we are, it's in a place of great peace, of utter harmony."

"Yes, of course." Morrissey remembered the terrible day when Nadia told him that she could no longer resist the spiritual communion of the aerial creatures, that she was going off to seek entry into the collective mind of the Ahya. All through the history of Medea some colonists had done that. No one had ever seen any of them again. Their souls, people said, were absorbed, and their bodies lay buried somewhere beneath the dry ice of Farside. Toward the end the frequency of such defections had doubled and doubled and doubled again, thousands of colonists every month giving themselves up to whatever mystic engulfment the balloons offered. To Morrissey it was a form of suicide; to Nadia, to Brannum, to all those other hordes, it had been the path to eternal bliss. Who was to say? Better to undertake the uncertain journey into the great mind of the Ahya, perhaps,

399

than to set out in panicky flight for the alien and unforgiving world that was Earth. "I hope you've found what you were looking for," Morrissey said. "I hope she has."

He unjacked the cube and left quickly.

He flew northward over the fog-streaked sea. Below him were the floating cities of the tropical waters, that marvelous tapestry of rafts and barges. That must be Port Backside down there, he decided— a sprawling, intricate tangle of foliage under which lay the crumbling splendors of one of Medea's greatest cities. Kelp choked the waterways. There was no sign of human life down there, and so he did not land.

Pellucidar, on the mainland, was empty also. Morrissey spent four days there, visiting the undersea gardens, treating himself to a concert in the famous Hall of Columns, watching the suns set from the top of Crystal Pyramid. That last evening dense drifts of balloons, hundreds of them, flew oceanward above him. He imagined he heard them calling to him in soft, sighing whispers, saying, *I am Nadia. Come to me. There's still time. Give yourself up to us, dear love. I am Nadia.*

Was it only imagination? The Ahya were seductive. They had called to Nadia, and ultimately Nadia had gone to them. Brannum had gone. Thousands had gone. Now he felt the pull himself, and it was real. For an instant it was tempting. Instead of perishing in the quake, life eternal—of a sort. Who knew what the balloons really offered? A merging, a loss of self, a transcendental bliss. Or was it only delusion, folly? Had the seekers found nothing but a quick death in the icy wastes? *Come to me. Come to me.* Either way, he thought, it meant peace.

I am Nadia. Come to me.

He stared a long while at the bobbing, shimmering globes overhead, and the whispers grew to a roar in his mind.

Then he shook his head. Union with the cosmic entity was not for him. He had sought no escape from Medea up till now, and now he would have none. He was himself and nothing but himself, and when he went out of the world, he would still be only himself. And then, only then, the balloons could have his soul.

It was nine weeks and a day before the earthquake when Morrissey reached sweltering Enrique, right on the equator. Enrique was celebrated for its Hotel Luxe, of legendary opulence. He took possession of its grandest suite, and no one was there to tell him no. The air conditioning still worked, the bar was well stocked, the hotel grounds still were manicured daily by fux gardeners who did not seem to know that their employers had gone away. Obliging servomechanisms provided Morrissey with meals of supreme elegance that would each have cost him a month's earnings in the old days. As he wandered through the silent grounds, he thought how wonderful it would have been to come here with Nadia and Danielle and Paul. But it was meaningless now, to be alone in all this luxury.

Was he alone, though? On his first night, and again the next, he heard laughter in the darkness, borne on the dense, sweet-scented air. Fuxes did not laugh. The balloons did not laugh.

On the morning of the third day, as he stood on his nineteenth-floor veranda, he saw movements in the shrubbery at the rim of the lawn. Five, seven, a dozen male fuxes, grim two-legged engines of lust, prowling through the bushes. And then a human form! Pale flesh, bare legs, long, unkempt hair! She streaked through the underbrush, giggling, pursued by fuxes.

"Hello!" Morrissey called. "Hey! I'm up here!"

He hurried downstairs and spent all day searching the hotel grounds. Occasionally he caught glimpses of frenzied naked figures, leaping and cavorting far away. He cried out to them, but they gave no sign of hearing him.

In the hotel office Morrissey found the manager's cube and turned it on. She was a dark-haired young woman, somewhat wild-eyed. "Hey, is it earthquake time yet?"

"Not quite yet."

"I want to be around for that. I want to see this stinking hotel crumble."

"Where have you gone?" Morrissey asked.

She snickered. "Where else? Into the bush. Off to hunt fuxes. And to be hunted." Her face was flushed. "The old recombinant genes are still pretty hot, you know? Me for the fuxes and the fuxes for me. Get yourself a little action, why don't you? Whoever you are."

Morrissey supposed he ought to be shocked. But he couldn't summon much indignation. He had already heard rumors of things like this. In the final years before the cataclysm, he knew, several sorts of migration had been going on. Some colonists opted for the exodus to Earth, and some for the surrender to the Ahya soul collective, and others chose the simple reversion to the life of the beast. Why not? Every Medean, by now, was a mongrel. The underlying Earth stock was tinged with alien genes. The colonists looked human enough, but they were in fact mixed with balloon or fux or both. Without the early recombinant manipulations the colony could never have survived, for human life and native Medean organisms were incompatible, and only by genetic splicing had a race been brought forth that could overcome that natural biological enmity. So now, with doom-time coming near, how many colonists had simply thrown off their clothes and slipped away into the jungles to run with their cousins the fuxes? And was that any worse, he wondered, than climbing in panic aboard a ship bound for Earth, or giving up one's individuality to merge with the balloons? What did it matter which route to escape was chosen? But Morrissey wanted no escape. Least of all into the jungles, off to the fuxes.

He flew on northward. In Catamount he heard the cube of the city's mayor tell him, "They've all cleared out, and I'm going next Dimday. There's nothing left here." In Yellowleaf a cubed biologist spoke of genetic drift, the reversion to the alien genes. In Sandy's Mishigos Morrissey could find no cubes at all, but eighteen or twenty skeletons lay chaotically on the broad central plaza. Mass immolation? Mass murder, in the final hours of the city's disintegration? He gathered the bones and buried them in the moist, spongy, ochre soil. It took him all day. Then he went on, up the coast as far as Arca, through city after city. Wherever he stopped it was the same story: no humans left, only balloons and fuxes, most of the balloons heading out to sea and most of the fuxes migrating inland. He jacked in cubes wherever he found them, but the cube people had little news to tell him. They were clearing out, they said: One way or another they were giving up on Medea. Why stay around to the end? Why wait for the big shudder? Going home, going to the balloons, going to the bush—clearing out, clearing out, clearing out.

So many cities, Morrissey thought. *Such an immense outpouring of effort. We smothered this world. We came in, we built our little isolated research stations, we stared in wonder at the coruscating sky and the double suns and the bizarre creatures, and we transformed ourselves into Medeans and transformed Medea into a kind of crazy imitation of Earth, and for a thousand years we spread out along the coasts wherever our kind of life could dig itself in. Eventually we lost sight of our purpose in coming here, which in the beginning was to learn. But we stayed anyway. We just stayed. We muddled along. And then we found out that it was all for nothing, that with one mighty heave of its shoulders this world was going to cast us off, and we got scared and packed up and went away. Sad,* he thought. *Sad and foolish.*

He stayed at Arca a few days and turned inland, across the bleak desert that sloped upward toward Mount Olympus. It was seven weeks and a day until the quake. For the first thousand kilometers or so he still could see encampments of migrating fuxes below him, slowly making their way into the Hotlands. Why, he wondered, had they permitted their world to be taken from them? *They could have fought back.*

In the beginning they could have wiped us out in a month of guerrilla warfare. Instead they let us come in, let us make them into pets and slaves and flunkies while we paved the most fertile zones of their planet, and whatever they thought about us they kept to themselves. We never even knew their own name for Medea, Morrissey thought. *That was how little of themselves they shared with us. But they tolerated us here. Why?*

The land below him was furnace hot, a badland streaked with red and yellow and orange, and now there were no fuxes in sight. The first jagged foothills of the Olympus scarp knobbed the desert. He saw the mountain itself rising like a black fang toward the heavy, low-hanging, sky-filling mass of Argo. Morrissey dared not approach that mountain. It was holy and deadly. Its thermal updrafts could send his flitter spinning to ground like a swatted fly, and he was not quite ready to die.

He swung northward again and journeyed up the barren and forlorn heart of the continent toward the polar regions. The Ring Ocean came into view, coiling like a world-swallowing serpent beyond the polar shores, and he kicked the flitter higher, almost to its maximum safety level, to give himself a peek at Farside, where white rivers of carbon dioxide flowed through the atmosphere and lakes of cold gases flooded the valleys. It seemed like six thousand years ago that he had led the party of geologists into that forbidding land. How earnest they had all been then! Measuring fault lines and seeking to discover the effects the quake would have over there. As if such things mattered. Why had he bothered? The quest for pure knowledge, yes. How futile that quest seemed to him now. Of course he had been much younger then. An eon ago. Almost in another life Morrissey had planned to fly into Farside on this trip, to bid formal farewell to the scientist he had been, but he changed his mind. There was no need. Some farewells had already been made.

He curved down out of the polar regions as far south as Northcape on the eastern coast, circled the wondrous red-glinting sweep of the High Cascades, and landed on the airstrip at Chong. It was six weeks and two days to the earthquake. In these high latitudes the twin suns were faint and feeble even though the day was a Sunday. The monster Argo itself, far to the south, appeared shrunken. He had forgotten the look of the northern sky while spending ten years in the tropics. And yet had he not lived thirty years in Chong? It seemed like only a moment ago now, as all time collapsed into this instant of now.

Morrissey found Chong painful, too many old associations, too many cues to memory. Yet he kept himself there until he had seen it all, the restaurant where he and Nadia had invited Danielle and Paul to join their marriage, the house on Vladimir Street where they had lived, the geophysics lab, the skiing lodge just beyond the Cascades. All the footprints of his life.

The city and its environs were utterly deserted. For day after day Morrissey wandered, reliving the time when he was young and Medea still lived. How exciting it had all been then! The quake was coming someday—everybody knew the day, down to the hour—but nobody cared except cranks and neurotics, for the others were too busy living. And then suddenly everyone cared, and everything changed.

Morrissey played no cubes in Chong. The city itself, gleaming, a vast palisade of silver thermal roofs, was one great cube for him, crying out the tale of his years.

When he could take it no longer, he started his southward curve around the east coast. There were four weeks and a day to go.

His first stop was Meditation Island, the jumping-off point for those who went to visit Virgil Oddum's fantastic and ever-evolving ice sculptures out on Farside. Four newlyweds had come here, a billion years ago, and had gone, laughing and embracing, off in icecrawlers to see the one miracle of art Medea had produced. Morrissey found the cabin where they all had stayed. It had faded and its roof was askew. He had thought of spending the night on Meditation Island, but he left after an hour.

Now the land grew lush again as he passed into the upper tropics. Again he saw balloons by the score letting themselves be wafted toward the ocean, and again there were bands of fuxes journeying inland, driven by he knew not what sense of ritual obligation as the quake neared.

Three weeks, two days, five hours, plus or minus.

He flew low over the fuxes. Some were mating. That astounded him—that persistence of lust in the face of calamity. Was it merely the irresistible biological drive that kept the fuxes coupling? What chance did the newly engendered young have to survive? Would their mothers not be better off with empty wombs when the quake came? They all knew what was going to happen, and yet they mated. It made no sense to Morrissey.

And then he thought he understood. The sight of those coupling fuxes gave him an insight into the Medean natives that explained it all, for the first time. Their patience, their calmness, their tolerance of all that had befallen them since their world had become Medea. Of course they would mate as the catastrophe drew near! They had been waiting for the earthquake all along, and for them it was no catastrophe. It was a holy moment—a purification—so he realized. He wished he could discuss this with Dinoov. It was a temptation to return at once to Argoview Dunes and seek out the old fux and test on him the theory that had just sprung to life in him. But not yet. Port Medea, first.

The east coast had been settled before the other, and the density of development here was intense. The first two colonies—Touchdown City and Medeatown—had long ago coalesced into the urban smear that radiated outward from the third town, Port Medea. When he was still far to the north, Morrissey could see the gigantic peninsula on which Port Medea and its suburbs sprawled. The tropic heat rose in visible waves from it, buffeting his little flitter as he made his way toward that awesome, hideous concrete expanse.

Dinoov had been correct. There were starships waiting at Port Medea—four of them, a waste of money beyond imagination. Why had they not been used in the exodus? Had they been set aside for emigrants who had decided instead to run with the rutting fuxes or to give their souls to the balloons? He would never know. He entered one of the ships and said, "Operations directory."

"At your service," a bodiless voice replied.

"Give me a report on ship status. Are you prepared for a voyage to Earth?"

"Fueled and ready."

"And the coldsleep equipment?"

"Everything operational."

Morrissey calculated his moves. *So easy,* he thought, *to lie down and go to sleep and let the ship take me to Earth. So easy, so automatic, so useless.*

Then he said, "How long do you need to reach departure level?"

"One hundred sixty minutes from moment of command."

"Good. The command is given. Get yourself ticking and take off. Your destination is Earth, and the message I give you is this: *Medea says goodbye. I thought you might have some use for this ship. Sincerely, Daniel F. Morrissey. Dated Earthquake minus two weeks one day seven hours.*"

"Acknowledged. Departure-level procedures initiated."

"Have a good flight," Morrissey told the ship.

He entered the second ship and gave it the same command. He did the same in the third. He paused before entering the last one, wondering whether there were other colonists who even now were desperately racing toward Port Medea to get aboard one of these ships before the end came. *To hell with them,* Morrissey thought. *They should have made up their minds sooner.* He told the fourth ship to go home to Earth.

On his way back from the port to the city he saw the four bright spears of light rise skyward, a few minutes apart. Each hovered a moment, outlined against Argo's colossal bulk, and shot swiftly into the aurora-dappled heavens. In sixty-one years they would descend onto a baffled Earth with their cargo of no one. Another great mystery of space to delight the taletellers, he thought. The Voyage of the Empty Ships.

With a curious sense of accomplishment he left Port Medea and headed down the coast to the sleek resort of Madagozar, where the elite of Medea had amused themselves in tropic luxury. Morrissey had always thought the place absurd. But it was still intact, still purring with automatic precision. He treated himself to a lavish holiday there. He raided the wine cellars of the best hotels, breakfasted on tubs of chilled spikelegs cavier, dozed in the warm sun, bathed in the juice of gilliwog flowers, and thought about absolutely nothing at all.

The day before the earthquake he flew back to Argoview dunes.

"So you chose not to go home after all," Dinoov said.

Morrissey shook his head. "Earth was never my home. Medea was my home. I went home to Medea. And then I came back to this place, because it was my last home. I am pleased that you're still here, Dinoov."

"Where would I have gone?" the fux asked.

"The rest of your people are migrating inland. I think it's to be nearer the holy mountain when the end comes. Is that right?"

"That is right."

"Then why have you stayed?"

"This is my home, too. I have so little time left that it matters not very much to me where I am when the ground shakes. But tell me, friend Morrissey, was your journey worth the taking?"

"It was."

"What did you see? What did you learn?"

"I saw Medea, all of it," Morrissey said. "I never realized how much of your world we took. By the end we covered all the land that was worth covering, didn't we? And you people never said a word. You stood by and let it happen."

The fux was silent.

Morrissey said, "I understand now. You were waiting for the earthquake all along, weren't you? You knew it was coming long before we bothered to figure it out. How many times has it happened since fuxes first evolved on Medea? Every seventy-one hundred sixty years the fuxes move to high ground and the balloons drift to Farside and the ground shakes and everything falls apart. And then the survivors reappear, with new life already in the wombs, and build again. So you knew, when we came here, when we built our towns everywhere and turned them into cities, when we rounded you up and made you work for us, when we mixed our genes with yours and changed the microbes in the air so we'd be more comfortable here, that what we were doing wouldn't last forever, right? That was your secret knowledge, your hidden consolation, that this, too, would pass. Eh, Dinoov? And now it has passed. We're gone, and the happy young fuxes are mating. I'm the only one

411

of my kind left, except for a few naked crazies in the bush.''

There was a glint in the fux's eyes. Amusement? Contempt? Compassion? Who could read a fux's eyes?

"All along," Morrissey said, "you were all just waiting for the earthquake. Right? The earthquake that would make everything whole again. Well, now it's almost upon us. And I'm going to stand here alongside you and wait for the earthquake, too. It's my contribution to interspecies harmony. I'll be the human sacrifice. I'll be the one who atones for all that we did here. How does that sound, Dinoov?"

"I wish," the fux said slowly, "that you had boarded one of those ships and gone back to Earth. Your death will give me no pleasure."

Morrissey nodded. "I'll be back in a few minutes." He went into his cabin.

The cubes of Nadia and Paul and Danielle sat beside the screen. Not for years had he played them, but he jacked them into the slots now, and on the screen appeared the three people he had most loved in all the universe. They smiled at him, and Danielle offered a soft greeting, and Paul winked, and Nadia blew a kiss. Morrissey said, "It's almost over now. Today's earthquake day. I just wanted to say good-bye, that's all. I just wanted to tell you that I love you and I'll be with you soon."

"Dan—" Nadia said.

"No. You don't have to say anything. I know you aren't really there, anyway. I just wanted to see you all again. I'm very happy right now."

He took the cubes from their slots. The screen went dark. Gathering up the cubes, he carried them outside and carefully buried them in the soft, moist soil of his garden. The fux watched him incuriously.

"Dinoov," Morrissey called, "one last question."

"Yes, my friend?"

"All the years we lived on Medea, we were never able to learn the name by which you people called your own world. We kept trying to find out, but all we were told was that it was taboo, and even when we coaxed a fux into telling us the name, the next fux would tell us an entirely different name. So we never knew. I ask you a special favor now, here at the end. Tell me what you call your world. Please. I need to know."

The old fux said, "We call it Sanoon."

"Sanoon? Truly?"

"Truly," said the fux.

"What does it mean?"

"Why, it means the world," said Dinoov. "What else?"

The earthquake was thirty minutes away—plus or minus a little. During the past hour the white suns had disappeared behind Argo. Morrissey had not noticed that. But now he heard a low rumbling roar, and then he felt a strange trembling in the ground, as if something mighty were stirring beneath his feet and would burst shortly into wakefulness. Not far from shore terrible waves rose and crashed.

Calmly Morrissey said, "This is it, I think."

Overhead, a dozen gleaming balloons soared and bobbed in a dance that looked much like a dance of triumph.

There was thunder in the air and a writhing in the heart of the world. In another moment the full force of the quake would be upon them, and the crust of the planet would quiver and the awful tremors would rip the land apart and the sea would rise up and cover the coast. Morrissey began to weep, and not out of fear. He managed a smile. "The cycle's complete. Dinoov. Out of Medea's ruins Sanoon will rise. The place is yours again at last."

MORE EXCITING READING
IN THE ZEBRA/OMNI SERIES